To Tuscany with Love

a novel

GAIL MENCINI

Capriole Group

To Tuscany with Love
by Gail Mencini

Published in the United States by

an imprint of Capriole Group LLC, Centennial 80161
www.CaprioleGroup.com

For information regarding special discounts for bulk purchases,
please contact Capriole Group Corporate and Premium Sales at
Books@CaprioleGroup.com.

Cover and book design by Nick Zelinger, *www.NZGraphics.com*
Editor: Patti Thorn, *www.BlueInkReview.com*
Book consultant: Judith Briles, *www.TheBookShepherd.com*
Author photograph by Ashlee Bratton, *www.Ashography.com*

ISBN 978-1-938592-00-3 (paperback)
ISBN 978-1-938592-01-0 (e-book)

Library of Congress Control Number: 2013907682

10 9 8 7 6 5 4 3 2 1

Mencini, Gail
To Tuscany with Love/Gail Mencini
1.Italy—Fiction 2. Friends—Fiction 3. Reunions—Fiction

First Edition

Manufactured in the United States of America

To Ray, my forever love

1

Present Day

Bella had bought her solid, rough-hewn table for David's first meal at home after their dreadful argument. She shuddered, remembering his anger and how she had been afraid that she had lost him.

Bella glanced at the stack of mail piled on the prized possession she had found at an estate auction. The previous owners had lived on Long Island and had shipped the table from the Italian countryside. They had discovered it in a vineyard estate undergoing renovation. It was a simple table, one that had silently shouldered decades of meals, conversations, laughter, arguments, and celebrations. Not stylish or valuable enough for their heirs, but perfect for Bella.

For her, it would always be David's table.

A square of black caught Bella's eye. It looked like sophisticated stationery stock, the expensive kind reserved for society party invitations. A swirl of silver calligraphy curled across it. She tugged on the black envelope, revealing an eight-by-eight-inch square with her name and address handwritten in a subdued yet elegant script. No return address.

Curious, Bella opened the envelope and found a cream-colored engraved invitation.

You are invited to rekindle the flame in Firenze
September 16-25
First class airfare and all expenses paid
No spouses, children, or friends allowed
Flight and lodging information enclosed

Regrets are for cowards

A photograph had slid out from the envelope along with the invitation. Bella knew the picture without looking. The eight of them had posed for only one picture together—the day they had left Florence at the end of that summer, thirty years before. When her copy had arrived in the mail, she had torn it into tiny pieces and flushed it down the toilet.

Bella had deliberately avoided contact with her classmates from that college semester abroad. But it was definitely time to set the record straight. No more hiding for her, or anyone else. Bella was determined to unleash her long-dormant anger.

2

Thirty Years Before

Who would have imagined that the punishment for a single night in the slammer would be spending the summer abroad?

Certainly not Bella, who'd be a junior this fall at City College and still lived at home with her mother. Bella had chalked up the notion of going to Italy as an impossible, idle threat of her mother's. Yet here she was, sitting in a tiny car in Florence, as in Florence, Italy. Even before she had climbed into the toy car, her stomach had tried to set a record for consecutive cartwheels.

Her new group of friends back home had likely already forgotten she existed. They were busy planning another summer of protests against U.S. intervention in Nicaragua, which they swore was still happening, in spite of the Boland Amendment. Plans were in the works for a series of demonstrations like the one that had landed Bella in the overnight lockup.

Even though she wouldn't admit it to a soul, she knew that she had a bigger issue than missing a summer with her friends. Bella had never, not even once, been away from her mother for longer than a day.

The woman driver of the miniature car braked to a sudden stop in front of a narrow, stone inn.

Bella was thrilled to see the end of their frantic race through the tight, cobblestone streets. At any moment, Bella had honestly expected one of the car's side-view mirrors to be clipped off as they squeezed past oncoming traffic. With her own brand of driver etiquette, the woman had leaned on the car's horn and screamed Italian obscenities out the open window at the driver of every car they nearly hit.

Bella released her grip on the seat and sucked in a gulp of air. The inn's open door, weathered sign, and sagging shutters were at least twenty years older than the picture Bella's mother had taped to their refrigerator. She sat motionless and stared.

The whining, coughing engine nagged her out of her trance.

Bella realized, with escalating panic, that her escort's duty ended here. She turned to the woman, who was probably in her late thirties, the same age as Bella's mother. Unlike her mother, though, whose tired eyes and pallid complexion had worried Bella as they parted, this woman was tanned, stylish, and oozed sexiness from her pores.

With a fluid wave of her manicured hand, the driver dismissed Bella to the curb, the only suitcase her mother owned clutched in her sweaty hand.

It served Bella right to be banished to summer school, albeit in Italy, for her transgressions. Bella had spent a sleepless spring night in the neighborhood lockup sitting on the cold, hard floor, shoulder-to-shoulder with her fellow protestors. And she had told her mother all about her plans to join the big demonstration in Washington, D.C., over the Fourth of July.

Four weeks later, her mother had handed her a plane ticket to Italy and a brochure for a summer college course abroad. How on earth had her mother found the money for the airfare and tuition? She worked two jobs, and even with Bella living at home and working at the diner, it seemed they barely scraped by.

Her mom insisted Bella go to Italy, as an early graduation present. But Bella knew the truth. This thinly disguised "gift" was her mother's method of keeping her away from anti-government protests and out of jail.

Bella tripped over the threshold of the tiny hotel that would be her home for the summer. Michael Jackson's "Billie Jean" blared out of a portable cassette player resting on the narrow reception counter.

On the left in the eight-by-eight-foot lounge area, four college men and a wholesome-looking girl Bella's age rocked to the music. One tall, lean guy strutted around the tiny lobby and sang along with the music. He looked like a movie star with his auburn hair and matching auburn eyes.

"Hey, babe," the strutter said. "Welcome to U of Miami Art in Florence." He belted out the chorus of "Billie Jean" with a Southern drawl and dipped his shoulders as he slid backwards in a passable moonwalk.

The chocolate-haired girl waved and kept dancing. Her big-boned shape bobbed like a guy's.

The other three jutted their chins and chimed in on the chorus.

If she could fly back home, this second, right now, Bella thought, she would. She would turn around, walk out the door, and do whatever it took to find her way back to the airport.

Hearing footsteps behind her, Bella turned around. Two beautiful twins with matching long, wavy blond hair stood at the open door. Each wore a backpack and held a suitcase far nicer and years newer than Bella's, and between them they carried a flattened jumbo rucksack.

They were perfect—skin, hair, clothes, teeth, and penetrating green eyes. The "perfect" twins.

"We've got company," one of the guys called out. He scrambled to turn off the cassette player.

Bella felt his arm drape over her shoulders.

"I'm Rune." His finger ruffled Bella's long curls. "If you give me a chance, I'll ruin you this summer." His slicked-back pompadour made him look older than everyone else in the lobby.

The twins giggled.

"Lee." A male voice piped up in self-introduction from the other side of Bella. Curly black hair surrounded his chinless face.

"I'm Phillip." One deep blue eye winked at Bella before he nodded to the twins. His sun-streaked brown hair fell in waves around his ears. Tanned, Phillip had the look—and muscled body to match—of a multisport athlete.

As much as she longed to escape, Bella knew it wasn't an option. She was stuck here. She sucked in a deep breath. At least these college kids acted friendly. Maybe she'd actually survive the long summer months ahead.

The auburn-haired guy danced his way in front of Bella. He stopped in front of the twins. "Stillman Jackson."

Bella held in a chuckle. Stillman Jackson was a Southerner with auburn hair who liked to dance the moonwalk. Stillman was a far cry from Michael Jackson.

"I'm Hope," the large girl called out from the back of the group.

Stillman turned around to face Bella. "You." He pointed both index fingers at Bella. "You look Italian. Can you speak the lingo?"

Bella tapped two fingers to her closed lips and shook her head.

Stillman smirked at her. "I'll bet you're Italian. Surely you know the naughty words, don't you?"

Bella shrugged her shoulders. People speaking another language were commonplace in her New York City neighborhood. Of course she knew the naughty words.

"Asshole," Phillip said.

Bella turned her head away from Stillman and winked at Phillip. He had come to her defense, after all.

Phillip threw his head back with laughter. "She got you, man." His palm slapped Stillman's back.

"Bella Rossini." She smiled at Stillman. "I only speak English. My Oral Comm prof claims even that's marginal. As far as Italian goes, I might know one or two nasty phrases, but that's it."

Bella looked past him at the twins. Their perfectness made her feel plain. And how could they be so perky after the long flights? Bella motioned to the empty rucksack. "Did you lose stuff already?"

She regretted her words and tone of voice as soon as they'd escaped from her mouth. Bella had promised her mother she'd give people a chance this summer and make new friends. Not much chance of that happening, if the first ten minutes were any indication.

The twin on the left answered with a shake of her long tresses. "No. It's for all the stuff we buy and want to bring back." She set down her end of the handle carefully, as if the bag held fragile treasures. "I'm Karen, and this is Meghan."

"We're from Chicago," the second twin said.

Rune's head ticked like a pendulum between the twins. "Karen … Meghan. Meghan … Karen." He rubbed his palms together in circles and leered at them. "I'm hoping there's a birthmark placed in a strategic—normally hidden—spot that we can use to tell you two apart."

Lee spoke. "Their eyes. Meghan's have flecks of brown."

Meghan's grateful smile zeroed in on Lee.

"I like my way of telling them apart better." Rune peered out the door and craned his neck to view the street. "God, it's hot in here. Let's see if we can find a beer. I'd even take a glass of wine. Our assigned babysitter isn't due back for a couple hours." His eyes canvassed their faces. "How 'bout it?"

They trotted out as a pack.

Bella followed them out the door. It was hot, and she was thirsty. Her eyes swept the ancient buildings that lined the narrow street, even narrower than those in Manhattan's Little Italy. She tried to soak in every detail—the pale-colored cornerstones, the window boxes of red geraniums, and the laundry that hung on line after line to dry in the hot shade of the five-story buildings.

Bella half-listened to the chatter about music, movies, schools, majors, and hopes for the summer. What did she have in common with this group? They all had more money and were all more rad than she was.

She thought of her mother. They had argued at the airport, and Bella had tried refusing to board the plane, but how could she do that after everything was paid for? Shipping her off to Italy was a major overreaction. Could Bella help it that the cops were on high alert after one of the stores near their protest had been looted and burned the night before? Her mother was acting as if she were a drug dealer or something.

Bella recalled their goodbyes at the airport. Even though excitement lit her mother's face, why had her eyes shied away?

3

After a stroll through the streets of Florence and a stop for beer and wine, the group returned to their hotel, dazed from the combination of alcohol and jet lag.

A tall, thin Italian man stood reading a paperback book beside the luggage they had abandoned in the lobby. He introduced himself as Paolo and nodded at them with a skeptical look on his face. Following minimal discussion and room assignments, he dispatched them to their rooms with keys and an admonition to be in the building's lower level for breakfast and coffee promptly at eight tomorrow morning.

Bella trudged up the stairs with her suitcase behind Hope, her roommate for the summer. Paolo had matched up Stillman with Phillip and Rune with Lee, and put the two perfect twins, Karen and Meghan, together.

Bella dropped her bag and backpack on the floor. Their tiny room held two single beds, a table barely large enough to hold the lamp on top of it between the beds, a wooden armoire, and a closet not much wider than Bella. The one window was closed, which made the room stifling.

She crossed to the window and leaned over the coil of hot water pipes to pry it open. It was stuck. Hope must have had the same thought, because a minute later, she stood next to Bella and tugged at the window, too.

"Damn, it's hotter than Hades in here," Hope said. She grunted and gave a ferocious pull on the window. The paint stuck around the frame made the upward progress a challenge. Sweat poured down the sides of the large girl's face. Finally, they had raised it to its maximum level.

Bella collapsed onto the closest bed, biting back her frustration and realizing that this summer would have fewer creature comforts than she knew in her mother's small apartment.

Hope had left the window and peered under each bed, opened and closed the armoire and then the closet. "God does have mercy." She held a small metal fan in her hand, which she had found on the upper shelf of the closet. Hope set the fan on the radiator in front of the opened window, plugged it in, and turned it on. She stood by the fan, letting the moving air wash over her.

Bella took a position beside Hope in front of the fan. It was a far cry from air conditioning, but at least the movement broke the oppressive, stale air. "Thank you. I didn't have the energy to think about, much less look for, a fan."

Rooming with Hope was off to a good start—the girl was a problem solver. "Do you want the bed next to the window?" It was the least Bella could do, since she was so exhausted she hadn't been able to think past opening the window.

"Do you mind?" Sweat still rolled down Hope's face.

"It's yours." Bella moved her belongings to the other bed. She opened her bag and stacked her clothes on her bed beside the suitcase. "I saw the bathroom at the end of the hall. I'm going to try to beat the crunch and go wash up. However you want to divvy up the storage space is fine with me. Go ahead and settle in."

"Will do." Hope turned to the armoire with a stack of underwear in her hands. "Good thing I didn't bring much clothes," she chuckled, "since a big girl like me has jumbo-sized everything."

An hour later, Karen and Meghan joined Bella and Hope in their room. The twins sat cross-legged on Hope's bed, in front of the fan. They already knew the basics about each other, from the group's time in the café, where they had exchanged info on colleges, hometowns, and majors.

Karen rubbed her palms together. "OK, girls, let's get to the good stuff—boyfriends. I've been dating Ed for two years, and he's jealous I'm here with other boys."

"None for me," Meghan said. "How about you?" She smiled at Bella and Hope.

Bella shook her head. She'd never really had a boyfriend. A casual date here and there, but work and school took most of her time. She didn't even have many friends, not until the group planning to spend the summer protesting about Nicaragua had befriended her.

Bella had met one of the girls when she was studying outdoors, beside the large fountain at the entrance to their urban campus. The girl had plopped herself down next to Bella and started chatting, soon inviting Bella to join her and her friends that night for pizza.

Their political fervor had been contagious, partly because there was lively discourse and teasing among the group. Bella longed to expand her family to include more than her mother; after all, it had been only the two of them her entire life. Following their politics had been more a means to be included in the group than an active decision to support their causes.

Hope spoke with quiet pride. "I've been dating Charlie since high school, and we'll be married after I finish college. He was in the Marines four years. He's got a great business job. We could afford to get married now, but he wants me to finish college first, since my folks will help pay for it if I'm not married."

Karen leaned forward, and her eyes had a mischievous look. "Did he like you coming to Italy?"

Hope shook her head. "Not at all." She dropped her head and gazed at her hands. "I almost backed out at the last minute, but the money was nonrefundable, and it was something my mom really wanted for me."

Karen nodded. "So it looks like you're off the market. Right?"

Hope nodded.

Karen jumped off the bed and held up four fingers on one hand and three on the other. "Good odds, I'd say. Four men, three eligible women."

"You're not eligible," Meghan said. "You're practically engaged to Ed."

"But I'm not. Not yet." Karen wiggled her hips back and forth. "And I intend to have fun this summer. Other than Lee, who I'll bet is a bookworm, they all seem to have potential."

Meghan nodded, a broad smile across her face.

Bella had to admit that the guys were a good-looking bunch. Lee was the most serious. Phillip, a total stud, acted a little standoffish. Was it because he had an attitude as an athlete? Stillman was definitely hot, friendly, and had that sexy Southern accent. Rune had kept them all laughing during their walk and had flirted with all of the girls.

These kids were friendlier than the students filing in and out of classes at City College. Maybe this summer in Italy wouldn't be so bad, after all.

"Woo-hoo," Rune said. "At UCLA, I'm used to the beach babes in California, but those twin blondes are hot. You can look at their eyes all you want, man," he nodded at Lee, "but I plan to find other ways to tell them apart, and then I'll be able to report on whether or not they're natural blondes."

Lee responded by throwing one of the hard, flat pillows at Rune's head.

Stillman had invited Lee and Rune to come to the room he shared with Phillip after they had unpacked.

Phillip seemed a little put off by the lack of air conditioning and having to share a bathroom down the hall, but Stillman didn't care. His first memories of the farm in Georgia with his mama and the preacher were when their only toilet was in a hot, airless bathroom added to the side of the house.

"I'm not sure I'd win if I arm-wrestled Hope," Stillman said, "but she seems like a straight-up gal. Bella, on the other hand, matches her name. Beautiful. I call dibs on Bella."

"Dibs?" Phillip scowled at Stillman. "There are no dibs."

"Ahh," Stillman said. "Every man for himself then?"

"Hell," Rune said, "it's always that way. I plan to frequent the locals, too. They're not so puritanical about sex in Europe, you know. If I focus on their tiny bodies and big tits, I'll be able to ignore their hairy pits."

Lee stood up, grabbed the pillow from the other bed and sailed it toward Rune. Phillip followed the pillow and tackled Rune against the bed. Not to be left out of the wrestling, Stillman piled onto Phillip. Lee landed on the narrow bed between the guys and the wall and whacked them with one of the pillows. The bed swayed and creaked as if it would collapse. Grunts and laughter punctuated the air.

Stillman wondered how they'd all pair up this summer. It seemed inevitable with four guys and four gals together in Italy. Hot weather, wine, and an ocean separating them from home.

This was a pass-fail class, a welcome break from Stillman's grindstone of pre-med courses and competition for the top grade in the class. He'd seen Lee before in large classes at the University of Michigan. Even though they were both aiming for medical school, on a campus that large it wasn't unusual that they hadn't met.

Lee was a natural enemy for him. With Affirmative Action in place and limited slots for med schools, a killer instinct was pervasive among white males in pre-med. Stillman would do whatever necessary to get the top grade in a class, and he suspected Lee was exactly the same way.

4

The next day, Paolo walked them for hours around Florence, reciting the city's history in professorial fashion. He had the common sense to include stories of wars, rivalries, love affairs, and *Mafiosi* to keep their interest. He wanted them to embrace the city and recognize its neighborhoods, storied churches and piazzas.

Bella was surprised at how easily her classmates conversed and joked with each other. Once drawn into a conversation, she knew, if she had to, that she could hold her own with any of them. But that first step terrified her. She didn't make friends easily and feared being the outsider all summer.

Bella stuck next to Hope. Having a roommate was a blessing, in that she had an excuse to tag along with the girl from Colorado.

The two girls followed Paolo, and halfway through the morning, Stillman appeared next to Bella. He asked her questions about New York and her family. She tried to quiz him back, but he wouldn't say much, only that his mother had died when he was young.

"Do you get home often, with Georgia being so far away?" she asked.

"Nah," Stillman said, "I usually stay in Ann Arbor and work over breaks. What's to go home for? The preacher— I live with him—just rags at me and makes me do chores if I'm there. We get under each other's skin, the preacher and I, so I'm better off staying north of the Mason-Dixon line."

He chuckled. "You know, that was the thing that I wondered about the most before I started college. I'd never met a Yankee, or been north of Atlanta."

Bella laughed. His polite, Southern manner put her at ease. "The Mason-Dixon line? Obviously, that's a much bigger deal to you than us Yankees. I hate to admit it, but I'm more sheltered than you—this is my first time out of the five boroughs of New York."

Sticking close to home might not be the only thing she and Stillman had in common. He never mentioned his father, which made her curious. Had both of their dads abandoned them?

Lunch was a slice of room-temperature pizza and an orange drink from a walk-up counter, and then off they trekked again. As they trailed behind Paolo, Phillip scooted up to claim the spot beside her.

He chatted at length with Hope first, asking about skiing in the Rockies and comparing Rocky Mountain National Park with Yosemite. Bella listened with interest and tried to imagine how those peaks and hiking trails and waterfalls looked. Such a different world from her own.

Bella felt Phillip's eyes turn to her. She looked him in the eyes and waited for him to speak.

"So you're a big-city girl."

Really, she thought? That's all he could think to say to her? Bella didn't know why, but his question rubbed her wrong. Surely after the detailed discussion with Hope he thought she was more interesting than merely being a "big-city girl," whatever that meant.

Her voice came out even more sarcastic than she had intended. "Seven million people? I'd guess that qualifies as a big city."

Phillip threw back his head and laughed. Not at all the reaction she'd expected after her snide remark.

"Seriously, I've always wanted to see New York City. Now I actually know someone who lives there." His voice sounded sincere rather than being a sleazy come-on. "Maybe you could show me around if I came to visit." He rubbed his palm over her bare biceps.

His touch on her skin sent a shiver that started at her arm and ran across her shoulders and neck.

Then Phillip's questions began. And not just about the usual sights, but about life in an urban environment. Did she feel safe with so many people around? What did city dwellers do for recreation besides Broadway and restaurants? Did young children play outside after school, and if so, where? Did she ever get out of the city to ski or hike?

She answered his questions and found herself telling him bits and pieces, between Paolo's walking lectures, about her favorite things in New York.

"Every season has its own charm. In the spring," Bella said, "Central Park comes alive with blooming trees and flowers. Summer brings the outdoor concerts and loads of street vendors. Autumn is a blaze of color, and, of course, there's the Thanksgiving Day parade, Rockefeller Center, and Times Square."

Telling him about it brought a wave of homesickness over Bella. She had to change the focus of the conversation for fear she'd cry. "Did you get a car when you were sixteen?"

Phillip nodded.

Bella quizzed him about it, and how it felt to drive. Wasn't it terrifying? She admitted to never having driven a car, and after hearing Phillip describe cruising along a beachfront road, for the first time she wished she had.

Hope, on the other hand, boasted of driving a tractor, although with a hearty laugh she said she'd vote for being behind the wheel of a convertible any day.

The afternoon flew by, and Bella wondered why she'd worried. Living together with seven new friends and being in Italy? This had the potential of being the best summer of her life.

Later, after they had washed off the sweat from the day's heat, they followed Paolo to a nearby *ristorante* for dinner.

Bella was famished. Inside the restaurant, after stopping to look at a wall of dusty cubbyholes holding equally dusty bottles of wine, she was the last to reach the small room where her group had gathered.

To Bella's chagrin, Paolo and her male classmates had remained standing, waiting for her to sit down. She saw that Phillip and Stillman had positioned themselves so that should she sit at the logical open chair, they would be on either side of her.

She couldn't remember why Phillip had struck her as standoffish yesterday; he had chatted with her all afternoon, even buying Hope and her gelatos.

Smiling at Stillman, then Phillip, Bella slid into the chair between them. A girl has a sense about these things, doesn't she? They wanted to compete for her attention? Let the games begin.

5

The days settled into a routine for Bella. Espresso with hard rolls and thinly sliced prosciutto or salami for breakfast, then an hour lecture and introduction to the day's lesson.

Following the classwork, they paraded out to the streets, Phillip and Stillman jockeying to be the one by her side through their stroll.

After the first few days, an easy rhythm developed, and, she thought, a truce between Phillip and Stillman. She loved her laid-back conversations with Hope and Meghan and would walk much of the day arm in arm, like the Italian girls did, with one of them. In the mornings, Stillman flanked Bella's other side, and in the afternoon, it was Phillip.

Lee had gravitated to Meghan. He clearly had the hots for her, and he walked next to Meghan whenever possible. Lee, like Stillman, was a pre-med student and the most serious of the group. Bella even saw him take notes on their lectures in the museums. Didn't he understand that a pass-fail class meant you didn't have to ace it?

One morning, after Bella had ducked into a *tabacchi*, a tobacconist, where she purchased stamps, Lee cornered her and asked how to send mail home. His mother, he admitted, had demanded that he write to her every day. With a guilty look on his face, Lee told Bella that he hadn't mailed anything yet and had a stack of letters to send.

Bella grabbed his arm and led Lee back into the store, pointing out the large white "T" on the sign overhead. After he had purchased enough stamps for his unsent letters, Bella showed him the correct slot on a mailbox in which to drop his mail, so—hopefully—his letters wouldn't end up lost in the Italian postal system.

"I'm close to my mother, too," Bella said when they stopped for a mid-morning espresso. "Are you the eldest or an only child, like me?"

"First born," Lee said. "And, unfortunately for me, my mother can lay the guilt on better than anyone. Anyone, that is, except her own mother. We may have that in common, you and I. Don't Jews and Catholics practically own the rights for laying guilt on their kids?"

Bella chuckled. "That's normally true. I'm lucky, though. I guess because my mom's parents disowned her for being an unwed mother, she never got into the "guilt" thing. Your mom's bad that way? I'm sorry to hear it."

His voice rose and he shook a finger at Bella, pretending to be his mother. "You must become a doctor. A specialist. Your grandfather, God rest his soul, was a respected surgeon until he died fighting Hitler. You must do this, not only for yourself, but for the family."

"Your grandfather died in World War II?"

Lee nodded. "He was in the Naval medical corps. Survived Omaha Beach, only to be killed a year later by a bomb."

"Oh, I'm so sorry!"

"My grandmother's a remarkable woman, but she won't rest until someone in the family becomes a physician—a specialist with advanced training, of course. My mom thought she had it taken care of when she married my dad."

Lee's face flushed. "My dad—he's a good guy—he went into business. He was pre-med when he married my mom, but then his grades weren't good enough. I'm next in line, and since I'm smart enough, that's my future. It's not an option for me; becoming a doctor is an ironclad obligation to my family."

Bella put her hand on Lee's arm. "You'll be a great doctor. You seem to really care about people. Have you ever thought that even without the pressure from your mother and grandmother, you might have picked medicine?"

"Actually, I've asked myself the same question. The answer is no. I'd pick something impractical, like art. But hearing you say I'll be a good doctor makes me feel better. Thanks."

Male voices from the piazza halted Bella and Lee's conversation. Three Italian men, looking only a few years older than they, chattered and peered at something, or someone, behind Lee and Bella. Suddenly, one of the men pushed through the seating area, brushing against Bella and Lee's table. Bella grabbed the edge to steady it.

The man stopped at the table where Karen and Meghan sat. He leaned over and kissed Karen on the lips, then threw his hands into the air and said, "*Fantastico!*"

Karen laughed and shooed the man away with her hands. He returned to the piazza, his arms overhead as if he'd won the World Cup, to rejoin his cheering companions.

Despite being practically engaged, Karen flirted with all the guys: the males in their class, the older museum guides, and the coffee shop baristas. It was no wonder the man had kissed her.

Karen had a technique of thrusting out her well-endowed chest while her eyes issued a playful dare. Her flirting was only topped by Rune's, who hit on all the girls, baited Lee with his audacious remarks, and disappeared during the quiet time. He spent his "study time" either looking for marijuana or finding a spot to make out with the latest Italian girl he'd attracted.

A week after Phillip and Stillman's "truce" began, Bella dragged herself uphill between Phillip and Hope.

They had crossed the River Arno that morning on a seemingly endless walking tour. After lunch, in spite of the increasing heat, Paolo had led them through the Boboli Gardens. Now they faced a long trek back across the river to their hotel, many blocks beyond the Duomo, the Cathedral of Florence. Bella and Hope didn't have the energy to chat. It had been a long day in the sun.

Bella felt Phillip's eyes on her. She knew her forehead was damp with perspiration and that her hair frizzed in tight curls around her face—not her best look, by a long shot. She sneaked a glance at him. How could he look so cheerful?

Suddenly, Phillip sprinted up the hill ahead of them. With a broad grin on his face, he flipped upside down into a handstand.

"Woo-hoo." Hope clapped her hands.

Bella had to laugh. Phillip stayed there, upside down and grinning, until she and Hope stood in front of him.

"Bella," Phillip said, "I'll flip for the chance to hold your hand." With that, he waggled his feet up and down to emphasize his words.

Bella giggled. Phillip could certainly make her laugh. She held out her hand. "I'd rather hold your hand than your foot, but it's your choice."

Rune clapped and said, "Good job, man."

Phillip bent his arms and sprang lightly to his feet. He beamed, brushed his hands off on his jeans, and clutched Bella's hand. With a hoot, he raised their clasped hands into the air in a victory salute. Their classmates, other than Stillman, cheered his success.

"I've never seen that approach," Bella said to Phillip. Her legs had new energy as they continued up the stone street.

Leaning closer to her, he winked and said, "Oh, I have a lot more tricks up my sleeve."

And he did. One day, he scaled the outside of a stone wall, finding handholds where none visibly existed; he later explained that he had learned bouldering and climbing skills during summer expeditions to Yosemite.

Bella wasn't sure if he did these stunts to make her laugh or to highlight his athleticism. Either way, he succeeded.

Betting he was on more than one sports team in high school, she asked Phillip about it.

"Tennis was my best sport. State singles champion my senior year," Phillip said. "But I played basketball and football, too. The thing I loved, though, was skiing, because I did that with my sister."

"I didn't know you had a sister. Older or younger?"

"Younger, but Anne died when I was in high school. She was the most determined athlete I've ever known. She pushed me, made me better."

Phillip pulled his wallet out of his pocket and extracted a worn photo of him dressed for skiing. His skis were spread in a deep "wedge", and he stood behind a grinning girl sitting on a low seat, which was mounted on skis. "She was disabled but loved sports—skiing, bicycling, and horse riding were her favorites. Before she got too big, I even took her hiking in a backpack. I miss her." He kissed the picture and replaced it in his wallet.

Bella squeezed his hand. "What happened?"

"Medical complications. She had a lot of operations and was often sick, but she never complained." He pressed his lips together in a tight smile. "She was always my cheerleader, my number one fan. It's why I was so competitive—for Anne."

He stopped walking and looked at Bella with a serious expression. "I don't talk about Anne much, and I'd appreciate it if you don't say anything to the rest of them. She was too special to be just another topic of discussion." Phillip's sincerity rang true.

"Of course."

Phillip ended any further discussion of his sister by asking Bella about her own high school activities. Bella could easily picture a young Phillip doing handstands, or jumps, or climbing a wall to make his sister laugh and cheer.

Two days later, Phillip upped the ante. He ran down a flat section of street and flipped over once, twice, three times.

Bella ran to him and hugged him. But then, while her arms were still around him, she caught Phillip looking at Stillman with a smirk on his face.

Was Phillip vying for her attention because of her or because he wanted to beat Stillman? The possibility that she was merely a prize to be won irritated Bella.

Regardless of their motivations, this attention was something she'd never known—an active courtship by two boys at the same time. Her experience had been limited to boys pulling her hair when she was a child, then disgusting, sweaty middle school kisses, topped by forward high school and college boys trying to grope her on a first date. She'd had as many first dates as she could tolerate, but rarely did she grant anyone a second.

She waited for the inevitable late-night advance from Stillman or Phillip. When it came, she wasn't prepared for it.

After two weeks of her ending the evening by walking and talking with the girls, Stillman and Phillip flanked her as she prepared to leave the restaurant. The guys looped their arms with hers and clutched her hands. Her mind raced. God help her, could they be imagining a threesome?

At her door, they stopped, released her arms, and stood in front of the door as if they were twin guards. Stillman looked confident, but she couldn't read Phillip.

"We talked about it," Stillman said, "and we came to a gentlemen's agreement. You must choose between us." He looked confident.

She was definitely attracted to them both—much more than merely *attracted*, if she was honest with herself. Choosing one would push away the other, and Bella wasn't sure if she wanted that, not yet.

Bella was twenty years old and had to admit that her body ached with longing for tender kisses and much more. Being close to them, having them flirt with her, brought surges of warmth and tingling over her body, a feeling starkly different from her repulsion during those sweaty, groping sessions with boys in the past. Now, her body begged to be caressed.

But how could she choose?

6

Later that night, Bella asked Hope how she knew that Charlie, Hope's steady boyfriend, was the one for her.

"During one of my high school summers," Hope said, "I met Charlie while I waited tables at a big truck stop along the interstate. We're both from Fort Collins, but I'd never met him before because he's older. He was already a Marine and had just got home on leave. Man, did he look sharp in his camo gear."

Hope bubbled with excitement. "We'd only met that night, yet he waited for me to end my shift. Charlie's buddy had picked him up from the airport, to surprise his parents. His friend left, and I drove Charlie home." Her cheeks flushed pink.

"So you liked him right away." Bella sat cross-legged on her bed. "But when did you stop dating other boys?"

"After I met Charlie, I never dated anyone else."

"But wasn't he away for long stretches of time? What about the dances, like prom? You were still in high school."

Hope looked down at her hands, and her voice got quiet. "I'm not pretty like you, Bella. Charlie is my one and only. I've never dated anyone else."

Bella was shocked. Hope was the first one who figured out how to navigate Florence's streets, the one who always came up with great ideas and plans for free time.

Hope was a natural leader, kind and honest. Maybe not what guys considered "cute," but she was a nice-looking girl. Bella suspected Hope's dress size and self-confidence were opposing forces. Charlie chose Hope, not the other way around.

Hope pressed one palm to her heart. "It's here, Bella. I can't say exactly when and how it happened, but I love Charlie and I'd do anything for him. And he loves me, so it's perfect."

Bella hoped her friend was right.

Maybe, Bella thought, she shouldn't worry about deciding between Phillip and Stillman. If she didn't choose now, it'd be fun to see what happened next.

Stillman stood with the rest of the sandal-clad group on the edge of Siena's shell-shaped Campo. The guided walking tour of the walled city—the reason they had come to Siena—bored him as much as listening to the preacher's broken-record sermons on the evils of sex outside of marriage. He couldn't wait for his free afternoon. Stillman knew what he wanted from Siena, and it had nothing to do with the history of this place and everything to do with sex.

Crowds of local Italians strolled the Campo. White and green Oca flags draped their shoulders, emblazoned with their mascot, the crowned goose. The celebrations following Oca's recent win in the Palio horse race continued in full, noisy force.

This morning, their guide had droned on about Siena's seventeen *contrade*, similar to city wards, or districts, each revolving around economics, faith, and social structure. People who wanted to rent an apartment within the boundaries of a *contrada* had to swear loyalty to that district and even raise their children as strong supporters. The rivalries between these districts resembled that of the Hatfields and the McCoys, or any other Southern feud.

The Palio—the highlight of competition between Siena's contrade—had run every year on July 2nd and August 16th since 1644, except for wartime suspensions. All day, drummers and costumed flag bearers had paraded through Siena, apparently to remind the losers of Oca's prized victory. The annoying pounding of the drums grew louder, then fainter, as the marchers' distance from the Campo changed.

The oppressive heat, trapped within the city's stone walls, sent rivulets of sweat down Stillman's back yet didn't seem to faze the costumed Italians.

The marchers reminded Stillman of his hometown's annual Fourth of July parade and picnic.

The parade featured contests for decorated floats and included the high school marching band. The band always seemed to follow the horses pulling wagons and surreys, which made marching an adventure, considering the inevitable horse manure littering the street. The town's old money residents dressed up in Civil War uniforms and carried Confederate flags to honor the noble veterans of the War of Northern Aggression.

His hometown parade and these costumed marching drummers seemed equally irrelevant to Stillman.

"Enough already." Rune wiped the sweat off his red face. "This reminds me of growing up in Nebraska and detasseling corn—ninety-four degrees and ninety-four percent humidity—and that's something I definitely don't want to think about. What I wouldn't give for Venice Beach now. How 'bout we find some shade and a nice cool beer?"

Hope rubbed her hands together. "I say we walk the city. We'll get exercise and keep our budgets intact."

Meghan shook her head. "Not us." She tilted her head to include her twin. "I saw too many leather stores in the back streets that had our names all over them." She giggled.

Karen chirped her agreement. "Not to mention the hot clerk that practically kidnapped us as we walked by." She looked at Bella. "You in?"

Bella shook her head. "No, thanks. I spotted a tiny shop on one of those narrow side streets," she waved her arm to the Campo's outer edge, "that had rad silk scarves. Thought I'd try to find it. I want something for my mom from Siena. She'd really love this place." Bella's eyes swept the Campo. Her lips pressed together, as if in determination, or maybe worry.

Stillman had tagged along with Bella all morning. He couldn't figure her out. She alternated between being aloof and flirty. But man, was she hot. He didn't make her out to be a tease. No, there was something deep about her. The mysterious part of her beneath that smokin' hot surface intrigued him almost as much as the prospect of bedding her.

The way Stillman saw it, that flirty side of her threw down a challenge to him. He thrived on competition, and he'd be damned if Phillip won her this summer.

His motor was revved. He went for it. "I know exactly where that shop is. It's next to a place with watercolor prints of the Palio." Out of the corner of his eye, he caught Phillip's scowl. "I'll show you."

Rune's head pivoted to take in the Campo. "I'll be here. It's where the action is, isn't it?" He nodded and muttered to himself. "God, I love these bitchin' babes."

Lee clapped Phillip on the back. "We seem to be the odd men out. Let's go for a walk with Hope."

Phillip's eyes shot to Bella, but Stillman stepped between them; he linked his arm with Bella's, her bare skin warm against his. He winked at her. "Ready to explore?" He didn't wait for an answer. Grinning, he pulled her with him toward the center of the Campo.

It couldn't have worked out better for him.

Stillman led Bella into the narrow street directly opposite the spot where they had left the others. He had exaggerated, of course. He remembered Bella checking out scarves and the art print store next to the shop, but he hadn't a clue as to which street it had been on. In fact, he thought it had been away from one of the piazza's spoke streets, down an almost hidden alley.

They'd find a scarf, any scrap of fabric that satisfied Bella, and then he'd take the grateful Bella to a dark alley and empty bench; he'd lost count of how many they'd passed this morning.

"I remember it being off one of these spoke streets." The deep-toned confidence sounded convincing, even to him. He let his hand slip lower to hold Bella's hand, and he pretended to lead her.

Off the main streets, narrow, cobbled alleys held more shops and restaurants, often with a handful of cloth-covered tables nestled against the building. One alley opened into a mini-piazza, complete with a fountain and park bench. Draped over the sun-drenched seat, a couple about their age groped each other and necked as if they were tucked into the back seat of a car hidden off a country road.

Stillman stopped, surprised they had chosen such an open, sunny spot. He muttered, more to himself than Bella, "What the hell?"

Bella tugged his arm to propel him forward. "They have nowhere else to go. More than likely, they live with their parents and grandparents in one house or apartment."

Stillman's groin perked to life. He had to focus on something else or his buddy would announce his thoughts to the world. His eyes roved the buildings, focusing on the architecture—surely a snoozer. He spotted a row of reliefs above them on the stone building: a lion adjacent to the arched doorway, a coat of arms, a martyred saint. "Look," he pointed at the guardians of the home. "Those are major stud."

Bella looked at him as if he were loco.

Stillman felt himself go flaccid. He shrugged. "When I'm a doctor, I'll have money to spare. I want to drive fast cars and own a big house—a mansion with a circle drive and carved reliefs."

"You'll be the rich doctor, why not?" Her head tilted back as she studied the medieval art. "You're from the South. Which do you prefer: animals or humans?" One eyebrow rose at him in a wicked, mocking challenge.

Perfect. He feigned indignation. Stillman leaned his torso backwards, away from her. He let his voice rise. "I can't believe you have to ask."

He stepped forward, slid one arm behind her lower back and supported the back of her head with his other hand, sweeping the startled girl backwards over his arm in a tango dip. "I prefer ladies. But only foxes, like you, of course." He pulled Bella upright, rested his palms on her shoulders and dropped his chin as if he were serious, and leaned toward her. Her smell—perspiration and baby powder—filled his nostrils. "You owe me an apology for the animal crack."

Bella's lips pecked his. Before Stillman had time to return the kiss, she skipped out of his grasp. She moved farther down the alley and giggled. Raising her voice, she said, "Excuse me. But you do like animals: foxy, lady animals."

He ran after her, only to have her sprint ahead. He caught up with her in a few feet. Stillman pinned Bella against the wall.

Her shoulders drew away from the wall as her bare arms met the cool stone.

One hand on her shoulder, he pinned her back to the wall. Stillman pressed his other palm flat against the stone, and stepped into her. This time, Bella met his mouth with eager lips. His hand had started to slide from her shoulder to the crook of her neck when she pulled out of the kiss.

"I still want to find that scarf for my mom."

He wanted to jump her right here and now. His thumb traced circles on her neck. "I like it here."

She smiled. "It is cooler, in the shade." Bella slid out from his arms and skipped two steps up the street. "The scarf. My mother, remember?"

He resigned himself to her singular focus. "You're pretty tight with your mother, aren't you?"

Bella nodded. "She was a young mom and worked her butt off to take care of me. Her family disowned her when she got pregnant." Her eyes lingered on his for a moment, as if she could sense the similarity in their mothers' past. Bella straightened with pride. "Mom put herself through college. She's a high school teacher. Somehow, she saved up enough to pay for my plane ticket over here. And she took on a second job to pay the rest." She looked down. "Summer abroad was her idea."

"Why?"

"She thought if I stayed in the States with all the demonstrations and protests, I'd decide to drop out."

Bella's shoulders trembled, as if a sudden chill had raced down her flesh. "But there's something else, too. I think something is going on with her that she's not telling me."

"A boyfriend?"

Bella shook her head. "Mom doesn't date much. Hardly ever, in fact. She seemed preoccupied when I left. Not sappy 'I've-got-a-new-boyfriend' preoccupied, more like, you know, distracted."

They walked in silence to the end of the street. Not looking at Bella, Stillman guided them down another street, one that sloped downhill. After the steep inclines they'd walked this morning, his legs had gotten heavier with each successive hill. Where was that damned shop?

"I appreciate your help. I really do." Quiet determination marked her words. "I refuse to give up on finding the store. I know there are a ton of other scarf shops, but it's a matter of principle at this point."

"What's my reward for finding this infamous shop?"

Expressionless, she studied his face. "How 'bout something soft and smooth?" Her husky voice hit him below the belt. She flicked her eyebrows up. The tip of her tongue pressed against her upper lip. "Something ... lickable?"

The wanting hit him hard. Stillman stepped back and jutted out his butt, afraid his arousal would scare her off. He nodded. "Let's go find that shop," he said, his words throaty with hunger. He wiped his damp palm against the back of his jeans and grabbed her hand. Stillman pulled her behind him. He had just made the best deal of the summer.

They wandered street-to-street; Bella's frustration with not finding the store became more evident as the afternoon wore on. Stillman dragged her into other stores, but she insisted none had the same selection of scarves.

Hours later, he no longer held her hand. The afternoon's heat closed in on them in the narrow passageways. They dragged their legs like wooden fence posts, heavy and unyielding after trudging the cobblestone streets.

Stillman attempted a methodical search of the side streets, without luck. Most of the shops had closed for the afternoon.

They rounded the corner of the street where they had started and spotted the twins exiting a building. The girls closed the thick wooden door behind them; they hadn't seen Stillman and Bella yet. Meghan's neck was draped with a pink and red scarf. Before Stillman could speak, Bella sprinted ahead to the girls.

Stillman caught up with them. His eyes traveled from the brass plaque on the door to the plate glass window of the neighboring shop. The window showcased large posters advertising an opera performance. Stillman could just make out the corner of the Palio print he remembered, peeking out from behind the posters. He heard Bella laughing with the twins and knew he had no time to waste.

He pulled on the wrought-iron handset. The heavy door, which the shopkeeper closed to keep out the afternoon heat, swung open. A glance inside confirmed his assumption. Stillman bent low and swept one arm toward the entryway in an exaggerated bow. "Your scarf store, I believe."

"Sure," Bella said, sauntering into the coolness of the store, "take the credit after Meghan discovers it."

"I found it, didn't I?" He pulled the door closed behind them. "You have to admit, we started on this street."

The scarves lay on tables just inside the door. Neat rows of fanned color, similar to playing cards spread to show a run in solitaire, covered the tables. A stiff plastic sleeve encased each swirl of color.

Beyond the tables in the narrow shop, leather coats, purses, and belts lined the walls. A small desk occupied the center, and beyond it stood a full-length mirror and tables of handbags. Opposite where they stood, the store opened into a wider, more traveled "spoke" street. They'd passed the store from the other side as well, Stillman realized.

He watched Bella poke among the scarves. Her long black hair fell in waves over her shoulders, which were covered enough by her blouse for admittance into the churches, but only just so. Bella's arms and legs had tanned during the weeks here, burnished to an olive brown.

"This one." She raised a plastic packet with a red, white, and black swirl scarf. "It's perfect."

Back on the street, Bella pressed him to her in a bear hug.

"I'm sorry it took so long." Stillman loved the smell of her hair, and the way the heat had intensified the natural scent of her body.

She shrugged and smiled. "No matter."

He dipped his chin. His eyes twinkled at her. "So when do I get to collect my reward? Tonight?"

Her lips parted wider. "No." She grabbed him by one wrist and tugged. Bella pulled him along, back toward the Campo. "Not later. Now."

The bright light of the open Campo made him blink to focus. The piazza had filled with people and a buzz of voices. He kept his voice light. "I was hoping for somewhere more private." His stomach flip-flopped. He couldn't think.

Without warning, she stopped behind a cluster of people, causing him to crash into her. Stillman's arms circled her to prevent them both from toppling over. Bella stepped away and spun to face him. She raised her eyebrows.

"What's your pleasure?" The corners of her eyes squinted with her smile. "Chocolate? *Limone*?" The cluster of people straightened into a queue in front of the gelateria.

Stillman remembered the specifics of her reward offer. He laughed. Regardless of the bait-and-switch, he knew she had thought about it. About sleeping together. And she wanted him. He could feel it. He also had a hunch about Bella. He'd bet she hadn't given in yet, that she still clung to virginity.

Bella handed him a cone with pale, yellow-white gelato.

Stillman lifted an eyebrow at her and made a show of oh-so-slowly licking the cool, refreshing lemon gelato. Tasty.

They were still enjoying the gelato-filled cones when the rest of their group joined them from across the piazza. The others had waited inside the museum in the base of the tower for over an hour.

Hope peeked inside the glossy red bag draped over Bella's wrist. "You found a scarf," Hope said. "It's beautiful."

Bella nodded, her pleasure still evident.

Meghan and Karen giggled.

"Did you have much trouble finding the shop?" Meghan's tone implied that an answer wasn't expected.

Stillman took a deep breath, aware of how Lee's and Phillip's eyes darted to him. He was embarrassed that it took him hours to find the scarf store. His pride would take a bigger hit if Phillip knew he'd spent the day leading Bella aimlessly through the streets instead of necking on a bench.

Stillman felt the heat first at his hairline. Phillip laughed. The burn slid around Stillman's eyes, onto his cheeks, and down his throat. Certain he was torch-red, Stillman turned his back to the growing laughter. He tossed the remainder of his cone into a trashcan. He felt a hand on his shoulder.

"You earned your reward." Bella's suggestive tone implied much more than the truth. The laughter behind them died.

He glanced over at her. Her back to the others now, she winked at him. She nodded her chin at him with one slow motion. She had rescued him.

Stillman put one hand on the small of her back, moved closer to her, and twisted her around to face their friends. His other hand covered hers, which held a cone of gelato. With slow, exacting deliberation, he licked an errant drip on Bella's cone. Stillman summoned a soft, throaty voice reserved for practiced lines in front of a mirror. "It was the best afternoon of my life."

Bella smiled, silent. A perfect "ladies don't tell" response.

Out of the corner of his eye, Stillman saw Phillip grimace.

"I'm starved," Rune said.

Phillip said, "Maybe we should have an early dinner."

Hope muttered something about munchies and bought Rune a gelato. She looked over at Phillip and motioned to the array of gelato flavors. Phillip shook his head.

Stillman draped an arm over Bella's shoulders. Phillip glared. He knew Phillip didn't give a rat's ass about dinner or food. No. Phillip was upset about Bella. Stillman smirked. He stood on second base and was poised to steal third. The preacher was gonna love Bella—he always did flirt with the pretty ones in church.

7

South of Atlanta, Georgia

Dust swirled across the long dirt lane. Hot, humid air pulled the sweat from Stillman's six-year-old head, frizzing his auburn curls and sending creeks of water from his forehead to his chin. The dirt clung to his cheeks like dew to grass on an early spring morning. He sat on the edge of the wooden front porch, waiting and watching the road for the rolling cloud of dust that signaled a car.

She started up again, with her cries. His mother moaned, a low, gasping moan, rising in pitch and volume. Then she screamed. "Oh God, oh God, help me! Help me!"

Stillman knew better than to run inside to her bedroom. He couldn't help her. Only the doctor and God could help her now. Thank goodness his daddy was at the church, so he couldn't hear her cry to God.

At last. The gray puffs appeared on the horizon. Stillman ran back to his mother's bedroom.

"Mama?" He stood outside her door. Her moaning stopped. "The doctor's coming. He'll be here soon, Mama."

"Come inside, honey."

Stillman stood by the door. She never asked him to come in alone.

"I need to … " Her frail voice faltered.

Stillman pushed open the door. The smell hit him harder than the sight of her. Stale, sour air filled the dark bedroom. He saw the window blind behind Mama's lace curtains pulled down to the sill to block out the daylight.

Mama's thin frame was curled on the bed, facing the door. She lifted one hand. Her fingers waved him toward her.

Stillman moved to the bed. He held her hand in both of his. "Do you need water, Mama?"

She shook her head. Her eyes took hold of his and jumped right inside his head. "He's"—her free hand patted the air over the bed next to her—"not your daddy. You hear me, honey? He's not your daddy." Her eyes wouldn't let go of him. "He'll take care of you, though. I made him promise … he promised on the Bible." The scratchy words seemed to make her chest cave in, as if she had to push them out one by one. "I loved your daddy."

This made no sense. His mama squeezed his fingers. Not his daddy?

As if she could read his mind, she nodded. "Your daddy was a college boy, from the North. Chicago. A big city, big as Atlanta. He was here for a year of college. He went to Emory." She smiled, like Stillman should know about Emory. He could see her pride. She collapsed back into her pillow.

Stillman bent over her. He rested one palm on her chest. "You need to rest, Mama. The doctor will be here any minute. We can talk later."

She shook her head, her lips in a tight line as if she'd caught him stealing a cookie before dinner, back when she had strength to work in the kitchen.

Her eyes closed for a second, then her hand fluttered in his, reminding him of a trapped butterfly. "He sold books door-to-door on weekends to help pay for his college. That's how we met. He came to town one fine, autumn day. The breeze that day was as gentle as a baby's whisper, and the night cooled down right proper. Cool enough for a sweater. I wore his."

Stillman had never heard his mother string so many words together in a row. Somehow, he knew she'd said these very words to herself many, many times.

"We saw each other every weekend after that. We loved each other. What we did together wasn't wrong. Don't ever believe him if he tries to tell you it was, preaching some Bible verse at you. No. It was beautiful. It's not a sin to love someone with your whole heart and body, that is, if you're not married to another person."

Stillman heard the doctor's old Ford pickup turn into the lane. He'd be here soon. Mama's hand tightened on his. She had heard it, too.

"You're smart, like your daddy. Study hard." Outside, the pickup's brakes squealed, and the engine stopped. The sound of the pickup door slamming closed seemed to sap Mama's last strength. She slumped back against the flat pillow. She nodded and her eyes flitted toward the bedroom door. She slid her hand out of his sweaty palm.

He turned to go.

"Stillman?"

He turned around. Her lips were pinched together.

"You study hard, and you'll get out of here. You can go to a big city."

"I will, Mama."

"Be a good boy. When you love someone, you do right by them." Her eyelids closed and opened, and then they closed and opened again like the long, swinging jump-rope the older girls played games with on the playground. "Promise me."

"Cross my heart and hope to die." His fingers drew a big "X" over his heart.

The doctor's fist rapped against the door. "Good afternoon." Stillman heard the door open and went to greet the doctor. The tall man's white hair was parted and slicked back like a movie star's. He bent down in front of Stillman and dropped one knee to the floor to look him in the eye. "I understand your mother's not doing well today."

"No, sir."

"Well then, maybe I should go visit her. Is that all right with you?"

"Yes, sir."

The doctor stood up. His fingers touched the top of Stillman's head, and then they scratched back and forth to muss his hair. Stillman looked up and smiled. His daddy— the preacher—never touched him except when it was time to punish him.

"All right, son, I'd best go tend to your mother." He carried his black bag into the bedroom and closed the door behind him.

Hours later, after his preacher-daddy had come home, Stillman sat on the porch steps again, wondering about the man who was his real daddy. He figured he shouldn't tell the preacher about Mama's story. Why else would she say those things when he wasn't around to hear? No, he'd best hide that all in the back of his brain and never, ever tell a soul. Stillman had a hunch that telling Mama's story would lead his preacher-daddy to bring out the leather strap, and he knew he didn't want that.

The fireflies had come out of hiding and tiny stars had appeared by the time he heard the men come out of the bedroom.

The doctor eased himself down on the step next to Stillman. His white dress shirt had big sweat rings under the armpits. His watch had a sweep hand that seemed to hitch onto every second mark and rest a moment as it circled on around. Stillman stared at that watch so hard he thought his eyes would bug out. He couldn't bring himself to look at the doctor's face.

The doctor cleared his throat, a raspy noise that sounded as if he needed a glass of water. Stillman watched another minute go by on the watch. Click-click-click.

"Your mama, Stillman, she's resting in heaven now."

Stillman nodded. His eyes burned as if he'd gotten soap in them. He could feel the tears and tried to blink them away. They kept coming, and he had to use the back of his wrist to clear them off his face.

The doctor put his arm across the back of Stillman's shoulders. The door to the house squeaked open and closed with a thud.

"Son," his daddy said, sounding perturbed, "what are you doing settin' here when there is chores that need doing?"

Stillman put his hands on the step to push himself up. He felt the doctor's arm heavy on his shoulders, pushing him down. The doctor's hand squeezed Stillman's shoulder. It felt right, somehow, sitting on the step next to him.

"The chores can wait. You don't have cows that need milking or animals to be fed. His chores can probably even wait until morning, if need be."

"I said now."

Stillman tried to push up, but the doctor wouldn't let him. He felt the big hand pat his shoulder, and then the doctor stood up and turned to face his daddy.

"I think the boy should come with me tonight," the doctor said. "I'll drive him out first thing in the morning. He can do his chores then." He stepped closer to Stillman's daddy and lowered his voice, but Stillman could still hear what he said. "That'll give you a chance to take care of things in the house. You can call the undertaker after we leave. He's only a child."

Stillman was afraid to turn around and look at the two men. He heard his daddy suck in air like Mama's vacuum and then snort it out.

"He should be here," his daddy said. "With me." The voice wasn't his Sunday preaching voice, or even his discipline voice that meant the strap. No, this was like the rattlesnake Stillman startled last summer when he crossed the ditch; it had hissed and reared its head up, its tongue flicking in and out.

"John," the doctor said, his voice low, but serious, "I'm taking him, and you're not stopping me. I did you and his mother a favor years ago, so I figure you owe me one or two favors back. You can count this as one." The doctor's big shoes stepped across the porch and he knelt beside Stillman. "Come on, son, you're coming with me."

The shakes came over Stillman, as if the weather had turned freezing cold, only it hadn't.

"Go on now." His daddy spit out the words.

Stillman stood up; afraid his daddy would change his mind, he tumbled down the porch steps and ran to the pickup.

Later, after a bath in the doctor's tub—and it wasn't even Saturday—Stillman stood in the little room that the doctor used as an office, right next to his examination room. Books lined half of one wall. He'd never seen so many books outside of the library. They had worn leather bindings; the doctor must read them often.

He reached out to touch one. His fingers traced the gold letters on the spine: *Anatomy and Physiology*. There were two books with that same name, one right next to the other—a worn one and a new one, with a spine that had hardly any creases in it.

Stillman jumped back from the books when he heard the floor creak behind him. He bowed his head and waited for his punishment.

But none came. "Which book interests you most?"

"I don't know, sir."

"Sure you do. Please call me Dr. D." He chuckled.

"Delacroix is a mouthful." He rested his hand on Stillman's shoulder. "Was it the *Anatomy and Physiology*?"

Stillman nodded. Then his words jumped right out of his mouth, although he hadn't intended to speak. "How come you have two? Is one better than the other?"

Dr. D reached up and pulled down the worn book. "This one is my favorite of all the books on the wall." He cradled the spine in his big palm. "I've studied it so often the pages are coming loose from the binding, so I bought a new one. I know it's frivolous, but I couldn't bear the thought of looking for a page and having it missing. Here," he said, opening it to pictures of naked bodies, "let me show you."

Stillman sucked in his breath. He knew he should look away, but his eyes stayed glued to the pictures. He'd go to hell for sure now. And if he was doomed to eternal damnation, he might as well get a good look, since he'd already sinned.

"This is a teaching book, not a sinful one." Dr. D must have read his mind. "Come closer, so you can read the captions. There is nothing more beautiful than the naked human body."

Stillman sat next to Dr. D on the upholstered bench in his office. Dr. D showed him one page and then another, sometimes explaining in his quiet, low voice and sometimes letting Stillman read and study it for himself.

"What do you want to be when you grow up, son?"

Stillman thought of his mama's words. Hot tears sprang to his eyes. He blinked hard and finally had to use the back of his hand. He lowered his chin and shook his head. "Don't know. But I'm gonna study hard." He gulped. "I promised my mama."

"Of course you will. You're a bright boy, just like your daddy."

Stillman's wide eyes shot up to Dr. D's.

He nodded solemnly. "I met your real daddy before he went back up North. He was book smart, but a fool to leave and not marry your mama." Dr. D stood up. "Time for bed. It's been a long day for us both, and I promised the preacher you'd do your chores in the morning."

Preacher. Dr. D knew his mama's secret. He scrambled to his feet.

The next morning, Dr. D drove him home early, while the dew still shone on the leaves of the weeping willow in front of the church.

The preacher stood on the porch, waiting for them.

Dr. D had his arm across Stillman's shoulders as they walked up to the porch.

"John," Dr. D said, "your boy is ready to do his chores, just as I promised. But before you send him out, I want you both to hear what I've got to say."

"Say it, then. He's got a passel to do today—two days' worth of chores—and I want him to sweep out the church, too."

"Then I'll be quick." Dr. D walked to his pickup and reached under the seat. He came back carrying his worn copy of *Anatomy and Physiology*. "Stillman," he said, holding out his prized book, "I want you to have this. You have a curious, bright mind. You'd make a good doctor. This book is for you to read and study."

Stillman clutched the big volume to his chest. His? To keep? He'd study it, too. Study it real hard, for Mama.

"John, I have two copies, so I'm giving the boy my old one. I know he'll respect it as a teaching book, to read and study, not to ogle or parade in front of other boys. Isn't that right, Stillman?"

Stillman looked at Dr. D. He nodded up and down three times. "Yes, sir. Thank you. I'll take real good care of it, so none of the pages drop out."

Dr. D leaned into the preacher until his mouth was right next to the preacher's ear. His voice got real quiet, but Stillman heard every word. "Don't even think about taking his book away, John. I'll ride you out of town myself if you do."

The preacher's face got white and puffy, then red as a wild strawberry.

"Stillman, you better take your book inside now and get to those chores." Dr. D patted Stillman's head.

Stillman clutched his book in one arm and hugged the doctor with the other. "It's the best present I've ever gotten."

After Stillman put the book on the center of the wooden crate beside his bed, he hustled out of the bedroom to start his chores. He heard Dr. D's pickup drive away from the house.

The preacher stood in the kitchen, his face even redder than it had been outside. He whacked the back of his hand so hard against Stillman's cheek that Stillman's legs buckled. His knees smacked the floor.

"After you're finished here, you'll sweep, then scrub, the church floor. You'll scrub that floor on your knees, boy. While you scrub you can ask the good Lord's forgiveness for saying that blasphemous book was a better gift than the Bible that I gave you for your birthday." He kicked Stillman's bottom, pushing him toward the door. "Now git, before I have to use the strap on you."

8

Siena, Italy

An Italian man in his late twenties sauntered up to the group. A cigarette dangled from the corner of his lips. He wore skin-tight jeans, leather loafers without socks, and a white T-shirt two sizes too small. He moved next to Karen—so close his T-shirt touched her breasts—and kissed her on both cheeks.

Stillman imagined fondling Bella's breasts.

Meghan got the double kiss next. Her cheeks flushed crimson when the Italian's hand lingered; his hand squeezed her butt.

Stillman's arm, still draped over Bella's shoulders, drew her into his side. The wholesome powdery smell of her punched him midline, jerking the breath from him. No way this Italian asshole was getting close to his girl.

Karen introduced everybody to the asshole. Massimo, a.k.a. the Italian with the playboy attitude, had met the girls in a leather store. Stillman would bet his dinner money Massimo had followed them into the shop for the sole purpose of meeting the beautiful, luscious American girls.

Massimo's finger pointed at each of them, and he counted in Italian. He nodded. "It is possible. We do not have too many to go together."

Wide-eyed, Karen turned to the puzzled group. "Massimo told us about an abandoned estate. He'll take us there and we can explore. I guess the place has Etruscan relics practically everywhere—"

"And Massimo said nobody really cares if you pick one up." Meghan's voice sounded convincing.

"That would be a radical souvenir." Rune nodded. He looked at his gelato cone. "I guess dinner could wait."

"Artifact raiding?" Lee frowned.

"Are you a coward?" Bella said.

Stillman studied his friends' faces—only Lee seemed to object. He couldn't read Bella's face at all. He thought of her words. Stillman knew that he would never steal. The preacher had drilled that into him. But let someone call him a coward? Not him. "I'm game," he said. "How do we get there?"

Massimo puffed up his small-framed chest. "I drive you." He swung one hairy arm around each of the twins' necks. "You beautiful ladies ride in front with me."

Phillip grimaced and looked at the others. "I believe in closeness, but how will we fit in one car?"

Meghan looked back at them as the threesome moved away. "Massimo's got a truck that'll hold you in the back. Let's get a move on."

At the parking lot, Massimo puffed out his chest and gestured to a pickup that had seen better days. Stillman vaulted into the back of the dusty truck and extended a hand down to help Hope and Bella. Before Lee and Phillip had a chance to climb into the truck, Stillman tugged Bella to the front of the truck bed. He sat down and patted the spot next to him, grinning at her. "You can lean on my shoulder so your head doesn't bang against the truck."

She slid in next to him and snuggled close, in spite of the blazing sun. Phillip's frown egged Stillman to rub it in. He nibbled Bella's ear. Phillip pouted and stared at the countryside.

The truck bounced over the cobblestones. It jostled them against one another and the truck's hard surfaces. Shock absorbers? What shock absorbers? Stillman clamped his teeth together so he wouldn't bite his tongue.

The cobblestones, thank God, finally ended when they reached the outskirts of the city. Massimo accelerated. The smoother streets soon gave way to the dust of the country. The afternoon sun and a swirl of dust smothered them. Everyone in the back—even the two girls—had stripes of sweat that made rivulets in the grit on their faces.

Stillman could hear the twins chatting and laughing with their Italian friend. The truck screeched to a stop at the crest of a rutted lane. Lee and Phillip, who had commandeered the rear sides of the truck, tumbled out first. Bella scrambled to the back and, aided by Phillip's eager arms, hopped out and skipped away from the truck before Stillman could jump out.

A rundown, abandoned house topped the hill. Around it, dead grasses and weeds evidenced past disruption. Newly turned earth showed signs of recent digging.

"The ground has zigzags." Meghan giggled after giving her apt description.

Rune put his hands on his hips and surveyed the land. "Gosh, it's great that we're the first to discover this site. With all the upturned earth, it seems like we're the last to the relic-hunting party. We'll be lucky to find anything."

Amen. Stillman's lips tightened, but he refused to complain.

Massimo kicked at a clod of dirt. "Perhaps one or two persons have also dug here for Etruscan relics." His flat palms rose up as if to ask, "How could one know?" He cast a beguiling look in Karen's direction.

Gag me, Stillman thought, turning away from the flirt. He trudged off toward the dilapidated structure, hurrying to catch up with Bella. "We may not want to go inside, Bella. It's probably rotten and home to a thousand rats."

She turned her head so he could hear. "Are you afraid?"

He had no choice. "Hell, no."

She grinned at him, all challenge. "Phillip's already inside."

The entry door hung on rusty hinges. Half of the door had broken off, which left jagged splinters along the edge. Stillman followed Bella inside. Rodent scat littered the floor and cobwebs masked the ceiling. Only the light that streamed through the window openings made the abandoned house seem less creepy.

"Phillip, where are you?" Bella stood four paces inside; her arms dangled limp at her sides.

"The next room." Phillip's voice sounded loud in the

empty structure, as if he were right beside them. "Be careful. There's junk and broken wine bottles everywhere."

Stillman followed Bella through the arched opening to the large room that occupied most of the structure's first floor. Phillip squatted next to a heap of clutter: large rocks, segments of rotten square timber, twisted rusty metal, broken and unbroken wine bottles.

"Lovely." Bella bent down beside him. "What do you think?"

"This place is a dump. It's probably been unoccupied, except for the occasional party, for a hundred years or more." He stood and kicked a wine bottle, sending it skittering across the room. "It's a wonder it's still standing." He beckoned with his hand. "Let's see what's upstairs."

"Not a good idea." Stillman's words shot out before he could stop them.

"Scared of ghosts?" Phillip leered at him.

"With all the water that's poured into here, don't you think the stairs might be rotten?" How many times had Stillman sat through the preacher's lecture on the dangers of abandoned shacks and how those dangers would punish sinners who entered?

Bella circled the room. "I think I'll take my chances." She pointed at the staircase. "Stone steps."

Stillman cursed to himself. He tramped past them to the stairs. A few window slits lit the narrow corridor by the stairs; he could hardly see. His toe jammed against the riser and pain shot through his foot. Hopefully, his shoe had saved him from a broken toe.

Stillman rounded the corner to the second floor. He pressed his back to the wall and sidestepped into the room. An enormous hole in the ceiling opened the room up to the sky—plenty of light here. The floorboards—where present—were warped upward in a crazy jumble of splintered lumber dotted with animal droppings. He heard Bella and Phillip step into the room behind him but didn't turn or speak.

"Ooh, look." Bella picked her way along the right wall until she reached an indented section. She untied the long, fringed, cotton sash around her waist, which released her peasant blouse. With it, she wiped the accumulated grime and dust off a relief imbedded in the niche. Her blouse, set free from the belt, swayed with her body as she scrubbed at the dirt.

Stillman edged along the perimeter of the room. He had a perfect view of her breasts jiggling braless under the gauzy fabric. He felt Phillip move beside him. He knew Phillip didn't give a crap about the relief. No, he and Phillip only had eyes for Bella's dancing breasts.

"It's Mary." Bella's fingers traced the face of the Madonna.

"It's a really old Mary," Phillip chimed in from behind Stillman. "The Italians really live their religion."

"With contradictions everywhere," Stillman said.

Bella turned to him.

"I don't get how Catholics can profess to adhere to the first and greatest commandment, yet practice idolatry." Stillman remembered many lectures from the preacher on this very topic.

Bella's eyebrows knit together. "I'm Catholic. I do not practice idolatry. This," she said, her hand sweeping in front of the relief, "is a figure of Mary. I pray to her, not a statue." A glare painted her face. "Take it back."

Bad choice on his part. A really bad choice. "Sorry. It's my interpretation, that's all. No offense intended." He studied Bella's face. He hadn't dampened her desire by mouthing off about religion, had he? Shit. Bella turned to the wall, kissed the relief, and then stomped past him and down the stairs.

"Smooth move, Casanova." With a chuckle, Phillip left him alone on the second floor.

Stillman's fist slammed against the wall adjacent to the relief. Dust flew everywhere from the impact and brought tears to his eyes. Moron. Then shouts of anger sent him running down the stairs.

In front of the house, Lee and Rune were wrestling; they tumbled over each other on the hard-baked earth, throwing out fists and curses with equal fervor. Rune had the edge on both fronts. What Rune lacked in fighting skill he made up for with innovative swearing that would have made a sailor proud. Stillman stopped behind Bella to watch the show.

A screeching whistle cut the air. Stillman turned to the noise and saw Hope's hand lower from her mouth. It was no surprise that a ranch girl from the West could whistle louder than he could. Rune's arm fell to his side. Time to be a hero. Stillman grabbed Rune and yanked him off Lee.

Lee scrambled to his feet, rubbing his puffy left eye. "Put it back." He craned his skinny neck, canvassing the others' faces. "He's got a relic—maybe Etruscan. Not to donate to a museum. To sell."

"This," Rune said, holding up a dirt-encrusted relic that might have once been a vase, "is sure as hell not doing any good out here. It's a souvenir. It's probably not salable, anyway." He walked away from them and examined the relic in his hands. He muttered to himself, loud enough for all to hear. "Piece of junk … not worth the trouble … " Rune bobbed it up and down in his hand, as if contemplating chucking it as far as he could throw it.

"Stealing, Rune?" Stillman remembered his lesson about stealing like it was yesterday, even though he had been in the seventh grade.

It had been exceptionally hot that year and his school didn't have air conditioning. His lunch had spoiled before he could eat it more than once. One morning, he had stolen a quarter from the change jar in the kitchen and bought himself an ice cream cone after school. Unfortunately, the heat had melted the ice cream faster than he could eat it, and telltale drips marked his shirt when he got home.

The preacher, after quizzing Stillman about the stains, had quoted Matthew, chapter 5, verse 30: "And if thy right hand causeth thee to stumble, cut it off, and cast it from thee: for it is profitable for thee that one of thy members should perish, and not thy whole body go into hell."

The preacher had grabbed a butcher knife and pinned his arm against the kitchen table. He had raised that knife in the air as if to sever Stillman's hand. Stillman begged for mercy, tears streaming down his face. The preacher hadn't cut his hand off, but as punishment, had taken Stillman's most prized possession—the *Anatomy and Physiology* book the doctor had given him after his mother died.

Ever since that day, Stillman had known two things with absolute certainty. He would never steal and he would never forgive the preacher, the mean, abusive man who had married his mother.

"I don't think taking that relic is a wise idea, Rune." Stillman's firm voice gave no indication of the pain stirred inside him by his memory.

Rune had stripped to his undershirt. He looked up from his rucksack; his hands were finishing the job of stuffing in the shirt he had stripped off. He cradled his pack under his arm. "You're right, guys. Only losers steal."

Stillman followed Rune to the pickup. Rune's pack, slung over one shoulder, bumped against his back. The bottom of the backpack curved out in the shape of its contents. The shape of the Etruscan pottery. Rune, asshole that he was, had the balls to steal the relic. Stillman knew, better than anyone, that thieves always get punished, one way or another.

9

Florence, Italy

Meghan, in a variegated coral blouse and white pleated skirt, followed the group into yet another room of the *Istituto e Museo di Storia della Scienza*. Why couldn't they tour a fashion exhibit, like the costume gallery in the Pitti Palace? No, she was stuck today in this science museum. Meghan had taken in way too many boring rooms filled with scientific instruments from the years of Medici influence.

She trudged along, and her mind wandered to imagining the fabrics used by the fashionable aristocrats of that era. She stood in front of exhibit after exhibit, but she refused to look at the one that held the middle finger of Galileo's right hand. Creepy. Why would anyone choose to display the finger of a dead guy—no matter how famous?

The beauty of the coiled glass spiral thermometers drew her eyes. The museum guide droned on about the mechanics. She tuned out the guide and studied the curled rings of the thermometer's glass "snail" stems, studded with colored buttons to mark the degrees. It was as pretty as a sheer beaded evening gown. The guide blew her warm breath on one thermometer, and water shot out of it into the air. Meghan giggled.

"Easier to look at than the finger of a dead scientist?" Lee's eyes twinkled.

She nodded; she thought about the finger and her lips clamped together to stifle a retch.

"This museum isn't your thing, is it?" His eyes didn't judge her.

"No way." She shrugged and then stepped closer to him to whisper next to his ear. "I'm good for maybe one more exhibit, then I'm splitting. I know my way back to the hotel, so don't let them call out the polizia. Those guys are like the Gestapo."

A grin lit up Lee's face. "Come with me to the medical instrument exhibit, and I'll split with you. I figure that since I'm pre-med, I have to check that section out. But that'll be it for me. I've had enough of museums, too."

"Deal." She had caught Lee drawing in an unlined notebook two days before. He had closed it too fast for her to see his work but confessed that he found the sculpture in Florence mesmerizing. Maybe they could plant themselves in a piazza somewhere and sketch together. She'd record ideas she had for clothing designs and he could draw, well, whatever someone planning to be a doctor draws. Organs? Body systems?

Meghan followed Lee to the second floor.

Boxes of instruments lined one wall of the high-ceilinged room. Lee grabbed her hand and pulled her along. His broad hand grasped her thin fingers casually, yet a warm sensation shot up Meghan's arm.

One box lined with velvet held saws that reminded her of those in her grandfather's garage, only these sported pearl handles, not paint-flecked red wood. The hacksaw looked ominous, conjuring up visions of surgeries on a battle's sidelines. The broad-bladed saw was similar to the one she and Karen had used to cut down a sapling in her grandfather's backyard. They never got in trouble for felling the little tree; their grandfather had a soft spot for them that seemed endless.

Lee muttered something about amputations.

Meghan ignored him. She moved closer to a series of life-size wax models mounted to the wall. Models of wombs, with babies in various positions, jutted out from the wall. She felt Lee's palms on the caps of her shoulders.

"They used them for obstetrics instruction. Pretty cool, huh?"

Meghan wondered how twins, like she and Karen, had looked inside a womb. Crowded, for sure. But do twins have their heads in the same direction, or are they yin-yang, one up and one down?

Lee's breath brushed her left ear. "Ready to bug out?"

She nodded.

They bolted hand-in-hand from the museum, away from the River Arno. Minutes later, the heat of the afternoon sun beat against their bare heads. They wove through the streets, Lee pulling Meghan along behind him. The streets opened into a piazza. Meghan knew where he'd brought her.

The Gothic white Santa Croce church presided over one side of the sand-covered piazza. It loomed like a smaller version of the Duomo. They had toured the church the previous week—the resting place of Michelangelo, Leonardo Bruni, and Galileo.

"Great." Meghan raised her hands in mock exasperation. "First Galileo's finger, now his tomb. You got a thing for him?"

Lee shook his head. "Nope." He grinned. One hand gestured to the piazza. "Check it out. For the Calcio, the football game that started centuries ago."

"Football?" Meghan had tuned out most of their guide's talk about Santa Croce.

"They brought in sand for a playing surface. The players all wear elaborate costumes, like from olden days. It started right here, at Santa Croce."

Sand covered the stone center of the piazza, and wooden bleachers lined one side of the square.

"There's a match today."

"Where'd you hear that?"

His mouth twitched. "I pay attention."

"This is pass-fail, remember? You don't need to nail an A in it. You and Stillman want to go to med school, so you need a high GPA, but this class won't matter, not unless you flunk."

"I dig Florence." His eyes looked serious, reminding Meghan of a professor. "I'll live here someday."

"Why?"

His head ducked low, as if he were embarrassed to

answer the question. "The art. Mostly the sculptures." He grabbed her hand and pulled her behind him. "C'mon."

They walked around the piazza, then down a tiny street off to the side. Shadows edged the narrow street. Lee stopped near a window that displayed a single black leather jacket and matching handbag. He pulled her inside the store.

Her eyes adjusted to the subdued light after the glaring sun of the piazza. Glass ceiling fixtures—identical to those in her grandparents' small frame house in Chicago—lit the store. Their cozy house always felt welcoming and warmed by love. This tiny leather goods shop had the same feeling. It was exactly what she hoped one day to capture in a boutique of her own.

Six jackets hung side by side on the left side of the shop. Narrow walnut shelves lined the opposite wall. A scant dozen purses and three belts comprised the rest of the visible selection. Below the shelves, splotches of color peeked out from narrow cubbyholes. Pink, yellow, tan, white, black, red, shades of brown and cordovan. The cubbyholes held leather gloves for every occasion— dress gloves, not the knobby knit mittens Meghan used to warm her hands against the blustery winter cold.

The rhythmic hum, punctuated by steady thumps, that came from the rear of the store suddenly stopped. Only the whir of an oscillating fan cut the silence.

"*Buon giorno.*" A thin man in his sixties stood beside the sewing machine in the back of the room. Thick, straight, steel-gray hair covered his head. He pulled his bifocals off, cradling the lenses in his palm. He grinned at Lee. "You are back, American."

"*Buon giorno.*" Lee moved with purpose to the older man. He clasped the man's right hand in both of his own. "I brought a friend. She likes leather and fashion."

Meghan's face erupted in a smile. She took her turn clasping the man's rough hand in both of hers. She bobbed her head to each side of his face as she gave him a double kiss. "Your work," she said, glancing back at the hanging jackets, not sure if he would understand her words, "is beautiful."

"*Grazie, grazie.*"

"*Prego.*" She smiled, then broke eye contact, afraid he'd speak Italian to her. She patted the sewing machine, identical to her grandmother's. Black, with a cord running from the wheel on the right to the foot platform below, the machine was powered by the pumping action of the operator's feet. Her fingertips traced a line along the smooth surface of the top. "Could we watch you work?"

Laughter erupted from deep within the man's chest. "Of course."

The afternoon flew by. Ideas for new designs bombarded her head. Shadows covered the street when Lee and Meghan stepped out into the cool air.

Meghan threw herself at Lee and kissed him square on the lips. "That shop was great."

Lee placed one hand under Meghan's long hair, sliding it up her spine to the back of her neck. "So was the kiss." His mouth found hers.

Her skin tingled all over. His left thumb traced a pattern up and down her right side, his hand finally lingering at her bra line. Shivers raced from his touch and extended to parts of her body that his hand was nowhere near. Lee nibbled on her lower lip. "Umm, this beats the middle finger of Galileo's right hand all to hell."

Acting like young Italians who take their love to the street, Meghan and Lee explored each other's faces, ears, and necks in the cool alley street. Time melted away.

The sound of beating drums, reminding Meghan of those in Chicago's St. Patrick's Day Parade, came from the nearby street, the Borgo Santa Croce.

Lee grabbed her hand and pulled her toward the noise. A crowd sat in the bleachers and circled the piazza. Cheers and clapping erupted when men wearing yellow and red tunics and black bloomers inset with yellow and red silk reached the sand field. Rows of marchers followed the drummers. They carried either blue and green flags or red and white flags–all embellished with designs of animals and symbols.

Meghan's fingers ran through the back of Lee's frizzy curls. "Now what?"

Lee slipped his arms around her waist. "It's the Calcio Storico. It's about to start." He bent his head, nibbling the side of her neck. He took a break from his playground to peer into her eyes. "It's today's event."

"Oh." Meghan frowned. "The event we're all supposed to watch together. Think the rest of the group is here?"

Lee's eyes sparkled. "We could watch five or ten minutes—maybe from over there, in the shadow of the awning—and then split. We can go to my room."

She thought about his roommate. "What about Rune?"

"He and Stillman are going to get stoned." Lee winked. "Besides, we have a signal when we don't want to be disturbed. We drape a towel over the doorknob. It means, 'I've got a girl inside, so don't come in.'"

Meghan peered at his face. "Have you used that signal this summer?"

"No." Lee blinked and his face was as solemn as if he were in church. "There's only one girl I want to use the signal for, and you're it."

Hours later, Lee walked her back to her own room. His mouth probed hers again. Meghan rested her palm against his damp chest. "You can't come in. I don't know if Karen's back yet."

"I know." He sighed. "Tomorrow?"

Meghan bit her lower lip. She nodded.

Inside her tiny room, the still air smothered her. Karen hadn't returned yet. Meghan ran to open the window, then flicked on the fan. Now the hot air moved. Sweat covered her face and body. She stripped to her bra and panties and danced around the narrow beds. Her hands moved to their own rhythm, the rhythm they had discovered together.

How had she not seen this coming? She had been drawn to Lee since the first afternoon they met, but never imagined she'd lose her virginity this summer.

The warm stickiness between her legs made her look down. A sheer smear of blood crossed her thigh. She remembered a bit of pain, but her passion had made her forget it. Karen seeing blood on her leg was not the way Meghan wanted to tell her twin about Lee, and how much she cared for him.

Karen knew all about having a boyfriend. Ed and Karen had dated for two years and had been having sex for over a year. Karen teased Meghan that if she didn't get busy, Meghan would be a virgin when they turned thirty.

Meghan grabbed a towel and fresh panties and threw a sundress over her head. At this hour, her odds with the communal bathroom looked promising. As she moved through the door, Karen's foot accidentally stepped on hers.

"Where were you?" Karen's lips pinched together. "You canned the museum. And I didn't see you at the Calcio, or at the phone booths."

Meghan grinned. "I had the most amazing time." With her wide smile, she probably resembled a circus clown, but Meghan didn't care. She waited for Karen to pump her for information. But instead of questions, Karen gave a whoop and her words rushed out.

"Meg, you won't believe it." Karen spun in a circle, her arms waving over her head. "Ed proposed." She stopped her spin and grabbed her twin by the arm. "I'm engaged."

The warmth of the lovemaking evaporated from Meghan's body. She froze. She couldn't tell Karen about Lee now. Karen's engagement trumped her news.

Disappointment washed over her as if it were a cool, slimy gel. Then, like she had so many times before, Meghan thought about Karen, about her twin's excitement. Meghan had a lifetime of Karen's triumphs outshining hers. Karen's part in the play was bigger. Karen, not Meghan, was soccer team captain. Karen's prom dress was more elaborate, and more expensive.

Meghan tossed her towel and panties onto the nearest bed. She hugged Karen and pulled her close.

The twins sat together cross-legged on the bed. Meghan had her face in control now. She widened her eyes. "Tell me everything."

Partway through Karen's recounting of her brief phone conversation with Ed, Karen stopped mid-sentence. "Hey, what happened to you?"

Meghan inhaled a deep breath. This was Karen's moment, not hers. "Lee and I watched a man make leather jackets and gloves. A real artisan."

Karen grinned. "Get some ideas we can use in the States?" They had long planned to open a boutique together someday.

"Of course." Meghan patted her sister's hand. "But tell me more. When are you going to tell Dad?" While Karen chatted on, Meghan's mind drifted back to her time with Lee. She thought of his gentle touch, his quiet whispers, and the fairy-tale future she had imagined while lying naked in Lee's arms.

10

Night train Milan, Italy to Paris, France

After running to catch the train, Bella and Karen collapsed onto a lower bunk. Stillman and Rune swung themselves onto the two top berths of the six-person couchette. The train jerked, then swayed side to side as it lumbered away from the loading platform in Milan.

Karen giggled. "I didn't think we'd make it."

Washed with relief, Bella sprawled on the hard berth, her arms and legs splayed out. "I know Lee wanted to be prepared." She gestured to the two bags crammed with food and bottled water on the floor of their couchette. "But those heavy suckers nearly cost us our train."

Bella laughed, thinking of their awkward dash through Milano Centrale with the guys carrying heavy bags of provisions, dodging fellow passengers, small children, and the occasional large pushcart stacked with luggage. Their stop at the small store a block from the station gobbled up precious time and nearly cost them the trip.

Stillman's head appeared above them over their berth, as he leaned into the center aisle. "By the way, thanks for the treat, Rune." He stretched one hand out toward Rune, who was perched cross-legged on the opposite top berth.

Rune slapped Stillman's hand in a "low-five."

"Thank the artists of Florence, whose paintings I resold at a profit."

Karen giggled again. She slid out of the berth and stood tiptoe next to Rune's berth. She grabbed the front of his shirt and pulled him toward her, planting a long, loud kiss on his mouth. "That's for your part in giving me a trip to Paris. This is going to be a blast, although you did take advantage of those painters."

Rune mocked offense. "You feel sorry for them? Because I purchased their watercolors at the going rate and sold them to Americans starved for a touch of Europe? Hell, they should thank me. I introduced their art to America. Thanks for the kiss, by the way, but won't the dude you're going to marry get pissed at you for stuff like that?"

"He'll never know," Karen said. "We're not married yet, and I intend to enjoy this last summer of freedom. I'd be stupid to not live it up while I'm in Europe. I have a lifetime to be married, but only one summer here."

Bella stood up next to Karen. She pulled Rune's head toward her and touched his mouth with a light kiss.

"Hell of an entrepreneur," Stillman said. He swung down next to Karen and Bella, so they stood side by side in the narrow space between the two triple bunks. Stillman wrapped an arm around each girl. "Now, as they say, it's a long train to Paris, and we can party down. Where's the wine?"

The sliding door to the tiny compartment jerked open.

"Hey." Phillip pushed his way inside, with a gloomy

look on his face. "This is no fun, being split up." He walked into the compartment until he stood beside Bella. "All eight of us could cram together."

Rune vaulted out of the top berth and stretched his hands toward the ceiling. "Nah. This is way better. I'd rather take our chances and play roommate roulette. Maybe we'll score and end up with only four and have extra room."

Bella felt Stillman's arm tighten around her waist. "Yeah. It's better. I bet no one shows up."

"Want to switch compartments?" Phillip asked Rune.

Rune leaned back. "I like it here."

"Me, too." Stillman answered Phillip's question before it was even asked.

Phillip scowled and looked at Bella. "We're three doors down, if you need anything." He tugged on the sliding pocket door to close it behind him, but it stuck halfway open. He swore, and jerked on the door.

"Leave it." Stillman's voice seemed to infuriate Phillip even more.

Phillip pounded his fist against the uncooperative door and then squeezed through the gap. He stomped off in the direction of his couchette.

Stillman, full of confidence, released Bella and Karen and addressed the door. He jiggled it back and forth until it broke free and slid closed. Bella and Karen sat side by side on one of the lower berths. Rune opened a bottle of wine, took a swig, and then passed it to Stillman, who drank and passed it to the girls. They took turns sharing the wine and discussing which of the cookies they'd try first.

Soon, they heard male voices muttering outside the door. Again, the door rattled and then edged open.

Two turban-clad men with dark complexions looked at the four students with obvious disdain. They consulted their tickets and then entered the compartment.

Stillman and the girls backed up to the window side of the couchette. The men gestured to two berths. They looked at Rune. Without waiting for a response, they tossed their black cylinder bags onto the bunks.

The taller and thicker man nodded in the direction of the girls and spoke loudly in an indecipherable language to his companion. Karen scooted closer to Bella.

Bella squinted at the two men. Following the president's lead, the U.S. had backed Iraq in its war with Iran. She wondered about the nationality of their cabin mates. They looked Middle Eastern, but that could mean they were from Saudi Arabia, Iraq, Iran, or a host of other Middle Eastern countries. Beginning with the boycott of the 1980 Olympics and now the Iraq-Iran War, the U.S. continued to take sides in that part of the world, meaning her country had made enemies. How did these two men feel about the U.S.? Friend or foe?

Karen whispered in Bella's ear, "They either think we're lesbian or want to rape us. But I'm not sure which."

Bella nodded, her eyes on the two strangers. Then, as abruptly as they had joined them, the strangers strode back into the corridor and disappeared. They left their bags behind.

Rune stuck his head into the hall, then pulled back into the couchette and closed the door behind him. He shot a glance up at Stillman. "You stand guard. I'll check the bags. Listen first to make sure there's not a bomb."

Stillman slid down and cocked his ear next to each bag, his mouth pursed as he concentrated. "I don't hear a thing." He took a position in front of the door.

Rune slid one of the bags to the edge of the berth. "Think it's safe to open?"

Stillman nodded, leaning his head next to the door to listen for anyone approaching in the hallway. His body swayed back and forth with the train's movement.

Rune pulled on the zipper and pried the top of the bag open. Examining the contents, he burst into laughter. "Contraband."

Bella slid off the bunk to see for herself. Grain alcohol, folded paper packets, and cigarettes filled the bag.

Stillman abandoned his post to inspect the bag, too. He pulled out one packet of paper, four inches square and half an inch thick.

Rune grabbed the packet from Stillman and opened it. A flat cake of dark brown rested on the white paper.

"What is it?" Karen asked, cowering on the opposite bunk.

Rune grinned at her. "Hashish." He smelled it. "Yup. Spicy as hell. Want some?"

Stillman moved back to the door and leaned against it to listen. He tipped his head at Rune. "Put it back, man. Those two would probably kill us if we stole from them."

Bella retreated from the bag and curled next to Karen on the bunk. "I'll bet they're Muslim. So much for them being pure in spirit and action."

Rune tossed the packet into the bag. He wolf-whistled and pulled out a long-stemmed wooden pipe. He waved the pipe in the air.

"Knock it off, Rune," Stillman said, his ear resting against the door.

Rune threw the pipe into the bag and zipped it up. "Get them away from home and those camel jockeys go berserk."

"What about all those rules they live by?" Bella wrinkled her nose. The strangers' bags stunk like perspiration and dust and old gym socks. She looked at Karen. "It may be a long night with them."

"I don't think I'll sleep a wink." Karen looked as worried as she sounded.

Rune, who had returned to his bunk, leaned his head over the edge and raised one eyebrow. "One or both of you ladies can share my bunk. We could give those junkies something to talk about back home."

Karen giggled and grinned up at Rune.

Stillman nodded at Bella. "We'll protect you. Don't worry." He plopped down beside her.

Bella felt Stillman's shoulder against hers. His hand draped over hers, easy and nonchalant.

The train rounded a bend, rocked, and then jerked left with a shudder. The sudden shift sent Bella sliding against Karen, who fell onto the bed. Stillman landed on top of

Bella. At that moment, the compartment door rattled open and admitted their two Middle Eastern couchette-mates. The taller of the two spat a string of words at the other, the contempt apparent on his face. He glared at the jumble of bodies. One word of his litany was crystal clear: *infidels.*

The shorter man rested one hand on the edge of the bunk and stared at the duffle bag.

Bella held her breath while the man studied the position of the bag on the berth.

The shorter man stepped in front of the bag. Bella heard the zipper open. The paper packets rustled. The zipper closed. The man gazed at his companion. No words were exchanged. The look in the near-black eyes of the man who stood by the door sent a cold shiver of fear down Bella's back.

Bella clutched Stillman's hand. "I'm sharing your bunk tonight," she said.

Stillman's eyes didn't leave the two men. The strangers stretched out on their bunks.

Bella saw Stillman's eyes flit sideways toward the two girls. He released Bella's grip on his hand and stood up in the narrow space between the columns of bunks.

Stillman looked at Karen. "Which bag's yours?" She grabbed her backpack in response. Stillman swung Karen's bag up to Rune, and then grabbed Karen by her waist and hoisted her up onto Rune's bunk. Bella tossed her backpack onto Stillman's bunk. Stillman's lift sent her flying onto the bunk, which prompted a stream of giggles from Karen.

Stillman moved to the door. "OK to cut the lights?"

Silence.

Stillman slid a horizontal palm across his throat and then pointed to the lights. "Lights. Cut. OK?"

The car fell into darkness. After Stillman joined her on the bunk, Bella felt his arms encircle her. He pulled her body next to his. She could hear Rune and Karen's bunk creak as they sought a comfortable position on the tiny, hard bunk.

Bella's mind raced. Thank God she was next to Stillman, his body shielding hers from the strangers. She heard the sounds of a zipper opening and then paper rustling. She sensed more than heard the two men slide off their berths into the narrow center aisle. Even with the sliver of light that seeped under the door, she could not see more than dark shapes. Their scent was strong, though, so she knew they were close to her bunk. She could feel the shallow evenness of Stillman's silent breaths. Bella pressed harder against Stillman, and his arms tightened around her. Good, he was awake.

Bella heard the creaking of a bedframe beneath her and Stillman. Low whispers and more rustling. She heard a match strike. The telltale smell wafted up, and Bella's nostrils flared. Rune coughed as if it bothered him. Bella had no doubt that pothead Rune was only trying to rattle the chain of the two men.

A stream of angry words in their native language silenced Rune's coughing.

Bella heard a second match strike. A cough threatened to erupt from her throat. She held it in. Stillman patted her hand, and then rolled off the bunk.

One of the Middle Easterners grunted in surprise.

"Stillman, no," Bella said. Two against one—bad odds. She had no confidence Rune would jump into the fight.

Stillman stood next to the bunks, as if daring the other men to attack him.

Nothing happened. No one moved.

Stillman stepped to the tiny window at the end of the compartment. He pushed and pounded on it until it gave way and slid open. He climbed back up into the berth beside Bella.

She snuggled against him, tucking her mouth next to his ear. "Thanks. That was stupid, but brave."

After they had finished the second pipe, Bella heard the two men settle into their beds. Soon, their snoring replaced the silence in the compartment.

The berth with Rune and Karen creaked. Rune whispered, "You two awake?"

"Yes," Stillman said in a quiet voice. "Do you think we should take turns sleeping, to make sure they don't try anything if they wake up in the middle of the night?"

"Damn straight we should," Rune whispered.

"I'll take first shift," Stillman said. "You sleep now. I'll wake you up in a few hours."

Bella felt Stillman's face nuzzle into her hair. "You can sleep," he said. His breath warmed her cheek.

She put one palm against his cool cheek, then rested her head against his arm. Her lips found his. Soft kisses at first, then harder, with insistence born of relief and, later, of desire. They kissed for what seemed like hours. Stillman slid on top of her, his upper body propped up on his elbows.

Bella couldn't complete their desire. Not here, with these strangers next to them, not more than an arm's length away.

Stillman didn't press her.

She patted her fingertips to her lips swollen from Stillman pressing against her mouth, kissing, nibbling, and sucking. She wondered if they'd still be swollen in the morning, for all to see. She hoped not, but kissing Stillman did more than merely wake the desire inside her. Kissing Stillman made her feel like she belonged. Kissing him, being here in his arms, eased the ever-present ache for her mother and the longing for a family that extended beyond just the two of them, which is all she'd ever known.

Stillman pressed his lips to her forehead and cradled her in his arms.

"Stillman." Rune's hiss startled Stillman, who turned his head to see the pair on the opposite bunk. "I can't sleep. If you want to, go ahead. I'll wake you up if I get tired."

"Deal." Stillman flipped back over and curled around Bella. "C'mon, pretty lady." His breath warmed her skin. Stillman's tongue flicked against her neck. "Let's try to sleep."

"Mm-hmm." Bella's exhaustion surprised her. She curled into his body and sank into the comfort of sleep.

Later, she heard a rhythmic noise. Her eyes flipped open to a darkened tunnel of stale air. Where was she? She felt Stillman beside her and remembered. Hot air hung above them and the hard bunk pressed against her shoulder. The sound of a moan widened her eyes and tightened her muscles.

Stillman's hand rubbed up and down her arm. "It's OK." His whispered words seemed calm; he was wide awake. "It's Rune and Karen. They've been at it awhile." His words didn't seem to disturb the others. The creaking from the opposite bunk kept its cadence.

Bella thought of Karen's faceless fiancé.

"Bitchin' way to celebrate her engagement to a guy 4,000 miles away," Stillman whispered. "The preacher would damn them both to hell."

Before she could respond, Stillman silenced her lips in the nicest way she could imagine.

"Stillman." Rune's whisper spanned the space between them. "Want to take over watch duty?" His words slurred from his sated state.

"No problem." Stillman shifted on the bunk, his arm encouraging Bella to curl her backside into him. "It's only a few more hours to Paris. I've got it covered." He kissed Bella's ear. "Try to sleep," he told her.

Bella nestled against him and drifted off.

Bella slept for several hours snuggled against Stillman. The couchette door rattled; Bella rubbed her eyes and lifted up on her elbows. Daylight streamed through the open train window. Their compartment-mates exchanged rapid-fire words. The two strangers rolled out of their bunks and crouched, facing the compartment door in a fight-ready position.

Another rattle and the door parted from the casing. Phillip led Lee into the cramped space. He stopped two feet from the larger stranger. Rune rolled over the top of Karen and vaulted to the floor.

"Hey, guys," Rune said. "Meet the charming gentlemen sharing our compartment. A couple of straight-up guys, but not too talkative." He pinched his fingers together like he was smoking a joint and pantomimed taking a drag. Rune glared at the taller man, as if daring him to take a swing.

The larger stranger grabbed both of the Middle Easterners' duffel bags and shoved Phillip out of his way. Lee moved to let the strangers exit. The two men disappeared down the corridor.

"Sociable fellows, weren't they?" Lee said.

"You met our couchette-mates," said Bella. "Who bunked with you?"

"Nuns." Lee's voice growled his disappointment. Then he laughed. "None of us dared share bunks with the two of them saying their "Hail Marys," "Our Fathers," and "Glory Bes" loud enough for everyone to hear."

Phillip laughed. He turned to clap Lee on the shoulder. "I counted twenty full rosaries before I fell asleep."

Lee grinned. "Beat ya. I probably heard fifty. After all that prayer last night, Phillip and I figured we should leave and give the nuns some privacy to get ready this morning. Meghan and Hope told us they'd wait there for all of us."

"The train is slowing down." Stillman nodded toward the corridor. "Let's meet up with the other girls and blow this pop stand."

Phillip's hand closed over Bella's arm when she passed him. "Let's switch room arrangements on the way back. How about it?"

"I like the way we split up this time," Lee said. "Maybe on the return trip we won't be stuck with nuns. I'd love to cozy up to Meghan on the ride home."

Karen giggled. "The girls should all ride together so we can compare our new lingerie."

"I want in on that action." Rune rubbed his hands together.

Bella felt Stillman's eyes on her. Phillip squeezed her arm and stepped closer to her. The train hissed and lurched to a stop.

Bella looked at Stillman, and then at Phillip. The two of them must be smoking something, she thought. They actually thought she'd do it with them on a train? Kissing and heavy petting was one thing, but no way she'd give up her virginity in a cramped couchette. No way.

11

San Gimignano, Italy

The following week, their chaperone drove them to San Gimignano to study the art and history of the famous hill town. Their van stopped far below the walls of the ancient towered city. Bella slid on her backpack. The morning sun warmed her bare arms.

Ugh. Without a doubt, her back would turn into a sticky sweat pool beneath the backpack's rough fabric before she had finished the long, uphill hike to the village entrance. Bella's pack, with her notebook and reference books on the culture and traditions of medieval Tuscany, dug into her back. Shifting the straps' position on her shoulders was of no help.

Bella dreaded the day. The deadline for her second research paper loomed in two days. The prospect of compiling her notes into annotated form and formal academic style seemed to her as much fun as cleaning a communal bathroom after a horde of middle school boys had used it for a week at summer camp. She'd procrastinated, thinking this visit to San Gimignano would somehow make finishing the paper easier. Wrong. Now she had no choice, but it was the last thing she felt like doing.

She knelt to tighten her sandal strap. Phillip and Stillman passed her. Neither wore a backpack.

Bella caught up with them and wedged herself into the middle. "What's up? Where are your backpacks?"

Stillman grinned. "I'm done. Finished my paper two days ago."

She searched Phillip's face. He nodded.

She pulled away from them. "You guys are too ambitious, just like Hope. My roomie finished her paper days ago. I'd hoped you two would pool resources with me and write through the night together. Hope will be sleeping, so we could use your room."

Stillman raised his eyebrows at her. "I'll spend the night with you."

Phillip draped an arm over her shoulders. "How 'bout I keep you company? I'll start the book I borrowed from Lee while you work."

"We can both keep you company," Stillman said, "and play poker or something."

"You can both go to hell," Bella said. They trudged the final stretch to the curved stone entrance of the city in silence. Inside, a few tiny shops showed signs of life. A rotund man wearing a starched white butcher's apron tugged on a four-foot stuffed wild boar. He positioned the taxidermy trophy to the side of his entry, proud of this visual advertisement for his meats. Bella shuddered.

Stillman and Phillip stopped at an espresso bar. Bella shook her head when they urged her to join them.

She continued walking up the dark, cool street. The

narrow space felt more like an alley than a thoroughfare. Bella reached the end of the street. It opened into the main stone piazza with a cistern in the center and the Cathedral of San Gimignano on one side. The sunny plaza was empty of people.

Bella walked around, looking for a place to sit and work, but found herself peering into the windows of the shops and thinking about which ones she'd enter later. She saw a wide outdoor stone staircase not far beyond the cathedral and wondered where it led. She started toward the steps.

"Bella, wait up," Phillip called out to her as he crossed the piazza toward her.

"I thought you were getting espresso," Bella said.

"One was enough for me." Phillip smiled. "I'd take you over Stillman any day." He pointed to the steps. "Want to find out where they lead?"

To her surprise, the steps led to a sunny rooftop court-yard at the edge of the city's wall. Beyond the low wall, green, rolling hills dotted with cypress trees, vineyards, and a few clay-roofed houses created an idyllic landscape. She exclaimed at the beauty of it.

Phillip moved behind her and tugged the backpack off her shoulders. He grabbed her hand and brought her to the wall. Phillip dropped the backpack and turned to Bella. Without a word, he cradled her chin in his hands and kissed her with tender lips.

Bella wasn't surprised Phillip had kissed her. He'd been flirting with her and vying for her attention every day.

What surprised her was the shock wave that ran through her body when his lips met hers.

After the night on the train to Paris, Bella was convinced that she'd sleep with Stillman this summer. True, Phillip had been attentive, funny, and charming when he would walk with her in the afternoons. But when they stopped for lunch and whenever he was near her at night, Stillman found a way to pull Bella into a doorway or side street to kiss her—the Italian groping kind of kiss. Stillman's kisses and hands had left Bella craving for more.

Every night, Stillman had asked her to come to his room, but how could she? Phillip was Stillman's roommate. The truth was that Bella wasn't ready to spend her time exclusively with Stillman, because she loved her afternoons with Phillip. With Phillip, she relaxed. Somehow, he managed to make her laugh and confide in him. She had even shared her worries about being so far from her mother.

After that kiss with Phillip—their first—he pulled his head away from hers. "Is this OK?" he said.

"Try that again," she said in a throaty voice, "and I'll let you know." And that's exactly what he did.

Phillip and Bella had the rooftop courtyard to themselves. They stood by the wall and kissed, not the sweaty, urgent kind she'd had with Stillman, but more soft and slow. Before long, he pulled away from her and asked if she needed to work on her paper. He volunteered to help her write it and pointed to the bench where they could sit and work.

Bella had procrastinated until she had no choice. If she didn't finish her paper, she'd flunk the course. She nodded, reluctantly picking up her backpack and moving to the bench. They reviewed her notes for a few minutes, and then Bella couldn't stand it anymore.

She looked out at the vineyards stretching away from the ancient city. She did homework back home. This was Italy, probably her only chance to come here, and it seemed a waste of a day to spend it compiling a paper. Bella knew Lee and Meghan were sneaking away together every chance they got. Her nights were spent in a tiny room with Hope. She said, "I'll study later. Want to see how many more rooftop courtyards we can find?"

Phillip and Bella explored San Gimignano together, hand in hand. She felt comfortable and at ease with him. He told jokes with self-deprecating humor and kept her laughing at his banter.

By unspoken agreement, they avoided the city center. They took turns tugging each other into doorways and even smaller side streets for quick, flirty kisses and hugs. They both kept it light and playful.

Eventually, their casual touring had to end, as it was time to join the group for lunch. As they rounded the last corner, Bella squeezed Phillip's hand and said, "It was a great morning." In truth, it had been the best morning of the summer. Looking ahead for signs of their group, she released Phillip's hand. Great morning or not, Bella knew she didn't want Stillman to see her cozying up with Phillip.

Phillip nodded. "I'd like more of these mornings."

So would Bella. The only problem was that now she had not one but two guys who turned her on.

After lunch, the guys stayed at the table to finish off the wine. The weather-bleached steps of the cathedral beckoned to Bella. She planted herself on the cool stone steps, her backpack beside her. She sighed. Time to work. She studied her notes about the city and museums. The sun, thankfully, dried her sweaty back.

Across the square, Bella spotted a tiny, stooped woman dressed all in black pulling a young boy by his hand. His mouth worked overtime, providing nonstop, lyrical Italian chatter to the older woman—probably his grandmother.

Bella watched them trudge past her up the steps and disappear into the cathedral. She glanced at the papers on her lap. She reread from the top of the page. Her handwritten notes swirled under her gaze. Crap. This wasn't working. She stuffed everything back into her pack and followed the woman and boy up the stairs and into the church.

The morning sun beat through the church's front windows, creating stripes of bright rainbow colors on the floor. Bella entered in time to see the grandmother push the boy into a confessional. The elderly woman knelt next to the curtained space, created from wood ornately carved to feature an oval relief of a battered Christ carrying his cross. Bella could hear the woman's soft cadence, praying Hail Marys in Italian.

Bella knelt on the wooden kneeler three pews back. She bowed her head over her folded hands and thought of her mother.

The confessional curtain slid open. The elderly woman finished her prayer, and then jumped to her feet. The boy stammered out something in Italian to the woman, and then hung his head, as if ashamed. She nodded, pulled him into the pew beside her, and thrust her rosary into his palms. The boy bowed his head. Bella could hear him murmur. She stared at the open confessional. She hadn't been inside one since her confirmation, years before.

Her legs propelled her to the tiny cubicle. Inside, she crossed herself, knelt, and launched into the words she was certain no one inside the sanctuary would understand.

"Forgive me, Father, for I have sinned. It has been seven years since my last confession."

Silence.

She shrugged and continued. "I have lustful thoughts for young men and I am not married."

Nothing.

The silence propelled her. It actually felt good to say her thoughts aloud. "I might even have sex with one of them this summer." She paused and thought about the rest of the summer. "I'm not sure which one, though." Damn. She was getting more confused rather than finding clarity.

Still silence.

This was silly. She started to rise. The feel of a folded paper in her skirt pocket stopped her. The letter from her mother. A lump of worry caught in her throat; her dry swallow erupted into a cough.

She whispered her fear—the unimaginable possibility that she had tried to push from conscious thought. "I'm afraid for my mother."

"*Madre?*" The priest's low voice startled her.

"Not Mother Mary. My mother. I worry … wonder … is she ill?" What was the point of this, anyway? He couldn't even understand her. Something drove her on. "Her last letter. It was only a couple of paragraphs. And the writing squiggled over the page, like … like she couldn't control the pen." She leaned forward. "She'd tell me, right? If something was wrong? She'd have to tell me."

Bella looked at her clasped hands. Her knuckles had turned white from the fierceness of her grip. She moved her lips, silently mouthing the next words. "She's the only family I have."

A chair squeaked behind the metal grate. The priest must have shifted his weight.

Bella closed her eyes to will away the fear.

The priest cleared his throat. "Pray." The rounded word hung in the air between them. Spoken in English, it made Bella wonder how much he had understood. As if to answer her question, the priest uttered a blessing, perhaps forgiveness, in Italian. She didn't understand the words, but it had the tone of someone offering comfort.

Bella wished his words, his tone, made her feel better. They didn't. But maybe his prayer could help her mom.

Two hours later, Bella sat again on the stone steps in front of the church. Now, after the afternoon break, the piazza teemed with life. Italian opera poured out of a gelateria.

Heat radiated from the stone steps. Clusters of people surrounded her. The steps provided a place to sit, to eat, and to rest.

Bella tried to concentrate on her notebook, but the words swam. She had no interest in writing her paper. Her mind kept returning to her mother. She decided to spend some of her emergency dollars for a phone call home tonight. She needed to hear her mom's voice.

"Almost done?" Stillman slid in next to her.

Bella shook her head. "I couldn't care less about this stupid paper." Without the paper, she'd fail the class. And she wouldn't graduate on time. Her eyes stung with tears. She turned from Stillman and swiped at her eyes.

Stillman slid his palm, cool to her skin, under her hair. He lifted the weight and heat of it off her shoulders and back.

"That's good." Bella smiled her appreciation at the breeze of cool air that hit her neck. "But it doesn't finish this." She flicked her fingernails against the paper.

"I'll make you a deal." Stillman tilted his head and raised his eyebrows. "I'll help you finish. However late we have to stay up, I'll do it. No fooling around, either. We'll write the paper."

Relief washed over her. "You'll help me?"

He nodded, solemn as a priest.

She studied his face and knew he meant it. "Good deal for me." She smiled with relief. "But why? What's in it for you?"

"This weekend we're all going to the Cinque Terre, the

five coastal cities along the Mediterranean. Let's go to the coast early. We can sunbathe, relax, and celebrate turning in your paper. Just us two. Deal?"

This would be it, then. Stillman would try to sleep with her before the others arrived at the coast. She wasn't sure if she was ready to choose Stillman over Phillip. She replayed his request in her head. All she was committing to was a day and a night with him, nothing more. She extended her hand. "Deal."

12

Bella woke to the sound of rapping on the wooden door to her room. Her eyes stung and felt swollen. She and Stillman had worked in the lobby until three on her paper before declaring it finished.

Stillman. The day he planned.

She squinted at the clock. Eight-fifteen. Late. She tumbled out of bed, still in her halter top and shorts from the previous night.

Not Stillman, but Phillip stood in the hall. He held two porcelain cups of espresso and offered her one. "Stillman's got the flu. Started upchucking about five. He finally got rid of everything in his stomach and fell asleep about thirty minutes ago."

Bella closed the door behind her. No sense waking Hope.

"I'm headed to Siena for a little shopping. Souvenirs for the folks back home. Want to come?"

Bella thought of her promise to Stillman. "I made plans—"

"He's down for the count, if you're worried about the old Still Man."

Her date with Stillman was postponed. But shopping? She deserved it after finishing her paper. "Give me five."

In Siena, they laughed, joked, teased, and flirted. Lunch brought cool panini of mozzarella, tomato, and basil, followed by gelato.

She put aside the worry that she hadn't reached her mother by phone the night before and succumbed to the day. They disagreed only once, when Phillip insisted they catch one particular bus out of Siena, which cut her shopping short.

The bus wound through curvy hills and valleys—a different route from the way they had come. The turns became tighter. They passed a cluster of cypress trees, and beyond the trees sat an ancient village on the crest of the hill. When they reached the edge of the town, Bella saw a sign for the city center that pointed to a narrow street flanked by stone buildings on either side. The bus screeched to a stop.

Phillip grabbed her arm. "Let's go. We get off here."

Bella scrambled for her backpack and followed Phillip, edging past a lady with dead chickens on her lap—she could tell by the chicken feet protruding from the shopping bag—and two elderly gentlemen who cackled together.

A Mediterranean goddess of seventeen-going-on-twenty-five grabbed Phillip's arm. Bella saw the young woman gesture to the empty seat beside her.

Phillip shook his head, then turned to Bella, planting a sloppy kiss on her mouth to make his point. The young goddess laughed and waved at them as they got off.

The bus pulled away before the door had even closed.

"The bus is running late. Not like the trains." Phillip picked up her backpack from the dusty street and brushed it off. "C'mon. I want to show you this place."

"You've been here before?" Bella swung in beside him and matched his pace toward the upward-sloped main street.

"Naw. Just asked about quaint villages close to Florence, something we could easily get to by train or bus. This place kept cropping up."

"Castellina-in-Chianti?"

He nodded. "I thought we could spend the afternoon here."

She grinned at him. She liked that he had planned a surprise for her. "Race you to the top." Without waiting for a response, she sprinted up the narrow cobblestone street that bisected the town center.

An hour into their shopping, Bella noticed the middle-aged pottery store owner glaring at them, her brows furrowed. Sparks from her black eyes flew first at Bella, then at the wall beside her.

Bella turned and scanned the wall, noticing a large ceramic clock. "She wants to close. It's past two already."

Nodding an apology to the store owner, Bella tugged on Phillip's arm and pulled him outside.

A gust of cool wind hit them. The sky, sunny and bright when they had started shopping, had taken refuge behind a thicket of charcoal clouds that hung low over the tiny village. A crack of lightning struck close to the wall behind the town. Thunder ripped the air, only seconds after the lightning.

Bella's hand clamped over Phillip's. "We've got to find cover. Now." She raced up the street, Phillip at her side. The stores had all closed for the afternoon, their wares tucked inside. She ran up to an enormous wooden door, arched at the top. It was a hotel. Bella tugged on the wrought-iron handle, at least a foot in length. Locked. She pounded her fist against the door. Nothing.

Slanting rain stung her bare legs.

Phillip pulled her back. "The church." His shout, although next to her ear, seemed a block away. He pointed to a church across the street. She ran beside him, her leather sandals sliding on the stones worn smooth by centuries of feet and rain. They took the church steps two at a time.

Phillip followed Bella into the cave-like interior, lit only by candle wall sconces and a table of prayer candles at the side. They stood at the back until their eyes adjusted, then slipped into the last pew and sat down on the hard wood.

The cool shadows of the sanctuary and Bella's drenched clothes made her shiver. Phillip's arm crossed her back; he pulled her next to him. Bella curled into his side. She shuddered and felt the cold prickle all the way down her spine and into the tips of her fingers and her toes. His arm tucked her in closer.

Bella felt his lips, warm and soft, against her forehead. Without thought, she tilted her face up. His mouth met hers full on. His slow, gentle kiss left her wanting more. She brushed his cheek with her fingers.

Phillip pulled her onto his lap. This time, his lips pressed harder against hers. The probing kisses brought tiny shudders of desire from her.

A man cleared his throat behind Bella.

She stiffened. Her face flushed hot. She hopped off Phillip and turned to face the stranger. She ventured an apologetic smile at the priest, who couldn't have been much older than they. She nudged Phillip with her hand and swung her backpack onto one shoulder.

Phillip scrambled out of the pew. He pulled a sweat-shirt out of his backpack and handed it to her. Under raised eyebrows, his eyes beat a path to her breasts. Bella's face flushed hot again. Her rain-drenched white peasant blouse over a braless chest made her a prime candidate for a wet T-shirt contest.

The priest ducked his head.

Bella wrestled the sweatshirt over her head. She grabbed Phillip's hand and pulled him behind her toward the door.

A crack of lightning lit the church windows. As quick as it came, the light disappeared, chased out by thunder so loud Bella jumped. She shuddered with cold and dreaded returning outside to the chilling rain.

"*Un momento, per favore.*"

Busted for making out in a church. Bella stopped, her head lowered. She felt Phillip's warm palm against the skin of her back underneath the sweatshirt.

She felt, rather than saw, the young Italian priest rush to their side. He thrust a paper toward them with a sheepish look on his face.

He had scrawled a map from the church to a building not far away. A large "X" crossed the building. Beside it, he'd written one word in beautiful script. "*Albergo.*" The priest had mapped a route to an inn.

Bella and Phillip murmured their thanks and bolted out the massive wooden door.

Rain came down in sheets, layer upon layer of large drops that blurred the line of shops across the tiny piazza. Bella felt the sweatshirt soak up water as if it were a mop, cold and heavy on her shoulders.

Phillip raised one forearm to shield his eyes. He grabbed Bella's hand and led her across the narrow pedestrian street. They turned into a narrow archway that marked a tunnel.

Out of the rain, they picked up their pace and ran down the sloping path to a lower level. Behind the row of shops, the corridor widened. The ancient town wall bordered the corridor on their right. The only light came from single blocks of gray—peepholes in the wall. The handful of doors on their left stood closed, and no windows or signs marked them.

"It's creepy." Bella edged closer to Phillip.

"Yeah, but it's at least out of the rain." Phillip consulted the priest's map. He stopped, counted the doors behind them, and then pulled her along.

The space between the peepholes lengthened and the corridor narrowed. The path angled down once again. The passage turned into a narrow, steep stairwell. Palms on the walls, they descended one more level below the piazza. A door on the left marked the bottom of the steps. Unlike the doors above, this one featured a wrought-iron ring hanging in the center.

Phillip swung the knocker against the door, which was plain except for large black pegs that protruded from the surface in parallel rows.

The door creaked open to reveal a stooped man with slicked-back gray hair. Every line in the man's face seemed to point to the dance of light in his eyes.

He stepped back, swung the door wide, and beckoned them inside. The man shuffled to a mahogany writing desk covered with papers. He held up a sheet for them to see that listed the room charge. Phillip paid for one night. The elderly gentleman extracted a key from a drawer and handed it to Phillip. Back in the outer corridor, the man swung open an adjacent door and stepped back. Wordlessly, their host shuffled past them back to his office.

Their room had one double bed. An embroidered quilt, white with orange and green stitching, covered it. Bella's hand traced the curves of the metal footboard. Other than the bed and two framed pictures, one of the Madonna and child and the other of Michelangelo's *David*, the room was devoid of furnishings. The Madonna was in her rightful place of honor over the bed's headboard, and *David* held court on the opposite wall. She heard Phillip opening the door on the interior wall.

"Score." He pulled his T-shirt over his head. "Private bathroom, no less. Tiny, but all the necessities—sink, toilet, and tub." He dropped his wet jeans to the floor. Standing in black jockey shorts, he rubbed his palms over his arms and chest.

"What are you doing?" Bella stifled a laugh.

"Trying to frigging get warm. You get first crack at the tub. But I'm warning you, more than ten minutes and I'm joining you." Without another word, he leaped onto the bed. The mattress creaked and swayed nearly to the floor.

Bella laughed. Phillip clawed at the thin comforter and curled up under the sheets. She pulled the heavy, sodden sweatshirt over her head, gave it one wring, and hung it by the neck from the bedpost.

Phillip's head followed her movements around the bed. "You sure gave that priest an eyeful. Probably made him regret his Holy Orders." He gestured at her shirt, still plastered like a barely opaque second skin to her breasts.

"You're a beast." Bella shivered from cold. "Screw it." She shucked her blouse and skirt, leaving them on the floor with Phillip's clothes, and dashed into the bathroom to run the water. Her hand tested the temperature. "It's barely warm. But it's still better than the air temp." She dropped her panties on the floor, stepped into the tub, and scrunched as low as possible. "Sorry. There's no room in here for you and probably not enough hot water for even one."

"Witch."

She heard the bed creak. Phillip entered the closet-sized bathroom naked. He bent over the tub. His lips met hers and she wrapped her arms around his neck. When he pulled away, she scooted to make as much room for him as possible in the tub. Phillip lowered himself in and settled Bella in front of him, her back to his front, which announced his intentions very, very clearly.

Much later, the heat from their passion had warmed them both. They lay together on the lumpy mattress; Bella nestled into the crook of Phillip's arm.

"Bella," Phillip said in a hesitant tone, "are you OK about this? This was your first time, wasn't it?"

She rose up on one elbow to look at his face. "Yes. You were the first." Being with Phillip, like this, felt too natural to be wrong. When she had been with Stillman on the train, it was simple lust. With Phillip, it was different, more than only the physical attraction. "Thanks for thinking about me. About how I feel. But, being with you, this way, is right for me. I can't really explain why, but I know it is."

Phillip caressed her cheek. "I know what you mean. It's right for me, too."

She coiled back into his arm and felt as if she were a cat ready to purr. Her eyes landed on the gilded wooden frame around the simple print of *David*.

"So muscled." Her fingertips traced Phillip's sternum.

"Thanks. But your parts are much more fun." His left hand tweaked her nipple.

She flicked his hand away and pushed back in mock indignation. "I was referring to *David*, silly."

He followed her eyes to the wall. Then he dove under the covers. His head went to her feet where his mouth and fingers sent her alternating between hysterical giggles and breath-sucking shivers of desire.

They didn't think about anything other than each other until a firm knock against the door woke them.

Bella squinted at her watch. "It's time for either dinner or breakfast, but I'm not sure which."

Phillip narrowed his eyes, and he made a show of counting the fingers on his right hand. "I'd say it's got to be breakfast, seeing as how I feel more rested than a bear after a long winter's hibernation, and … " A second round of knocking interrupted him.

Bella giggled and pushed Phillip out of bed. "You better get some clothes on before he comes in." She threw the quilt over her head and curled into a ball over the warm spot in the center of the bed.

Bella heard muffled male voices. She couldn't pick out many of the words, but she thought Phillip said "*due,*" followed by a double "*grazie*" from the other man. A few more words were exchanged, and then she heard the door close.

"Since we obviously missed the train to the beach, I paid for a second night here. I figure by tomorrow we might, just might, be ready to come up for air."

"Aren't you forgetting something?" Bella pulled the covers tighter over her head.

She felt the bed tilt when Phillip sat on the side of the bed closest to the door.

"Not a chance."

"I … need … food." Bella sang the words, tossing off the covers and throwing her arms into the air as if she were in the finale at the grand opera.

"Madam." Phillip swept his arm in the direction of the door. On the floor in front of the door sat a wooden tray holding a plate of hard rolls, a tiny saucer of fruit preserves, and two cups of cappuccino topped with caramel-colored foam. "You're in luck. Our host decided it was time to deliver our breakfast."

By lunchtime, they needed to venture out for more food. They devoured roast chicken so tender it fell away from the bone. It was juicy and flavorful, satisfying and seductive. Two full carafes of house wine disappeared before dessert. Their conversation bounced between formulating giggly concoctions of why they had missed the trip to the beach, teasing each other, and marveling at the food, all punctuated by intertwined fingertips and smiles.

Sunday afternoon, they stood hand in hand, waiting for the bus to Florence. Bella's cheeks warmed under Phillip's stare. She was falling for him. Hard. She silently asked him the question they'd skirted all weekend. What now? Had what started as a sodden, spontaneous romp evolved into something that would continue after they returned home?

Phillip nodded, as if he had heard her question. "We'll see each other after we leave Italy. We will."

"We live on opposite sides of the country." The logistics of that kind of long-distance relationship were challenging, but so was the immediate issue. Stillman. Bella didn't want to be with Stillman anymore. How would she tell him? What would she tell him?

Phillip's arms circled her, his hands clasping at the small of her back. "Have faith." His lips brushed hers. A grin split his face. "Hey, aren't you the Catholic girl I picked up in a church?"

13

Bella dreaded seeing Stillman. What could she say? You didn't show up, so I climbed into bed with Phillip? She'd been flattered that the two of them had competed for her attention all summer, and yes, she was attracted to both. If Stillman cared for her as a person, rather than merely as a girl to have sex with, he'd get over it.

So why did she dread seeing Stillman?

The truth of it was that while this weekend with Phillip might have started as a spontaneous roll in the sack, for her now, it was something altogether different. It surprised her. More than that, it shocked and scared her. How could she feel this way after only one weekend together? Maybe it was because he was her first. That's what she tried to tell herself, anyway.

Bella knew one thing. She didn't want to sleep with Stillman, not now. All she wanted was to be with Phillip, to feel the warmth of his hand holding hers, the touch of his fingers tucking her curls behind her ear, and the caress of his palm on her back. She wanted to climb back into bed with him and not surface until the end of the summer. Beyond that, she didn't allow herself to think about everything she wanted, because everything involved him. Involved Phillip.

Bella sat in the lobby of their building, waiting for the group to join her for the walk to the bar for espresso. She prayed that Phillip would be the first to come downstairs, so they could face the others' questions together. Maybe Phillip had even talked to Stillman late last night after the others returned from the beach.

While she and Phillip had gotten back in time for dinner, the rest of the group didn't show up until after midnight. When Hope had returned to their room, Bella had glanced at her bedside alarm clock while her roommate undressed. She had pretended to be sound asleep, since she wasn't ready to share details about her weekend with Phillip.

Damn. Just her luck, Stillman was the first to join her in the lobby.

He paused for a moment, and then walked over to Bella. He leaned down and raised her chin with his hand. Without a word of greeting, he touched his lips to hers. "I'm sorry I missed our date. When I rejoined the land of the living Friday, you had already gone."

He kissed her again, parting her lips. His tongue flicked against hers, as his fingers stroked the tender skin under her chin. He pulled back and leaned close to her ear. "Forgive me? I want a rain check on our date—a day *and a night* with you." His whispered words and tone asked for more than forgiveness. The insinuated invitation hung in the air between them.

Not at all what she was expecting from him. She had steeled herself for anger and accusations, or maybe the cold shoulder treatment, but not this. Didn't he know about her weekend with Phillip? "I … I'm glad you're OK." He looked rested and tanned from the weekend on the beach. His Friday flu bug must have passed quickly for him to join the others when they left on Saturday.

She didn't know what to say to him. His eyes bore into hers as if he could read her mind. She had to change the subject. "How was the beach? Were the Italian ladies nude, or merely topless?" It had been the center of the guys' discussion the week before—the mode of dress of the Italian girls, and if their unshaved armpits would be a turnoff.

He took a step back and snorted. "Topless—even the saggy-boobed old ladies, who had no business exposing their chests or fat bellies." Raising his eyebrows, he said, "There were a few knockouts, though. Too bad you couldn't join them." His finger snaked down her shoulder, over her collarbone, circling lower and lower toward her breasts.

Damn, her nipples came to attention with his touch. She grabbed his hand. "Stillman—"

"Good morning," Phillip said. He crossed the small lobby and stood next to Bella.

"Hi." Bella's voice squeaked as if she were a boy whose voice was changing. She looked up at Phillip but couldn't read him. He didn't kiss her, didn't even touch her, in fact. Her eyes pleaded with him to say something.

Stillman clapped Phillip on the shoulder. "You missed a hell of a good time at the beach." He gave a low-pitched wolf whistle. "Those Italian chicks were something." He nodded at Phillip with a wink. "I'll fill you in later, man."

"Sure." Phillip fake-punched Stillman. "Love to hear it."

Was Phillip going to pretend nothing had happened? Worse yet, did it mean nothing to him? His silence and distance shocked her. Here she was, breathless with desire at the mere sight of him, and he all but ignored her. Where was her tender, sexy lover of the weekend?

Confused and hurt, she stood up and stumbled to the front door. She had to get out of there. She needed time alone to sort this out. Did he regret their lovemaking? Or was she merely the sought-after prize that was won and then discarded?

"Wait." Phillip crossed the room in big steps. He grabbed her hand and stopped her exodus. He looked back at Stillman and said, "Glad you had a good weekend." Then he led Bella outside by the hand.

She waited until they were almost to the corner before her anger erupted. "Why didn't you tell Stillman about us? You pretended like nothing happened. Didn't this weekend mean anything to you? You know he was coming on to me." Her chest heaved, and her face flushed. Was she mistaken about Phillip? "I thought something happened, more than just sex, this weekend. But I guess you don't feel that way."

Phillip stopped. He put both of his hands on her shoulders. "First off, a gentleman never kisses and tells.

Second, I know he was coming on to you, which is why I got you the hell out of there. Third, you don't know what I feel, so don't assume I don't care, or that this weekend didn't mean anything. I do care." He looked away and lowered his head, his whispered words now aimed at the sidewalk. "I care about you."

And how was that response supposed to make her feel? His words were exactly what she wanted to hear, but why did he look away when he spoke? Why couldn't he look at her eyes?

He pulled her into a bar and walked up to the counter, ordering and paying for two espressos and ciabatta rolls. They downed the espressos while standing at the bar. Phillip handed her a roll. "Let's walk."

They ate their rolls in silence as he led her to the Piazza della Signoria. He stopped in front of the replica of Michelangelo's *David*. It took all the patience she had to let him talk first.

"The weekend took me by surprise. Despite what you think, I didn't take you to Castellina-in-Chianti to sleep with you."

But that's sure as hell what happened, she thought. So, tell me what you're thinking and why you're being evasive. Please.

Phillip studied her face. He traced his thumb over her forehead and smoothed her hair over her ears. "I admit to the competition thing with Stillman. But it wasn't only about beating him. I wanted time with you. Alone." He kissed her nose. "But I never thought we'd have that kind of a relationship. I didn't plan to sleep with you. I merely wanted one day to be with you, and no one else."

He wanted a day. Instead, he got her virginity.

A sick feeling swept over Bella. Damn it. She'd projected her feelings onto him. That's why he acted so aloof in front of Stillman. Was this where he'd say, "I really care about you, but what I said about staying together isn't realistic"?

She stomped to the nearest trash container and chucked in her half-eaten roll. She spun to face him. "So why did you sleep with me? What was that about? A leading home run in the contest with Stillman?"

He joined her in fast, long strides, finally grabbing her forearm and pulling her into him. His lips crushed against hers. His other hand pushed the back of her head, trapping her lips against his.

Locked tight against Phillip, Bella felt the rhythmic pounding of a heart. Was it hers, his, or merely the coursing of her blood through her veins? As suddenly as he had locked her in an embrace, he released her. Bella stumbled back, rubbing her bruised lips.

"You don't … know … what I feel," Phillip said. "You can't. So, stop it. Stop pinning things on me." He reached for her, kissing her again with an urgency that startled her.

When he pulled back his head, Bella didn't move. She opened her eyes and stared at him.

"Did I hurt you?" Phillip asked.

When? Bella thought. With the bruising kiss? When I lost my virginity to you? No, and no. Her chest heaved with her breaths. He was giving her mixed messages. Kissing her like that, but then accusing her of pinning things on him. "Please, tell me how you feel, so I don't 'pin things on you.'"

His right hand slid up her arm toward her face. When his fingertips reached her cheek, she pulled her head away.

Phillip met her fiery eyes. "Oh, Bella." Pain laced his whispered words. "If I've hurt you, please forgive me." Anguish shadowed his face. "Bella. I am so sorry."

He caught his breath and then the words rushed out as if in a downhill tumble. "I didn't intend to sleep with you, because, well, for a lot of reasons. I wanted to, though. I've wanted you all summer, but I figured I couldn't be with you, not that way. You were off-limits. But then, the rain, and your shirt, and … and I couldn't think of anything but making love with you. Bella, please forgive me for hurting you. I hate myself for letting that happen. But I can't control how I feel."

Something about his tone of voice and his eyes comforted her. He had apologized and seemed sincere about it.

She knew one thing. She had to find out how he felt about her. Being this close to him took her breath away and planted a gut-deep need to spend every waking and sleeping moment with him. If he didn't feel that way about her, it was better that she knew it sooner rather than later, wasn't it? She inhaled sharply and kept her voice as level as possible. "So. Phillip. How do you feel about me?"

His eyes met hers. "I love you."

14

Late that afternoon, Bella did it. She asked Stillman to go for a coffee with her, and she told him about Phillip. Well, not everything. She told him that she had decided to be with Phillip and that she couldn't date two guys at the same time.

Stillman slammed one palm against the tiny table in the coffee bar. "Did Mr. Wonderful tell you why I wasn't there on time for our date?"

Bella nodded. "He explained how sick you were, and I wanted to come see you, to find out if I could help. But Phillip told me you'd finally fallen asleep after throwing up for hours and said I should let you rest." She grabbed one of his hands. "I felt awful you were so sick. Thank God it was only the twenty-four-hour flu."

Stillman's face turned red. He opened his mouth to talk but closed it without saying anything. Then he looked down at her hand holding his. He squeezed her hand and looked up at her. "He told you I was really sick, and yet you wanted to come see me?"

"Absolutely."

"Why?"

"Because you're my friend and I love you." Bella knew she had to choose her words with care. He was her friend, and she did love him, but it was different from the way she felt about Phillip.

She drew a deep breath. "This weekend, I realized I can't be with two guys at once. I'm going to date Phillip, which means I can't be with you, not like we've been. You guys asked to me choose one of you, and I didn't want to do that, because I care for you both. You were right, though." Bella squeezed his hand. "I hate this. Please know that I you love you, but as my very dear friend."

"So there's no chance for me? None? Under any circumstance?"

"No."

Stillman looked out the window. After what seemed an eternity to Bella, he turned back and faced her.

Stillman spoke in a quiet, even voice. "I promised my mother two things before she died. To study hard, and to do right by those I love."

This was it, then. The end of the summer semester in Italy. These last days of the semester, she and Phillip had been inseparable. They had spent nearly every waking hour together, making love in the few stolen moments when they knew they had a room to themselves and talking about how Phillip would come to visit her before the end of the summer. Bella couldn't wait for her mom to meet Phillip. He was everything her mother would want for her.

Not surprisingly, Bella hadn't spent much time with Stillman since her talk with him. They were all together for the group lessons and activities, and Stillman was always friendly, even joking with her and Phillip. But that was all. Bella and Stillman had never been alone again.

Bella sighed, half-heartedly folding the last of her blouses and tossing it on top of the stack of clothing that rose four inches over the rim of her worn suitcase. She remembered the empty bag Karen and Meghan had shown up with that first day and how foolish she had thought they looked. She didn't need an entire empty bag, but she'd bust the hinges on her suitcase if she didn't shrink that messy pile of blouses and skirts.

A light rap of knuckles against her door sent her skipping to open it.

Bella launched herself into Phillip's arms. She clutched him as tightly as she could, her lips insistent against his, demanding. How could she leave Italy when it meant leaving Phillip? He met her kisses with matched fervor. His hands roved over her backside, pressing her even tighter against him. A groan escaped Phillip's lips.

"Excuse me, lovebirds." Meghan's soft voice next to them finally pried them apart.

Phillip turned, drawing Bella against his side.

"I'm rounding everyone up for a group photo in fifteen minutes," Meghan said. "And the driver said we need to have our luggage with us so we're ready to blast off after the picture."

"Shit." Phillip's arm slid off Bella's shoulders. "I better pack. It'll take me at least fifteen to finish."

Bella playfully pushed him away. "Get cracking, then. I've got a towering mound of clothes to deal with myself."

"I'll help you, Bella." Meghan smiled with a wistful look on her face.

Once back in the room, Meghan took one look at Bella's messy pile and scooped the clothes out of the case and onto the bed. Meghan turned into a packing machine, folding and sorting clothes with precision. Neat stacks, sorted by type of garment, covered the bed. Army precision guided the mechanics of Meghan's folding and sorting, but her face bore a weary sadness.

Bella recognized herself in Meghan's expression. "You're going through the same thing, aren't you? Leaving Lee, I mean." Bella sat with her legs folded underneath her on a corner of the bed, out of Meghan's way.

Meghan shook her downcast head. She stopped folding and met Bella's gaze. "We're breaking up."

"What? Why?"

"I told him we had to. He wants to get into med school, and when he does, it'll be even tougher on him, with studying and trying to work on the side whenever he can. He doesn't need, and can't afford, the luxury of an out-of-town girlfriend." Meghan inhaled so deeply that her chest rose and fell visibly. Her voice dropped to a whisper. "We agreed that if we're meant to be together, it'll happen someday. Just not now." She bit her lower lip and silently returned to folding Bella's summer garb.

Bella sprang up and threw her arms around Meghan. "No. Don't give up so easily. You could always go visit him at school, couldn't you? And can't you move to be with him in med school?"

Meghan shook her head. "I'd be a distraction, and I love him too much to do anything that would hold him back. Besides," she added, her somber face breaking into what was almost a smile, "I need to help Karen plan her wedding. We're going to design all the dresses ourselves, and I'm going to help with the arrangements and planning. She needs me."

"Right. I guess you do have to do that."

Meghan looked up, her eyes lit with excitement. "While Karen and Ed are honeymooning, I'm going to be looking for a place to lease for our boutique. Our dad's giving us some seed money, and Ed's going to be a partner in the business, too, putting in some of his own money. You see, I have to be where Karen is so we can start our boutique. That's always been our dream. To open our own shop after college."

Bella nodded, but she could not imagine breaking up with Phillip. Thank God Phillip was in sync with her and was going to move heaven and earth to be with her. Bella watched as Meghan miraculously tucked the last blouse into the suitcase and closed it with only a gentle push.

Meghan patted the lid of the closed case. "So, I guess you and Phillip are going to try the long-distance romance?"

"He's going to transfer as soon as he can figure out the money thing. Hopefully, this semester."

"Lucky you. No, I should say, lucky him."

Bella and Meghan were the last to tumble into the courtyard, lugging Bella's suitcase and backpack.

With their chaperone chiding them to deposit their bags by the van and to hurry and line up for a photograph, the group laughed and jostled each other as they complied. Bella hugged each of her friends in turn by the van. She couldn't imagine not being with them next week or next month. These seven kids were the best friends she'd ever had.

Bella punched Stillman on the shoulder to get his attention as he tucked his suitcase into the back of the van. "Hey, I need a hug from you."

Stillman turned around. "Nope. You're rationed. You get one at the airport, and that's it." His face was dead serious.

Bella pretended indignation. "After sharing a couchette with me on the train to Paris, you're rationing me to one flippin' hug?"

Stillman nodded in the direction of Phillip. "Doesn't he get all your hugs?"

Bella rested her hand on his forearm. She leaned close, so only he could hear her words. "That's bullshit. I hug who I want." Bella wrapped her arms around Stillman. "You're my friend, and I'm going to miss you like crazy."

"Friend." Stillman snorted. "The hot ones always want to be my friend."

Phillip appeared at Bella's side, tugging her free hand, pulling her into the line being formed for the picture. Laughing and joking, the group lined up—Phillip, Bella,

Stillman, Hope, Lee, Meghan, Karen, and Rune. Summer abroad was officially over.

Phillip held her tight. Bella glanced sideways at him, giddy with the thought that he'd soon meet her mom. She couldn't wait to be home and see her.

Being so far from her mom this summer had been harder than she'd imagined. It had become even worse when the letters from her mother stopped coming. Bella had shared her worry with Phillip, who had shrugged and chalked it up to the unreliable Italian postal system. For now, Bella pushed away the nagging worry. She'd see her mom in less than a day.

Bella daydreamed about being back home with both her mom and Phillip, all three of them together at the kitchen table. Her family.

15

JFK Airport, New York

Bella twitched with excitement in spite of her exhaustion from being up twenty-four hours straight. Her mother stood somewhere in the waiting area.

"I'll take off work, honey. I can't wait to see you." Her mother's lyrical voice, her cadence slower than usual, had crackled through the lines during her telephone call two weeks before.

Bella couldn't get back soon enough. This was the longest she had ever been apart from her mother. Ever since Bella had started college, she and her mother had been best friends, often talking and giggling together late into the night.

Bella blinked at the harsh airport light and breathed deeply to force out the stale airplane air. Her pace, which had been a sprint from the steps of the airplane to the shuttle bus, and then on to the terminal and the lines in U.S. Customs, had turned into a crawl in the waiting area.

Around her, voices chatted in English, not Italian. English meant home. Bella's eyes danced through the curtain of eager faces waiting for loved ones. Light bounced everywhere; it welcomed her home. Finally.

She skipped forward at the sight of her neighbor, Mrs. Kowalski, but the swarm of passengers slowed her progress. Her eyes searched for her mother as she walked toward Mrs. Kowalski, twenty feet away. Wrinkles framed the woman's eyes, not just from the passage of time, but also from hours and hours of laughter. Today, though, Mrs. Kowalski's eyes, accustomed to smiling, seemed clouded with sorrow.

Bella stopped. She felt someone slam into her from behind; hot breath swept the back of her neck, and garbled words marked the person's sudden redirection.

Bella clawed and swam through the people still blocking her path until she reached Mrs. Kowalski. She could see that red puffiness had turned Mrs. Kowalski's laugh lines into creases of pain. "Where's my mom?" The breathless words echoed, too loud, too harsh.

Mrs. Kowalski clutched Bella to her.

Bella couldn't breathe.

"I'm so sorry, honey." Mrs. Kowalski's husky voice against Bella's ear excluded all other sound. "She got so weak. Your mother went into the hospital a week ago. They found cancer everywhere. I didn't know how to reach you."

Bella wrestled away from the fleshy arms. "Where is she?" She tugged on Mrs. Kowalski's arm. "Let's go. What hospital is she in?"

Mrs. Kowalski shook her head, and tears wet her eyes. "I'm so sorry. She's gone."

Bella stared at her.

Her knees trembled. Voices ping-ponged around her. The lights dimmed …

Bella's eyes fluttered open. She was sprawled on the floor. Dirty male toes in Jesus sandals stood a foot from her nose. She remembered. Her eyes squeezed closed. Her cheek pressed against the cold, hard floor. It smelled like dust and lemon industrial cleaner.

Mom.

A few weeks later, Bella sat in a molded chair, back at JFK. The terminal's vast empty space loomed around her. Even the bright summer colors of passengers' clothes couldn't warm the sterile cavern.

The previous few weeks blurred in her mind. Endless paperwork, tears until she could only hack and choke up air, and a swirling fog that circled her every movement and thought. Exhaustion gripped her, even though she had fallen into deep chasms of sleep every night in her mother's bed. The burn on her left hand caught her eye. She wondered if it would scar, a constant reminder of ironing the dress she had buried her mother in.

She hoped the oppressive fog surrounding her might lift today. Or at least not surround her until she gagged and choked, like it had each of the days since she learned that her mother had died all alone. At the same time, she, the dutiful daughter, had flirted and made love with Phillip in Italy, relishing the idea of introducing him to her mom. She had known that her mother would love Phillip.

She clutched her purse in her lap, the precious letter tucked inside. Bella sighed and pulled out Phillip's note.

So sorry to miss the funeral … need to see you … had a long talk with my parents about transferring out East … love you … can't wait.

I love you.

Phillip

Bella refolded the paper, weak along the fold lines from countless readings.

"Meeting a boyfriend?" a petite woman nearby asked. She wore a stylish black suit and crisp white blouse, with a black-and-white silk flower pinned to her left lapel. Her hair was twirled behind her head in a French twist. The woman smiled.

"Yes."

"Lucky you. I'm picking up my boss. Fine thing to do on a Friday night when you're single, isn't it?" The woman moved one seat closer. She extended her hand. "I'm Edie Bernstein. Actually, I'm divorced. I was married seven years to an attorney who liked to jump into bed with his clients. Literally." Her face lit up with a teeth-exposing grin. "But I know a few sharks in Manhattan legal circles, so I came out just fine, thank you very much."

Bella couldn't help but smile. "Bella Rossini. Nice to meet you. Sorry about the ruined Friday night."

Edie leaned closer and lowered her voice. "My boss hates airport shuttles, and the company won't approve a limo. I volunteered to pick him up." She flashed another toothy grin and winked. "I got my husband's Cadillac in the divorce."

Edie snapped open her slim leather briefcase and exposed a pad of paper, a silver card case, and a clutch purse. As she extracted a business card from the card case, she used only the pads of her fingers; her manicured fingernails glistened.

She handed the card to Bella. "Editorial assistant. I'll be a full-fledged editor before the year's out, with my own author clients. A huge promotion up from gofer, don't you think? At twenty-nine, a girl in the city has to scramble to get ahead. So you donate your Friday nights to airport runs in exchange for a promotion." She winked again. "A hell of a lot better than fucking him, I say."

"Amen." Bella smiled. "My boyfriend's going to transfer out here. Or at least he hopes to. He's got interviews with three schools."

The public address announcer's garbled words prevented Edie from replying. Bella and Edie stood and edged toward the gate door being opened by two blue-uniformed women.

A balding, rotund man exited the gate third. Edie raised her left hand and waved. It was her boss, apparently. A fixed professional smile had lodged on Edie's face. She moved behind a pillar toward the spot where her boss would enter the waiting area. Edie half-turned to call back to Bella. "Nice meeting you. Remember to come up for air this weekend, Bella." Another wink and Edie and her boss disappeared into the crowd.

Bella turned back to study the faces of the people arriving. She rocked up on her toes and found herself smiling at all the exiting passengers.

A thin, tired-looking man with wire-rimmed glasses appeared in the door. With a suitcase in one hand, a diaper bag slung over his shoulder, and an unusual, folded-up stroller in the other hand, he spanned the width of the doorway. Ten seconds later, a woman, obviously his wife, walked out, a toddler holding one of her hands and a tiny baby cradled in her other arm.

No wonder he's tired, Bella thought.

After the mother, one, two, and then a third flight attendant exited the gate.

Bella watched the uniformed woman at the door speak into a walkie-talkie. The gate attendant closed the door.

Bella's face turned cold, her smile frozen in place.

"Bella Rossini?"

The male voice behind Bella made her spin around.

Bella nodded.

A man in his forties handed Bella an envelope. He wore a gray, short-sleeved shirt and matching shorts. The words "Airport Courier" and his name, Walt Smiley, were embroidered on his left chest pocket. He nodded at Bella, then turned and hurried away as if he had just punched out for the weekend.

Bella lowered her head and studied the envelope. She took a deep breath, then opened it. Inside was a piece of paper with a short typed message on it. Key words jumped out.

Didn't mean to deceive.
Engaged.
Planned to break up.

Business considerations.
Her father ... great opportunity.

Bella read the page twice. The typewriter's "e" character had a flaw in the top curve, so every "e" had a break in it. She thought it odd that she noticed the broken curve, but then, why wouldn't she notice? Every word, every letter, burned into her mind.

Forgive me.

Phillip's name was typed at the bottom, one space below his closing lie. The biggest lie of all.

I'll always love you.

Bella folded the page into thirds, the same as the letter in her purse. She creased the folds twice with her fingertips. She pulled Phillip's hand-scrawled letter out of her purse and folded the new, typed missive inside it. Bella pressed her eyes closed, to stop the stinging tears. She felt hot, stale air on her face. When she dared to open her eyes, she tucked the letters into the bottom of her purse.

Bella lifted her chin, swiped her wet cheek with the back of her hand, and swept her hair over her shoulders. Her eyes scanned the terminal filled with strangers.

She, and she alone, would have to cope and somehow survive. But how?

16

Ann Arbor, Michigan

L ee sat inside the Blue Coffee House with a half-drunk
cup of cold coffee. The swarm of students around
him had one topic of discussion—the upcoming annual
Michigan football game against their archrival, Ohio State
University. This year, Lee had no time for football. Having
grown used to strong espresso during his summer in
Florence, the University coffee tasted weak in comparison.
The only good thing about this coffee was the caffeine.

A letter from his mother had arrived this morning.
They never changed. The standard letter consisted of three
parts.

First, study hard or he wouldn't get into med school.
For as long as Lee could remember, his mother and grandmother demanded that he become a physician.

Second, Lee must learn how to be at the top of his class
now, so that he would excel later in med school. Following
med school, his mother would remind him, Lee must
secure an internship, and then a residency in one of the
specialties. Cardiology. Plastic surgery. Anesthesiology.
Something that garnered prestige and a high paycheck,

restoring the family to their rightful position, which had been lost with his grandfather's death in World War II.

His mother's last demand? Write to her more frequently.

Lee concentrated on the Organic Chemistry text open before him. With practiced effort, he tuned out the chatter and laughter around him. Not his ideal study location, but this was where Stillman had suggested they meet. A clap on his back startled Lee; his glasses slipped down his nose with the sudden motion.

Stillman dropped his books on the round table, jostling Lee's cup. He slid into a chair. "Hey, dude. How's it going?"

"Shitty. My deadbeat lab partner dropped. Of course, he could have bailed before he'd taken on half the responsibility for our labs."

Stillman shook his head. "Tough break, man. So did you get his work before he rode off into the sunset?"

Lee's disgusted look answered the question. "Zip. Nothing but piss and promises."

"That sucks. You know, it freaks us out now, but someday we'll be living the life of rich doctors driving fancy cars, and O Chem will be ancient history." Stillman leaned back in his chair and eyed the large-chested co-ed at the counter. "Have you talked to Meghan since the summer?"

Lee looked away. "Nah. You know, MCATs this year, plus this friggin' organic." He shrugged. "I miss her, though. Who knows? Maybe I'll call her."

Stillman, motionless, seemed to be studying Lee as if he were an alien to be wary of.

"How 'bout you? Have you talked to anybody? You were pretty tight with Bella." He was fishing.

Stillman pursed his lips and gave one decisive shake of his head. "Not really."

"But I thought for sure you two did it before she and Phillip became an item. I remember you guys burning the midnight oil at least once or twice alone together. Plus, of course, the train." Lee leered at him. He remembered how Bella and Karen had shared berths with Stillman and Rune out of fear of their Middle Eastern couchette-mates. "Those couchettes were something, weren't they?"

"I haven't spoken to her since we left Italy." Stillman's thumb rubbed the binding of his organic book. "She and Phillip were going to keep dating in the States."

"Really? I never caught that."

"Guess it was hard to see anything beyond Meghan's tits." Stillman chuckled.

Lee wanted to snap back. He cared about Meghan. He really did. It just wasn't their time. Not with MCATs and then med school applications looming. But he knew Stillman spoke the truth. During those last weeks, his world had consisted of Meghan and Florence, two beauties he had hated to leave. He grinned. "Guess I'm guilty."

Stillman straightened his stack of books on the table, as meticulously as if he were being graded on it. Expressionless, he looked up and his eyes caught Lee's. "What're you going to do about the labs? The final project with all the lab results from the semester is worth thirty percent."

Lee's posture stiffened. "Can I tag with you and your partner? I've lost some ground but I'll do most of the work from wherever you are if you'll share data with me. There's no way I can start from scratch and finish in time. How 'bout it?"

Stillman pursed his lips and leaned back, the perfect study of contemplation. "Nah."

Stillman collected his books and pushed away from the table. "I'm sorry. You know I'd do it, but it won't fly with my partner. Every one of us is competing for the top grade and those coveted med school slots. He won't share. He's paranoid about the competition for grades. I don't even trust him to give me the full analyses. I use his data and write my own."

He clapped the back of Lee's shoulder again. "Hey, good luck, man. I wish I could help you. You have natural luck with the ladies. Maybe one of them will share their labs."

Without a word, Lee watched Stillman duck through the crowd of wind-chapped faces that entered the coffee shop.

Three weeks later, finals loomed as if they were a phantom lurking around the campus. The campus pubs, normally overflowing at night, were as empty as ghost towns. Only a handful of fraternities hadn't broken stride in their social schedule.

The library reigned as the campus hot spot. Lee sat in his regular top-floor cubicle, his head buried in the messy stack of papers and printouts in front of him. He returned, for the twentieth time, to the chart of lab results he had checked and rechecked. Suddenly he slammed one fist against the laminated cubicle desk, scattering his papers in a tornado to the floor. The noise drew angry whispers from the cloistered students at neighboring study desks.

Lee dropped his head into his hands in frustration. The final lab report was due by four o'clock the next afternoon. He opened his backpack and stuffed his lab results, charts, notes, and rough draft inside, oblivious to the sound of wrinkling paper.

Then he methodically started his rounds, covering every floor, cubicle, table, and low-slung chair in the library. Finally, he caught Stillman charming the girl who staffed the checkout desk, his backpack slung over one shoulder and a smile on his face. Lee waited until the proper moment, then fell in step beside Stillman as he left the building.

Lee braced himself against the frigid north wind that gusted through campus. "How's it going?"

"Same as you, I'm sure. Lots of worry, too much caffeine, and damn near a stranger to my bed." Stillman grinned at him. His eyes showed no evidence of exhaustion.

"Got your O Chem done?" Lee couldn't help himself. No sense making idle chatter since that's all anyone in the class talked about.

"Yep. Gonna turn the packet in tomorrow morning. Sherry's typing up the report and lab data for me. How about you?"

Lee felt as if he'd been punched in the stomach. He had flown through the labs because of the compressed time schedule. Now he lacked confidence in his conclusions, since his data wasn't complete. With the deadline looming, he had no time to rerun labs.

Although it was a long shot, maybe Stillman would let him read his finished lab packet before turning it in. No doubt, Stillman had aced it. If Lee knew the correct conclusions, he could do what the students called "dry lab"—tweak the data to match the conclusion.

Could he convince Stillman to share his report? Sometimes, lying was necessary. "My packet, at least, is going great. I do final changes tonight. Only I'm doing my own typing tomorrow. Guess those years of piano lessons paid off for something."

Lee had seen the flyers on his dorm bulletin board for Sherry's typing services. Poor thing, he'd met her once—major acne plus headgear braces. No life, but a fat bank account.

"You done for the night?"

"Nah." Stillman stopped at the junction of two sidewalks. "I'm studying for my Art History final with a girl over in West Quad." Stillman winked at him. "How's your quota on tail these days?"

"Hah. My steady date is O Chem."

"And she's butt ugly. But at least you pulled it out." Stillman rubbed his gloved hands together. "I gotta get out of this cold."

Lee went for it. "Think I could read your packet before you turn it in? I would love to double-check my conclusions, since I had to rush the labs. I could look at your paper first thing in the morning, and you could turn it in afterwards."

Stillman frowned. "Sounds like you want to dry lab. I can't do it. That would be cheating. After growing up in a

Bible-beating preacher's house, there's no way I could lie, cheat, or steal. You're so conscientious, Lee, I'll bet your paper's great the way it is." He motioned toward the Quads. "I gotta go now. After Christmas, let's grab a beer."

Shit. Lee felt as if someone had punched him in the stomach, but he couldn't let Stillman know it. "Nah, I wouldn't know how to dry lab. I just thought it'd be good to compare our reports." He shrugged to indicate that it didn't matter, although the polar opposite was true.

Lee clapped Stillman on the shoulder. "Right. You're on for a beer when we return from break. But now, I need fuel. Thought I'd grab a burger, then bury myself back in the library."

"Later." Stillman bowed his head against the wind and moved in the direction of the West Quad without waiting for Lee's reply.

Lee pulled up the hood of his coat and started in the direction of the university beer and burger hangout two blocks off campus. By the time he reached the edge of campus, the anxiety consuming him had taken over.

His lab results were sketchy; he could massage them all night, but it wouldn't help. He needed to ace the paper to save a decent grade in Organic Chemistry. Everything he'd ever worked for rode on this class. Everything. His family was counting on him, and failure was not an option.

He staggered off the sidewalk to the line of lonely, barren trees. Lee clutched his midsection and bent over with nausea. The remnants of food and coffee in his stomach spewed out onto the ground. He vomited again and again until he had nothing left. Still, dry heaves racked his body. A jackhammer pounded in his head, and his belly ached. Shivers of cold and exhaustion shook him. He wiped his mouth across the sleeve of his coat. Tears burned his eyes.

It wasn't fair.

He had done his part, and his lab partner had dumped on him. He knew it was fruitless to appeal to "One Letter Grade Johnson," his O Chem prof. Late, even one minute late, turning in an assignment cost you one letter grade. Excuses cost you one letter grade. More than one grammatical error in an assignment cost you one letter grade.

Lee sucked in the frigid air. Why bother to finish? It was impossible to get an A with the data he had scraped together the last three weeks. Dropping it now would look so bad on his transcript that he'd be denied admission to any reputable med school. Lee knew in his heart that he'd make a decent physician, even though it was an obligation rather than a choice. Stillman, on the other hand, seemed driven to achieve the income of a doctor, nothing more. The injustice of it burned in him.

He had two choices: give up or take control and seize what was rightfully his.

Lee looked at his watch. Although it seemed like an eternity, only minutes had passed since he parted with Stillman. He knew what he had to do, and even though it violated his every principle, sometimes Machiavelli was right. The end justifies the means.

An hour later, Lee waited outside Sherry's window. He shivered and paced under the row of oak and maple trees beside the dormitory. Surely she'd be asleep by now. He'd given it thirty minutes after her window had darkened. Luckily for him, he'd been an RA in this dorm his sophomore year and knew every inch of its floors. He had looked Sherry up in the directory; it had been a cinch to count off the windows to her room.

He pulled his coat up to his chin and swung his backpack over his shoulder. A girl Lee had known from his Calculus II class last year lived in this dorm. She'd flirted with Lee all year and last week asked him to meet for coffee between finals. Although Lee had put her off initially, now she became his ticket inside.

Lee waltzed inside to the dorm's front desk and called her room. When the girl arrived, two other students were studying in the main lounge, so Lee followed her to the back recreation room. Admitting that finals were swamping him now, Lee suggested that they meet for lunch the first week after Christmas break, and they agreed on a day. Then Lee volunteered to exit the dorm by the back door—it was closer to the library.

The heavy-duty tape Lee had used to reinforce a textbook was still in his backpack. The girl didn't notice when he slapped a piece of tape to the bolt as he pulled the door closed behind him.

Lee knew this moment was his chance.

He waited five minutes and re-entered the building. He quickly removed the tape from the bolt on the dorm door, then found and pulled a fire alarm. Lee slipped into the utility closet on the first floor. He heard the fire alarm ringing and footsteps running past the closet. Alarmed girls' voices rose and fell in volume as the residents headed out of the building.

When the footsteps died down, he ran up the stairwell farthest from the door and peered down the hall, looking in both directions. No one. Lee relied on Sherry to have had the good sense to leave the building. He ran down the hall. He'd pretend to be a "sweeper," one who looks for people not yet evacuated, if anyone saw him.

He turned the knob to Sherry's room. Yes—she'd left it unlocked. The light was on, but to Lee's luck, curtains covered the windows. He closed the door behind him and rushed to her desk. There, on the far side, sat a stack of large envelopes. He ripped the top one open, careful not to damage the contents. It was Stillman's typed lab packet and report.

Beneath Stillman's report, he noticed two more large envelopes, no doubt with other students' papers inside. Next to the stack of envelopes, a voluminous research paper sat in a pristine cover. He flipped through it. It was Sherry's British Literature final paper. He let it weigh in his hand as he considered the alternatives. Could he risk destroying her paper in the fire he was going to start?

A photograph of Sherry, her faced scarred by acne, smiled at him. In the picture, her arms were draped over two brown mutts. The three faces watched him. Lee thought of her, forced by bad dental luck to wear braces with headgear in college, and he couldn't put her paper in jeopardy. Her life was tough enough. He placed her re-search paper back on the desk, but closer to the center than it had been before.

Lee had to work fast. He tucked the envelope with Still-man's project into his backpack.

He didn't feel remorse for what he was doing. Stillman had the raw lab work; he could easily re-create the report, turn it in a day late, and lose only one letter grade. Stillman had the highest grade in the class, so if he got a B on the labs, he could still get an A for the semester.

Lee placed the other two envelopes on the edge of the desk, sliding them out so that a corner of the envelopes hung over the wastebasket below. Lee knew it was possible that these two envelopes, with students' term papers inside, would be destroyed. He wouldn't allow himself to think of those students. Hopefully, flames from the fire he was about to start wouldn't rise high enough to burn the envelopes.

In the distance, the horn of a firetruck sounded. Fire-men would soon be here to control the blaze. He grabbed the campus newspaper, threw it into Sherry's metal wastebasket and then topped it off with a handful of typing paper. He lit the blank paper with his lighter.

It had to look as if Stillman's paper had slid off the stack of envelopes and fallen into the wastebasket, or been consumed by leaping flames. Please, he thought, don't let the flames leap that high. Even though Lee could live with Stillman losing a letter grade, he didn't want to burn anyone's paper.

Lee ran out into the hall. It took less than five minutes for him to exit through the side door and slip out into the dark night. He heard the girls tittering in fear and excitement. He could picture them clustered on the grass circle in front of the building. Lee ran for a clump of trees.

High-pitched screams drew him back to the dorm.

He circled wide, so if anyone saw him, it would look as though he had come from the library.

The screams intensified.

Lee saw the reason. Black and gray smoke seeped from around the window in Sherry's room. Had the desk ignited? Why hadn't the firetrucks arrived yet? The sirens had sounded so close. Last month, a prankster had pulled the fire alarm and the trucks had arrived in less than ten minutes.

He thought of the hard work of the students that he had put in jeopardy, now likely consumed by flames. He felt nauseous. What had he done?

The wail of the firetrucks split the air. Closer. Closer. The pitch of the girls' screams changed, and he saw why. Sherry had run back into the building. His stomach clenched. He sprinted toward the dorm. He had to stop her.

Firemen raced toward the building from the back, where the trucks had rumbled to a stop. The firefighters dashed inside, splitting between the front and side doors.

Lee stopped his race to the dorm. They would reach her first. He leaned against an oak tree and caught his breath. Please. Find Sherry. Bring her out safely. He repeated his silent prayer over and over.

The back door to the dorm opened. A firefighter walked out with his arm around Sherry.

Lee collapsed to his knees and thanked God. The fire sirens silenced. He knew he had to leave and distance himself from the fire. He stood and stumbled away. Sixty paces later, he stopped. With one hand on a tree, Lee bent, racked again by dry heaves. Guilt and fear consumed him, and he shivered as if he'd fallen through the ice of a frozen pond.

Sunrise was peeking through the blinds in Lee's room by the time he finished.

He'd spent the night retyping and rewriting Stillman's paper, changing the descriptions into his own language. Now even Stillman couldn't guess Lee had stolen his material. Stillman's work impressed Lee. He couldn't imagine a more precise and well-worded document.

His eyes wandered to the window. The sky had the typical Midwest gray pallor, but streaks of color brightened the horizon.

He pulled a trash can lid from the bottom of his closet. Black soot caked the inside of the lid. Last winter, he had had the brilliant idea of sharing s'mores with a coed. Bedding her had become an obsession and a distraction. Unfortunately, even building a small fire in his dorm room hadn't loosened her morals. He'd kept the lid because he was proud of his idea—the Residential Housing Department never had a clue he had built a fire in his room.

Lee ripped Stillman's typed report and the envelope into halves, then halves again. He laid the ripped pages of his friend's labors in the center of the trash can lid and pulled out his cigarette lighter. Then, Lee cracked open the windows in his room, letting in the frigid air. Bending over the lid, he lit the papers. The flame grew immediately. After a few minutes, he doused the fire with a cup of cold coffee.

Ten minutes later, the ashes had been flushed down the toilet. No evidence remained of his criminal act.

A couple of hours later, his final lab packet hand-delivered to his professor, Lee stood in line at the Blue Coffee House for an extra-large cup of the high-octane liquid fuel. He hoped to get by with coffee for another few hours, rather than the caffeine-laced pills that many students used during finals.

The remainder of the day loomed, his duties a blur of library time and one final that night. Everywhere he went, students buzzed with stories of the dorm fire. He pretended to be focused solely on his books, but he strained to hear every word.

The next night, Lee stood outside the Organic Chemistry room; he scanned the ID numbers for his own. His gut felt like an acid pump on steroids. Even though his finals had ended the day before, he couldn't join the end-of-term celebrations. He felt no joy.

"Mr. Mostow, may I have a word with you, please?" The deep voice of his Organic Chemistry professor echoed behind him.

Lee forced his face into a stoic expression, turned, and nodded. He didn't trust his voice. He followed his professor's brisk march to the stairwell. Lee's breaths came shallow and silent.

"Mr. Mostow, I must tell you, I read your final labs last night. It was the finest packet I have seen in my thirty years of teaching at this institution. And to think you did it without a lab partner. I am confident your application to medical school next year will be successful. Down the road, don't rule out research. Your attention to detail and analysis is remarkable for an undergraduate."

"Thank you, sir." Lee shook his prof's hand.

"Now go. Enjoy your holiday. You've earned it." A broad smile spread across the man's face.

Lee turned toward the stairs, stopping a foot short of running smack into Stillman, who was leaving the chemistry lab. A putrid shade of gray blanketed Stillman's face. His shoulders slumped. Only his eyes showed signs of life.

Stillman gave Lee a dark, penetrating stare that sucked the air right out of Lee's lungs.

Behind Lee, footsteps scuffled against the floor.

"Mr. Jackson, have you resurrected your report yet?" The professor's voice made both Lee and Stillman jump.

"No, sir. We're reassembling the data. Unfortunately, some of our charts were lost in the fire." Stillman's voice broke. "If we could just have to the end of the break—"

"Absolutely not. That would be unfair to those who managed to complete the work in a timely fashion."

Lee edged around Stillman, desperately trying to avoid eye contact. The professor's next words followed Lee through the hall.

"Mr. Jackson, I'm afraid because it is the end of the term and this paper counts as your final, if you don't turn it in today, you and your partner will have to accept zeroes on it, which means you fail my Organic Chemistry class. I suggest you either take it again next summer or fall, or drop out of pre-med."

Lee took the stairs down two at a time. He ran to his car parked a block away. Gusts of wind pelted snow through the campus. Other students were also racing to their cars, so the storm wouldn't strand them. Lee guided his VW Rabbit, already packed for the holiday, to I-94. His foot pressed down on the accelerator as he headed home for Christmas.

No matter how loud Lee cranked the volume on the car's tape player, he couldn't drown out the professor's words to Stillman.

17

Los Angeles, California

Rune, one year after college, rocked his head in time to the blaring music. The walls shuddered from the bass and the crowd's screams. He eased open the back stage entrance, peeked outside, and slammed it shut again behind the broad backs of the body-builder duo who guarded the door. The groupies spilled like vomit over the sidewalk outside the back entrance. His hands rubbed together.

Mick ran up to Rune from the edge of the stage. A shit-ass grin stretched across Mick's face. Coked already.

Mick's entire body jiggled in time to the finale. He shouted to be heard. "Last encore. Be ready to run. Grab the hottest two chicks on your way through the crowd. I'll do the same. The muscles fill the last limo with anybody that'll blow them."

Mick grabbed Rune's cheeks between his palms. "I told you, dude. Metal bands are the ticket." Mick's head tilted back, sending his high-pitched scream to the stars. "Sex … drugs … and rock-and-roll!"

Bodacious girls and a weed cloud. Entering the band's hotel suite, Rune scoped pairs and threesomes sprawled in marathon sex. The dudes outside on the balcony sucked joints, snorted coke, and diddled with needles. Beer bottles littered the floor.

Rune slid down against a wall. He tapped out a line of coke on the table next to him. A topless blonde with cantaloupe tits crouched in front of him. She eyed his coke. Her head dove. Awesome. Mick was right.

Rune's head lolled back. His eyes wandered to a couple on the balcony. A guy long on hair and short on body fat straddled a bimbo lying on chair cushions. She shouted obscenities in rhythm with his thrusts. Her hands clung to his protruding hipbones.

After sucking him off, the blonde pulled up from Rune's crotch and crouched over the coke. Rune saw Mick sprawled on the couch. His friend cinched a band around his biceps. A redhead, likely jailbait, sat next to Mick. She injected her arm, then passed the syringe to Mick.

"Don't do it, man." Rune's eyes widened. "Dirty needles are no good, man."

Mick didn't hesitate. He jabbed the needle into his arm.

Rune watched Mick flip the strap off his arm. Mick's eyes rolled and he slumped back against the couch.

The cantaloupe-titted chick flopped against Rune's side, her left boob smashed into his ribs. Rune's eyes drifted closed. This was the life.

18

Chicago, Illinois

Meghan, in her mid-twenties, lounged in the middle of ten women sitting cross-legged on the floor. Glasses of champagne sat next to them amid opened boxes and crumpled wrapping paper. The giggling and laughter drowned out Ravel's *Bolero* in the background.

The boutique had closed an hour early so that Karen could host the lingerie shower for Meghan here in their store. Meghan couldn't keep the grin off her face. Life was perfect. The twins, along with Karen's husband, Ed, owned this growing boutique, and now Meghan was getting married.

"Ooh, hoo-hoo. Look at this one." Karen held up a filmy black lace panty and swung it in the air. "This is destined to become one of Jason's favorites." She moved on to a matching camisole, swishing it through the air by its satin straps. "I really blew it, getting married right after college. No one had money to buy sexy lingerie for me."

Meghan's eyes sparkled. "I thought you liked the kitchen gadget shower I threw for you."

"Are you kidding?" Karen laughed. "What could be sexier than a sand-colored toaster?"

Meghan pursed her lips. "Guess you have to toast bread naked then, don't you?"

"Shh. You'll give away my secrets." Karen succumbed to a fit of giggles.

Howls of laughter erupted at the banter between the twins.

Karen leaned over and whispered to her sister. "I told you things would work out when we left Italy. That you were better off without Lee."

Meghan kissed her sister's cheek. "You're right. If I'd left Chicago to be with Lee in medical school, we wouldn't have the shop. And without the shop, I wouldn't have met Jason." She had met her fiancé at the deli across the street from the shop one day when they each had run in for a quick take-out lunch.

She tingled all over at the mere thought of him. He was sexy in a bad-boy way. Jason supported her career, too, never complaining about her night or weekend shifts at the shop. The day they met, he had followed her back to the boutique, quizzing her about her interests and the store as they ate their lunches. It had been love at first sight for him, he'd brag to anyone they met. Jason traveled most of the time, selling medical equipment to hospitals from Chicago to Los Angeles.

Meghan remembered that she hadn't completed the purchase orders for the upcoming season. "We have to go through the new order tomorrow. I'm not letting this wedding stuff ruin our profits because we didn't pay attention to business."

"Ed's not sure it's wise to bring in the two new lines," Karen said.

Meghan covered Karen's hand with her own. "Tomorrow, come an hour early. I'll have the coffee on and we can go through the budgets. We need the new lines to stay on the forefront. If we want to move to Pine Street and be part of boutique row, we've got to be avant-garde trendsetters. We need those lines." She sat back, the matter settled. "I'm not leaving on a honeymoon until the new order is in."

"Ed's worried about the money." Karen's eyes dropped to her lap, where one palm rested on her belly.

Meghan's eyes followed her sister's. Karen's champagne sat untouched beside her. Meghan's mouth gaped open at a sudden suspicion. "Are you pregnant?"

Karen looked up. A flush ran up her cheeks. She nodded twice. Meghan's arms flew around her sister. "I'm so excited!" She waved her arms back and forth in the air, calling for the attention of the group. "Karen is having a baby. I'm going to be an auntie."

The women clustered around them and hugged Karen. Karen's eyes met Meghan's. "I'm sorry. This was supposed to be your day."

Meghan flicked her hand, dismissing her sister's comment. But inside her, the giddy feeling from the wedding shower deflated by one-third. Her mind traveled back to the day she first fell in love—the day she lost her virginity to Lee. That day, too, Karen's news of her engagement to Ed had put a lid on her own milestone. Meghan felt Karen's eyes on her face. She smiled and nodded at her sister. "I'm happy for you."

Meghan scooted around the floor, gathering up the satin and lace undergarments. The girls' giggly banter shifted from sexual innuendos to talk of babies and motherhood. The camisole on the top of the pile, fire-engine red with white lace trim, glistened under a spotlight. Meghan remembered that the florist wanted final approval for the table centerpieces on Monday: red roses surrounded by lily-of-the-valley.

Her smile widened. In one week, she'd be married.

A bell tinkled when Meghan pushed open the door to the florist shop and was hit by the immediate sensory overload. Vibrant colors splashed from every corner. The fragrance of the flowers tickled her nose. Her eyes settled on the sales counter. Papers were scattered on the surface, but no one manned the desk.

"Hello?" she said.

Meghan peeked into the walk-in coolers. Empty. She heard a muffled voice from the back room. "Harvey?" It didn't sound like Harvey's nasal tone, the only thing about him she didn't like. She opened the door to the back workroom.

Only one light, a yellowish bulb by the alley door, lit the crammed space. Meghan heard a muffled noise on the left side of the room. It came from the passageway between the floor-to-ceiling metal storage shelves.

Maybe Harvey had fallen and was hurt. Was it an intruder?

She shuddered and grabbed a stoneware vase by the lip; it was the only thing she saw that was heavy enough to be a weapon. She eyed the back door and calculated an escape route, in case she needed it. Her feet padded against the linoleum floor.

Meghan thought about calling the police, but what if Harvey was bleeding or had suffered a heart attack? Every moment might count, and she'd heard far too many horror stories of Cook County 911 operators putting callers on hold.

She leaned to her left and peered around the storage unit. The shelves, crammed full of vases, wires, and florist foam, allowed only ribbons of amber light into the space.

Meghan's gaze dropped from eye level to the floor.

She saw not an injured Harvey, but two bodies curled together. The man's freckled ass moved in time with his grunts. A freckled body Meghan knew all too well. Underneath him, the spindly legs of a girl jutted out.

Meghan had seen the girl before, an eighteen-year-old beauty who helped Harvey with the cash register. Not a brain trust, but the girl had a pretty face with a bust that made Meghan look flat. The girl's wide eyes peered over the man's shoulder and broadcast horror at being caught. Her long green and black fingernails dug into her partner's shoulders. His thrusts sped up, apparently taking her clawing as a sign of passion.

Meghan remembered giving Jason the address of Harvey's floral shop a month earlier so that he could order her bouquet. *Her wedding bouquet.* The slivers of light created stripes across Jason's skin as his backside moved up and down with each thrust.

She let the vase slip from her fingers. It crashed against the floor and split in two. A retching cough erupted from her throat. Somehow, by sheer will, she kept her nausea in check. She'd be damned if she'd give him the satisfaction of seeing her toss her cookies.

Meghan chose her words with care and then spit them out in a voice both clear and strong. "I should have looked at your flabby ass from this vantage point before, Jason; it would have saved a shitload of heartache."

19

Lower Fork of the Salmon River, Idaho

"Woo-hoo." Phillip, athletic at age thirty-two, dug his paddle into the swirling water.

Their guide, a tanned young woman with chiseled muscles, perched on the back of the raft and shouted commands. "Right side back. Dig in. Harder. Left—forward. Hard."

Spray hit Phillip's face; the cold, rising water drove his arms deeper into the current. The second day into their five-day vacation, they faced the first Class III rapids of the trip. He glanced over his shoulder at Jewel, his pre-teen daughter.

What he saw sank his heart. Not joy, fear, or concern. No. Not Jewel. His daughter hung onto the safety rope, inspecting her fingernails. God knows what she had done with her paddle.

The raft bounced and bobbed. Water smacked the front riders' faces. The chilly blast of river water brought shouts and cheers.

Phillip turned back and dug harder. He gritted his teeth and surrendered to the physical task. His heart hammered in his chest. The paddle rubbed across the blister from yesterday, but he didn't care.

They emerged from the rapids. The water smoothed out in a wide stretch of river.

"That's it," their guide said. "You did it. Take a break." They pulled out their paddles and rested them across their knees. She steered them to a calm eddy at the river's edge. "Great work, team. Last group I brought through here dumped the front two riders after the big rock."

"When's the next one?" Phillip rubbed his palms together. "That was great." He refused to let Jewel's bad attitude spoil his fun.

Ruth, the tall, athletic woman across from Phillip, raised her arm and slapped the hand of her son, a boy a little younger than Jewel. His red ball cap had worn through at the edge of the brim, exposing white underneath. Ruth then slapped the outstretched hands of the rafters on her side and reached across to Phillip. She stretched to extend her palm to Jewel.

Phillip caught her eye and shook his head. Jewel hadn't raised her eyes to acknowledge the woman. He mouthed the word, "Sorry."

At the end of the day, Phillip sat in the calm, shallow water on a three-legged stool. His bare feet rested in the water, his toes curling over the smooth pebbles as he nursed a beer. How different this was from his normal high-pressure corporate life. This was another world— relaxing and sitting in the water after an exhilarating day in a raft.

Ruth sat next to him on a similar stool. The other adult rafters were nearby in the shallow water on stools or wading, each with a cool drink in hand.

The sun lingered over the horizon, not ready to relinquish its grasp on the day. Here the canyon widened to expose a broad white sand beach. Two-person tents dotted one end of the beach. A guide led the kids in games at the far end of the sandbar.

"Rafting must not be your daughter's thing," Ruth said. "It's not for everybody, you know." She tilted her head to take a big swallow of beer. "I'm just glad my James seems to be having fun. It's a splurge for us to be here on a teacher's salary, but I wanted to do it for him. It's tough for him, without a dad."

Laughter from the younger group peppered the air. Why couldn't Jewel let herself be a kid here? Phillip's eyes drank in the jutting rocks that lined the canyon's walls. He looked at Ruth. "Divorced?"

"Widowed."

"I'm sorry. Was it recent?"

"When James was three. Thanks for asking. I focus on my son and my kids at school. It's enough." Ruth stood. "Anybody want another beer?"

Phillip stood and stretched his legs. "No, but I'll help carry. I want to check on Jewel."

After Ruth got the beer count, she splashed out of the water toward the cooler. "Leave her be." She rested her hand on Phillip's forearm. "You know your child. But if you don't think she's depressed, I'd let her sulk. If she's bored enough, maybe she'll join the games."

As if to answer the unasked question, Phillip saw Jewel crawl out of her tent. She had changed into dry clothes. Jewel turned back into the tent and tugged her large, waterproof gear bag outside.

Above them, a whirring sound cut the calm, still evening. The noise grew louder. The distinct air-chopping sound of a helicopter stopped the children's jumping game. Everybody stood and craned their necks to see it.

"Clear the area! Everybody, clear." One of the guides ran to the group of youngsters and shooed them toward the tents. "It's coming down."

The helicopter hovered twenty feet above the now-empty section of the sandbar. The wind created by the chopper blew the plastic cover off a table by the campfire. The guides scurried to retrieve the blowing supplies and cover the food from the swirling sand. Those wearing baseball caps or river hats held onto them to prevent them from being blown into the river. The whirling air ruffled Phillip's hair and whipped up the long tresses of their guide.

The helicopter shut down, and silence blanketed them.

Phillip had a hunch the surprise landing brought bad news. He would bet the cost of a charter into these canyons exceeded the national average annual salary.

"Dad. We're going." Jewel stood with one hand on her narrow hip. "The helicopter is for us."

Phillip's mouth suddenly went dry. "What?"

"Mom promised me. If I came on this stupid trip with you, she'd take me to Rodeo Drive. She said all I had to do was wait until a helicopter could land. This is the first spot where the dumb river's wide enough. Get your stuff. C'mon."

Phillip gritted his teeth.

Beside him, Ruth's voice spoke only for his ears. "It sounds like the decision's been made."

"Not for me, it hasn't." Phillip opened his mouth to berate his daughter but swallowed his words unspoken. "Let me talk to the pilot."

Once he verified that Angel, his wife, waited at the helicopter's hanger for Jewel's return, he turned to his daughter. "You didn't give rafting a fair shot."

"Sleeping on the ground? No shower or bathroom? Get real, Dad. This is so … primitive. I told you I didn't want to come." She dragged her bag behind her. After two steps, she stopped and pouted at the pilot. "Help me," she said to him.

"Don't touch that bag." Phillip's eyes locked with the pilot's.

The pilot shrugged. "Sorry, man. Your wife's paying my tab." He lifted Jewel's bag and tossed it into the helicopter. He turned back to Phillip. "You coming?"

"No."

"Want me to tell your wife anything?"

Phillip stood erect and silent.

The helicopter roared to life and kicked up more sand. The guides scrambled again to cover the food.

Phillip spoke to the retreating helicopter. "Thanks for the father-daughter bonding, Jewel."

20

Los Angeles, California

At age thirty-five, Rune figured he was due for some good luck. He kept his face impassive and let his eyes case the starlet who stood in his office. Short, tight skirt and tits ready to burst out of her blouse.

"Mr. Adams." She offered him a file folder. "Please. Look at my resume and photos, even if you aren't interested in my screenplay. I have acting experience."

Her voice carried a professional tone, but her eyes betrayed her. She eyed his roast beef sandwich. Kid probably hadn't eaten.

"If you wanted me to look at your script, why bother dangling your boobs at me?" Rune leaned back, a smirk tightening his lips. This was a piece of cake. He wanted to savor the anticipation before indulging.

She squinted, as if to fight back tears. Her lips quivered.

The girl's words came out whisper-quiet, but her enunciation left no doubt of her intent. "I've tried making a contact every day for two years. Every day. First a business suit. Then a modest dress. Stylish pantsuit? Not a chance. I hand-carried my script to every agent I could find an address for. I brought one here, too, hearing that you would look at unagented work. You mailed it back the same day, with only a "no" scribbled on the front page."

Her back straightened. "I tried everything. This," her left hand grabbed her breast, "is my last resort." Her eyes met his dead-on.

"How old are you?"

"Twenty-four." She extended the folder toward him. Her eyes narrowed.

Rune took the folder. She had a nice package, all right. Dynamite photos, a script presented in standard industry format, a professional resume—equally impressive in amateur acting and screenwriting credentials. He closed the folder; his head bowed over it.

He looked up at her and nodded. "I admire your perseverance."

"Will you read my script?"

Rune stood and moved to her side of the desk. "I'll read it, but no promises."

She extended her hand. "Shake my hand, Mr. Adams, and we have a deal."

This girl had all her chips on the table. No way he'd read now. He had one hell of a hard-on.

Afterwards, he read. She paced his bedroom while he lay in bed. The script fell to his lap. The sound of the ruffling pages stopped her movement. She rushed to the side of the bed. She looked sexy in his robe. This girl paid a huge price for her ambition. He respected that.

"It's good. Bankable."

She had the sense to wait for him to continue.

He grinned. "I'll option this with me as the director and see if I can get one of the major studios to back it."

She sat beside him on the bed. Her left hand lowered to the sheet covering his groin. "Thank you."

He removed her hand and returned it to her lap. "You paid your price. From now on, I'll get my reward from a piece of the action."

"I'll do whatever I have to. I want a part in the film, even if it's a small one."

"I can't deliver that. If I can sell the script, I'll try to get you a screen test, but no promises. I'll ask. That's all."

She stood and extended her hand.

"What did you say your name was?" Rune met her grasp.

"Sunny."

"Sunny what?"

She straightened her back. "Just Sunny."

Two months later, Rune knew the deal had gasped its last breath. The studios wanted the script. Screen test for Sunny? Only on a "no promises" basis. But nobody wanted to bankroll him.

Rune stood by the Porsche convertible in the MGM parking lot. It was a lousy sign. The only place Frankie would meet him was here—at the end of the day. Christ, it must be over ninety. Why in hell had he worn black? Rune wiped his forehead with his fingertips; he smeared the sweat from one side to the other.

"Rune." Frankie's velvet voice came from across the lot.

Rune slapped a grin across his face and spun to face him. "Frankie." He lifted one arm in salute.

Frankie tapped a rolled-up script against his left palm. He stopped beside Rune, tapping the script in a staccato rhythm. "I want it."

Just like that.

Rune tried to appear confident even though acid shot into his stomach at a breakneck pace. He puckered his lips. Let Frankie think he was contemplating the nuances of a deal.

The tapping stopped. "What do you need to let me have this?"

"I direct and Sunny has a part. A speaking part."

"She'll get a screen test. If she has anything, she gets a part. No promises, though, on whether we see her face or hear her voice on-screen."

Sunny had expected this. All he had hoped for was to get her a screen test; the rest was up to her. Rune's eyes narrowed. He went for the deal. "And I direct. With a piece of the action, of course."

Frankie's guffaw split the air between them. "Who the fuck do you think you are? Steven Spielberg? Here's the deal. You direct the first month of production. If the takes don't look good, you're out. If they're good, you get to keep going. You get a quarter of a million. Period. No percentage. If the movie tears up the box office, you'll have press worth millions."

Rune threw back his shoulders. "I found the script. I get a piece."

"You get jack shit." Frankie leaned into him. His sneer uncovered two gold crowns. "I'm willing, for the next two minutes, to give you a shot at directing. After that, I'll wait until Sunny comes on her knees to me with the script between her bare breasts. Then I'll get the script and a piece of ass without you as part of the deal."

Rune had only one choice. He extended his right hand. A one-month test? No problem, man.

21

New York, New York

Bella, who at forty-one still garnered wolf whistles when she passed construction sites, straightened the faded linen table runner for the fourth time. She thought of all the nights her son David had sat here, eager to tell her about his day. This was where they ate, he did homework, and she'd clean and bandage his scrapes and cuts from the neighborhood bullies.

David and his girlfriend—*the* girl, he said—were due any minute.

Now a college junior, David had said he'd pop for a taxi from the train station with money saved from tutoring freshmen at Tufts. Three loud raps from a fist hitting the wooden door startled Bella. They were here.

Bella opened the door and smiled.

David rushed in and raised her off her feet in a waist-cinching bear hug. Bella closed her eyes; she drank in the smell of him—clean soap with hints of cedar. Her arms crossed around his neck. His height struck her first.

His arms dropped and she pulled back to study his face. "I haven't seen you for two months, and you grew again."

She tweaked his chin, a gesture she'd picked up from Nonna Maria.

"Mom." His voice chastised her.

She took the hint and dropped her hand. Bella then turned and pulled the tiny blonde to her in a breast-flattening hug. And the girl had a lot to flatten. Definitely a boob job—too firm and too perfect. Bella's smile stiffened. She had to say something. Something nice. "I'm delighted to finally meet you, Crystal."

The girl's eyes flickered. One deliberate, practiced eye blink, and Crystal smiled.

She's good. I bet she spent hours in front of the mirror practicing her expressions, Bella thought.

"It's great to meet you, too, Mrs. Rossini." Crystal's perky smile and fluttering eyes suited her baby doll pink cashmere sweater.

"It's Ms. Rossini, not Mrs."

"Oh, of course." Crystal tucked her matching pink fingernails into the crook of David's arm. "My apologies. Davie told me you hadn't been married. I just said 'Mrs.' out of habit."

Davie?

David circled the waists of the two women with his strong, wiry arms. Black hairs, thicker now than two months earlier, curled over the wide band of his watch.

"Your dinner smells outta-sight, Mom. It was a siren call coming up the stairs." David propelled them all forward, closer to the kitchen table, only a few feet in from the door. "Put us to work. You know I love helping you cook."

Bella laughed. "That's only because you snitch food the entire time you help." She reached out and grabbed her apron, a faded, threadbare, flowered cotton print, with ruffles on the shoulders.

She'd kept all of Nonna Maria's aprons after she died. Maria, a tiny, generous Italian grandmother to the world, had lived next door to Bella and David for eighteen years. Bella had cleaned Maria's apartment and run her errands. When he was too young to be alone and Bella couldn't bring him to work, David had stayed with Maria. Maria had taught them both Italian and shamed them into relentless practice.

They had become each other's family. Maria had lost her two sons and husband in World War II. After the war, she had immigrated to the United States in a moment of defiance.

Bella eyed Crystal's expensive clothes. "I'll get you an apron, Crystal."

Crystal shook her honey blond hair over her shoulders. "Oh, I don't cook." She giggled. "But I'm a pro at making reservations."

Bella nodded. The words that begged to come out lodged like a jagged potato chip in the back of her throat.

"By the looks of it," David said, rushing to his girl-friend's defense, "there's not much left to do, anyway. Right, Mom?" His eyes pleaded with her.

He always could melt her. "All that's left is setting the table, mashing the potatoes, and making the gravy. You're my masher, buddy."

"Always." He smiled at Bella.

"Crystal." Bella touched the girl's pink sleeve and nodded at the antique sideboard. "Would you mind setting the table? Today there's just the three of us. I'd like to use our good dishes, in honor of you joining us today."

"Now that," Crystal giggled, "I can do."

Bella tackled the gravy while David smashed the potatoes with the same aggression he had used against the Puerto Ricans he grew up fighting, two streets over. Bella heard the sideboard doors opening and closing. A quick glance told her that only the silverware had found its way to the table.

Crystal wrapped her arms around David's waist from the back. Bella couldn't help but notice she was curving her pelvis against his backside.

"I'm such a goof, Davie. I can't even set the table. I couldn't find the good dishes, just old cracked ones."

A scarlet flush raced up David's cheeks to his hairline and down into the crew neck of his T-shirt.

Bella couldn't stand it. "Those are the good dishes. We inherited them from the kindest woman in the world. They're irreplaceable. Nonna Maria brought only the clothes she wore and her dishes when she emigrated from Italy."

"Oh." Even Crystal could see the faux pas she had committed.

"She didn't know." The chill in David's tone hit Bella smack in the gut.

Bella fumed inside and busied herself with setting food

on the table. Hoping to redeem herself with her son, she enlisted David and Crystal in selecting a record album to put on the stereo. Thank goodness, vinyl records were slowly resurging in popularity, or she suspected that Crystal would have commented on that as well.

At the simple wooden table, Bella crossed herself and bowed her head. David bowed his head but kept his folded hands in his lap. She resisted the temptation to pop the side of his head with her knuckles. He'd done this before—abandoned the visible practice of Catholicism in favor of the Protestant habits of his friends. He's an adult now, she told herself. No head pops allowed.

"So what do you do?" Crystal's smile broadcast her desire to win Bella's approval in spite of the rocky start.

"I clean houses for a living. I started it when David was born. I didn't have enough money for rent, food, and a babysitter. It was work I could do and bring him with me when he was first born."

"You're a maid?" The words burst from Crystal's mouth as if she had spewed vomit in a sudden attack of explosive flu.

Bella watched her son—handsome as a Greek god—cast his eyes down, away from his mother and his girlfriend.

Bella met the girl's wide-eyed stare head on. "Yes."

Crystal's palms pressed against the table. "Davie, is this true? Your mother's a … a maid? And you never told me?"

David grabbed Crystal's hand. "It's not what you think." His eyes glared at Bella.

Shocked by her son's disloyalty, Bella's eyes darted from

David to Crystal and back to David. Their faces hid no secrets. They were all on some cockeyed carousel run amok. How could they all feel betrayed? This couldn't be happening. David, looking at her that way, like she'd done something wrong. Bella had always held him first in her priorities. Always.

Crystal forced her wooden chair back; it crashed to the floor when she stood.

David slid out from the table, moved to face her, and put his hands on her shoulders.

Crystal's face flushed crimson. Her voice trembled. "You never told me."

Bella couldn't help herself. She had fought down all the ugliness she wanted to fling at this shallow leech of a girl. Now, she kept her voice calm and soft, the voice of reason. David needed to see the truth about his little girlfriend. "It shouldn't matter."

David's voice, frigid with anger, shocked Bella. "It's not your business, so keep out of this."

"David—" Bella said.

"Shut up."

His words struck her with the force of a slap to the face. Bella pushed herself up from the table. "Don't speak to me that way."

His soft, enunciated words cut like a dagger. "Be glad I didn't tell you to fuck off."

"David." Crystal's whining voice brought his full attention back to her. "I ... I can't." She shook her head. "I can't be with someone whose mother is a maid."

"I'm not my mother."

Crystal's eyes darted around the room. Then, with an apparent sudden moment of clarity, she stomped to her calf-length cashmere coat and proceeded to bundle herself up. She ignored Bella as if she were no more important than the twenty-five-year-old stove.

"Can you imagine our wedding? Dear Mrs. Gates, this is my mother-in-law, Bella Rossini, whom you may have run into cleaning someone's toilet?" She flung her matching scarf around her neck. "Not on your life. I'm out of here. And you can forget I ever knew you." She tromped over to the phone, picked it up as if she feared catching a debilitating disease, and called a cab. She looked at David only to ask the apartment address.

"Crystal." David's hand stroked the back of her shoulder. "Take five. You're overreacting. Just chill a minute, will you? Let's not go somewhere we can't return from."

Crystal spun to face him. An evil sneer erased her beauty.

"Oh. We've already gone way too far. And believe me, I will never, ever, be here again." She stormed out, slamming the door behind her so hard the cups in the sideboard clinked together.

David moved to the door.

"Let … her … go." Bella's voice left no room for negotiation or discussion.

David stood facing the door, at a crossroads.

Bella couldn't allow the attack that was boiling inside her to spill out. Count to ten, a slow ten, she thought. "I'm sorry."

David rested his forehead against the door. When he righted it, he faced the door, his back to her. "Can I ask you something?"

"Anything."

"After I started school, why didn't you get another job? I could have stayed with Nonna Maria after school until you got home."

Bella studied how the hair at the back of his head curled over his collar. His hair always had a wave to it. He got it from his father. She wanted to run her fingers up his head, from the nape to the crown, and then kiss his forehead, like she'd done when he was a little boy.

He turned to face her. His eyebrows knitted together. "You're smart and witty and work harder than anyone I know. Didn't you ever want to be more than a maid?"

Pain creased his face.

"Is it my fault? Did being out of the workforce because of me hinder your job prospects? Was being a maid more lucrative than your other alternatives?"

Not shame, but a lack of understanding tinged his questions.

Bella pulled out a chair for him. "You didn't do anything wrong. Nothing is your fault. Don't ever think that." She stared at David. The pain on his face seared her. She knew it was now or never. "I'm a writer."

Bella inhaled deeply, then let the flood waters loose. "Books. Two action/adventure series, plus children's books. I started writing before you were even born. Got lucky by meeting someone in publishing very early." She nodded. "She initially was one of my housekeeping clients, and later my editor." The relief of finally spilling her secret washed over her.

He sat down. His face broadcast his confusion.

"I didn't tell you at first because you were so little." Bella reached out her hand to rest it on his arm. "Then it seemed a fluke, not something that would ever support us."

The reason she had kept this all a secret stemmed from the devastation she had felt long before, when Phillip chose to marry another woman. He had married for money, and for an easy ticket up the corporate ladder. Bella wanted David to learn that money can't create happiness, only love can. More than anything, she *needed* him to understand this.

"How successful are you?" With his stony expression and flat tone, he could have been asking directions from someone in the train station.

With a smile, Bella said, "I passed the million books in print mark when you were twelve."

Thank God. The deception had ended.

"So all this while, you've been writing books, doing book signings, the whole bit? Am I the last to know you're a successful writer?"

"Oh, David. No one but my editor, Edie, knows. I've never done a book tour or a signing. I write under a pseudonym. I kept it that way to protect you." Protect you from becoming like Phillip, she thought.

"Protect me?" David snorted in disgust. "You don't clean apartments at all anymore, do you?" Ice tinged his words.

"Yes, I do."

"Just ours?"

"Yes."

David pushed up from the table and leaned forward on it. He slammed the bottom of his fist against the table-top. "Why the charade? Why the hell couldn't you tell me?"

He paced up and down across the tiny kitchen. "Do you have any idea how many rich kids from my honors classes I took to the alleys? How I beat them up as payback for mocking me at school? And there were always the poor kids who laughed at me for caring so much about my homework." He glared at her. "I got it from both ends. Because of you."

Those strong hands gripped the edge of the table. He leaned forward toward Bella. "Why? Why couldn't you tell me?" David's voice grew quieter. "Why not let me celebrate with you? I would have been so proud of you."

After all my efforts, did I still fail? She couldn't bear that thought. Had David become as two-faced and money-grubbing as Phillip? She had to ask the question. "And you weren't proud of me as a maid?"

His face crumbled and his head bowed. When he looked up, his face had softened. "I was. Proud of you. But—"

"That's why I did it." She jumped up from the table. "You have always been more precious to me than life itself." She paused to frame her words. "I've known people who used others, and lied, just for money." Her voice dropped in volume. "I've seen firsthand how valuing money and position can hurt a person, or hurt someone who loves them."

She swallowed, choking down the hurt and loneliness that threatened to surface from those dark days when she was alone, the days before David was born. "I loved you so much. I always will."

She touched his face with her fingertips.

"I wanted to teach you to respect people in all walks of life. And it worked. Look at you. You're intelligent, at college on an academic scholarship. You have always cared about people, regardless of whether they were rich or poor."

David stood erect as a statue, his arms still and limp at his sides. She couldn't read his face.

He spoke so softly that she strained to hear his voice over the traffic noise, the music, and the muffled voices from the apartment next door.

"What was your number one rule for me?"

Oh, no. Don't make me say it. Bella bit her bottom lip.

"What was it, Mom? Tell me, would you?"

Her eyes sought his. She blinked to halt the tears that floated over her eyes. She'd said it so often that she didn't even need to think. This time, however, her words broke and she stuttered halfway through. "Whatever happens, the most … most important thing is to always," she paused, "always be honest with people. The t-truth is always better."

David turned and walked out of the apartment without a word.

"No. No." Bella pounded her fist against the door. She flung it open. "David." She yelled down the stairwell. Bella listened for his footsteps. She ran for the steps. Her foot slipped. She tripped and tumbled down, banging her elbow, knees, and shoulder.

Bella collapsed in a heap on the landing as if she were a pile of rotting garbage. "David." She listened.

No more footsteps.

The silent balloon of loss and loneliness surrounded her; it pressed and pushed against her. This same suffocating weight had hovered over her once before. That time, it had been the day she learned that Phillip didn't choose her.

22

New York, New York

David, a year out of college now, had called her this morning. Talking to David always gave her a reason to celebrate.

He had refused to speak to Bella, or meet her, for months after that fateful dinner with his shallow girlfriend. Thank God that girl never resurfaced. Eventually, Bella had worn David down. Finally, one day when she had called, he answered. They had met here the first time, in Central Park. A long walk had mended the rift, at least enough for him to allow Bella back into his life.

Today was a perfect spring day for a jog in the park, and Bella joined the throngs doing just that. The warm afternoon stretched out her stride, and Bella decided to double her normal jog around the reservoir. Brilliant pink and white cherry blossoms lined the path. A slight breeze fluttered through the trees, lifting stray petals off and sending them drifting down as if they were lazy confetti. She filled her lungs with the roselike scent and lifted her face to the sun.

Heavy footfalls, likely belonging to a man, approached her from behind. Bella edged to the side of the narrow path. The male jogger came up beside her and matched her stride. Bella kept her eyes on the trees, hoping he'd get the hint that she wasn't interested and run on ahead.

"Bella?" the man said, a hint of a Southern accent drawing out the question.

It was a voice from long ago. Stillman. Bella glanced at the man beside her and saw an older version of her friend from that summer abroad. His hair, once auburn, had morphed into a close-cropped white. But his handsome face, now with wrinkles at the corners of his eyes, was the same.

She grabbed his arm. "Stillman!"

They both slowed their pace, and then she lurched into him in an awkward hug. Another runner swerved to miss them. Stillman pulled her to the very edge of the path. Once safely out of the way, he drew her into his arms.

The warmth of his body next to hers was both comforting and, she had to admit, exciting. Bella hadn't had sex with a man for more years than she cared to think about.

Stepping out of the embrace, Stillman moved his hands to clasp hers. "This is incredible," he said, "running into you—no pun intended—here in Central Park. Do you live here?"

She nodded. Smiling at him, Bella asked if he lived here, too, and where he was practicing medicine.

"I'm an entertainment attorney with a big firm here in the city," he said. "Decided law suited me better than medicine." He chuckled. "Judging by my bank account and those of my physician friends, it was a good choice."

His fingers rubbed the ring finger of her left hand. "Does the absence of a ring here mean you're not married?"

Bella burst out laughing. "You cut to the chase, don't you?"

"Just getting the ground rules established, my dear."

"Not married. Actually, never married."

"Perfect," Stillman said. "Same for me." He glanced at the chronograph watch on his wrist. "Damn, I'd love to stay and talk, but I've got a client meeting. Will you let me take you to dinner, so I have a chance to find out what you've been doing all these years?"

They arranged a dinner date for Saturday night, planning to meet at a well-known restaurant on the Upper East Side.

Bella watched Stillman speed away on the running path. Her body prickled with anticipation. She knew one thing for certain. After her run and a shower, she was going shopping for a new dress.

Bella loved the way candlelight made a man look sexy.

Stillman, she decided, didn't need the candles. He was sexy in his running shorts and was beyond sexy in his tailored suit.

They covered all the easy subjects, which meant she didn't mention David. He likely assumed that since she'd never married, she was childless. If she was going to see Stillman again, Bella figured she could tell him about

David then. Well, maybe a slimmed-down version of the truth. And if this was it—no second date—Bella saw no merit in opening that can of worms.

Before he had a chance to ask her more questions, she brought up that summer abroad. "What happened to us, Stillman?"

His eyes narrowed. "Phillip got there first."

Something in his tone of voice disturbed her. "You were ill. The flu. That's why he was there."

Stillman lifted his wineglass to his lips and took a sip, all the while staring at her with an intensity that sliced through the distance between them.

The chill in the air was palpable. "Stillman?"

Cold, steel eyes met hers. "Phillip turned off my alarm."

She sunk back against her chair. "You weren't sick?"

He shook his head.

"Phillip told me you were dreadfully sick. Married to the porcelain god. You never seemed upset, with either Phillip or me. If he did that to you …"

"Believe me, he did it." Stillman cleared his throat. "I went through the gamut of emotions that weekend, while you were off with our buddy Phillip. Disbelief, anger, hurt. Eventually, I realized that if you were with him all weekend, it was because you wanted to be. That for some incomprehensible reason, you chose him over me, regardless of how he arranged it."

He shrugged. "It became an easy choice for me. I lost your love. I didn't want to lose your friendship, too."

She reached out and placed her hand over his on the table.

He cocked one eyebrow. "Typical of Phillip, wasn't it? To lie?"

An icy chill ran from Bella's temples to the tips of her nipples. What did Stillman mean by that? Had he, somehow, found out that Phillip had lied to her, too? While Phillip was with her in Italy, he was engaged to someone else. Did Stillman know that Phillip had dumped Bella for the promise of a cushy job?

She lowered her head. "So true. So very true." She had to change the subject off this dangerous ground. "What matters," she said, squeezing his hand, "is that today you and I are here, together. I can't believe that all these years we lived so close to each other but never knew it. I'd like to renew our friendship, if that's OK with you. Could we meet again soon?"

Stillman smiled. "How about Tuesday night? One of my partners' wives is curating an exhibit at a small art gallery. There's going to be an opening-night cocktail party. Can you join me? We could have a late dinner afterwards."

Honesty was imperative. She couldn't bear the thought of being deceived again, and so asked the question that would set the ground rules going forward. "Yes, I'll meet you at the gallery. But I don't want there to be any misunderstandings between us. I have to ask. Are you dating or in a relationship with anyone now?"

"Whoa, girl." He chuckled. "Aren't you the direct one? Don't get me wrong—I love you taking it to the hoop. No. I'm not dating or in a relationship with anyone now. And, yes, in case it's your next question, I'd love to be dating you.

We'll figure out the relationship part as we go along, if that suits you."

After the art gallery party, Bella and Stillman had a late dinner, followed by a tender kiss goodnight. That kiss left Bella wanting more.

They had dinner together almost every night for the next two weeks, being apart only when Stillman had a business dinner. Even though they met at the restaurants, Stillman insisted on seeing her home afterwards. Each night, Stillman kissed her goodnight as they parted but always refused to come into her apartment. It drove Bella mad.

Finally, she asked him why he refused to come inside.

"My dear," Stillman said, "don't you really know why? If I walk into your apartment, I won't want to leave until morning. So, be kind to me, will you? Don't invite me inside anymore, not unless you're inviting me into your bedroom."

With that knowledge, Bella turned and unlocked her door. She held out her hand to Stillman and led him inside.

Bella and Stillman settled into a routine. On most week-nights, Stillman slept at her apartment, always leaving early in the morning to go home to shower and dress for work. On the weekends, she'd pack a bag, and they would be at one of his places, either his Manhattan apartment or his house in Connecticut.

He refused to keep clothes at her place, stating that he was an "all or none type of guy" and that their clothes shouldn't cohabit until they did.

During those first weeks of intimacy, Bella told Stillman about David. Most of what she told him was true.

David had been the product, she claimed, of a one-night stand shortly after that summer in Italy. She had been devastated by the unexpected loss of her mother, and all alone. To fill the hole that her mother's death had created, she told Stillman, she had taken up with a boy she had met a month after her mother's death.

She shared how it had been a struggle—being a single mom and trying to work, take care of her baby, and finish college all at the same time. Bella confided that she had a career as an author and even how she had shielded David from this knowledge. It had been for security reasons, she claimed, that she had kept her identity secret.

"So, my darling," Stillman said, running his fingertip over and around her bare breasts, "when do I get to meet your son? How about if he joins us this weekend at the beach?"

Thank God for small favors, Bella thought. "That might be a little difficult. David's in an MD-PhD program at Stanford. It's a grueling schedule, and he rarely comes home."

"Too bad. Maybe next time I head to LA for work, you could tag along. We could fly up to San Francisco and see him on the weekend."

"That might work." In truth, she had no intention of taking Stillman to meet her son.

David's relationship with her was improving, but she had lost so much ground after their blowout over Crystal that Bella was afraid to do anything that might drive her son away. Throughout David's life, it had always been only the two of them. No men. Just Bella and David. Besides, if Stillman met David, he would know that her story about the one-night stand was a lie.

To get Stillman's mind off the subject of her son, she distracted him. Bella ran her fingers through the white hair on her lover's chest, down his stomach, and then lower, until she had him moaning with pleasure.

Bella loved being with Stillman. Always the chivalrous gentleman, Stillman never let her buy dinner, and he held open doors, walked on the street side of her on sidewalks, and helped her on and off with her coat. Little gifts—flowers, a book she might enjoy reading, a scarf that matched her eyes, a delivered box lunch on a busy day of writing—appeared at unpredictable intervals from Stillman.

As a lover, he was tender and considerate. She tried not to compare making love with Stillman to the playful and passionate times she had shared with Phillip. That was different, she told herself. Phillip had been her lover a quarter of a century earlier, when she was young and her sex hormones raged. Stillman truly cared for her, and Bella believed him when he'd whisper in her ear that he would never do anything to hurt her.

Three months after their first meeting in the park, they marked the occasion by having dinner together in Bella's apartment. Well, they actually started the evening in the bedroom, as they often did.

Afterwards, they were ravenous. Stillman had promised to provide everything for the meal, and he was true to his word. Their dinner had been delivered from Bella's favorite Italian restaurant, and Stillman had unveiled a different wine to taste with each course.

Bella loved every meticulously planned part of the meal. Some, such as the *Linguine ai Frutti di Mare*, were her favorites. Stillman surprised her with new items, too, like the tender butter lettuce salad with truffle dressing, which seemed to melt on her tongue, and its heady fragrance made her want to head back to the bedroom.

Now, with candles burning around the partially drunk wine bottles on her coffee table, the two of them nestled beside each other on her sofa.

Stillman raised her fingertips to his lips and kissed them. Then, without a word, he slid off the sofa to kneel before her. He clasped her hands in his. "I love you, Bella. And I will always take care of you," he said with a smile, "if the independent woman that you are will let me."

No, she thought. Don't do this.

"Bella, will you marry me?"

Her heart sank. It was too soon. Bella truly cared for him and knew Stillman was the best thing that had happened to her in years. Did she love him? Yes. Enough to marry him? Bella didn't know the answer to that question. She did know, however, that she wasn't ready, and their relationship wasn't ready, for Stillman to meet David. She looked down.

"My dear, this is where you're supposed to tell me that you love me, too, and say that you'll marry me."

Bella's eyes lifted and met his. Stillman's face still held a smile, but it looked as if it had frozen on his face. She blinked. "I love you. I do. But it's too soon for me. I've been single so long. I'm not ready for marriage."

Stillman stood up and walked to the window. He stood there, his back to her, looking out at the lights of her neighborhood, for what seemed an eternity. When he turned around, she saw that his face had relaxed and his smile was genuine. He returned to sit beside her on the sofa and positioned himself so that his body was open to hers. A good sign, she thought.

"We've been dating three months today," he said. "I knew by the third date that I wanted to marry you, but that's me. You're cautious because you have a son. I get that. Since I'm a problem-solver by nature, I have a solution."

She saw, with dread, where he was headed.

"I'll arrange flights. This weekend or next, whatever works for David, we'll go out and you can introduce us. We'll spend whatever time with him that his schedule allows. And we'll keep flying west on weekends until you feel he and I know each other well enough for us to get married."

Bella knew she couldn't let Stillman meet David. What she knew, and wouldn't tell Stillman, was that David bore a strong resemblance to his father. The most striking thing was that David had his father's piercing blue eyes. No one, other than herself and her long-time friend and editor, Edie, knew that Phillip was David's father.

"I'm not ready for that. My relationship with David is still too fragile."

"How long will you make me wait?" His soft voice could not hide the intensity behind his words.

She shook her head and shrugged. She whispered her answer, afraid of his reaction. "I don't know."

"There is either a reason you're keeping me from meeting David, or you're using him as an excuse. So which is it?"

She looked at her hands, which were clenched in her lap.

"Bella, look at me."

Bella raised her eyes. Tears threatened to spill. Why was he pushing this?

"Today, next week, or in a few months, will you marry me? Yes or no? Tell me."

Agreeing to marry Stillman meant Bella had to show her hand—all the cards—not only to Stillman, but to David as well. How could she? Her mouth opened, but no words came out.

Stillman stood up, crossed to the door, and walked out.

23

Fort Lauderdale, Florida

Meghan lifted her face to the sun. A perfect spring-break day for tanning. She wore a two-piece suit and was proud of how she looked in it.

Meghan rolled to her side and studied April, her eighteen-year-old niece, Karen's only child. April had Karen's charisma but Meghan's eye for color, fabric and style. Last night over dinner, the two of them had plotted April's path to join Meghan at the store. First design school, then an internship in New York, and finally Chicago with her aunt.

Karen would have approved.

It had been an emotional yo-yo for Meghan since they lost Karen to breast cancer five years before. Karen was her twin, her best friend, and her business partner.

After Karen died, Ed, the store's majority owner and Karen's widower, never set foot in the store and declined to meet Meghan in person to discuss the business. He made Meghan submit her ideas for the boutique to his accountant for review, who questioned every expense and was wary of every new idea. Annually, Meghan offered to buy Ed out. But why should he sell? The store paid him a handsome distribution each year.

Meghan loved April as if she were her own child and was thrilled that her niece wanted to join the business. Sharing the shop with April would be almost like it was during those early years, when she and Karen first opened it.

April's eyes flipped open. She turned her head to grin at her aunt. "Awesome day, isn't it?" She propped one elbow on the blanket to look over at Meghan. "This spring break trip is the best birthday present you could ever give me."

Meghan smiled. "Don't you realize it's a present to myself? I don't get to see you enough."

April's eyes followed the jumbo striped beach ball overhead, being volleyed down the beach by a group of laughing, screaming college kids. "I know. I wish we still lived in Chicago, with you. It took me a long time to understand why Dad moved us to Texas after Mom died."

Meghan bit her tongue. She had given Ed the benefit of the doubt and imagined Chicago held too many memories of Karen for him to stay. Now she knew better. It was because he hated her. She had lived and Karen had died. It was as simple as that. That explained why Ed limited April's visits with her to twice a year.

She would have gladly sold the store and moved to Texas with them if she could have been present in April's life. But no. All Meghan could do was send April airplane tickets twice a year for visits preapproved by her father.

April's face turned serious. She nodded at Meghan's bikini top. "Have you talked to a doctor yet?"

Meghan pretended to mark her page in the paperback novel beside her. "No. But I do my breast self-exams religiously." Something we both know that Karen didn't do, she thought. "I'm fine. No lumps. Nothing out of the ordinary."

"One of my friends at school has breast cancer in her family, too." April rushed on, as if afraid her courage would dwindle. "Her mother had a double mastectomy because she lost two sisters and her mother to the disease. She had reconstruction. I saw her before Christmas. You'd never guess."

"Maybe, but it seems pretty radical to me. You never feel the same." Meghan lathered sunscreen over the exposed curves of her breasts. "It's hard enough being a single woman today. If I had the surgery, who'd take care of the store?"

"I would." April reached out to touch Meghan's arm. "I'd stay with you over the summer. I could drive you to the doctor's appointments and manage the store. We'd have a blast."

"I'll think about it." Meghan's promise sounded hollow, even to herself. She knew Ed would never allow April to spend her summer in Chicago. Meghan shifted the conversation to plans for dinner that night at a dockside restaurant within walking distance of the hotel.

At dinner, April bantered about her series of boyfriends at school. The sweltering heat of the day drifted out to sea with the receding tide. Quick-moving clouds shadowed the sky by the time they walked out of the restaurant. Meghan gazed up and hoped they would reach the hotel before it started raining.

"Maybe we should get a cab," she said. "It's going to rain."

April skipped ahead. "It's only a couple of blocks. We'll be there and in our jammies by the time a taxi gets here. It's spring break, remember?"

Cars whizzed by on the two-lane road that led to their beachfront hotel. "Let's walk single file. There's more traffic now, and it's dark. You go first."

April stared at the dark sky. "Too bad we can't see the stars. I hoped we could pick out constellations again, like we did in Chicago during the summers when I was a kid."

Meghan pushed April forward, her palm against the girl's back. "C'mon. No stalling. We can study the stars once we're back at the hotel."

April's giggle reminded Meghan of how her niece had always managed to stall when bedtime came. As a little girl, she'd leave her bed and find Karen and Meghan, insisting that she wanted "girl talk" with them; she ate popcorn and giggled one minute, and then lay curled up asleep on the couch the next.

Meghan pulled her cotton shawl tighter around her shoulders. They walked on the shoulder with the flow of traffic, because the road was too busy to cross two lanes at night. The cars zoomed by. Meghan caught up to April and nudged her forward. "Let's keep moving, honey. I want to get away from these cars."

A massive bolt of lightning struck the lake on the other side of the road. The sky split with the shudder of thunder chasing the lightning a mere second behind. Rain—big, pelting drops of rain—sheeted down, soaking their thin cotton sundresses.

A car veered closer to them. April jumped to the side. She squeaked with fright, then jogged ahead, soon settling into a brisk race-walk speed. Meghan picked her way along the rain-slick shoulder as April widened the gap between them.

Suddenly, Meghan froze at the whine of squealing tires.

A car in the approaching lane had come up too fast on a motorcycle. The driver slammed on the brakes, then veered toward them.

Meghan's eyes widened. She heard a car behind her and felt a splash of cold water hit her back as it sped past.

It seemed like a slow-motion blur. Meghan opened her mouth to scream. The word choked her as it came out. "April …"

The screech of metal on metal split the air when the cars collided. They spun on the wet pavement and careened toward the ditch.

April's body flew into the air when they struck her, ten feet in front of Meghan.

The two cars lay in a crumpled heap in a ditch alongside the road. One wheel of the closest car spun crazy circles in the air, around and around. Meghan scrambled and slipped down the embankment to the cars. Her ankle twisted beneath her. Hot pain shot up her leg. Tears burned her eyes. The rain blurred everything. She screamed April's name, over and over.

At the bottom of the ditch, her knees buckled and Meghan fell to the wet clay.

One jackknifed human leg, partly covered by a cotton sundress, protruded beneath the twisted, steaming metal.

April.

The day of the Texas funeral dawned with low-slung clouds and, once again, the threat of rain. Meghan stood at her hotel window. The sight of the putty-gray clouds seemed appropriate. The rain had stolen April from them, and it was destined to carry her on her journey.

Hours and hours after the mangled remains of the beautiful child had been carted away, Meghan had found strength to string three words together. She had called Ed. Meghan's words had cut her throat raw, yet she delivered them without emotion, the only way she could get to the end of the story. A freak accident. Couldn't be helped. Blinding rainstorm. Chain reaction.

How could they bear this? First Karen. Now April. Ed didn't speak.

Meghan had continued with the details.

When she had finished, dry, racking sobs took control. Soundless, jerking gasps shook her body.

Ed had hung up the phone without saying a word.

She would face him today. She knew he blamed her. Of course. She blamed herself. Spring break in Florida? Too crowded. Too many people. Too much drinking. Why hadn't she taken April to the Caribbean, or the Bahamas, or Montana, or Tennessee, or Chicago? Why had she agreed to go where all the college students go? Why?

At the church, Meghan found Ed in a private room. He knelt by the closed casket. She walked up behind him, her eyes long since exhausted of tears. Wordless, Meghan rested one hand on the shoulder of his black suit. He didn't speak.

A friend of April's gave the eulogy. The girl spoke of April's unabashed joy of life, her love for her friends, her mother, her aunt, and her father. The girl's funny anecdotes prompted a dozen of April's friends to walk to the front and share their memories, their love.

Through it all, Ed bowed his head. His hunched shoulders shook with silent sobs.

Meghan sat still, her hands clasped in her lap. She alternated between smiling—just a little—at the stories and pranks and offering silent, somber pleas to Karen for forgiveness.

Ed stood with difficulty. His white-knuckled hands gripped the front railing for support. He didn't look at Meghan.

She climbed into the black limousine and sat next to Ed.

Neither one spoke.

At the graveside service, Meghan didn't speak to anyone. She could cry no more. In her mind, she repeatedly asked herself the question, "Why wasn't it me?"

After the burial, on the silent journey to the car, Ed raised one palm, signaling her to stop walking. "The next limousine will take you to your hotel," he said. Then he sighed.

Meghan strained to hear the words.

"I want to be alone. Thanks to you, that's what I am now. Alone."

Meghan opened her mouth. She closed it. She knew he spoke the truth for them both.

"I want you to leave." His head bowed.

Meghan watched him stumble to the door of the first limousine. He turned his head back to look at her.

"Ed, I'm—"

His hand rose to stop her. His eyes narrowed. A deep breath launched his words, and his solemn voice, like a poison-tipped sword, delivered her punishment. "I sold the store. The proceeds from your thirty percent share will be sent to you. Transfer happens next week. An independent firm is inventorying it today." He tightened his lips into a grimace. "I don't ever want to see you or speak to you again."

Meghan's legs quivered. An icy chill ran down her arms. Dull thunder sounded. The sky gave up its protection, and big drops of summer rain speckled her face and her black linen dress. Meghan didn't shield herself. She stood with her arms hanging limp by her side and watched Ed's limo drive away.

24

Durham, North Carolina

Lee, now forty-five and a physician specializing in reconstructive plastic surgery, hung up his lab coat and slipped his arms into the sleeves of his sport coat. Established in his position on the medical staff at Duke University, Lee didn't feel guilty about ducking out early on occasion. Surgeries were scheduled for the morning hours, and he'd already rounded on his patients today. He was pleased that the tough congenital defect case from last week, a three-year-old girl, was healing well and would soon go home.

A traveling exhibit of Rodin's smaller sculptures was ending its short visit to Duke's Nasher Museum of Art today. He had reserved his spot on the guided tour as soon as it had been announced. The Nasher held a highly regarded medieval collection, which Lee visited whenever his schedule allowed. But his visits to the museum were never often enough, between his long hours, call schedule, and the seemingly endless activities of his two children.

He turned to lock the door to his tiny office, which he had rights to only because he used it to consult with patients before their surgeries. Damn. His phone was ringing. Should he answer it?

A glance at his watch revealed that he still had enough time to handle the call before his tour started. If a nurse monitoring one of his patients had a question, he'd rather answer it now than when he was enjoying the tour.

"This is Dr. Mostow."

"Lee," his wife, Merry, said, "thank goodness I caught you." She explained that Anne, their fifteen-year-old daughter, had a soccer game that night. The statewide semifinal match had been rescheduled after a lightning storm cancellation earlier in the week. The game was in Charlotte, over two hours away. Merry and Anne were already on the outskirts of Charlotte.

Lee knew that if he went to the Rodin exhibit, he wouldn't make the soccer game. His life had been a series of compromises, and Lee had always opted for choices made to appease someone else—first his mother, then his wife, and now his children. Not anymore.

Merry, a psychiatrist, was a pro at conversation. In one breath, she acknowledged how inconvenient it was for them both to drive all that distance; in the next breath, she reminded him how important it was that they support their children.

Why had he picked up the phone? Truth was, it didn't matter. If she hadn't reached him at the office, Merry would have redialed his cell until he had answered. It was one of the many things about his wife that made him crazy.

Lee took a deep breath and told her he couldn't drive to Charlotte. "I wish I could," he said, "but one of Duke's VIPs wants me to meet his nephew tonight. The family's visiting from out of state today, and apparently, the boy's previous surgeries had poor results."

"For once, can't someone else do it?"

"He wants me, and you know how political it is here. Ignoring requests from the powers-that-be is a fast ticket out." Lee pulled his Nasher tour ticket out of the breast pocket of his jacket. He rubbed circles on the glossy ticket with his thumb.

The crazy thing was that he didn't feel guilty at all about lying to Merry. Maybe medicine had to be his life, but art—sculpture in particular—was his passion. It was time he did something for himself. Short of flying to Paris, this was his only chance to see these Rodin pieces.

"Please hand the phone to Anne, so that I can wish her good luck," he said.

One lie after another.

Lee relayed his fabricated excuse to his daughter, and even her obvious disappointment did not alter his story. He wished her luck, and then he ended the call before Merry could return to the phone.

After the guided tour, Lee walked through the exhibit a second time, studying the sculptures, one by one. He marveled at the musculature of the male figures and sensuality of the women. Staring at each piece in succession, he tried to cement into memory the angles and curves that brought the figures to life.

When he finally walked to his car, he realized he was starving. He knew Merry and Anne would be gone for hours and his son, Max, a computer whiz, was spending the night with one of his eighth-grade friends. He didn't want to go home, not because he'd be alone but so he could preserve the buoyant energy that had filled him at the museum for as long as he could.

Being in the presence of great art always reminded him of his semester abroad in Florence. Already on the pre-med track then, he hadn't allowed himself to consider pursuing a career in art. His mother would have never allowed it.

Tonight, his dinner choice was obvious. Italian food. It was his favorite cuisine, but Merry had a way of reminding him that the carbs in pasta weren't good for his waistline. She was right about that, but he suspected the truth behind her anti-pasta tirades. One night in a moment of blazing stupidity, having drunk more than a bottle of wine himself, he had told Merry that eating pasta reminded him of Meghan, his first love. What an idiot.

After enjoying his pasta dinner and responsibly drinking only one glass of wine, he drove home to finish the bottle there. He was dozing in front of the television when Merry and a very tired Anne got home. Anne, who volunteered that she had played only in the last three minutes of their losing game, stumbled up to bed.

"How was the VIP's nephew?" Merry asked, after grabbing a glass of water for herself.

"Definitely a bad result, but I can improve it," Lee said. "Not sure if they'll schedule surgery, though. I guess they're visiting a few places across the country before they make the final decision on who they want to handle it."

Merry had an intent look on her face. "Do you want to tell me about his underlying problem?"

"Nah. I can fill you in if they decide to go with me." Over dinner, Lee had come up with the story he'd tell Merry. Something enough to satisfy her polite questions, but nothing that would come back to bite him.

Merry bit her bottom lip and looked away. She stared at the television, which he had muted after Anne had awakened him on their return. "Right. Who can ever predict what someone like that will do?" She turned her head to face him and her eyes glared. "Cut the crap. How was the museum?"

Lee choked.

"I wanted to see how elaborate your lies would be," she said.

"How did you find out?"

"I've been searching your pockets and car for clues to explain your behavior. You've been excited one moment and removed the next. I knew something was happening that you hadn't told me." She snorted and her nostrils flared. "I'm glad it was museum tickets I found in the glove box, rather than a pair of panties that don't belong to me."

"What's the big deal?"

"The 'big deal' is that you made it one, by hiding it and lying to me. Not once, but twice."

It was only a museum, for God's sake, he thought. He shrugged.

"Let me guess, you had pasta tonight, didn't you?" She looked venomous.

"So what if I did? You don't approve of my choice of cuisine?"

She slammed her hand against the coffee table. Her arm trembled as she leaned on the table. "Lee," she said, her quiet, level voice rocking him harder than if she'd screamed, "these things are symptomatic of significant issues." She was using her psychiatrist voice, the calm demeanor that enticed her patients to spill their life's secrets and angst to her.

Lee's chest heaved with rapid, deep breaths. "You wanna psychoanalyze me? Go right ahead. Tell me how fucked up I am."

"No." She shook her head. "You're not 'fucked up.' You are, however, unhappy in your job, and maybe in your marriage, too, although I'm still trying to get a read on that one."

She stood up and started pacing; her words increased in tempo to match her stride. "I know you often wonder about Meghan. Where is she? Is she married? Beyond the pedestal you'll always place her on as your first love, she's a symbol of all you sacrificed to follow your family's behest and become a physician." Merry stopped pacing and stood in front of him with her hands on her hips. "So, you tell me, Lee, what is it you truly want? Do you want to leave me? Leave, and go chase a dream?"

Lee wondered if the dream she referred to was Meghan or art. Either way, he was screwed. They depended on his salary to pay the mortgage, the car payments, the private school tuition, and, soon, college. Merry's income paid for everything else. He couldn't afford to chuck it all.

"Every day I pray this is a midlife crisis you're going through. But know that in spite of everything, I still love you. I want you to stay. Yes, you deserve happiness, but I've seen it time and time again. Men and women get to a certain age, and they panic. Stay the course. Let's get the kids through college and then, if you want to run off to Italy with an old or new girlfriend, so be it."

She was asking him for eight years of being a good father and provider. Eight years, Lee thought. To him, it sounded like a life sentence.

25

Fort Collins, Colorado

Hope wondered when she first knew she had a lousy marriage. I'm forty-five now, she thought, so it's been fifteen, or maybe twenty years? It had been after Erica, her daughter, was born. That's all Hope remembered, because she had buried most of those early memories of Charlie's meanness.

"You're the hostess tonight," Charlie said. Her husband stood inside their bedroom; his hands rested on his hips and he spread his legs wide in a fortress of opposition. "You should be downstairs, mingling."

Hope turned away from the mirror and dropped her comb to the counter. "I came upstairs because I had something in my eye. I took the chance to pee while I was up here." Her stomach burned. She ducked around him to the hallway and scurried down the stairs as if she were a child caught snitching cookies an hour before dinner.

"Try to restrain yourself at dinner," Charlie said to her retreating back. "I don't want you making a pig of yourself. Grant's mother won't stuff her face. And take it easy on the wine, too. You don't want anyone to think you're a lush."

Hope cringed. A sharp stab of pain hit her gut. She bit back the words that soured her tongue. At the base of the stairs, Hope stopped. She composed her lips into her best smile and walked outside to join the party.

Grant stood in a pack with his groomsmen under the oak tree. The men's voices were low, but their leers at the bridesmaids were as obvious as if they were shouting. Hope's face tingled with heat. Grant, the ringleader, dangled a cigar from his hand. Hope watched him bring it to the corner of his mouth, gangster-like. She shuddered.

Erica, sweet and glowing in her pink summer sundress, skipped past her mother to join her fiancé. Hope stared at her daughter, who cuddled next to Grant. Erica kissed him on the cheek and linked her arm in his.

Grant turned to look down at her, the girl a head shorter and not much more than half his width. "Not now," he said, loud enough for Hope to hear. "Can't you see I'm with my buddies? Christ, I'm going to have my whole life with you."

Erica backed away. One step, then two.

Grant returned the cigar to his mouth and dismissed his bride-to-be with a flick of his fingers. He nodded at the most voluptuous bridesmaid. Gesturing for his friends, Grant raised his hands in tandem and twisted imaginary breasts; he cackled loud enough to make the bridesmaid turn around. The girl flushed crimson and scampered in retreat to the bar.

Hope's mouth gaped open. Her daughter had seen everything. Erica turned and stumbled away from Grant.

Hope intercepted her and wrapped one stout arm around her daughter. "Hey, pumpkin," Hope said. "Want to go inside and talk?"

Erica brushed her mother's arm aside. She turned around with slow deliberation. "Mom, this is my rehearsal dinner." Erica gulped. "I ... I've got people to see. You know, socialize." Her shoulders straightened. "Thank them for coming."

Good Lord, she's just like me. Hope nodded. She lowered her voice. "What about Grant?"

Hope saw calm acceptance take command of the young face. Erica's hand flicked away the accusation as if it were a fly. "He's only being a guy." Her chin rose. "You ought to know. He's just like Dad." Without waiting for a reply, she waltzed to the table of seated guests. Erica draped her arms over the shoulders of her future in-laws and bent to kiss them each on the cheek.

Another fiery bullet shot through Hope. She forced her eyes wide to halt the tears. Hope picked at her food during the dinner. Her first catered dinner party in years. Charlie liked it when Hope cooked for their parties; somehow, her culinary skills became his accomplishment.

Since they lived out of town, Grant's parents had asked Hope to work with the caterer. But now, she couldn't even enjoy the meal she had taken such care in selecting. She pushed aside the green beans, "crunchy haricots verts with fresh dill," as the caterer called them. The "herb-crusted sea bass resting on a swirl of beurre blanc"—delicious at her tasting—sat cold before her.

The bridal couple sat across the table from Hope and Charlie. A line of empty glasses stood in front of Grant's plate. Hope had watched his beer consumption increase throughout the night.

Grant stood up and rapped his fork against an empty beer bottle. "Thank you all for coming." Leering at Erica, Grant hauled her to her feet by slinging one arm behind her back and under her armpit. Grant grinned at his buddies. His eyes bugged out; a sloppy half-sneer crossed his face. "I'm happy you came, and I'm happy to now be able to do this," he grabbed Erica's breast with the hand lodged under her arm, "in public."

Hope heard the horrified gasp from Erica's godmother. She elbowed Charlie for assistance.

Charlie rose in slow motion. He clapped one hand to Hope's shoulder. His vise-like grip ratcheted down on her, making her flinch. "Grant, we know you're excited to be marrying my beautiful, intelligent daughter. A toast to the happy couple." Charlie lifted his glass of wine in Grant's direction, which prompted the young man to release Erica's breast and reach for his beer.

Erica slumped back on her chair. A glare from her future hubby sent her scrambling for her wineglass. Erica stood up. She kissed Grant's cheek and clinked his glass. She brought her glass to her mouth. Hope watched her daughter return the glass to the table without the wine even touching her lips.

A foul lump lodged in the back of Hope's mouth. She forced it down. Her hand reached for her wineglass but stopped short, remembering Charlie's admonitions. Her fingers curled into a fist and dropped to her side. Erica had learned her lessons well.

Present Day

26

Fort Collins, Colorado

The invitation to the reunion sat open on the kitchen table between Charlie and Hope.

Charlie pushed his large, hairy hands against the thick maple table. "I can't believe you'd even consider this. You can't go without me. It'd be ludicrous. And then there's the matter of the company picnic. We always host it the fourth weekend in September. Always."

Hope lowered her head and her voice. "Maybe we could have an Oktoberfest this year."

Charlie's palms pressed harder against the table, his fingers turning a splotchy red. Tension rippled up his arms. "You can't go." He sneered at her over the table. "You traveling alone? You'd get lost."

She felt like she was facing her father rather than her husband. "You forget. I made this trip alone before."

"The world is different now. I can't believe you'd even want to go if I wasn't along. It's ridiculous."

Hope studied his balding head, the only place on his body where the thick mat of hair had disappeared. She spoke in an even, quiet tone. "It was a remarkable time for all of us. A key part of our college evolution. We were the best of friends."

"Right. And how many of these great friends have you kept in touch with?"

Hope's stomach flopped over on itself. After their marriage, Charlie's friends had become her friends.

"It's settled, then." He reached for the trip itinerary and invitation to Italy. "Maybe we can cash this in for my Canadian fishing trip or something."

Hope's hand darted to the papers for Italy. "No." She flipped them into her lap. "Let's wait a little. Sit on the decision."

Charlie pushed up from the table. "You're not going. Now give me that." He motioned to the invitation.

Hope clutched the papers in her hand. She ran upstairs to the bathroom and locked herself in. She sat on the closed toilet lid and dropped her head to her hands.

The brass door lever jiggled.

"God damn it. Open the door." Charlie wiggled the lever again. His voice grew louder. "You should know by now. You can't solve problems by running away. That's why your business failed. Why you don't have any friends."

Hope studied the wrought-iron shelf in the corner. It held a scented candle, a faded silk flower arrangement purchased at the school's auction when Erica was a senior, and one spare roll of toilet paper, the ends of the tissue folded into a point. Seashells from the previous summer's reward trip to the Caribbean leaned against each other at jaunty angles, yet even they couldn't disguise the lack of personal touches in the room.

Everything in this house was a prop—an orchestrated prop in the life she had designed for Charlie.

"What? Are you so worthless you can't even talk?" Charlie thwacked his hand against the door. "What is it? You think one of those old farts is going to think you're beautiful and charming? It'll take five minutes for everyone to see you for what you are—a fat, do-nothing housewife who's lived on the gravy train of her husband's hard work."

Hope bit the inside of her lip. She closed her eyes to force back the sting of his words. *You're worthless. You're fat. You're hopeless.* She steeled herself against the pain. Pain—that's what he wants. To hurt her. Hurt her where no one else can see it.

"You want to go to Italy? I'll tell you what'll happen."

Hope visualized him leaning in closer to the door. She suspected that a sneer marked his face.

"You'll go with your unrealistic hopes and wild ideas of a charmed reunion. But some won't show up. Why? Because they have a life. They're successful. Happy. So who makes the schlep to Italy? A couple of fat, balding old farts, either losers looking for an easy lay or con men after a quick financial score with a rich widow or a divorcee who earned her dough the old-fashioned way—on her back."

Hope slumped off the toilet onto the floor, her back to the door as if she could turn off his litany.

"Enter Hope—fat, hopeless, a dame with no skills and only the money her hard-working husband gives her."

Hope's hand stifled a sob. He was right.

"Here you have a home. A purpose. You're my wife. We have a life that works. If you go, you'll be ignored by the men and jealous of the women who are skinny, the ones focused on catching a new victim."

Her eyes bore into the itinerary in her hand. "A Firenze Reunion" in beautiful cream script danced across the top. Delicate, graceful and screaming with confidence. Everything she wasn't. Maybe Charlie was right. Maybe she shouldn't go.

"Hope." Charlie's voice had softened to a coaxing tone. "Open the door. Let's put this foolishness behind us. If you don't want me to use the money from the ticket, fine. I won't. We could fly Grant, Erica, and the kids here with that money."

Hope studied the itinerary. First class to Florence. Not just the overseas segment, but the entire flight, starting in Denver. Someone wanted her presence enough to spend a small fortune on this ticket.

"We'll talk about how best to use the money. I'll let you have input. OK? Now I have to go. My tee time with Bob is at ten, and I don't want to be late. I'm going to tell him we're on for hosting the company picnic again in September as usual."

She heard him start down the stairs, then retrace his steps; he stood again outside her fortress door. "I'll be home at eight tonight. We're going to have a couple beers after our round, but you can plan dinner for me then."

Hope studied the pale beige tones of the seashells she had brought to add life to this room. White, tan, beige.

She thought of the clay-colored dome of the Duomo in Florence and the colors in the market. Three or four shades of green—artichoke, arugula, and fava beans. Ruby Roma tomatoes lined up in perfect formation. Purple eggplants the color of royalty. Pale yellow beans nestled next to golden squash. Hope remembered the tiny wine grapes kissed with dew.

Her thumb rubbed the glossy brochure that came with the itinerary. She looked down at her hand. The words printed on the slick paper seemed to swim before her eyes, never quite legible.

The girl inside her, long forgotten, screamed in protest. The girl from Colorado who had journeyed alone all the way to Italy for a summer. The very same girl who had made great friends because she had brimmed with confidence and embraced adventure.

That girl wanted to go. That girl *needed* to go.

27

Los Angeles, California

Rune stood underneath the marquee, two blocks off Hollywood and a world away from success. He waited for Steven. Rune wished the management had fixed the sign. The dinner theater's marquee advertising his current production read "Pha–t–m of the –p–ra." God knew where the missing letters had gone. He was grateful to Steven for agreeing to meet him at all.

Rune watched a red-and-yellow, jumbo-sized fast-food cup roll along the sidewalk, pushed by the wind. His latest script must have some merit, or Steven wouldn't have agreed to meet him, right?

A yellow Lamborghini swerved to the curb beside him. The rumbling engine cut, leaving a sudden sound void in the early morning air. Rune's ears focused on the scraping roll of the empty cup and the click of the Lamborghini's door releasing.

Steven, dressed in blue jeans, T-shirt, and sandals, slid out of the car as if he owned the city, not just a fine driving machine. He tossed a crisp script at Rune.

Rune caught the script. It looked as if it hadn't even

been opened. No crease marked the edge to indicate someone had read it. He jutted his chin forward. "Great, huh?"

"It sucks. Just like the last twenty you insisted I look at." Steven gazed up at the marquee. "Phat?" He chuckled at his own joke, and then brought his eyes to meet Rune's. "What the hell happened to you, man?" He shook his head. "I read your crap because of Mick. The three of us were friends. But you know what? Those days are gone. I saw Mick yesterday. He's in the hospital. First it was hepatitis, now he's got liver cancer. Poor sucker."

With one foot inside the car, Steven narrowed his eyes. "I won't walk across the street for you, let alone read or, God forbid, finance your projects. I lost a fortune the last time I invested in your films. Not anymore. Stick to run-down dinner theater and call yourself lucky anybody still wants you." He slid into the car and roared away.

Only the scrape of the cup against the sidewalk remained.

An hour later, Rune sat at the laminate-topped table in his furnished studio apartment. Grime-filled knife cuts from previous tenants marred the table's surface, where unpaid bills fanned out in front of him. Directing dinner theater was hardly lucrative.

Rent. Car payment. Medical bills. He could cover only one, even if he reverted to college days and ate nothing more than a cup of noodles for breakfast, lunch, and dinner, with an occasional fast-food burger. He shoved the bills away from him. He shifted on the metal-framed chair and stared out the dirty window at the building across the alley.

His cellphone rang. Rune answered it without looking at the number. The woman who jabbered at him on the phone made no sense. He asked her to repeat her request.

"When would you like to come in for more tests?"

Tests? Bits of her words punched him.

"Several of the biopsy sites were suspicious for malignancy."

It was as if a kid with a toy gun had fired plastic darts at him. Rune could only focus on bits and pieces of what the woman said. Pop. As if a toy dart had hit him, he registered a phrase.

"An operation will be necessary."

Pop.

"Possible issues with impotence."

Rune dropped the cellphone to his lap. This was it. The Big "C." He had cancer.

His hand rubbed over his chest. Hearing this kind of shit could give a person a heart attack, he thought. Papers in his breast pocket crinkled under his fingers. He pulled out the folded card. The reunion invitation.

His knuckles smacked the table. The invitation slipped from his fingers. Rune's eyes bounced between the invitation and the mocking, unpaid bills.

He straightened in his chair, flipped open his temperamental old laptop, logged into his bank website, and studied the numbers once more. Rune's eyes swept the studio apartment, imprinting the faded colors in his mind.

No money. No insurance. And now, since paying rent was only a pipe dream, no place to live.

28

Newport Beach, California

Sweaty and flushed from three sets of outdoor tennis, Phillip eased the Porsche convertible onto his Newport Beach driveway. After besting last year's senior club champion, he planned a few laps in the pool before showering and dressing for the biggest night of his life.

Half a dozen pickups and one flatbed trailer jammed the drive, all labeled with the name of the area's premier construction company. An enormous blue Dumpster camped in the extra parking spots. The pounding of jackhammers and buzzing of saws filled the normally serene air.

Plastic draped the foyer of the sprawling ranch home; cardboard covered the white marble floor. Phillip followed the sound of the jackhammers to the rear of the house. Plastic drapes hung everywhere.

He exited the house through the bank of sliding glass doors and found the source of the noise, or most of it, at least. No swim today. Fractured slabs of the pool's concrete littered the backyard. Phillip stomped over to the apparent supervisor, a man who wore a golf shirt and carried a clipboard. Designer sunglasses covered the man's eyes.

"What's going on here?" Phillip had to shout over the noise.

The man extended a tanned hand to Phillip. "Are you Mr. Krueger? Nice to meet you. Harvey Casson."

Phillip looked around. Dust flew everywhere. "What the hell's going on?"

One cool eyebrow lifted on Harvey's face. "I guess Angel wanted to surprise you."

Phillip spoke with precise words. "Where is my wife?"

Harvey lifted one hand and gestured to the house.

Phillip stormed back inside. He found her in the exercise room, decked out in skintight white shorts and a sports bra. The music video channel played on a television. It entertained her while she pumped the elliptical machine. The vertical blinds that covered the plate glass windows facing the pool stood open.

Phillip glared at the windows and realized Angel had opened the blinds to give the workmen a view of her. Heat crept up his neck and then engulfed his face. He grabbed the six-hundred-dollar master remote off the elliptical trainer and turned the television off with one jab at the remote's touch screen, then pivoted to face her. "What the hell is going on?"

Her feet continued their punishing pace. "I'm giving myself a birthday present. Harvey's designed a fabulous new master suite for me—bed and bath, of course, plus a sitting room, study, and exercise room. The pool practically screamed for a redesign. Of course, now I'll have my own access to the spa."

Her words slapped him. "So that's it? Your own wing? Your own bed?"

"Turn the TV on. I still have forty-five minutes left." She prided herself on her movie-star shape, and after years of strenuous exercise, the rigorous pace did not even wind her.

"Tell me one thing. Did you deliberately plan this—" his arm cut the air in the direction of the windows and the pool, "—this construction project to coincide with my being named president?"

A tight smile crept onto her face. "That would have been delicious, wouldn't it? No, it's just a happy coincidence."

"Don't you think you need to get ready for the share-holders' meeting?"

"I'm not going. Daddy will vote my shares. But I'll show up for the dinner, since we're at the head table. I want my own car there anyway. I'm leaving early. I have a morning flight for Maui."

He clenched his fists by his sides. "We have a ten o'clock meeting tomorrow with the attorneys."

She stared at the blank television screen. "I won't make it." Her tanned legs didn't miss a beat on the elliptical.

It was as if she had punched him in the gut. He knew her answer before he asked the question. "Did you sign over the shares?"

She turned her head to look at him, expressionless. "I changed my mind."

A wave of icy chill swept over him. "That was the deal. I make president and I get your shares. The deal your father made when he offered me the job. You agreed to this before we got married."

She turned back to the blank television screen.

His stomach churned acid; it burned and threatened to send his post-match protein bar north. "My deal is for ownership."

She didn't trouble herself to look at him, apparently finding the blank screen more interesting. "So sue me."

He turned, afraid of throwing something at her. He stopped short of the door and spoke but didn't turn to face her. "How long will you be gone?"

"Three weeks. Maybe longer. All this dust and noise will be intolerable. I'm meeting Jewel and her boyfriend in Maui. With a friend along and a credit card that I pay for, she'll be happy."

He ignored her comment about the credit card for his almost thirty-year-old daughter. He knew exactly who'd pay the bill, and it wasn't Angel. He'd long abandoned the hope that Jewel would be inclined to get a job and support herself.

"Who's going with you?" He heard himself ask the question but knew he didn't really want the answer.

A rare thing, an honest laugh, came from Angel. "No one. But I'm sure I'll find company."

Of course you will. Phillip spun away from her. He grabbed the fifty-inch flat-screen television and pulled. It didn't budge.

"Are you crazy?"

Phillip glared at his wife.

"I'm not doing anything you won't do on that 'come bang your old girlfriend' reunion in Italy," she continued.

"I'm not going."

"Maybe you should. A good lay might loosen you up." As she tilted her head back with laughter, she reminded Phillip of the Wicked Witch of the West.

"I can't imagine you've gotten any since the last time I let you do me. Not with the presidency on the line." She cackled again. "Oh, my poor husband has had to be such a good boy. You lusted for my shares more than you ever did for me."

Phillip snorted air through his nose. He picked up a ten-pound pink neoprene-covered hand weight and threw it with anger-fueled adrenaline at the television. Whack. The screen crumpled under the force, listing sideways on its hinged bracket. He walked away without turning to face his wife. Her barrage of swearing followed him down the hall.

29

Fort Lauderdale, Florida

Meghan turned to greet the incoming customer. One of the regulars at the natural food store, a tall, thin woman in her mid-thirties, stood in the entry. Meghan smiled at the woman, one of the many she had converted to healthful ways. The woman returned Meghan's smile with a glare. Meghan moved a step closer to her, concern replacing her smile. "Are you OK?"

"No, I'm not OK." Anger underscored the woman's words. "I'll never be oh-kay again." Her voice rose and quickened. "I should have never listened to you and believed your tree-hugging, hocus-pocus mantra. Breast cancer. I got the call yesterday."

Meghan sucked in a breath. That sick feeling that she knew too well returned. "Do you know—"

"Do I know what? What kind? What stage?" The woman spit the words in Meghan's direction. She stomped to the closest shelf and with one toned arm swept the contents onto the floor. The shelf above met the same fate. The jars and boxes crashed to the floor, sending powder and pills and glass everywhere. She lowered her arm to attack another, lower shelf.

"Stop." Meghan ran to her. She grabbed the woman's arm with both hands.

The woman wrestled her arm free. "Damn you." She scooped the third shelf's neatly arranged goods in one deft move to the floor.

The angry act sent chunks of broken glass flying toward Meghan. A piece of glass stabbed Meghan's leg. She jumped back and bent over. Blood oozed from around the shard. She pulled the glass wedge from her leg. With a body-fat percentage rivaling elite athletes', she had no buffer of tissue to absorb the cut; the glass had sliced deep into her leg, and now blood gushed from the wound.

The customer shouted at Meghan, her red face contorted with anger. "Damn you."

"I'm sorry," Meghan said. She hated that this had happened to her customer, but she knew that a healthful lifestyle could only improve, not totally beat, the odds. "There's no guarantee. You know that."

"Bullshit. I believed you. But it's all a scam. A big fat scam to make you money."

"That's not true. Studies have proven positive outcomes."

"I trusted you. But you don't know anything." Tears dropped from the woman's eyes. "I have two young children. What happens to them when I die? You ought to be drawn and quartered for promising people that you can make them cancer-free."

"But I don't. Promise."

"Oh, really? Think about it. What you say, how you act, the purer-than-thou way you live. Right. You damn well do promise." The woman pointed her finger at Meghan. "And because of you, I'm dying." Before Meghan could speak, the woman ran from the store.

Tears filled Meghan's eyes. Cancer. Her leg throbbed. She ran to the back of the store. She found the first aid kit but threw it to the floor at the sight of the puny bandages. Meghan jerked open the cleaning cupboard. Her hand closed over a folded rag, and she jammed it against her calf.

Her breath came fast and hot. The bleeding wouldn't stop. She rushed to the telephone on the counter. Her finger shook as she stabbed out 9-1-1 on the keypad.

Meghan opened her eyes and squinted at the bright fluorescent lights. Noise all around. People talking, paging gibberish overhead, and machines whirring. She was in a hospital. Her leg hurt. She remembered. Remembered the angry customer. The woman with breast cancer.

Meghan knew she had never said that green tea and organic products and the right supplements could prevent a person from getting cancer. She passionately believed that they would reduce the odds, and that was all she ever said to customers. *One in eight.* One in eight U.S. women get breast cancer. She always told them, "Do whatever you can to beat the odds." But this customer was the unlucky "one." Just like Karen.

"Meghan? Meghan, love, I know you're awake. Your eyes are open." It was Talli, her store's co-owner, a New Age hippy and the wife of a mega-wealthy hip-hop musician. Her tone was soft, apologetic.

Meghan's tongue felt fat and useless.

"Hey, love, the doctor says you'll be all right. Your leg's fine, just a gash that needed stitches."

Meghan turned her head toward Talli. "Hi."

"Hi yourself." Talli's face lit up with a smile. "You should have heard the scrubbies tsk-tsking over your weight. I say they're jealous bitches because you're thin and they're definitely not." She chuckled.

Meghan tried to smile, but she couldn't. The memory of the customer's swollen, angry face and the sound of the inventory crashing to the floor made her flinch even now. She closed her eyes. The woman's accusations reverberated in the small, curtained-off space. The words pushed down on Meghan, trying to force the breath out of her lungs. They played over and over, sounding like an old vinyl record with a scratch.

One week later, Talli drove her to the airport for the reunion she had insisted Meghan attend. "This will do you good." Talli's cheery voice didn't match the worry that crinkled her waxed eyebrows.

Meghan stared out the window. She thought about the trip. Should she go? If she didn't, what would she do? She didn't think she could work in the store anymore. How could she? What if someone else came in with accusations? Meghan couldn't stomach the thought.

Words formed inside Meghan and she blurted them out. "I may not come back."

Talli coughed out her stunned reaction. "What?"

Why had she said that? Meghan repeated her words, slowly, to hear them herself. "I may not come back."

Talli blinked. "Shut up." Her head pivoted between Meghan and the interstate traffic. She leaned on the horn. "Dammit, asshole. Drive." She glanced at Meghan. "What do you mean? To the store? Or to Florida?"

"I think I may stay in Italy."

"Why? To eat cheese? To find love? Need I remind you that you're vegan? You don't even eat most of the food they cook in Italy. And as far as love goes, I'll bet there are more hotties here on the beach than where you're headed." Her tone was flip, but Talli's knuckles were white on the steering wheel. She leaned her palm on the horn again.

Meghan felt a mounting urgency to insist on her new plan. It was as if she were racing to beat a train to the intersection. "I'm leaving Fort Lauderdale. I can't bear the thought of another customer coming to me with cancer. I want you to have the store. My computer has the phone number of my lawyer. Call him. Set it up."

"Really? Are you sure? Just like that?" Talli looked at her with worry written on her face.

Meghan whispered her answer. "Yes. Just like that."

"You're probably still in shock or something. We can laugh about it when you get back." Talli's foot slammed the accelerator pedal to the floor. She swerved right, cut through three lanes of traffic, and darted down the exit ramp toward the airport.

Meghan shook her head at Talli's fearless driving antics. Maybe her partner was right about her being in shock. Where did that thought, and her own words, come from? Perhaps she, deep down, wanted to do something fearless herself. She doubted Talli's boldness would ever be her style.

What was her style, anyway? One word slammed into her head. Afraid.

Meghan couldn't imagine something worse than being afraid. When it came to business, she was proud that she had been willing to take risks and twice been rewarded with success. When first Karen, and then April, died, Meghan had been convinced that she would soon follow them. That fear had propelled her into opening the store with Talli and had driven her to adopt a healthy lifestyle.

After all the suffering she'd endured, she thought she deserved more than a life governed by fear.

"Do it," Meghan said. "Call my lawyer." Staying here was no longer a choice.

"Look, if you change your mind when you come back from the reunion, however long you stay, I'll tear up the papers. I swear, I will." Talli's voice echoed with calm reason. "I don't want you to rush into anything you'll regret later. This is emotional for you, seeing everyone."

Without Karen. Talli didn't say it, but to Meghan, it was if she had screamed it through one of her husband's microphones. Without Karen.

Meghan nodded. "Do it."

"What's in Italy for you?"

Meghan couldn't say it, but she had a hunch that what she needed was an escape from her cautionary life. Now, her focus was on avoiding death rather than living. Could Italy help her embrace life and all of its roller-coaster ups and downs once again?

30

Florence, Italy

Bella leaned against the cool, timeworn stone wall that flanked the interior marble steps to the courtyard. The *palazzo*, her mansion residence for the reunion, occupied a hilltop perch less than an hour south of the old city of Florence. The arched doorway that led to the outdoor patio loomed ten paces ahead. She stopped and closed her eyes. Bella could hear their voices—murmurs and laughter.

"Anybody heard from Stillman?" A baritone voice clipped out the words.

Bella waited for the response.

The man continued. "I was really looking forward to hooking up with him again. Counting on it, actually. Did you know he abandoned med school and took up law? I heard this from someone—maybe Bobby. You know," the voice paused as if for emphasis, "*Bobby DeNiro*. Stillman specializes in creative rights. He's a player in the entertainment world. Would love my new project. You all would."

"Is that why you brought us here, Rune?" Another man's voice, quieter, asked.

"Outstanding," Rune said. "Fly everyone first class to Italy to put together a backer group. Hell of an idea, man.

Wish I'd thought of it. Simpatico with West Coast style. Hell of an idea."

Bella's eyes dropped to her watch. Her entrance would be at exactly fifteen minutes past the appointed hour, fashionably late, but no more. The new curve-clinging red blouse and skirt showed off her figure and legs—both still good. She pushed aside the panic about the reunion that had blanketed her during the flight. Too late for that. It's now or never. How about never?

Bella considered her options. Then she remembered the invitation and its taunt about cowards. She'd come this far, all the way to Italy. Bella patted her black, shoulder-length hair, lifted her chin and sauntered down the stairs with fake confidence.

Rune, facing the mansion, saw Bella first.

"Bella. *Bellissimo.*" Rune rushed to her, folding her in arms hairy enough to vie for an honorable mention in a Ripley's book.

Bella returned the hug, and then pulled back to kiss his bronzed cheek. "Hello, Rune. Great tan. Is it faux, or are you competing for the melanoma hall of shame?"

Rune's head flipped back, and laughter erupted from him. "You haven't changed a bit, sweetheart. Still as sassy and foxy as ever." He squeezed her again, this time ensuring that her breasts smashed against his chest. "It's 100 percent fake, you'll be happy to know. Goes with my nose job, tummy tuck, and lid work." He cocked his head to the right. "That's your specialty isn't it, Lee? Plastics?"

Bella followed Rune's gaze to her left. Lee slouched in a colorful chintz chair, a sweating glass of pale white wine in his hand. Silver streaked the fringe of drab gray hair anchoring his bald scalp. Thick-lensed glasses perched on his nose. Bifocals, Bella silently bet. Even without his curly hair, she found the Lee she remembered in his kind eyes and receding chin.

"Yes," Lee said. He pushed up from his chair. "But I specialize in reconstructive and medically indicated surgeries." He held open his arms. "Bella, you are a walking testimonial as to why people do not need plastic surgery to age with beauty and grace."

Bella stepped into his embrace. "Lee, you can pitch a line of malarkey with the best of them." She clicked the tip of her tongue. "But I appreciate the compliment." His warmth made her think this might not be so terrifying after all. Only five classmates left, but the thought of the two men she had yet to see set off her internal panic alarm.

Lee chuckled. "Bella. I meant it. Seriously." He draped his arm around her waist and escorted her to the white-linen-covered table a few steps beyond the chairs.

Bella saw a tall, white-haired woman standing at the edge of the courtyard with her back to them.

"First things first." Lee reached for a bottle of wine. "Pinot grigio? We're waiting to break into the Prosecco until everyone arrives."

"Lee," Rune said, apparently determined to stay in the conversation, "are you crazy? 'Medically indicated surger-ies?' The tits and ass market's a gold mine. No shit. Plastic surgeons may not be top of the food chain, but damn close. Models and actresses start under the knife when they're still jailbait and keep on until they croak."

Lee flicked away Rune's argument with his hand. He smiled and offered Bella a wineglass, which she declined. "Bella," his voice raised in mock drama, "our aged group awaits."

The woman with the head of brilliant white hair walked over to join them. Rounded in frame, she looked stout enough to be a high school heavyweight wrestler. A worry line creased her forehead, and her makeup couldn't hide the dark circles under her eyes. A smile, at first tentative, then honest, brightened her face. "I'm Hope."

The two women embraced. "Fabulous hair," Bella said. Wow, had Hope changed. She looked at least ten years beyond their calendar age.

"I turned early," Hope said. "White as snow by thirty. Dyed it for a while, until it started falling out in droves. Then I surrendered." She shrugged.

"It's distinctive," Bella leaned back, inspecting Hope further. "Memorable." One eyebrow perked up. "Sexy."

"Cow poppy." Hope looked down, her hand smoothing nonexistent wrinkles in her ankle-length black-and-tan silk skirt.

Bella heard footsteps on the stone path that led from the central fountain. She turned to look.

A too-thin solo version of the twins approached them. She had a pixie haircut and wore beige cotton capri pants and an unbleached cotton T-shirt that hung loosely over her bony frame. The woman's left hand drifted to the hem of her shirt. Her fingers picked at the fabric edge, the same unconscious fluttering that Bella recalled from their summer together.

Bella rushed to meet her at the edge of the patio and gave her a hug. The woman's angular bones protruded through her cotton shirt. "Hello, Meghan," Bella said. "It's great to see you. Is Karen here, too?"

Meghan's eyes shifted down.

Then, stone-faced, Meghan's eyes drifted back to meet Bella's. "Breast cancer. She died about ten years ago."

"I'm sorry." Bella's arms surrounded Meghan again, this time with a gentle embrace of sympathy. Silence draped them. Words—Bella's trademark—escaped her. The heavy door of grief opened to the black void beyond while Bella quietly held her friend from the past.

"It should have been me." With that bombshell dropped, Meghan stepped away from Bella and took refuge in slowly filling her glass with aqua naturale.

Bella began to speak but swallowed the questions nagging at her. She remembered swapping bras with the twins as the three of them had raided Paris lingerie shops on their mid-semester break. Karen's breasts had betrayed her, becoming the carrier for her fatal disease.

Remembering the scanty lace bras and panties she had fallen in love with in Paris brought back other memories of those months. Bella forced those unwanted thoughts away, returning them to the deep crevice to which she had banished them.

"Meghan," Bella said, "are you married?"

Meghan shook her head. "Karen married."

Karen's excitement over her long-distance proposal percolated in Bella's memory. "Are you close to her family?"

Pain tightened Meghan's eyes. "Her husband hasn't spoken to me for six years."

"What an asshole," Rune said. He put one hairy arm over Meghan's narrow shoulders and kissed her cheek. "Sweetheart, you're better off without him."

A weak smile rested on Meghan's face. "Where were you when I needed you?"

"Let's see, six years ago? I had just inked a major deal. I mean major. Then I promptly blew my advance on a sweet young thing whose ass wasn't near as high and tight as yours." Rune made a show of casting his eyes to Meghan's bottom.

Color radiated from Meghan's cheeks and a spark ignited in her eyes.

"Rune, you are still every bit the lecher you always were," Hope said.

Meghan seemed to relax. "And isn't it great that some things haven't changed?"

"What hasn't changed? Did I miss a revelation?" A brown-haired man with silver at his temples and striking blue eyes ambled in from the sidewalk that led to an overlook. A black cotton sweater was draped over his shoulders, Italian style; the top two buttons on his white linen shirt gaped open, exposing curling salt-and-pepper chest hair.

Bella stood silently, hidden in the shadow cast by a potted lemon tree. Phillip looked as she had expected. Styled hair, expensive clothes and shoes. She recognized his Italian designer footwear from her research for the last manuscript that she'd sent to her editor. Requisite California tan—check. Simple gold wedding band—check.

Lee helped himself to another glass of pinot grigio. "Teach you for wandering off, Phillip."

"Just had to say hello to my old lover, Florence." Phillip poured the pale yellow-green wine into his empty glass. "What hasn't changed?"

"Rune, of course." Hope edged over to the table of libations. "Lee, the pinot grigio is finished. I say, let's pop that Prosecco. It'll feel like a celebration then."

Lee aimed the bottle of bubbly into the grassy garden. He let the cork fly with a grin.

Checking the anger that threatened to burst out, Bella forced her voice into something akin to the tone of a policewoman asking for a driver's license. "Hello, Phillip." She stepped into the light of the curved iron wall sconce beside her.

Phillip spun to see her; his sweater slipped over one arm. He reached for it and wine splattered his shirt.

"Shit." Phillip studied the nipple-high wet spot on his otherwise immaculate shirt.

"Now that's a greeting that could give even a completely balanced person a complex," Bella said.

Phillip slid his three-quarters-empty glass onto the table. He turned to face her. "Hello, Bella. You look good."

"Good, hell, she's beyond that. She's fab-u-lous. Do you need eye surgery?" Rune said. Behind Phillip's back, he raised one eyebrow at Bella. "Look, man, I know a laser eye doc. He's done all the A-list stars."

Without a word, Phillip glided over the dust-flecked stones with the erect bearing befitting the president of a three-generation, multibillion-dollar company. He leaned forward and hugged Bella as if she were a china doll.

"That was worthless." The words came out of Bella before she could stop them. "Have you forgotten how to hug?" Even though Phillip was pond scum to Bella, how dare he show everyone how little he thought of her?

For one agonizing moment, Phillip stared at her.

Bella wanted to slap him, but her pride wouldn't let her. She relished the opportunity to tell Phillip exactly what she thought of him. Unleashing her anger was a private matter, though, and it wouldn't happen in front of the others.

Phillip laughed. "Worthless? Since my memory on hug etiquette seems lacking, perhaps you can teach me." He rubbed one of her shoulders with his palm. "May I have a mulligan on that hug?"

Bella shrugged and forced a smile to her lips.

This time, he folded her into his arms like she'd never left them.

A shudder rumbled inside her, propelling her back and out of his arms. She pretended to stifle a sneeze and waved him off with her hand.

"I love reunions." Rune poured himself a Prosecco. "Where else does a horny guy have carte blanche to kiss and grope all the women in his reach?" He locked one arm around Meghan's neck and the other around her waist and crushed the shocked woman into a French kiss.

Meghan pulled away, sputtering and coughing.

Phillip stepped back and looked over his shoulder at Rune. "Speak for yourself." He scanned their faces. "I'm assuming Stillman is our host for this reunion. Has anyone heard from him?"

Heads shook a negative response, and murmurs indicated the same.

Bella moistened her lips. "My last contact with Stillman was several years ago." The words came out quiet and tentative.

Phillip's shoulders stiffened. He moved to the table and poured two glasses of the Italian effervescent wine. He extended one glass to Bella.

"And how was Stillman?" His precisely enunciated words sliced the air. "When you last saw him."

Bella remembered their last night together at her apartment. Their comfortable routine of tender sex, light conversation, and dinner had culminated in a marriage proposal. Stillman had pushed her for a commitment, which Bella hadn't been able to give him, and he had walked out. He didn't say anything, not even goodbye. Stillman had left that night and disappeared from her life.

Bella gulped a large swallow of the wine; the refreshing coolness washed inside her. Her eyes roved across the faces of her former classmates.

"He's the same," she said. "'Still Man'—calm, warm, effectively hiding the forty-two plates he spun constantly."

Rune stepped forward.

Bella felt their eyes on her, all trying to decipher the connection. She tried to keep it light and noncommittal. "Stillman and I reconnected in New York, years after we left Florence."

She moved to the table and added a negligible amount of wine to her glass to regain her composure. She knew they waited for the details. No more stalling. Bella picked up her glass and turned to face the group.

"I haven't spoken to him for years. At one point, I heard he went to Prague for an extended visit." Bella shot a meaningful glance at Rune. "A client of his was producing a film there."

"Which one?" Rune's cool façade evaporated.

Bella shrugged.

"Really, he was on location in Prague?" Rune leaned forward.

Bella watched Hope chug her wine.

Hope's eyes drifted to meet Bella's. The empty champagne glass twisted in Hope's fingers. "It's supposed to be a great city," Hope said. "One on my list." Her words tumbled out. "Hell, I wanted to travel all over Europe after being here."

"Have you been back to Europe since our summer, Hope?" Meghan asked in a kind voice.

Bella hid her relief that the conversation had moved off Stillman.

Hope's face flinched. "No. I never left the States after our summer here. I married an asshole. Remember me talking about Charlie?" She tramped to the libation table and refilled her glass. Before anyone could try to salvage the situation, she turned and raised her glass skyward. "To freedom from assholes."

The others stared at her.

Meghan lifted her glass of water in salute. "I'll second that. Freedom from assholes."

"*Scusi.*" A man stood in the arched doorway to the hotel. His face and complexion looked more Roman than Florentine. He held a paper in his hand. In Italian, he asked if anyone could speak the language.

"*Sì.*" Bella nodded and stepped toward him.

His melodious voice rattled off a string of Italian that Bella immediately understood. He has a message from Stillman? Bella's heart jolted. She had two goals for this trip: one regarded Phillip and the other was to figure out whether she and Stillman could have a future together. She reached for the paper. "*Grazie.*"

"*Prego.*" The Italian stepped back into the arched doorway and waited in silence.

Bella's eyes shot to the page. She raced through the words. She looked up and knew her eyes broadcast her disappointment. "It's a message from Stillman. He's been detained on an errand but promises to arrive before long. He sends his love."

"Love?" Rune asked. "That's touching, isn't it? We haven't seen the man in thirty years, and he still loves us.

Hell, I'm used to the kind of love that disappears before morning."

"Not everyone has your emotional dysfunction, Rune," Bella said. She felt her cheeks flush but couldn't stop herself. "Stillman cares about people. When he arrives, maybe you can learn something from him."

Rune saluted her with an index finger.

Phillip stared at her.

"*Signora?*" The Italian had stepped toward Bella.

"*Prego?*"

The Italian phrases tumbled from his smiling mouth, a lilting description of their dinner arrangements. Bella responded in Italian, promising that the group would adjourn soon to the rooftop garden.

"*Prego.*" The man tilted his head sideways and accented the all-purpose word with a flip of his hand.

Bella felt the others' eyes on her.

Hope spoke first. "You learned Italian. After being here, I wanted to. But there was never time for taking classes."

"Are you fluent?" Lee asked in Italian, his voice tentative.

Bella shook her head. "Am I fluent? Not really. I understand conversation better than I speak."

Lee smiled at her. "You're modest, Bella. Your accent sounds like a native."

She felt their eyes locked on her and shrugged in response. She addressed her answer to Hope. "I lucked out. An Italian grandmother who refused to speak English lived next to me when I first had my own apartment in New York." Bella turned to Lee. "How about you?"

Lee's smile widened. "I dabbled with lessons over the last couple of years. Even toyed with the crazy idea of spending a year here."

Bella lifted her head to the view beyond the courtyard. A smile drew up the corners of her mouth. "Not so crazy." She turned back to the group. "A dinner has been set up for us in the rooftop garden. It's ready for us now."

"Thank God." Hope moved toward the archway of the building. "The last time I ate was on another continent."

"I did damage to the Chianti and Parmesan in my room," Rune said. "Rustic, but a nice touch."

"I wish I had," Hope said. "When I got here, I had no appetite." Her eyes bounced between them. "Travel stomach, I guess. Not that it's such a bad thing." She slapped her hips. "Hear that, hips? You can shrink anytime now." She linked arms with Meghan and pulled the slight woman along. "Let's go renew our love affair with Italian cuisine. Remember the ribolitta and tortelloni we had in that little trattoria by the Duomo?"

Meghan laughed. "Remember it? It took me six months after going back home to lose all the weight I'd gained."

Hope plowed through the group to the courtyard entrance. "Which way to the roof?" She looked at the man who waited in the doorway. The Italian smiled at her and gestured up the stairs to the left of the doorway.

Phillip and Lee motioned Bella ahead. Behind her, she heard Phillip's voice.

"How was your flight, Lee?"

"Noisy. My luck to finally fly first class and have a screaming child behind me. How 'bout you?"

"Long. I couldn't sleep. Luckily I brought an E.V. Tate thriller with me to pass the hours."

Bella's hand tightened on the wrought-iron railing that flanked the narrow, curved stairs to the roof. She forced herself to keep moving upward.

"Are you a fan?" Lee's baritone echoed up the winding stair.

"They're entertaining. I travel a lot and prefer Tate's novels to the economic reports that fill my briefcase."

Bella ran up the stairs to escape the sound of Phillip's voice. Hearing him talk sent her spiraling back to that summer. The searing memory of standing in JFK airport with his typed message in her hand pummeled her, filling her churning stomach with acid.

31

A massive square lookout tower at the far corner of the
rooftop courtyard overshadowed the rectangular
dining area. Through the rooftop's railing, Bella saw the
edge of the palazzo's garden down below. The lights of
Florence peppered the distant horizon.

"Amazing." Hope's breath came in loud, short bursts as
she tried to catch her breath from the trip up the stairs.

"It's calming, isn't it?" The view soothed Bella. Her
shoulders relaxed.

"Look at that tower," Rune said as he approached the
women. "This is even more radical than the ones we used
in *Knights of the Blood Order*. How thick are these walls,
do you think?" He patted one dust-covered stone with his
palm.

"Two meters. Same as the cornerstone." Phillip slid by
Bella without even a glance in her direction. "*Knights of
the Blood Order*? I must have missed it."

Rune coughed and cleared his throat. "You and the
rest of the free world." Rune's voice dropped lower. "But
we had great numbers in a handful of up-and-coming
locations."

He looked back at the group clustered by the stairs and shook his head. "Hell, you guys are my friends. It bombed. Big time. But we had one radical castle, complete with five towers. I should have kept the bloody towers. Those five— not four, like everyone else gets by with, but five—monster towers lapped up the last of my funds quicker than a high school cheerleader sucks off the quarterback following a big game."

Hope chuckled. "I bet your towers looked grand, Rune."

Rune grabbed his crotch. "Sweetheart, they were an instant hard-on."

Hope linked her arm through Rune's and guided him toward the table. "Come on, Rune. I want to sit by you so I won't feel intimidated by our wildly successful class-mates."

Bella chewed the inside of her lip. "Who says we're all wildly successful?"

Hope's smile inched across her wide face. "Honey, I have a sense about these things. That's what made me a wicked fundraiser for the school. I can smell who's got the money." She chuckled.

Bella shook her head in denial. She realized that Meghan wasn't at the table. Her eyes turned back to the stairway and then peered through the dusky light. She thought that Meghan must have stopped short of the dining area. Her eyes paused on Phillip. He tipped his head to the left, nodding to the wall behind her. He could still read her actions, damn it. She looked over her shoulder. Meghan stood away from the back wall, studying the subtle-hued fresco painted on it.

Bella moved beside Meghan. In her soft, querying mother's voice, she asked, "What moves you about the fresco?"

Meghan smiled but didn't cease her methodical study of the painting. Her voice came slowly, in an awed whisper. "That it's here. Still. That once people valued art and chose to live surrounded by beautiful creations." Her bony shoulders raised in a shrug. "It warms me."

Bella placed her hand against the center of Meghan's back and matched Meghan's whisper. "Me, too."

Meghan turned to look at Bella. She offered silent thanks. Bella gave a tiny nod in return and took in Meghan's eyes. Eyes that looked like they were searching for something.

The women turned in tandem. Bella copied Hope's gesture that the girls had adopted during their summer here—she linked arms with Meghan and led her to the table.

Sienna-colored runners straddled the wooden surface of the table, which was laden with trays of antipasto. Olive branches with silvery green leaves framed the platters. A large bowl of fresh produce—shiny purple eggplants, crimson plum tomatoes, burgundy and white radicchio, yellow squash, and indigo grapes—decorated one end of the table, occupying the space rightfully belonging to Karen.

"Do we go ahead and eat without Stillman?" Rune rubbed his hands together and looked as anxious to start dinner as Hope.

"We can all eat together," Stillman said from the top of the stairwell. In his black Armani clothing, he looked tanned, rested, and oozing with the confidence that success brings.

Bella rushed to Stillman and wrapped her arms around him. She whispered in his ear. "I've missed you. Thank you, both for this trip and for coming back into my life."

He pulled back and brushed his lips against hers. "It is truly my pleasure."

Bella percolated with an excited, nervous joy, as if she were a fifteen-year-old on her first date. She smiled. "I'm glad you've forgiven me."

"What makes you so sure?" He punctuated his words with a boyish grin.

Hope's booming voice rang out. "Quit hogging him, Bella. The rest of us would like to say hello, too, you know."

Stillman stepped away from Bella and extended both arms. "I'm all yours, ladies."

Hope and Meghan hugged Stillman. Their quiet laughter and words were interspersed with his. Lee remained beside the table, in a conversation with Rune about the teams headed for the World Series.

Bella's head turned to meet Phillip's scrutiny.

His face showed no emotion, and his tone was equally flat. "Looks like you and Stillman got to know each other better after we left Italy."

Bella flicked her hair back from her face with a shake of her head. Her voice lifted in affirmation. "We did."

She returned to the table and reclaimed her wineglass.

Bella tipped it up to wet her lips and watched the strained greeting and stiff handshake extended by Lee. Stillman clapped Lee's shoulder and bet that collecting fees with a JD, rather than an MD, behind one's name met with greater success. Though their razzing seemed like standard water-cooler fare, the pained expression on Lee's face never wavered.

Phillip asked Stillman why he ended up choosing law instead of medicine.

"Bombed Organic Chemistry," Stillman said, "and for a semester, I thought it was the end of the world. It was a freak thing, actually," he said, looking at Lee, "but ended up being a blessing in disguise. I love what I do." He shrugged. "I wasn't cut out to be a doctor, anyway." He clapped Lee on the back. "Not like Lee, here. He's nationally renowned, you know."

Lee's face relaxed. "Thank you."

Stillman gazed straight at Lee. "I'm glad it worked out the way it did, with you in medicine and me in law. Besides," he laughed, "we have law to thank for this re-union." Stillman admitted to hosting the trip, saying he'd come into a windfall on a film on which he'd taken his fee as a percentage. With a fiftieth birthday approaching and having no family, he told them, he couldn't imagine a better way to celebrate than with them at this reunion.

As if she sat in a theater seat watching a performance, Bella felt removed from the banter around her. Her mind was muddled by the surreal nature of the week ahead with people, other than Stillman, whom she hadn't seen for thirty years. Bella relished the idea of being with her old friends again—that is, except for Phillip. The prospect of spending a week in his company was as enticing as being thrown into the belly of an outhouse.

At Stillman's urging, they limited their conversation to suggestions on how to spend their time in Italy. He insisted that the sharing of their personal histories occur through-out the days ahead. The unveiling would be as if they were unwrapping cherished gifts. Until all was known, he claimed, they could be as they were thirty years ago when they first met, before they had their own families, successes, and failures.

The evening unfolded with course after course of Tuscan comfort food. Antipasto gave way to pasta filled with squash and amaretti cookie crumbs. Wine and herb-infused roast chicken melted on their tongues. Crunchy roasted new potatoes sat largely untouched, except by Hope, who vowed to sample everything. Field greens dressed in wild strawberry vinaigrette finished off the dinner.

Even Hope had to put up her hands in defeat when the Roman who brought plate after plate of food produced an enormous platter of almond pastries, pine nut cookies, cheeses, and fruit. They all declined espresso and limoncello in favor of sleep after their twenty-four hours of travel.

"Say," Lee said, tapping four fingers against the wooden tabletop, "what are the plans for the morning?"

"Breakfast will be available in the courtyard from 8:00 to 9:30. Then," Stillman added, his eyes crinkling as he grinned, "I've arranged a hidden treasures tour of Florence."

Curious murmurs accompanied the group down the stone steps and echoed through the stairwell. They reached Bella's room first. She unlocked it and turned to face the others. "Good night, all. Sleep well."

Stillman lifted her chin with his fingertips and lightly kissed her lips.

The others filed past, offering hugs and kisses on the cheek before following Stillman down the hall.

Phillip drew up the rear of the group. He watched them move around the corner before he turned to Bella.

"I owe you the apology of a lifetime," Phillip said, "and an explanation."

You pompous ass, Bella thought. She kept her face expressionless and said, "*That* is the understatement of the year."

Phillip pulled her hands into his.

"Is that an attempt to prevent me from slapping you?" Bella removed her hands from his grasp. "If so, you needn't worry. Slapping you might be temporarily satisfying, but it wouldn't come close to paying you back for what you did to me."

Meeting her gaze, he said, "I know. I will never forgive myself for what happened. Even though you have a right to despise me, please let me explain."

Bella had fantasied about unleashing her anger on him, but something made her wait. Maybe she was emotionally and physically exhausted from the travel and the anticipation of seeing everyone, especially him. Perhaps it was his insistence on explaining his money-grubbing decision. The thought of listening to his excuses was unbearable.

"I can't. Not now." She turned, unlocked her door, and stepped inside.

"Bella, please wait."

The door swung closed behind her. Its heavy thud echoed in her room.

32

At seven the next morning, Bella confronted the copper-plated espresso machine in the parlor adjacent to the courtyard. The machine resembled a small steam engine. No attendant in sight and Bella needed coffee. She climbed onto a wooden chair in order to look down on it. Were beans already inside?

"*Scusi.*" A man's voice.

Bella's back jerked straight. Damn. Caught straddling this thing with her butt pointed sky high. Certain of the flush on her cheeks, she turned and climbed down from the chair. It was the young Roman from the previous night. Bella explained in Italian that she wanted an espresso but did not want to trouble anyone.

"I speak English." He grinned.

"But last night—"

He moved closer and rested one hand on the chair back next to her. "Last night I wanted to test your Italian."

He stood close enough that she could feel his breath. Bella resisted the urge to insert more space between them and reminded herself that flirting was a national pastime in Italy. "Why?"

He leaned closer to confide a secret. "Stillman told me you were fluent." He pulled away, smug and sure of himself.

Two can play. She stepped in closer, though no part of her body touched his. "And what did you decide?"

Laughter tumbled out. "Your Italian is very good." He extended his right hand. "I'm Giacomo."

The calluses on Giacomo's slender hand rubbed against her palm.

Bella took stock of the man, who smiled at her with that Italian "I-could-make-love-to-you-like-you've-never-known-before" gaze. He looked in his late thirties and wore no wedding ring. His pale ginger linen shirt and black slacks draped his body with the telltale mark of expensive Italian fabric and construction. Giacomo's tanned arms, visible with the short-sleeved shirt, showed the sinewy muscles of someone who used his body for physical work.

She remembered feeling tacky during her semester abroad, wearing her peasant blouses and denim skirts. The twenty-year-old Italian girls resembled tiny femmes fatales in pencil skirts that showed the lines of their sexy under-wear and clingy, low-cut blouses. Fashion and seduction—it's what it is all about.

Giacomo waited, not stepping away from her. Bella felt his palpable appraisal of her—her age, her looks, even her smell—and bet his animal instincts could guess she hadn't slept with a man for years.

Bella blinked, as if she could back him down with the slight movement. "Espresso?"

"But of course."

While Giacomo drew an espresso for her, she quizzed him about the estate. One espresso led to a second and a light, historical discussion of the property. Giacomo fell into the easy banter of a tour guide. Bella learned of a looped footpath around the property, which Giacomo recommended that she explore.

A blanket of low morning mist clung to the slopes. Cool, moist air lent a shine to Bella's cheeks as her rubber-bottomed flats met the cobblestone road in front of the palazzo. The world here, an ocean away from Manhattan, felt fresh, not cloyingly claustrophobic like her lonely home had become. Out here, with a wide sky above, she couldn't wait to venture out.

Bella turned to her right, away from the driveway, and walked to the farthest building. More recently constructed, it must serve as some kind of machine shed, she decided, as it stood two stories high and had a monstrous double wooden door. Bella's fingers slid down the building's wall, which was constructed with ancient stones. She admired the attention to detail. Although Giacomo had said it was a new building, meaning built in the last century, it matched the rest of the estate.

Beyond the crest of the hill, an apple tree marked the footpath. It extended in two directions, both of which wound down the hill and disappeared into olive trees. Bella chose left. Delicate pink wild roses marked the path's edge. This direction led away from Florence, and the morning sun yielded to a landscape vista dotted with hilltop villas, vineyards, and olive groves. Gold, orange, pink, and dusty greens unfolded in a rolling patchwork.

Rosebushes gave way to a crumbled stone retaining wall on her left. She stopped to examine a scooped stone protruding from the wall. Long ago, the bowl had caught the flow of a natural spring. Below the cracked basin, she saw tiny black spiders and their webs. Bella ran her index finger inside the stone spout—dusty, but not overburdened with dirt. She wondered if restoration of the wall, or at least the spring, was underway.

"Good morning, Bella." Stillman's voice came from above the retaining wall.

Bella peered up the slope. "Good morning. I can't see you. Where are you hiding?"

Stillman chuckled. "Not hiding. Merely contemplating the day."

Bella saw him now. He stood behind a clump of rose-bushes. He invited her to join him, pointing out the tiny side path that meandered up the slope. Once she reached him, she saw a small graveled area behind the rosebushes, where Stillman had been sitting on a cast-iron bench.

Smiling, she drew her cashmere sweater closed. A gentle breeze cooled her. "What a lovely spot."

His arms opened wide, inviting her in for an embrace. "And even better now that you're here." He pressed her against him in a warm, but not passionate, embrace. He gestured to the bench and they sat down. He didn't waste time getting to the conversation she had fretted over. "You know, after you refused to marry me, I was convinced I never wanted to see you again."

Bella nodded. "I know. I tried everything I could think of to get your assistant to put me in touch with you, but all he'd say was that you'd left the country and couldn't be reached. The part about not being reachable was obviously a lie. But I got the message—you wanted to avoid me." She rested one palm on his arm. "I can't say that I blame you. My situation with David at the time was so … complicated."

"Being honest, you were both the inspiration behind this reunion and the primary reason I didn't want to do it." Stillman gazed out at the postcard-perfect landscape.

Inspiration? That held promise. "So what tipped the balance?"

Stillman laughed. "Turning fifty." He smiled at her. "It's a time to take stock. Make sure you don't have regrets."

Bella nodded. The thought of her approaching birthday had accentuated her loneliness.

David was on another continent, serving as the lone physician for an African town and the surrounding area. Her son had been bitten by the missionary spirit and was thriving, content with the aid he provided to needy people. Last year, at the end of his commitment, she had hoped he'd return to the States. Instead, a foundation gave him a grant to build a clinic and it reenergized him, making it impossible for him to leave.

Without David, and without a partner, lover, or spouse, Bella was alone. She had regrets. Plenty of them. And one was that she had driven Stillman away.

"Thank you," Bella said. "For the bold, generous gift of

this reunion. And for being willing to see me again." Her heart thumped inside her chest and she felt her face flush.

"Willing, yes. Pleased about it?" He chuckled. "Maybe not."

Bella rapped him on the arm with her knuckles. "Right. I seem to remember you kissing me last night."

He laughed. "So I did. I guess that means that I've forgiven you for casting me aside." Stillman winked. "Or maybe I did it just to infuriate Phillip."

Bella jumped to her feet. "I could give a rat's ass about Phillip." She paced in front of the bench. She stopped and, with her hands on her hips, faced Stillman. She had fallen into a deep well, and a lone rope from above offered a chance for survival.

Fearful of Stillman's answer, her words came out slow and soft. "Is that the only reason you wanted to see me again? To use me to get back at Phillip?"

On his feet, Stillman grasped her hands. "No. Don't think that. A few years ago, I didn't want to see or talk to you because you crushed me. Twice. I like to think I'm not a fool. But that's how I felt. I'll not make that mistake again."

Bella bowed her head. He was right, of course. She had stupidly chosen Phillip over him during that long-ago summer, and then, because she was afraid to tell him the truth about David, she had rejected Stillman a second time.

But it was different now. Not merely because she dreaded entering the last segment of life alone. No. She loved Stillman. She figured that she always had, but thirty years ago, lust and love had swirled together, complicating everything. That one weekend with Phillip had shattered the rest of her life.

No matter how much she wanted Stillman to love her again, Bella couldn't, and wouldn't, beg him to take her back. Begging wasn't in her DNA. She had to win him back. That's what she would do.

"You're certainly no fool," she said. "I'm the one who's been the fool. But, honestly, when you're almost fifty, it's a brand-new ball game, and all bets are off. I say, let's be friends, good friends. Then you don't have to worry about being hurt again."

And if you think I'm going to be content with being only your friend, she thought, you don't know me.

"So," she said, holding out her hand to him, "our generous and dashing host, care to join me for some breakfast?"

He looked at her for a long moment, then stood and held her hand. He started walking, but she didn't move forward. He turned back to look at her. "I thought you mentioned breakfast."

With a grin, she said, "I'm trying to decide whether we should walk together, another great opportunity for you to shove it in Phillip's face, or," she continued, dropping his hand, "race back!" She took off jogging up the side path, betting it would lead back to the palazzo.

His laughter and footsteps followed her up the hill.

Stillman caught up to her at the top of the path. Instead of heading for the front of the palazzo, however, he motioned to a smooth pebble path that skirted the rear of the building.

"In the invitations," she asked, "why the 'Regrets are for cowards'?"

"Who could resist that?"

"Good point. So when did you first think of having this reunion?"

"When the preacher died, a couple of years ago. The bitter old man finally checked out. It's funny how one thinks about old friends when there isn't a generation standing between you and death."

"I'm sorry to hear about the preacher."

"Don't be. To tell the truth, I was relieved. Lucky bastard died in his sleep one night. He'd preached a hell of a sermon that morning, I was told."

Bella remembered her feelings when her mother died. "Regardless of circumstance, a person becomes an orphan when their parents are both gone."

"I've felt like an orphan for years. But enough of that." Stillman lightened the conversation with an exaggerated British accent. "My dear, I brought all of you here to help me celebrate my birthday. I'm devastated you don't remember that it's this week."

"But your birthday's in July. We spent it together in San Gimignano."

Stillman's laughter carried them as they walked through an archway and into a wide, terra-cotta-floored corridor. Stillman stopped before they reached the central garden and courtyard and grabbed her arm. He leaned in toward her and whispered as if he had a secret to share. "I fibbed in San Gimignano. Part of my failed seduction attempt. My birthday's really this week."

She giggled. "And why should I believe that it's this week?"

With a laugh, he wrapped his arm around her waist, propelling her onto a garden path that led to a cluster of round, wrought-iron breakfast tables. "Because if it's my birthday, I can get you to kiss me again."

Bella grinned at him. OK, she thought. You want to play kissy-face around Phillip? Fine with me. Somewhere during this flirty week, though, you'll discover that I won't reject you this time. And I will get you to love me again.

"Bella, Bella." Rune's voice rang out over the background of Andrea Bocelli singing "Immenso". "I've got room here." He patted his thighs and laughed. "How about a lap dance?"

"You should be so lucky." Stillman answered for her.

"What's this about Bella giving lap dances?" Phillip's dry voice came from behind her.

Bella turned to Phillip. "Do you always sneak up on people?"

As he smiled, wrinkles appeared at the corners of Phillip's eyes. "I can't seem to let go of the view of Florence from the outer garden paths. It's hypnotic." He crossed by her and extended a rigid hand to Stillman. In a flat voice, he said, "Thank you again for the reunion. Great idea."

Bella wondered how long Phillip had lived without passion.

Stillman turned to the group by the tables. "I'm going to dig into that plate of meats," he said, motioning to the salumi, prosciutto, and mortadella, "have a doppio espresso, and I'll be ready for the day." Without even looking back, he said, "Bella, have at it, princess, or there won't be anything left." He layered thinly sliced meats onto his plate. "Anyone seen Meghan this morning?"

"I've been down here since seven-thirty," Hope said, "and I haven't seen her."

Lee pushed up from the table. "I'll go knock on her door. Maybe she slept in." Without a glance at any of them, he slipped into the building and disappeared.

"Uh-*hmm*." Hope's voice raised on the second syllable.

Bella remembered the connection between Lee and Meghan during that summer. She wondered whether their love affair had continued after Italy or ended, as Meghan had claimed, on that last day. Bella layered her plate with three paper-thin slices of the cured meats.

"Today we head into Florence for a special treat and a little touring," Stillman said after downing his breakfast with an obvious appetite. "A small touring van will ferry five of the group down. I'll join you in a second car, since our large van isn't here today. Unfortunately, one of you will need to ride with me. Logistics, I'm afraid."

Bella spoke quickly. "I'll ride with you, Stillman."

Stillman beamed at her. "*Grazie.*"

"*Prego.*" She answered with a soft voice.

Phillip leaned in toward her. "Did Stillman take you on a private tour of the estate this morning?"

Phillip's query felt like an accusation. Damn it. How dare he? Her relationship with Stillman wasn't his business. He had given up that right a long time ago.

33

While they rode into the city, Stillman chatted about the changes in Florence over the previous thirty years. Television accounts of ongoing art restorations following the Arno's 1966 flood—a yawn-provoking topic of discussion in every gallery they had visited during their long-ago summer—still continued. Full of energy, he described how the Mafiosi still popped up across Italy, creating havoc and leaving unsolved crimes in their wake.

Stillman boasted about visiting Florence many times since their last weekend together. He told her that his favorite moments of those vacations were when he explored the surprising villages south of Florence. One small hill town, he told her with a secretive smile, was the inspiration for the reunion.

His reference to the hill towns reminded Bella about that infamous weekend with Phillip in Castellina-in-Chianti. A Tuscan village had set her life on a brand-new course thirty years ago. Would Stillman's inspiration in a hill town now change her life as dramatically?

Bella could see acres of gardens scrolling past her window. Their car slowed down. They drove down a driveway shaded with a row of cypress trees and stopped beside a villa. She rested her hand on Stillman's forearm. "I'd like to visit some of your favorite hill towns during this trip. After all, it sounds like I have them to thank for bringing you back into my life."

"We'll see," Stillman said. "I'll have to decide if I want to share them with anyone."

That was a kick to Bella's stomach. She had thought she was making headway and returning to Stillman's good graces, but his comment indicated the opposite. Getting him to love her again might be more of a challenge than she had anticipated.

"When do you plan to tell everyone about David?" Stillman's face was expressionless.

Sharing that part of her history thrilled and terrified her. She had dreamed of flinging barbed words at Phillip, telling him exactly what he had given up when he ditched her. He had abandoned not only her love, but also his son. The problem was that when that happened, Stillman would know the truth about David, too. Once Stillman knew the secret she had hidden from everyone, that Phillip had fathered her son, could he accept David?

Bella tagged with Meghan through their private tour of a small but storied non-public garden inside Florence's walls. As they walked, Meghan chatted in wonder about the magnificence of the garden.

Giacomo had driven the van carrying the rest of the group. The wiry Italian's arms gestured nonstop as he spoke. His tailored slacks moved fluidly with him, exposing hand-made leather loafers when he walked and eliciting an admiring, and perhaps envious, muttered comment from Rune. Bella let Giacomo's explanation of the gardens melt into background music.

Her mind zigzagged with indecision. When, and how, should she disclose that Phillip had fathered her son? Possible scenarios raced through her mind. It was impossible to pay attention to their guide, as he rambled on about the scattered sculptures and manicured botanicals. The group paused in front of a giant ginkgo biloba, which dwarfed the garden's gazebo. The tree's magnificent height contrasted with the sparse branches along its trunk.

Meghan's cold fingers on Bella's elbow pulled her to the back of the cluster of people. She whispered in Bella's ear. "Are you all right?"

Bella shook off the question. "Probably jet-lagged."

Meghan reached into the hemp bag that hung from her shoulder and extracted a slim bottle of water. "Drink more water." Her hand slid into the bag again. This time she produced a bottle of pills. She tapped a couple into Bella's hand. "They're herbal. No side effects. Aid with digestion, travel stomach, bloating, and sleep."

Bella gazed at Meghan. Her skin, while pale, did appear rested. But other than for her alert eyes, Meghan, in a new unbleached T-shirt and cotton skirt, didn't broadcast a picture of health.

Bella returned the pills. "Water, yes, pills, no."

The group moved ahead. Meghan charged forward to hear the explanations.

Bella felt Stillman's eyes on her. Her feet propelled her forward with the rest of the group. Stillman's surprising reticence at the end of their ride together replayed in her head. How would he react when he learned about David?

34

To Bella's relief, Meghan took Bella's place in Stillman's car when they left the garden. The tightrope of flirting with Stillman to return to his good graces and, at the same time, wanting to blast Phillip had twisted Bella's stomach into a knot.

They would all soon, perhaps today, talk about the years between college and the present—their work and families. Contemplating the onslaught of questions that would occur after she told them all that she had a son terrified Bella.

Damn it, even if it cost her Stillman, Bella was tired of hiding her past. If Stillman couldn't deal with it, then so be it. Yes, she loved him and was tired of being alone. But she was almost fifty, a time for action. A second chance at life. What had been her biggest complaint about Phillip? His lying to her. Going down the path of dishonesty was not an option for Bella. On life's chessboard, it was her move. But when? Her timing had to be perfect.

They drove across the Arno, up Via Cavour, and through the Piazza San Marco. Bella's eyes found no joy in these landmarks. She fought to steady her breathing and, with it, her anxiety.

Their drivers let them out a few blocks beyond the *Galleria dell'Accademia.* Giacomo waltzed them past the masses of tourists standing in clumps along the sidewalk adjacent to the museum. Fiats and Vespas breezed by them, oblivious to the pedestrians who spilled onto the street as if they were last week's garbage.

Kiosks of T-shirts, aprons, and boxer shorts featuring the lower anatomy of Michelangelo's famous statue cluttered the sidewalk along the queue. American tourists in shorts, crew socks, and tennis shoes snapped up the tacky souvenirs, their voices tittered in a suffocating muddle of sound. Tour groups clustered, perspiring and weary, at the entrance. Each set of bobbing heads huddled behind a guide, who spouted out instructions.

Giacomo's voice competed with the background singsong of several foreign languages spoken simultaneously. Other guides held props—a red umbrella, an enormous sunflower, a sign, or even a striped clown hat perched on a stick. Bella silently thanked Giacomo for saving them from a similar fate, although she couldn't imagine Rune tolerating any such humiliation.

They bypassed the long line of tourists waiting to buy tickets. Giacomo's flirtatious banter with the woman guarding the door then moved them ahead of the other ticket holders. No queue for them, just a quick VIP saunter into the museum. Bella heard Rune emit a soft hoot of delight. Once inside, they needed no instruction from Giacomo, who handed them each a guidebook. Without hesitation, they bolted for *David.*

Bella stopped twenty feet short of the base. She wanted to take in the sensuality of the whole sculpture—alone. Perhaps the statue's quiet strength could rein in her emotions. This marble *David* calmed her. The statue stopped her breath with its beauty.

During the ride here, Giacomo had hinted that controversy surrounded the restoration performed prior to his 500th birthday. It was hard to remember exactly what he had looked like thirty years before, but removing all those years of grime from his surface did add brilliance to his finish. Bella heard Rune up ahead.

"My God, they did clean up his act." Rune circled the statue. He tromped around the nearly fourteen-foot piece as if it were a prop in a movie. "To my mind, this is a great example of edgy art."

"Because he carved a massive sculpture from what others had discarded?" Hope asked.

"Because he rejected the effeminate style," Rune said, consulting his guidebook, "of Verrocchio's and Donatello's *Davids*. No secret about Donatello's proclivities, by the way. Their art was more the style of the day. But hey, Michelangelo carved a guy who actually could slay a giant."

Lee stood riveted in front of *David*, his head tilted back. "Michelangelo certainly did his anatomical homework. I have a much better appreciation of that now, after med school." He took two steps back. His head cocked to one side. His voice softened. "Sculpture has been my one enduring love."

Behind her, Bella felt a presence.

"I like him better without the crowd," Phillip said in a low voice, so that only she would hear.

She didn't turn around. "So do I," she said.

Phillip rested his hand on her shoulder. With effort, she fought the urge to step away from his touch. He traced her arm down to the tips of her fingers, sending a warm torrent rushing down her spine and over her cheeks. He quickly squeezed her hand and then let it go. Good thing—two more seconds of him touching her and Bella would have jerked away.

Happy that he couldn't see her face, she forced herself to breathe slowly and act normally, as if it had been Lee or Rune who had touched her.

Meghan turned back and gestured for them to come closer. Thankful for the excuse to escape from Phillip, Bella said, "Let's get a better look." She raised her voice loud enough for the others to hear. "Giacomo, tell us about that restoration controversy you mentioned in the car."

Stillman raised a silent eyebrow at Bella when she and Phillip moved to join the group's semicircle in front of the famous statue. She felt her cheeks flush with heat. Damn it—that flush made her look as if she were a schoolgirl caught kissing by the lockers.

After they raced through the Galleria finding the highlights of the museum, they headed for a tiny ristorante that sat in the shadow of the Duomo. The packs of Americans—

who always lunched at noon—had come and gone. The tiny space held no more than a dozen red-cloaked tables under the awning and another dozen inside.

Jet lag hit Bella, and she sank onto a vinyl-padded metal chair with relief. A twenty-something, longhaired Italian beauty passed out menus, took beverage orders, and then retreated into the dark recesses of the restaurant.

Meghan straightened in her chair and opened her menu. "We should order when she comes back. I think they want to close soon for the afternoon."

Lee opened his menu. A sheen of perspiration capped his forehead. He sighed. "What's on tap for the afternoon? The Duomo is open, as is the Uffizi, although we may want a day for that. If we go separate directions, I'll visit the curator of a Leonardo da Vinci treasure discovered here in Florence. I'm hoping to see it while we're here, and we've been exchanging e-mails."

"Not me." Rune stretched his arms over his head. "I've done my museum deal for the day. Hell, I'm done for the week. I want to check out the enotecas. I want wine, a place to sit," he grinned, "and, if I'm lucky, interaction with the natives."

"Shopping and exploring," Hope said. Her brow furrowed with determination. "The Uffizi is too much for today. I say we browse artisan streets and shop in places that don't close for the afternoon."

"I'll shop with you, if you want company," Bella said.

"You'd come with me?" Hope's face reminded Bella of a puppy craving affection.

"I'd love to. Meghan, want to join us in our quest for merchants who are open?"

Meghan shook her head. "No, I think I'll find steps somewhere and relax. People-watch."

Rune chuckled. "Pigeon-watch, you mean."

Their waitress appeared at the table. She set down liter bottles of aqua naturale and glasses and opened the two bottles of Chianti Riserva that Rune had ordered.

"*Grazie.*" Bella smiled at the woman.

"*Prego.*" The woman kept her head lowered, attentive to her task.

"We lived in Firenze thirty years ago," Hope said to their waitress. "A man named Pino worked in this restaurant then. Do you know him?"

Their waitress stopped filling glasses and straightened. She held the wine bottle in one palm. "Pino? He's my uncle. He's here every night, passing out limoncello and our own liquor made with bay leaves. He is the boss now. Did you know him well?"

"I loved that bay leaf liquor." Meghan smiled at the younger woman. "We knew him well enough that even though we were students, Pino gave us as much of the liquors as we wanted, on the house."

Hope snorted. "We paid for it with our lasagna consumption."

"Then you should come see him. We are closed Monday. Come any other night."

"Your English is very good," Lee said.

"Here," the woman gestured at the Duomo, "it has to be." She shrugged. "English, French, German. Let me put your order in. My father, the chef, gets cranky if he doesn't get to close on time."

Giacomo leaned forward to scan his charges. He smiled at Hope. "In the direction of the Uffizi and Ponte Vecchio, I suggest Ciancibella for handmade jewelry and Bella Arte for beautiful handmade objects, the Ponte Vecchio itself for gold, of course, and Tesoro, across the river on Borgo San Jacopo. This tiny shop carries some of the most beautiful jewels in the city. I will check their store hours." His index finger tapped the cellphone resting under his palm.

Hope grinned. "No need. Just give me directions and I'm ready to wander. I can window shop if all else fails. Trust me," she said, patting her large leather bag, "I've got my husband's money to spend, and I plan on doing just that. I'll find shops open." She winked at Bella.

"For you," Giacomo said to Rune, "there is a reasonable enoteca near where we were earlier, Enoteca Tre, on Via degli Alfani. I'll give you directions after lunch."

The wine relaxed Bella. A warm haze settled over the table.

Citing a piece they saw this morning, Lee launched into a description of the restoration processes used on paintings and marble. Only Meghan and Giacomo appeared to be listening.

Underneath Lee's voice, Bella heard the sounds of the piazza—voices in passionate conversation, church bells, scooters, and cars. The fragrant mingling smells of meat, tomato, garlic, and baked cheese brought her focus back and made Bella realize she was hungry. The young waitress placed plain white pasta bowls in front of them all except Meghan, whose lunch was a small vegetable salad.

Bella savored the delicate noodles of her pappardelle with rabbit and porcini. "I tried to cook rabbit at home. Deboning it was more of a challenge than I imagined. And mine never tasted like this." She closed her eyes on the next bite. It melted over her tongue.

Murmurs of delight rounded the table.

Meghan picked at her salad, dressed with only vinegar and oil. Her words burst out over the table, too loud for the moment. "After Karen's daughter was killed in a car accident, I turned vegan. First I lost Karen, then her daughter. I decided to do all I could to be healthy."

Rune paused with his fork halfway to his mouth. "I don't call that healthy, sweetheart."

Bella shot Rune her parent "disapproval" glare.

He responded by topping off Bella's wineglass. "You need to loosen up. More of this will help."

Bella pushed her wineglass away. She looked at Meghan. "Is it difficult finding adequate protein?"

Before Meghan could answer, Giacomo raised one hand in the air in front of him, smiled, and nodded. "With your permission, Signora Meghan, I have a place to show you after lunch. I think, perhaps, you would enjoy this shop very much."

Meghan shook her head. "No. No, thank you. I'm tired. Sitting and watching people. That's what I'll do."

"You're tired because you don't fuel the engine." Rune gestured to Meghan's salad. "Rabbit food sucks."

Hope swatted Rune's shoulder with the back of her hand.

"No problem." Giacomo smiled at Meghan. "I'll keep you company, then." Meghan lowered her head. She stirred her salad with her fork.

Bella ate too much—over half her entrée, far more than normal. She glanced at the other bowls. Everyone but Meghan had demolished lunch. Stillman met Bella's eyes, lifted his wineglass by the stem, and sipped the last swallow of his Chianti.

Rune reached for the bottle to refill Phillip's glass, but Phillip shook his head. "No thanks. One of the boards I'm on, dealing with therapeutic sports for the disabled, meets today, so I'll phone into it. I would duck out if it was business-related—especially now—but this is one board I never miss. I need to prepare this afternoon, so I'll head back now. I apologize in advance, Stillman, but I may miss dinner, too, depending on how long the meeting goes."

Bella remembered that Phillip had told her about his disabled sister, who had died at a young age. He had carried a picture of her in his wallet. No doubt, his sister was the reason he was so dedicated to this organization. So the man had a heart after all.

Stillman nodded at Giacomo. "You'll arrange a car to drive Phillip back to the palazzo, correct?"

Giacomo nodded quickly.

"Good," Stillman said. "I'll join you, Rune, at Enoteca Tre. I've read great reviews about the place but haven't had a chance to check it out myself."

The knot in Bella's stomach had returned. Her deception clawed at her. There would be no chance to confront Phillip today, which meant she couldn't bring up David to Stillman or anybody else. Bella felt as if a major league pitcher had just fired a fastball into her chest.

35

At nine o'clock that evening, Bella stepped inside the ristorante. The low, arched ceilings made it feel like a cave. The pale colors of the rough plastered walls hinted at long-ago frescos whitewashed by well-meaning owners. Sixteen white-cloth-covered tables filled the room with Manhattan bistro proximity.

Lee paced around the center table, his hands clasped behind his back. A heap of fruits and vegetables covered the table with no apparent design. "Arcimboldo's *Summer*, don't you think?"

"Archee what?" Rune asked.

"Exactly my thought, Rune." Stillman walked to the tables pushed together to accommodate their group. "The art is in the preparation of the food, not the garden."

"It's a painting." Lee claimed a chair on the side opposite Stillman. "He created faces out of clustered produce."

Bella slipped into a chair next to Stillman. In her peripheral vision, she saw Lee beckon for Meghan to sit next to him, which sent a pink flush up Meghan's cosmetic-free cheeks. Rune and Hope entered the room and slid into the open seats next to their friends.

Elderly waiters appeared from the kitchen carrying trays with Prosecco and champagne glasses. Again, Meghan declined the bubbly.

"Is Phillip coming?" Rune asked.

Stillman looked at his watch. "I suspect not. He'll miss a great evening." He nodded to Bella.

Rune lifted his glass, making a show of inspecting the color. "This looks richer than what we had the first night." His voice dropped to a stage whisper. "Or did it just gather dust in the cellar for a few more years?"

"And when did you become a master sommelier?" Bella's words sounded harsh, even to her. "Oops. Sorry how that came out."

Rune winked at Bella. "You're mighty quick to defend our host."

Stillman raised his Prosecco, all smiles and warmth. "To our long overdue reunion." His eyes shot to Bella's, as if insinuating that he spoke only to her.

Bella tipped her glass against Stillman's. She felt Rune's eyes on her. She didn't care. She had a history—a recent history—with their host. The night before, with the Tuscan stars winking at her, she had drifted to sleep remembering Stillman's passionate lovemaking during their last weekend together.

Platters of crusty Tuscan bread spread with a thick brown paste appeared before them.

The most weathered of their waiters, no doubt the owner, announced the appetizer.

"Wild hare crostini," Bella interpreted. "It smells heavenly. Forest meat of the season."

The proud gentleman motioned for them to eat. "*Cioccolato*." His kissed his fingertips.

Hope claimed one for her plate and chuckled. "Even I can translate that. Meat mixed with chocolate—now that's my kind of appetizer." She eyed the platter and waited for it to circle the table. When it returned to her, she snatched a second piece.

Bella's sympathies went to Meghan, steadfast in her refusal of meat.

As if sensing Bella's thoughts, Meghan smiled at her and mouthed her words: "It's OK."

Bella turned her head. She couldn't look at Meghan when she bit into the crostini. She closed her eyes and savored the delicate yet decadent flavor. The pâté melted on her tongue, and the toasted crunch of the bread provided a perfect texture contrast. And the hint of chocolate? Definitely an undertone that added complexity. Poor Meghan, she had no clue what she was missing.

Giacomo bounded into the ristorante, flustered and flushed. He rushed to Stillman's side. While he whispered to Stillman, one of Giacomo's hands gestured behind his back. Stillman nodded several times in the brief exchange.

Giacomo stood and spoke in hushed tones to the waiters. He grabbed a chair from another table and wedged it between Meghan and Lee.

Lee scowled.

Grinning, Giacomo sat down and twisted on the chair to face Meghan.

The wait staff swooped away the appetizer plates and, moments later, slid small bowls of steaming ribolitta, a bread, bean and vegetable soup, in front of each of them.

"Can I get it without the bread?" Meghan asked.

"Oh, signora," Giacomo said, patting Meghan's arm, "not to worry. The bread in this soup is perfect for your vee-gan diet."

Lee spoke in a soft, authoritative tone. "You only had that bit of fruit from the market after lunch. Traveling, with exposure to unfamiliar germs, is an undetonated bomb. You have to eat if you want to stay healthy."

Meghan shook her head. "Do they have minestrone?"

Giacomo conferred with a waiter in Italian. He patted Meghan's arm. "No, no, signora, only this soup today. Please, you should try it." He looked sideways at Lee. "It is very nourishing."

Bella raised a spoonful of the thick soup to her mouth—delicious and hearty. If she ate more than a spoonful or two, she'd be done for the night. Across the table, Meghan filled her spoon but avoided any morsel of bread.

With the spoon halfway to her mouth, Meghan paused and looked at Giacomo. "What about meat? In the broth?"

Giacomo's hands flew in front of him in denial. "No, no. No meat. Just vegetables." As Meghan put her spoon into her mouth, Giacomo's eyes shot over to Bella. The ferocity in his eyes silenced any rebuttal she might have uttered about the contents of the ribolitta.

Meghan dipped her spoon into the bowl again, this time without hesitation. She smiled at Giacomo. "Thank you for the delicious vegetable soup."

Bella tasted the soup again. The spicy smokiness of pancetta added complexity that could never have come from vegetables alone. She smiled at Giacomo and affirmed their conspiracy. She agreed with Lee about Meghan's diet.

Hope dug into her soup, her bowl already nearly empty. "Best damn vegetable soup I've ever had."

Lee entertained the table with details of his afternoon meeting with the curator he'd mentioned. A forgotten workshop of Leonardo da Vinci had been discovered in the Santissima Annunziata convent. Long ago, the convent had housed artists in a wing that eventually was split by a wall that sealed the secrets behind it. Lee was more animated than Bella had ever seen him.

While Lee spoke of one of the five hundred-year-old frescos, which contained a white silhouette similar to da Vinci's Archangel Gabriel, Bella felt Stillman's eyes on her. She met his gaze.

A Cheshire cat smile slid over his face. He leaned toward her and whispered in her ear. "Too bad. Phillip is missing not only a gourmet meal, but another shot at seducing you."

She whipped around to look at him. Seduce me, she thought? Phillip had been mildly apologetic, the jerk, but that was the extent of it. Stillman was toying with her, baiting her. Why? She had a sinking feeling in her stomach. Was it love for her or the old competition with Phillip that motivated Stillman now?

Before she could respond, Stillman turned to Lee and quizzed him on some aspect of the da Vinci find, as if he had been listening to Lee the entire time.

Bella picked at her food, her appetite lost. Phillip never joined them for dinner. Her head throbbed. She didn't want to believe it but had to wonder if Stillman was using her.

The table conversations had elevated in volume with the wine consumption. Stillman, Meghan, and Hope discussed the lack of support for youth interested in the arts and contrasted life today with the Renaissance period. Rune and Lee debated whether a film treatment could be developed around the discovery of lost artistic treasures in Italy. She felt as if she were in a *Peanuts* movie with the adults' nonsensical "blah blah blah" suffocating her.

Bella pushed the chicken around her plate with a fork and lectured herself. Stillman could play master of ceremonies all he wanted, directing when they shared information about their jobs and families. It didn't matter. Bella was going to control her own timing.

She needed to catch Phillip alone and have the conversation she swore she'd never have—revealing to him that he has a son. Then, she'd tell everyone else about David. After that, it was likely that neither Phillip nor Stillman would have anything to do with her. Passionate memories may have driven her dreams the night before, but right now, rekindling a love affair while here in Italy seemed as far away as her days with David when he was a toddler.

Beautiful, warbling laughter caught Bella's attention. Following the sound, she saw that it was Meghan, her cheeks flushing as she laughed. One of Giacomo's palms rested on Meghan's bare forearm, and the other opened upward beside a plate of arugula, pomegranate seeds, and slivers of cantaloupe.

"Fruits and vegetables, no?" Giacomo's wide grin broadcast his joy at pleasing the strange American.

"*Grazie.*"

Giacomo leaned into Meghan, as if sharing a secret. "*Prego.*"

Loneliness swept over Bella. A steady, drought-driven Oklahoma wind engulfed her. Other than her friend and editor, Edie—who threatened to retire and move to Florida every other day—and David—far away on another continent—she had no one.

36

A misty shroud draped the estate at breakfast. Bella joined the others in the courtyard, where they huddled over morning espresso.

Stillman clapped his hands to silence the morning chatter. He explained that he had details to arrange while they embarked on a scavenger hunt in Florence. He waved off their questions with a smile. "I'll be there in time to judge the winner."

Maybe she could get Phillip alone, Bella thought, since Stillman wouldn't be around.

"Giacomo will explain when he drops you off. Our van has arrived, so you'll go in that today. It's out front now. You have a strict timetable and rules for the hunt." Stillman's eyes sparked with delight. "I'll meet you tonight at eight in front of the Duomo. Good luck and be safe. And no cheating."

On the drive into the city, Bella heard her voice—shrill to her own ears—laugh at Rune's monologue of jokes over the possible nature of the scavenger hunt. Behind her, Phillip chatted with Lee in the back seat as if they were regular golfing partners. Getting him alone, she realized, might be a challenge.

Giacomo headed toward the train station, *Stazione di Santa Maria Novella.* Cars, taxis, and Vespas jockeyed for position in a crazed frenzy around them. Giacomo slammed on the brakes to avoid a car that darted in front of the van in a roundabout. When the vehicle cleared the path and exited the traffic circle, Giacomo's foot slammed to the floorboard and the van lurched forward.

At the next intersection, Giacomo copied the car's maneuver and changed lanes without a turn signal, causing a taxi driver to staccato-punch his horn at them. With each near collision and swerve of the van, Bella heard gasps of alarm from Hope and Meghan.

The van entered the next roundabout. At the second entrance, two side-by-side Vespas cut into the flow and motored across both lanes of the traffic circle without a pause or glance in their direction. Giacomo swerved right to avoid the scooters. Bella saw how close the van came to one of them and she clutched her seatbelt. Giacomo ceased the litany of rapid-fire Italian that he was speaking into his cellphone headset, leaned his head out the window, and shouted a string of obscenities at the clueless drivers.

"Holy shit," Rune said. "There must be some real jack in auto insurance here. What's the accident rate in a city like Florence?"

"Not many accidents," Giacomo said, "but when they happen …" He clucked his tongue and shook his head.

Across from the train station, a grassy piazza housed two marble obelisks anchored on turtles. Beyond the piazza, they could see Alberti's façade for the church of Santa Maria Novella.

"Many tourists do not respect our monuments." Giacomo glanced over his shoulder. "One time, not so long ago, tourists used a fountain near Santa Maria Novella for their washing of clothes."

"Wish I'd seen that," Hope said.

"What do you say ... clothes soap?"

"Detergent?" Meghan said.

"Yes. Detergent. They poured detergent into the fountain." His right hand arced in the air. "Bubbles everywhere."

Bella watched as Rune howled with laughter and recorded the story in his smartphone. A future scene in some movie, no doubt.

Giacomo gestured to the right and dropped his voice. "You do not want to venture through those dismal streets. They are known for their prostitutes."

"Maybe I'll come check it out later," Rune said.

"Do you want to get a case of the cooties?" Hope asked.

Lee chuckled.

Giacomo cranked the steering wheel and made a U-turn. The careening motion rocked Bella forward and her shoulder belt smashed her chest. Another abrupt turn, this time down a narrow side street. The van jerked to a stop by a row of slender shops.

"Aha." Giacomo seemed satisfied at their destination. He vaulted out of the van and held open the door for the group. He pointed to an ancient wooden door. "Before the hunt, we stop here." He clasped Meghan's elbow. "Beautiful lady, I go with you."

Meghan nodded, but she did not speak.

Bella pretended to study the marker for the store, the *Officina Profumo Farmaceutica di Santa Maria Novella,* so she could eavesdrop. No window advertised the store's wares, only the simple sign and ancient door.

"A pharmacy?" Meghan said.

"It is a special treat for you." Giacomo's voice rose. "This, beautiful lady, is very famous. One of the world's oldest, and most honored, pharmacies."

His arm cradled the back of Meghan's waist, and they moved side by side toward the door. "Dominican friars first began creating their potions in 1221, but the farmacia officially opened in 1612. In the eighteenth century," he added, opening the door for the two women, "these special potions were traded as far away as China."

"Their formulas must be remarkable." Meghan smiled at Giacomo.

Bella closed her eyes. The scent of flowers and herbs tickled her nose and enveloped her with a foreign smell.

A golden-frescoed ceiling reigned above antique wooden display cabinets filled with bottles and packets of herbal concoctions. "What do they use to create that unique smell?" Meghan's head twisted to survey the room.

Giacomo urged Meghan forward, his arm returning to its perch around her tiny waist. Although slight of frame himself, Giacomo's muscular forearm could easily span Meghan's back. "The smell is from the best herbs and flowers picked from the hills around Florence, then mixed and dried in terra-cotta vessels. This method and the formulas, they are the same as those developed by the friars and used through the centuries."

They moved in front of a display of soaps in a cabinet, individually wrapped in white paper printed with gold letters and designs. "Each is hand-wrapped. They are only sold after a sixty-day aging." Giacomo touched Meghan's arm. "Perhaps you would like some eau de cologne?"

"No, thank you," Meghan said. "I don't like the chemicals in beauty products."

Giacomo moved in front of Meghan. He stroked her shoulders with his hands. Giacomo glanced at Bella. "How do you say it? From nature?"

"All natural products?" Bella guessed at the phrase he wanted.

Giacomo nodded. "All natural products. No chemicals, not here. The eau de cologne was first brought to Paris by Caterina de' Medici, developed for her in 1500."

He abandoned the women and rushed to a tiny man who was straightening the wares in a cabinet across the room from them. Even though he spoke in a whisper, his words echoed in the cavernous room. In response to his request, the elderly shop clerk shuffled to an adjacent cabinet. The upper shelves extended far above the clerk's head. He returned to the group of shoppers holding a small bottle with a handwritten label.

"What's that?" Lee had joined them. He sidled in next to Meghan.

"Cologne." Meghan smiled at Giacomo.

"All natural." Giacomo puffed out his chest.

Bella saw Lee's shoulders stiffen under his pressed cotton shirt.

Lee placed his fingertips against the small of Meghan's back. "Shall we see what it smells like?"

Meghan looked to Giacomo. "May we open it?"

Giacomo took Meghan's hand and pulled her along with him to the counter-height, glass-topped wooden cabinet. He opened the fragrance, and his free hand held her chin as he raised the bottle to her nose.

Bella tilted her head and watched Lee's reaction to this. His left cheek flexed, just once. Quite the drama unfolding here. Lee hadn't forgotten Meghan through the years. No, he hadn't. His attraction to Meghan was very, very clear to Bella.

"You're missing the other rooms, Bella." Phillip stood in an arched doorway; one hand leaned against the wood casing.

Bella crossed the smooth marble inlaid floor to Phillip, imagining how she'd like to tear into him. But she couldn't. Not here. It was too public. But if she brushed him off now, she thought, he might not give her a chance to be alone with him. "The architecture is remarkable."

Phillip led her into a green hall, where they paused to admire paintings in gilded frames. Majolica chemist jars lined the shelves, each one more splendid than the next. He nudged her on. They entered the old spice shop. Burnished walnut shelves rose to the ceiling and ended in a line of delicate carved wood. Above, frescoes covered the vaulted ceiling, which was adorned in pink, ivory, gold, and even purple.

"It's magic." Bella whispered the words to herself. She tilted her neck back to study the handiwork above. Noblemen had commissioned this, no doubt. For the sake of the artistry, she wondered, or as a testament to themselves? She studied each section of the ceiling in turn, allowing herself to soak in the rare beauty above.

Phillip cleared his throat.

She turned to him. A hot flash bolted across her face and chest. Crap, why now? Bella hoped he wouldn't notice her flush. "I love it."

Phillip smiled. "I knew you would."

"Thank you—for sharing this."

Silence. He stood there looking at her with that stupid smile on his face.

Bella felt as though she were trapped in a naked dream.

"We used to be close." Phillip looked down for a moment, and then his eyes lifted to hers. "I wondered if we might be able to be friends again."

Friends? Bella thought. He bloody wants to be my friend after what he did to me?

"What's in here?" Rune bounced into the room with Hope by his side.

"There's incredible beauty here," Phillip said. He gestured to the ceiling, but his eyes remained locked on Bella.

37

Bella's stomach churned. She broke Phillip's gaze and looked at the ceiling, pretending to listen as Rune and Hope discussed it.

Hands clapped together in the next room. A loud, insistent summons.

"Come, come," Giacomo said.

Another series of claps.

Bella, Phillip, Hope, and Rune returned to join the others.

"We must go outside now. Please, everyone." Giacomo glanced at his wristwatch, as if nervous about their schedule. He rushed through the rules of their scavenger hunt.

Stillman had planned a challenge for them. Each was to borrow a method of transportation and ride it to their rendezvous tonight at the Duomo. No buying or renting allowed. They, not someone else, had to drive their borrowed vehicles. The mode of transportation must have wheels and must belong to someone else. Creativity counted.

Bella stood outside the pharmacy and watched the others walk away. Meghan laughed at something Lee said.

Meghan and Lee walked away together and headed left. Giacomo stared after them, his hands on his hips.

Rune placed a bet with Hope, certain of his success in finding a more unusual vehicle. They had all seen how Hope's husband's abuse had eroded her self-confidence.

Bella had her own doubts about Hope's prospects of beating Rune. Thankfully, Bella thought, Hope had bet only a single euro. Rune and Hope walked a short distance together, and then split into different directions. Phillip strode off alone without a word to anyone.

The low-hanging mist of the morning had burned off. Bella let the warmth of the sun bathe her face. She had a day to explore Florence by herself; she might as well try to enjoy it. Bella headed toward the Arno. The shops that lined the streets between the Duomo and the Ponte Vecchio waited for her.

All the usual shops beckoned her—stationery stores with handmade papers, art galleries, leather stores with their butter-soft designs, and tiny shops with silk scarf-laden tables. Her feet drove her past each store with only a glance.

Bella realized that she couldn't shop. Not yet. The transportation challenge had awakened the competitive spirit within her. She had a mission. The hunt was on. A shocking idea rushed into her head. She did have some-thing unique to trade for her borrowed transportation. That is, if she had the courage to follow it through.

Finally, she spotted it—a bookstore. Bella stood inside the open door and looked around. Italian volumes on the first floor, English on the second. Her feet carried her with purpose through the store. To her delight, E.V. Tate action/adventure novels appeared on both floors. Her heart skipped. Bella spoke to the store manager. The woman led Bella into a back room and pointed to the telephone.

Bella waited, the handset pressed to her ear. After several transfers, Edie got on the line. Bella's words cascaded out. "Edie, I'm here in Florence, in a bookstore. It's time. You've begged me to do this for years. I'm ready. I want the world to know I'm E.V. Tate, and I want to start with a signing now in Florence."

"Why the epiphany?" Edie said. Her voice sounded curious.

"Long story. You can take me to lunch when I'm back in the city and I'll tell all." Well, maybe not everything.

"How's your nemesis?"

"What nemesis?" Bella said.

"You've disparaged the man for thirty years, ever since he chose his LA girlfriend over you. So how is he?"

"He's boring."

"Give me the dirt. All of it."

"There isn't any. We've hardly spoken. Probably because we haven't thought about each other since we split."

"Right," Edie said. "No, not at all. You haven't thought about him. And I'm Christie Brinkley."

Bella thought of the petite woman with her Katharine Hepburn hair and tailored pantsuits. She laughed. "He and I have nothing in common."

"Umm. Right." Edie sighed into the phone.

"Can we talk about my book signing?"

"If you insist."

"I need you to convince the manager—her name is Sophia and she speaks English—that I'm E.V. Tate and it's a once-in-a-lifetime opportunity to have me willing to sign books today, in her store."

"Today? Don't you want her to do some publicity so you have a good turnout?"

"It has to be today. Now."

Edie's throaty laughter filled the phone. "I've heard that at some point every author goes wacko, and now, with this phone call, I believe it."

"Edie, you know I've been wacko for years. I need this. Please?"

"Yes, of course." Edie sighed. "Put Sophia on. I want the name and phone number of the store so I can run it up a flagpole in Times Square. The reclusive E.V. Tate has been revealed, and he's a woman. This should raise your books at least two or three lines on *The New York Times* bestseller list."

Bella handed the phone to Sophia. She watched the woman bob her head as she made notes. She asked Edie a few questions to verify that the woman standing in front of her in Florence was E.V. Tate.

Sophia returned the phone to the cradle. She hugged Bella enthusiastically. Clapping her hands with excitement, she asked, "Why do you do this?"

"Keep my identity a secret?"

"No, no, come to my store and want a signing today."

Bella smiled. "Do you own a Vespa?" Before entering the bookstore, she had walked through the alley behind it and seen a Vespa chained to a rack by the back door.

Sophia nodded. "Yes. Why?"

"In exchange for the signing, I want to borrow your scooter for the evening. I'll be here later, when you reopen, and I'll sign books until nineteen-thirty. You get the world's first E.V. Tate book signing, and I have use of your Vespa for the evening. Deal?"

Sophia hugged Bella, followed with a double kiss.

Bella had never imagined that she'd do a book signing. Years ago, keeping her identity a mystery had been nothing more than the natural progression in her life of secrets.

Bella returned to the bookstore a few minutes before it reopened for the evening. As she approached, she heard the noise first. When she rounded the corner of the block, she stopped, her feet frozen to the sidewalk. A line of people, starting at the bookstore's door, snaked back to the far end of the block and disappeared around the corner. Many held books in their hands. Her books.

Sophia unlocked the door to admit Bella. "Good evening. Isn't this grand?"

Bella nodded. The thought of facing all these people terrified her. What if they were disappointed?

"Simone, my clerk, thought of having her two young brothers walk the old city with signs announcing your signing."

Bella gulped air.

"Come, come. We will have you here," Sophia said, gesturing to the back room, "and people can enter as others leave." Her eyebrows bunched together, as if she were worried. "I hope we have enough books. I brought them in from stores all over Florence. I do not wish to disappoint."

She rubbed Bella's arm with her palm. "This is so exciting for us. I telephoned your editor to tell her the wonderful news—how the queue is around the corner."

Within minutes, Bella stood in front of a rectangular table piled with stacks of her novels—Italian translations on her left and English on her right. Her copies, their pages marked with the selections she planned to read, sat on the table in front of her.

An excited buzz filled the air as a group of people filed in to sit in the two rows of folding chairs and stand in the back and sides of the room. She heard Sophia calling to the people still outside that more would be admitted when some departed.

Bella smiled and quizzed the audience as to whether they preferred English or Italian. The majority preferred English. She had come up with a logical public reason for her suddenly revealing her identity. Bella explained that as this novel had scenes in Florence, it was appropriate for her very first public appearance to be here.

She began reading the selection she had marked. Her voice cracked once or twice, and then she settled into a normal rhythm. Bella heard rustling and whispering in her audience. She glanced up, only to be met with smiles and nods. Her eyes dropped back to the book and she continued, but the whispering resumed.

Sophia stood at Bella's side. Her face, though smiling, showed concern. Sophia leaned closer to whisper. "They wish to start the signing now."

"But normally, I mean, in the States, an author will read a selection from their novel and speak about themselves or the book. Don't they want—"?

Sophia shook her head. "The signing. They are here to have their books signed and to speak to you. Many more are waiting outside for their turn."

"Oh." All they wanted was her autograph. All these years, she could have kept her identity a secret and merely hired an actor to stand in for her? Bella nodded and grinned at the crowd. Her smile still plastered on her face, she whispered through her teeth to Sophia. "Bring them on."

An hour later, Bella rubbed the lowest juncture of her thumb. She sipped water, but it didn't satisfy her dry mouth. She picked up the pen again. A cramp shot up her arm.

The line of people still snaked somewhere beyond the front door. It seemed endless. Books and more books.

She should have taken a pain reliever before she came. But how could she have known? Finally, the line of people ended. Bella stood and stretched her back. She shook her legs. Only a few copies of her novel, the Italian translation, remained.

Sophia walked the last group of customers to the door and locked it behind them. The Italian storekeeper hooted with delight. She raced back to Bella and kissed her on each cheek, thanking her for the grand success.

Humming a tune, Sophia sashayed back to the front cashier area. From a locked drawer, she extracted her shoulder bag and fished out a vehicle key. "My Vespa is parked at a rack in back of the store. It is white." Sophia extended the key to Bella.

"Will you need a ride home?"

Sophia shook her head. "Tonight I'm meeting friends to celebrate the unveiling of E.V. Tate."

Bella hugged the woman, palmed the key, and moved to the door. When she walked outside into the cool evening, a thought smashed her festive mood.

On the surface, the night had been a rousing success, but was it really? No one she cared about—David, Edie, or even Stillman—had been there to celebrate this once-in-a-lifetime moment with her. Was this a predictor of her future?

38

Hope spent the day shopping. Actually, it was more aimless wandering than anything else. Luckily for her, Charlie hadn't cut off her credit cards.

After a few hours of spending his money on items she didn't need and couldn't use, she quit buying things. It hadn't been as much fun as she had imagined. And she couldn't bear the thought of trying on clothes, not when his voice calling her "fat" still echoed in her mind. Their last argument haunted her; his words had been carved into her: "fat," "you don't have any friends," "no skills," and, worst of all, "worthless." Her eyes stung with tears she couldn't stop from falling.

Having found a quiet, tucked-away bench in a small piazza, Piazza dei Rossi, Hope sat and stared at the foldout map of Florence. She had no clue where to go next. What could *she* possibly offer someone in trade for a mode of transportation? Nothing. No skills, remember?

Hope decided to wait here, where none of her friends was likely to stumble on her, until it was time to meet at the Duomo. What would happen if she showed up on foot, rather than in something with wheels? Nothing. Not a damn thing. Her friends would pity her—they already did—and she'd pay Rune his euro. That's it. Then, the night would go on as if there hadn't ever been a hunt for transportation.

A touring van crept into the piazza where Hope sat. It stopped in the street beside a sign reading "Hotel Americano," blocking traffic behind it. The vehicle was so tall that it couldn't fit into the arched alley entrance to the hotel.

Eight women stumbled out and stood by the rear of it, no doubt waiting to claim their luggage. A thin, hard-looking Italian man, the driver, joined them at the back of the van. He opened the door and then beckoned for one woman to follow him into the hotel. The remaining women pulled the suitcases out. They looked American and wore comfortable clothing of the type one finds in travel catalogs. One by one, they carried the luggage into the hotel.

Loud voices from the direction of the hotel drew Hope's attention. The driver stomped into the street, waving his hands and cursing in Italian. The American woman who had accompanied him inside stormed out a step behind him. Her voice carried to where Hope sat. "This is abominable!" With her hands on her hips and her face red, she leaned toward the Italian and yelled louder. "We will *not* stay here. You have to fix this."

The driver yelled back. It was obvious to Hope that the man had no intention of fixing anything. He paced back and forth by the van, and the woman continued her insistent demands that he must correct the situation.

A taxi behind them started honking, since now they, as well as their vehicle, partially blocked the street's traffic. The Italian tromped over to the taxi and spoke to the cab driver. Then, to Hope's surprise, the van driver got into the taxi and left.

The American tourist ran across the piazza after the cab, pleading and swearing. The taxi didn't slow down, and soon it was too far ahead for the woman to catch it. She walked back with her head lowered. When the woman reached the stranded van, she kicked the side of it in apparent frustration.

Screw Charlie and his rants that she was worthless. Hope didn't know if she could help these women, but she had to try. She crossed the piazza and stood by the crying woman who had kicked the van. "I saw what happened. You're American, aren't you?"

The woman looked at Hope. She nodded. "The bastard stranded us because we refused to stay in this dump. We prepaid as part of our tour. He told us it was a four-star hotel."

Even from the outside of the building, Hope could tell that rating was inflated. "Tell me what happened when you went inside."

"I always go in and look at a room first. None of the places he booked us in has been four-star by my standards, but this one is awful. The room I saw was dirty and the bathrooms are down the hall. Unacceptable. I asked him to book us somewhere else, since he's our guide as well as our driver. He refused to change our reservation or give us our money back."

"Have you talked to the hotel personnel?"

"No."

Unfortunately, the group had no leverage over the hotel. These American women had been wronged, and it made Hope spitting mad. Maybe she wasn't good at sticking up for herself, but she'd go to battle for an underdog every time. "I don't know if I can help, but do you mind if I try?"

"Please," the woman said, "anything you can do, even a partial refund, would help."

Hope walked to the hotel entrance. In the minuscule lobby, a man stood behind the counter with his arms crossed. A sneer was plastered on his face. This doesn't look promising, Hope thought. The man had to know that the women wanted a change of venue. This will be a challenge.

Hope smiled at the man and approached the counter. "Good afternoon, sir."

The man stared at her.

Hope noticed the tour group's confirmation in front of him had been printed in English. Taking that as a sign that he understood some English, Hope launched into her attack, praying the women standing near her wouldn't blow her story.

"We have an issue." Hope leaned over the counter and lowered her voice, as if she had something discreet to share.

She grabbed the notepad and a pen from the counter. "One of our members has, uh, a problem. She has a very contagious foot fungus." Hope drew a foot with sores all over it and an exclamation point beside it. "And with the communal bathroom"—Hope drew a picture of a hallway with one open door and a sink inside—"I don't think you want the fungus in there." Her picture now included a circle with a slash through it, the sign for "no" or "do not enter," over the bathroom.

Hope looked at the man and was thrilled to see a horrified expression on his face. It was all she could do to keep a straight face. She picked up the confirmation and circled the amount prepaid for their rooms, an amount likely three or four times the going rate for this hotel.

"To save you from this terrible disease entering your hotel," Hope said, "why don't you transfer these women to another hotel and forward their payment?" She tapped the circled number.

Hope dug out the brochures from her purse that she had collected during her wanderings today. One of them, she remembered, had advertisements for several hotels, all much nicer than the Hotel Americano. Hope pointed to one of the hotels she had walked past, a very respectable-looking place. "Call here."

The man looked uncertain. He glanced at the cluster of women in his lobby.

"You don't want this in your hotel." Hope pointed to her drawing of the infected foot. "Call." She pointed to her brochure.

He picked up the phone and spoke in rapid Italian. At the end of the call, he pulled a Hotel Americano check-book out and wrote a check made out to the new hotel. He offered it to Hope. "Go. Get them out of here."

Of course he spoke English, Hope thought.

Luckily for the tour group, Hope had experience driving big vehicles. One time, she'd even driven a school bus.

Hope slid in behind the wheel of the van, adjusted the mirrors, and thought, God, please guide my hands so I don't hit anything. She checked her map one more time. The maze of tiny side streets in the vicinity of the hotel left her clueless. The vehicle had a navigation system, but to Hope's eyes, it seemed far from state-of-the-art. Still, it was better than nothing. Hope entered the new hotel's address and was pleased when it plotted a route.

She turned her head to face the women seated behind her. "I say we leave this dump and go find a decent hotel. OK with you?"

The women cheered and clapped. In minutes, they started chattering, leaving Hope to both the driving and the navigating.

Hope was relieved to learn that the device gave audible directions. Negotiating the corners was a bit of a challenge, but she didn't care. These women had been abandoned by their driver, booked to stay in that dump, and overcharged. All the fury that she couldn't muster to defend herself against Charlie burned in her now. These women needed her, and she refused to let them down.

While stopped at an intersection, Hope glanced at the map displayed on the guidance screen. It showed them to be almost at their destination—a little farther straight ahead, and then a block or so to the left.

She slowed the van to a crawl as their path traveled up a steep, narrow stone street. Hope hated going uphill with a stick shift. She had bad high school memories of rolling downhill backward with a carload of hooting, cheering friends onboard while she attempted to juggle between the clutch, brake and accelerator. Today, at least, there was no one behind them on the hill. "Whew," she said in relief when they had reached the top.

At the crest of the hill, the street leveled out and three cars had been parallel-parked directly in front of Hope, two facing right and one facing left. She realized it was a "T" intersection. Sure enough, the navigation system instructed Hope to turn left. Fortunately, in this intersection, the street was wider.

Hope pulled the van forward and then backed up, so she could make the ninety-degree turn. The one-way street ahead angled steeply down, with one narrow walkway to the side and no second lane. Hope couldn't see the end of it but imagined it opened into a piazza in front of their new hotel. She cautiously steered down the narrow street. With her foot more often on the brake than the accelerator, they crept forward. The tour group had stopped talking in the "T" intersection, when Hope had backed up to make the turn.

It can't be, Hope thought. The street narrowed more. Now, the space between the van and the building to her right wasn't even wide enough for a single pedestrian, and the passageway on the left could only accommodate the width of two.

One of the women squeaked in alarm. Two men in their thirties walked side by side toward them. Leading them was a leashed greyhound that meandered side to side.

Hope stopped the van to allow them to pass safely. The closest man practically brushed the side mirror as he walked by. The hotel better be ahead, she thought. She glanced at the rear-view mirror. Holy shit! If this was the wrong street, it would be impossible to turn around, and she'd have to back uphill—with a stick shift. Hope groaned at the thought.

She turned off the engine, grabbed her brochure with the hotel's address, and got out. She jogged up to the men who had walked by and showed them the brochure. Hope pointed to the address of the ladies' hotel and then down the street that the van sat on. She asked them if the hotel was ahead.

One of the men chuckled. The other shook his head. He turned and faced the spot where Hope had made the last left-hand turn, opposite to the direction that she was now piloting the van. He gestured straight, then left and up the hill.

Wrong, she thought. There was no road that went up the hill from the "T" intersection, only right or left. Should she have taken a right instead of a left at the crest of the hill?

Hope tramped back to the van and then walked beyond it. Maybe, she thought, he was sending her in the wrong direction as a sick joke. She decided to walk farther down the street and, hopefully, find the hotel, or at least a sign for it, ahead.

What Hope found made her heart sink. No hotel. No sign for the hotel. Only a dead end.

She drew a deep breath. These women depended on her. She had no choice. She would back that van uphill.

When she reached it, she asked for one calm volunteer. Emphasis on "calm," Hope thought. The woman who had gone to inspect their hotel rooms before check-in raised her hand. Hope explained what she needed. The woman's job was to walk backward and direct from the uphill position, pointing to the right or left, to keep Hope from clipping one of the stone buildings that loomed on each side.

Hope knew how to back up a vehicle. But this was uphill, with a stick shift, and in quarters so tight one could practically touch the buildings on each side.

Hope instructed all of the other women to be quiet. The last thing she needed was a chorus of instructions. "Ready?" she asked the woman who stood behind the van.

"You're a little to the right," the woman said. "Go a tad this way." She gestured with her arm to the left as if she were a traffic cop.

Hope knew that her direction changes had to be in inches, not feet. I hope there's insurance on this sucker, she thought. She put the van in reverse, moved her foot from the brake to the accelerator and eased it down while letting the clutch up, until the engine caught and propelled the van backward. Thankfully, they rolled downhill only a short distance before the engine caught, and there was nothing in front of them. Hope bit her bottom lip and focused on the woman behind her.

"Straight. Right. More right. Too much—stop! Left now."

And so Hope edged that van, inch by inch, uphill. Finally, she reached the "T."

The two men with the dog whom she had asked for directions? They stood at the top of that cursed alley and had been watching her back uphill. Laughing, no doubt, at the crazy Americans.

Hope was shaking. She pulled the van off to the side as much as possible and turned off the engine. The ladies in the tour group clapped and cheered.

"How about we look for the hotel on foot?" Hope asked. She was met with whole-hearted concurrence from the group.

An elderly Italian woman entered the intersection on foot. Hope went over and asked directions, pointing to her brochure. The woman spoke no English but pointed up the hill. Looking more carefully, Hope realized there was a footpath that snaked up the hill from where she had parked. Their hotel must be at the top. Hope helped the women get their luggage out of the van. She sized up the group and then picked up the suitcases for the oldest two women. Together, they trudged up the path.

Embarrassment swept over Hope when they reached the hotel. A wide, two-way street ran by it. The street she should have found. Breathless from carrying the suitcases,

Hope started to apologize to the women.

"Are you kidding?" one asked.

"You saved us," another said.

"You're our hero."

From the looks on their faces, Hope believed them. She went inside with them and verified that the new hotel would honor the check from the Hotel Americano and the women's rooms were waiting for them.

A gold clock in the shape of the sun hung over the reception desk. It was almost time for her rendezvous at the Duomo. Hope had two choices. Show up without a vehicle, or take the van.

39

Bella leaned with the Vespa as it rounded the street corners. She dodged pedestrians who lingered on the narrow streets. She pursed her lips and chewed on the foul air of loneliness. She knew she was feeling sorry for herself but couldn't seem to break out of it.

Bella recognized the shops she passed. The Duomo emerged in the gap of converging streets. Bella throttled down the Vespa. People swarmed the sidewalks and streets for the ritual nighttime stroll. Her pace slowed to a crawl.

An overweight man in plaid orange-and-brown shorts and a white stretched-out T-shirt stepped in front of Bella. She braked. She lurched forward on the seat. Bella felt the scooter's weight shift to the right. Instinctively, she planted a foot on the street to steady herself. A car honked behind her. Bella clenched her hands on the scooter grips and glared at the oaf who blocked her path.

"Bella." She heard Lee's voice.

Where was he? A feeble horn tooted to her right. Bella whipped her neck around and tried to pick him out of the crowd.

"Wanna race?" Lee's jovial tone ratcheted down her pity party.

There. Behind her in a banana-yellow Smart car. Lee's head and arm protruded from the window. He waved at her, and a grin lit his face. "Love the Vespa, Bella."

"Nice gas guzzler you found."

"You, too. I'll follow you in." He tapped his horn again.

Bella saw an opening in the crowd. Without hesitation, she gunned the Vespa and shot through. Shadows crept around the Duomo. Bella aimed for the bank of steps by the tourist entrance. She and Lee ignored all parking restrictions and left their vehicles at the base of the Duomo.

Meghan stood in front of the steps, her face tilted to the sky. Lee and Bella walked over to join her. Meghan's hand steadied a bicycle. Bella's neighbor, when she was a child, had a girl's bicycle with big, dented fenders identical to the one Meghan held. Even the ratty woven front basket was the same.

"Wherever did you find this?" Lee pulled the lever of the silver bell on the bicycle's handlebars.

The sound of the bell brought a rush of warm memories to Bella of her mother. Using their neighbor's bike, her mom had taught her to ride. Oh, how Bella had loved to ring the bell.

Meghan giggled. "I helped the owner of a natural products store find new supply sources on the Internet." She patted the bike seat. "The owner couldn't believe I'd actually work to borrow this."

"Good eeev-ning, Florence!" Hope's voice bellowed from the window of a touring van.

Hope parked the van right behind Lee's Smart car. She sauntered over to them and slapped Lee's raised hand in a high five.

Meghan, Lee, and Bella all burst into laughter. Meghan hugged Hope. "You've certainly got us beat, at least on the creativity angle."

"How did you pull that one off?" Bella asked.

Hope shrugged. "Dumb luck. I wandered around aimlessly for a while. Mostly, I stuffed my face with gelato and charged things to Charlie's credit card. Then I came across this." Her hand swept toward the van. "A group of tourists was stranded by their driver, who also happened to be their guide. A piss-poor one, I might add. Here they were, at this dive hotel: no air conditioning, no elevator, yellowed threadbare sheets, and a bathroom down the hall. Four stars? Try a measly one star. They asked him to find another hotel. First he swore at them, and then he ditched them."

"What did you do?" Meghan asked.

"What anyone would do. I went in and sweet-talked the Italian behind the desk into booking the group into another hotel, a nicer one with private bathrooms and air conditioning. He was very willing to cooperate when I explained that one member of the tour had a highly contagious foot fungus. And, of course, he wouldn't want that spread through his hotel via the communal bathroom."

They all doubled over with laughter. Tears escaped Bella's eyes. She released herself to the laughter. Bella could picture Hope weaving her tale as the unsuspecting clerk took it in.

The obnoxious roar of a high-speed motorcycle sliced through the normal evening buzz of cars and voices. A red Ducati slowed to a stop in front of them. The rider tugged off his black and red helmet.

"Nice wheels, Rune." Lee's tone spoke his admiration. He moved in for a closer inspection.

Meghan approached the Ducati with caution, as if mere proximity might be life-threatening.

"Splendid choice, Rune." Stillman's voice came from behind them.

Turning to look at Stillman, Bella saw that their own touring van was now parked behind the roped-off area on this side of the Duomo. Rested and dashing in a cream-colored silk shirt and handmade loafers, Stillman walked toward them.

The roar of an approaching engine pulled her eyes to the sound. A black Ferrari spun to a halt next to the Ducati. Phillip unfolded himself from behind the wheel and leaned—oh so casually—against the car.

Everyone except Bella and Stillman rushed to examine the Ferrari.

The sound of slow clapping made everyone turn to look at Stillman. His deliberate, hollow clapping mocked Phillip's choice. Bella knew Stillman had grabbed the final word.

"I give the award to Hope, for bringing the most unpre-dictable mode of transportation." Stillman's voice brought quick seconds of agreement from Meghan and Lee. Phillip couldn't care less, it seemed. He had his showy prize and didn't care what price he had paid to get it.

Stillman moved beside Bella and rubbed her shoulder. "By the way, love, how did you get your Vespa?"

"I volunteered at a bookstore."

"And how did it go?" Stillman said.

Bella stared at him. She had a hunch he knew something about her afternoon. Had he seen a placard for the signing? She steadied her voice before speaking. "It wasn't quite what I expected, but I did come away with the Vespa."

She heard the uncertainty in her words and suddenly got angry with herself. Bella didn't need another person to validate her. The signing *had* been a success, damn it, and she should be proud of it. "It went very well, thank you. Did you see signs this afternoon for an event at a bookstore?"

"Yes, and it took all my willpower not to come and be a mouse in the corner." Stillman wrapped an arm around her shoulders and gestured to her with his other hand, saying, "Everyone, I want you to meet the reclusive but very talented and successful author, E.V. Tate, who earned her Vespa by doing a book signing this afternoon."

Congratulations and cries of surprised delight came from everyone. Even Phillip sounded excited in his congratulations, but Bella couldn't bring herself to look at him. Questions started peppering her, but Bella waved them off. She wanted to turn the attention to someone else and so asked Lee, "What about you? How did you get the Smart car?"

"I gave a talk at a hospital nearby on state-of-the-art surgical procedures."

"Good for you," Meghan said. "I'll bet they appreciated it."

Lee shrugged. "I guess so. Physicians are nerds and like to talk medicine." He nodded at the car. "But I could use one of these at home. It certainly would make parking easier."

"And what about Mr. Playboy? Did you buy the Ferrari?" Stillman's eyes cut into Phillip.

"No, I bartered for it, like everyone else. No money could change hands, wasn't that the rule?"

Another Ferrari, this one red, rumbled in next to Phillip's. A man got out of the passenger seat. Without exchanging a word, Phillip passed off his key to the man, who nodded and then climbed behind the wheel of the black sports car. The two Ferraris snaked away through the crowd.

"Well, I'm sure as hell ready for dinner." Hope rubbed her hands together.

Stillman, with his arm still around Bella, whispered in her ear. "Do you think Phillip lied about how he got the Ferrari? We both know he double-crossed a friend thirty years ago. What do you think, love? Is Phillip the kind who would lie or break a promise to a friend?"

A millipede with icy feet marched across Bella's neck. She had told Stillman that she and Phillip had broken up by mutual agreement. Stillman made it sound like he knew that Phillip had ditched her. And if he knew that, did Stillman suspect that Phillip had fathered David?

40

The next morning, Meghan and Rune stood outside the window of a shop that featured shirts and blouses of all colors. The display's vibrant hues derailed their search for a holistic remedy shop. Meghan was surprised when Rune had suggested that they search for the alternative medicine store. He hadn't explained why, and she hadn't asked. Some things were private. Who knew that better than she?

Now, Rune grabbed Meghan's hand and pulled her into the clothing store. Inside, they gravitated to opposite sides of the narrow shop. Meghan's fingertips explored the fabrics—fine cotton and silk. The rich tones of the fall season sent her eyes skipping between the garments.

Meghan felt a presence behind her. A tiny, wizened man, the store's owner, cradled a silk blouse of sapphire blue. He grinned under a thick gray moustache. He gestured to the back of the shop, where a parted curtain marked a dressing room.

Meghan's hand fluttered up. "Oh, no, I couldn't."

She felt Rune's palm push against the small of her back. He tucked the blouse and Meghan into the dressing room, despite her sputtered objections.

Meghan gasped as the cool silk draped over her shoulders and chest. The drape and line of the fabric, which crossed over in front, showed her cleavage. The color complemented her blond hair streaked with silver; it warmed the tone of her cheeks.

"Come out, my dear, before I come in after you." Rune's playful tone announced his intention to see her in the garment.

Her fingers trembled. The curtain's wooden rings slid over the rod. She stepped out.

Rune wolf-whistled.

The shop owner grinned and nodded. He trotted to the wall and returned bearing four more silk blouses, some with patterns but all in colors Meghan knew would flatter her.

Rune put his hands on his hips. "You are one beautiful woman, Meghan."

Meghan blushed. She turned to face the three-way mirror. Even her red face couldn't detract from how stunning she looked. After wearing unbleached cotton, Meghan had to admit that she loved the look, and feel, of the silk blouse.

Meghan smiled as she and Rune returned to the street with two bags of tissue-wrapped blouses. She grabbed Rune's wrist to check his watch. "Do we still have time? I don't have to find the alternative medicine store. I brought all I needed for the trip with me."

"I'm still a go. I'm, ah, thinking I should learn more about homeopathic therapy and treatments. Thought you might be able to teach me stuff." He rubbed the center of her back with one hand and gestured ahead with the other. "It's this way, I think."

Meghan turned to study him. "Really? That surprises me. What do you take now?"

"Nothing. Not yet."

"What's wrong?"

Rune's color washed out of his face.

"What is it?"

He shook his head.

She grabbed his arm. "What is it?" She knew what he would say. It had to be cancer.

"Prostate cancer."

"Is there an alternative treatment for it?"

"I don't know." His voice deepened. "I hoped you could help with that."

"Have you had surgery?"

His face flushed. He avoided her eyes. "Not yet."

She took one of his hairy hands in both of hers but was interrupted before she could say what she had intended.

"Signora Meghan." A male voice called to them from between the buildings. Giacomo scurried toward them, his face one-third grin.

Rune's eyes pleaded with Meghan.

Giacomo glided up to Meghan. His eyes danced. He tugged on her arm. "Come. You must see."

They followed Giacomo as he wove through narrow streets and ancient alleys.

Meghan heard a drum. They moved toward the sound.

Cheering, laughter, and clapping gave way to a lilting music played on some sort of flute. The three rounded a corner and ran into a wall of people, nearly all of them women and children. Where were the men? Meghan's eyes canvassed the street until she found them—a cluster of cashmere-coated, white-haired gentlemen anchored the street corner.

Musicians strolled by in the center of the street. A groom and a bride, who was dressed in a filmy, white, ankle-length dress, walked ahead of the musicians. The groom's right arm extended high over his head in a jubilant wave to the crowd that lined the street.

Meghan clutched Giacomo's arm. On her tiptoes, she strained to see the couple.

Rune's hands circled her waist. With ease, he lifted her straight up. The last of the musicians passed them. The crowd filtered away.

Rune lowered Meghan back to the street. She felt his palm trail over her bottom. As she stepped forward, away from Rune, she bumped into Giacomo. The Italian grabbed her shoulders to prevent a full collision.

"Oh." Meghan said, flustered.

Giacomo studied her face. "I am happy you enjoyed the wedding celebration."

"Where are they going? To dinner?"

"The wedding and feast were yesterday. Until late hours, I am certain. Today is the feast for the closest family."

"With a band?" Rune asked.

"Of course, of course."

"How many people?" Meghan stepped forward to draw herself side by side with Giacomo.

"Fifty or sixty people. Just the closest family."

But of course, this was Italy. Fifty or sixty people—just the closest family. Family. It was as if a massive boulder had fallen on Meghan. The word family reminded her of April.

Fifteen minutes later, Meghan and Rune sat on the steps of the Church of Santa Croce. Giacomo had disappeared with a promise of gelato.

"He's hot for you." Rune threw out the accusation.

Meghan shook her head in denial.

"You can ignore it if you want. But trust me, he's just warming up with his flirtation."

Meghan looked away. "I love weddings."

"So how come you never got married?"

Meghan flushed. "Never the right guy, or the right moment."

"So you believe that 'finding-your-life-partner' crap is possible."

"Of course." She spun her head to face him. "Look at Karen and Ed. They met at freshman orientation and were madly smitten from the first day."

"Yeah, right." He licked his lips and gave an ugly laugh. "Karen and I had a thing. I guess you didn't know."

Meghan popped up to stand before him. "When?"

"On the night train to Paris."

"You had sex?"

Rune nodded. A snort escaped from his nose. "Oh, yeah. My legs were so weak walking around Paris there was no way I could climb the friggin' steps up Notre Dame." He rubbed his palms over his thighs. "It was the moment. Nothing more." He mumbled the words as if he meant them as an apology.

Meghan bowed her head.

"Jeez, I'm sorry I told you."

"That's all you're about, isn't it? Sex."

His face drained of color. Meghan thought about what she had said. Wrong words to a man with prostate cancer. Was he imagining the possible repercussions of his surgery?

Rune's eyes searched her face. "I've heard prostate cancer is somehow related to breast cancer. Was it awful for Karen?"

"Karen's death was ugly. Painful. Hard to watch. Her death—and then her daughter's—was like a beacon. Something flipped in me. I decided I would do whatever I needed to survive."

Rune clapped one palm against the stone step. "Survive? Hell, I want to live. I refuse to turn into a sorry excuse for a human being. My world rocks, and I can't lose that."

"A sorry excuse for a human being?" Meghan's palm met his cheek with a jarring force that shot up her arm.

"Shit." Rune's eyes watered.

Giacomo cleared his throat. He held three cups of gelato in his hands.

Meghan set her cup down on the step.

"You wasted your euros on her. She's too pure for gelato." Rune sucked on the plastic spoon of chocolate gelato; he made a great show of his pleasure.

Meghan glared at Rune.

He ignored her. He turned from his gelato to gawk at a young American blonde with a size E cup who bounced up the steps to the church. More cleavage bobbed above her top than rested beneath it. The modesty patrol at the entrance to the sanctuary stopped her. With a giggle, she draped a shawl over her shoulders. Once the blonde disappeared inside, Rune returned to his gelato. He licked the tiny pink spoon for every drop of chocolate.

"We should start for the Duomo." Giacomo stood. He gestured with his half-eaten gelato cup.

Meghan picked up her untouched gelato. She glared at Rune. Take this, you cretin. She brought one cautious sample to her lips. The fresh scent made her salivate before it even hit her tongue. A cool explosion of flavor rushed through her mouth, both sweet and tart. How many years had it been since sugar had passed her lips? She gulped it down so fast that only half remained when she heard Rune's low whistle of surprise.

Meghan chucked her cup of gelato into the nearest trashcan without a glance in Rune's direction. She scooted up to Giacomo and tucked her hand into the crook of his arm. She could already sense the sugar rush in her body, but the interesting thing was that the lapse from her rigid diet felt empowering. It felt defiant.

What else about Karen didn't she know? Had Rune been the only one to bed her sister?

41

Rune hovered near the edge of the rooftop bar of the Hotel Elegante. A violet and rose sunset washed the clay tile roofs of ancient Florence. The air turned from the thick warmth of the day to the cool of an autumn night. The first to arrive for their pre-dinner cocktails, he clutched a glass of Chianti Riserva close to his chest. He psyched himself up for the pitch.

Hope and Bella arrived. They jabbered about their designer outlet excursion and the endless lines at the stores as if he gave a shit. Their words fell on Rune's ears like pesky droplets of rain. By the looks of them, they wore some of their purchases tonight. Ah, the almighty power of frivolous consumption. Hope's smile was plastered to her face.

Stillman walked in and sat with his back to the falling sun. Rune sauntered over.

Then a wolf whistle made Rune pivot. Hope's fingers lowered from her mouth. Meghan stood at the crest of the stairwell. She wore the blue silk blouse he had helped her pick out. Bella and Hope rushed over to Meghan, squealing and swapping compliments.

It was Rune's chance to hit up Stillman. He sat down on a chair across from him. "While they're gabbing, let me bend your ear." He tried to calm his nerves. "I've been holding back a property waiting for the right market, right backing."

Stillman's eyebrows rose.

"It's very high-concept. Think *Saving Private Ryan* meets *The Bridges of Madison County*, with shades of *Seven* layered in."

"What's the setting?"

Rune shifted forward. "That's the great part. It's set in the Sahara Desert."

"Sounds sandy."

"But great, right?" Rune edged to the lip of the chair. "I'm thinking a couple big names, budget maybe fifty to seventy mill for three stars, plus a half dozen on-the-edge-of-greatness actors. It's an ensemble piece, so the bankroll's a bit pricey, plus we'll need the best stunt guys we can persuade to eat sand for the better part of a year."

Stillman's lips puckered. "Got a script?"

"In the van. I can get it now or bring it out at dinner." He leaned in toward Stillman and his chair scooted out from under him on the fine crushed pebbles of the roof. Rune tumbled forward in a sprawl to the ground. His knees cracked against the ground and his palms jammed onto the sharp pebbles. Stillman's laughter covered him like a blanket of thorns.

Bella, Hope, and Meghan crowded over him. He pushed aside their hands, stood up, and brushed off his knees, his left knee showing under the ragged tear in his best slacks.

He leaned over Stillman and rested one hand on his shoulder. "I'll go get it now. That way we won't forget to discuss it later."

"No." Stillman's hand shot out and grabbed Rune's wrist. "It's time for dinner. The van is waiting."

Rune gestured to his leg. "I should wash this off. I can do that and grab the script, so we can talk about it on the ride. Besides, Phil and Lee aren't here yet."

"We're going now." Stillman's firm tone left no room for discussion.

"Your party, man."

"Where are we going?" Phillip asked as he glided out of the elevator.

Rune eyed Phillip's designer-label jacket. He cringed as Phillip's eyes flicked to his ripped slacks.

"Where's Lee?" Stillman sounded more perturbed than concerned.

"Couldn't tell you." Phillip accepted the glass of Prosecco offered by the silent attendant. "He and I split ways earlier. Said he had something to investigate."

On the ride to dinner, Giacomo mentioned that Lee had said he was going to research more rumored locations for lost works of art.

Platters of roasted meats crowded the table at the tiny ristorante on San Jacopo. The owner had pushed small tables together to seat them, which left only a border of booths for other patrons. They laughed and drank glass after glass of Brunello di Montalcino. Still, no Lee.

Rune patted the screenplay on the table between him and Stillman. He hadn't sat near Stillman in the van, so he couldn't discuss it on the ride over, but Rune had brought it into the ristorante. "You'll love it. Luckily, I happen to be available soon. The project I was working on got postponed due to an unplanned pregnancy of the female lead." He smirked. "You've probably seen that the tabloids already picked up the news about her."

"You're full of shit." Stillman's calm but harsh words silenced the table. He rested the tips of his fork and knife against his plate. "You're directing dinner theater at a run-down, second-tier house. Unless the father of the baby is famous, I suspect your female lead's pregnancy isn't making the news. This," he said, gesturing to the crisp screenplay beside him, "is the same horse crap you've been peddling for three years." He picked up his utensils and attacked the wild boar sausage in front of him.

Rune opened his mouth. Words failed him. He slid the screenplay onto his lap and picked up his fork. Sausage, chicken, and veal blurred together on his plate. Had the whole table heard?

Meghan spoke first. "That was rude."

"Are you a dinner theater fan?" A smirk marked Stillman's face.

"Why be so hurtful?" Meghan glared at Stillman.

"His screenplay is unbankable." He rested his hand on Rune's arm. "Sorry about coming on strong. You're my friend, Rune, but you're desperate to land a sucker. It's not going to be me."

"Maybe he's desperate because he's facing a health crisis," Meghan said.

Stillman looked at Rune. "What?"

Rune didn't speak. His eyes pleaded with Meghan across the table. He didn't want pity from his friends.

She misunderstood the silent request to keep his disease a secret. "Prostate cancer." She ratcheted up her volume as if she needed to be heard in the cheap seats. "Rune's having surgery after this trip." Her words silenced the table.

Bella, on the other side of Rune, rested her palm on his arm. "I'm sorry. I didn't hear anything except that you're having surgery. I hope it's not serious."

Shit, Rune thought. Thanks a heap, Meghan. "Prostate cancer. Pretty advanced, I guess." Rune spit out the words. "Even with the surgery—which will undoubtedly fuck up the few things that work well in my body—my long-term survival prospects aren't great."

Phillip's business tone surfaced in his terse question. "Do you have insurance?"

Rune looked at his plate. He shook his head.

"Rune," Phillip said, "I can help if you can't cover your treatment."

Rune stared at Phillip. "You'd do that?"

Phillip smiled. "I can give it to you or, eventually, to my wife's attorney. I'd rather give it to you."

"Man, you're incredible." Rune shook his head in disbelief. He saw Bella stare at Phillip.

"Rune, it's my pleasure," Phillip said. "At our age, everybody has something—health, work, or family issues. If we can help each other, maybe we should. We used to be close." His eyes darted to Bella. "Close enough to know each other's dreams."

Stillman's eyes circled the table, finally settling on Rune. "Sorry, Rune. You took me off guard. I resented you hitting me up on your screenplay." He cut a healthy piece of meat, stabbed it with his fork, and paused, the meat suspended in the air. "I'm really sorry."

"Thanks." Rune looked Stillman square in the eye. "Wanna change your mind about producing my work?"

"You don't give up, do you?" Stillman downed his forkful and reached for seconds of the wild boar sausage. "I think you should concentrate on beating the disease and not worry about work."

Meghan pushed up from the table. "I'm sorry, I'm exhausted."

Rune wiped his mouth with his napkin. He stood up. "I'll go with you, doll."

Ten minutes later, a sedan arrived to drive them. Rune marveled at Giacomo's ability to produce an extra car without advance notice. He wished he had half as many connections.

Back at the palazzo, Meghan fumbled with the key while Rune pressed his lips to her bare neck. It was cool and soft and beckoning. "I think we need to be together tonight." His raspy voice projected his desire and his desperation.

Meghan opened the door and took one step into her room. Her hand held the door firmly. "Look, I enjoyed shopping with you today, but I'm not your type."

Zing. After Stillman's routing at dinner, Rune couldn't take more. He exploded. "Not my type? It doesn't matter. Soon I'll have a limp dick. My take on sex is changing already. I'll bet you haven't gotten laid recently."

Meghan's eyes grew dark. She spit her words in his face. "I feel awful that you have cancer. You're my friend. But I'm not going to have sex with you. And for the record, my sex life is none of your damn business."

This doesn't look promising, Rune thought.

Before he could say another word, Meghan disappeared inside the room. He stood facing the closed door. First Stillman, and now Meghan, had slammed a door in his face. Worst damn day of his miserable life.

42

L ee ventured into Florence alone. He'd risen earlier than the others, who had slept in after their dinner on San Jacopo. He grabbed espresso at a stand-up bar near the University; his face crinkled at the bitterness. He had done the research yesterday and into the night, but uncertainty plagued him.

His mission today was the key to his escape. Today, he'd begin his new life. He chastised himself for his doubt and strode with purpose out of the bar and into the morning shadows of the street.

Only a few people walked the city center streets, still wet from a nighttime rain. As he passed a bakery already open to customers, the smell of breads, rolls, and sweet pastries tugged at Lee. Next door, an older, balding man stooped beside a roll-up metal garage door. He unlocked it and then lifted it to uncover the wood and glass façade of a butcher shop.

Lee ducked down cool, shaded side streets, left and then right, until he reached his destination. He ran up the steps and into the building marked by a modest sign. Inside, the light and airiness struck him first. Lee found only one person in the studio, a warehouse-like

room with support posts in lieu of interior walls. A
bent-over man swept the cement floor between the statues
with a straw broom. He looked all of eighty. Lee called out
a hearty greeting.

The man ignored him.

Screw it. He'd look around.

Ten-foot windows extended down from the ceiling on
two sides of the room, which allowed natural light to flood
the space. Clay models and half-finished reliefs crammed
the room's outer edges, with bare floor and unoccupied
easels in the center. A huge metal trough extended from
one wall. Lee's hand rubbed the inner surface to capture
the feel of the clay traces remaining. A water faucet hung
out of the wall above it.

Lee ignored the janitor and positioned himself in front
of an empty pillar stand in the room's creative center. He
imagined himself working here. He lifted his hands to cup
a pretend statue in process. His fingers moved—shaping,
molding, and bringing life to his art.

This was his future. The certainty of it burned inside
him as hot as the habanero chili peppers he'd once eaten
on a dare from his son. The energy of the light-filled studio
lifted him. He closed his eyes and let his hands continue
their molding of the imaginary clay.

A low, scratchy cough to his right brought Lee back to
reality. His hands dropped to his sides. He felt the color
rise on his cheeks. The elderly man stood beside him, his
broom no longer in his hands. Lee could not understand
the Italian words shot at him, but he could tell that he
wasn't expected. Or welcome.

"Student," Lee said. He tapped his chest.

The man flung his arm in the direction of the door. His intent was as clear as if he'd picked Lee up by his shirt collar and thrown him out of the studio.

Lee tried again to introduce himself as a student. The elderly man again threw his arm with obvious disgust in the direction of the door, accompanying the gesture with a string of Italian that spewed out too fast for Lee to understand. But he didn't need to interpret the words; the meaning was clear enough.

Lee slunk to the door. All those calls and e-mails he'd sent from the States—only to be thrown out by the janitor? His faxes were never answered, true, but this studio had the reputation of training the best new sculptors in Italy. It would be worth coming back, to meet the maestro in person. Then Lee would have a chance to convince him that he was a worthy student.

Since dropping in uninvited hadn't worked, he'd talk to Giacomo; maybe he knew someone. After all, this was Italy. There was always a way to get something done, right?

He turned to soak in one more glimpse of the studio— its light and energy and creative excitement. What he saw surprised him.

The elderly man stood erect in front of an easel on which a canvas had appeared. Bold charcoal strokes of a woman's reclining body already graced the canvas. The artist moved quickly, his arms sweeping through the air with the fluid grace of a dancer. All vestiges of age disappeared as his work, his passion, consumed him. Was this the maestro himself? If so, Lee knew he'd crashed and burned on his first impression. He lowered his head and pulled the door closed behind him.

After downing two more espressos and sitting by the Duomo for over an hour, Lee walked to meet the others in the Piazza della Signoria.

The open square had already filled with tour groups clustered around their guides, their patterned umbrellas stuck straight over their heads as if they were lightning rods. The middle-aged tourists bobbed their collective heads as they listened to their guides describe the *Museo di Palazzo Vecchio* that stood behind them, the statues that bordered the large piazza, and the history surrounding this Florence landmark.

Lee saw Meghan first. She sat on the steps underneath Cellini's bronze *Perseus*, in which the mighty Perseus holds the severed head of Medusa.

Giacomo sat beside her, his arm brushing hers. Giacomo's mouth moved in rapid explanation; his hands flew in wild gestures.

Meghan's head tilted back in laughter.

A pang from nowhere hit Lee in his sternum. But he couldn't let jealousy derail him. If he wanted Giacomo's help, he'd have to ask for it. He moved to join them.

Meghan curled forward in fits of laughter. "Stop," she said. "Just stop." She swiped at her eyes with her fingers. She winked at Giacomo. "You are wicked and perverted. You know that."

The handsome Italian bowed to her. "It is necessary, you see, to sometimes be most wicked to bring laughter to a pretty lady."

Lee raised an eyebrow at Meghan. "Is that the secret to unlocking Meghan?"

Her face flushed hot pink.

Lee smiled at their guide. "Giacomo, I could use some laughter this morning. Care to share your story with me, too?"

Giacomo rubbed Meghan's arm. "My apology. The moment has passed. It is time to join our group." He motioned at the others, who sat clustered across the piazza at outdoor tables, nursing espressos.

Lee knew he had only a few minutes to make his appeal. He blurted out his story of searching for the studio, his hope of finding information about classes, and his run-in with the elderly artist. He hadn't even told Merry, his wife, his vision of sculpting in Italy. Yet, to Giacomo and Meghan, his whole dream rushed out.

"You are lucky to meet the maestro." Giacomo beamed. "He is very famous in Italy and Europe."

Lee shook his head. "So that was the maestro. It was a disaster. He threw me out of the studio. I'm going to need connections, Giacomo. I'll pay whatever it costs. Can you help?"

Giacomo nodded. "But of course." His face solemn, he stood and patted Lee's shoulder. "Do not worry. His work always comes first. Perhaps I can arrange for you to speak to his son, who manages the financial part of his business."

"Does his son speak English?"

"Yes, of course." Giacomo reached down and pulled Meghan to her feet. "I will tell you a story about the maestro. One day I went to visit him. A friend of mine had helped the maestro secure a commission. I go to see the maestro to take pictures of his work for my friend. He was late for our meeting, which was unheard of for this man. When he arrived, he excused himself, saying he was very upset. His brother had died that morning. He wouldn't accept my condolences, or questions after his brother, as he was late starting work. 'There's always the work, you see,' he told me. His brother dead less than an hour, and the maestro was already back to work."

"In Italy," Giacomo said, grinning at Meghan, "only artists and tour guides work with such dedication. Yes, I will help you."

Lee clapped Giacomo on the shoulder. "Thank you. You don't know what this means to me."

"It is my pleasure." Giacomo grinned and then folded Meghan's small hand into the bend of his arm, leading her toward where the rest of the group sat.

Relief washed over Lee.

Instead of rounding up the group, though, Giacomo and Meghan disappeared inside the espresso bar. Lee followed them to the counter, where he heard Giacomo order an espresso and a cappuccino. Moments later, the clerk behind the counter offered the latter to Meghan. Surprised that she would indulge, Lee watched her cautiously taste it; the golden froth stuck to her upper lip until she licked it off with her tongue.

Giacomo had obviously gotten her to abandon the strict vegan approach. And Lee knew how it had happened. It'd take a blind man to miss the chemistry between the two of them. He wasn't sure what he felt about Meghan, but he hated imagining her with anyone else.

Lee ducked outside to the street. He breathed in the cool, humid air. Thoughts of his wife slammed into his temples. He decided he'd call Merry—now. He stared at his watch and realized it was the middle of the night in Durham. Not the time to phone. Maybe later, he told himself, he'd call. But he knew he wouldn't. He'd find an excuse. The truth was that he didn't know what he'd say to her. I want to stay in Italy without you? No. That confession was not ready for prime time yet.

After he and Meghan had finished their drinks, Giacomo led the group to the Palazzo Vecchio. He promised a special tour. Lee noticed how Giacomo positioned himself next to Meghan, so close that their shoulders and arms brushed against each other.

An hour into the tour, Giacomo introduced them to a gem. It was Lee's favorite discovery on the tour, a room that had belonged to Francesco I.

The small chamber bore the curved ceiling of a treasure chest and was built for that exact purpose. Behind the artwork hinged to the wall were narrow shelves that had held the duke's treasures—jewels, gold, alchemy potions, and ingredients. Francesco I, it seems, had studied the science of alchemy. The artwork gave clues as to the treasures previously held behind each painting. Lee found himself studying the paintings and guessing at the ancient secrets they had contained.

Prying the group from this mysterious room, Giacomo led them up a hidden stairway to another secret room. Lee and Meghan brought up the rear.

"Do you ever wonder?" Lee blurted out the words. Damn it, she'll think I'm crazy, asking a question that seems to make no sense, he thought.

Meghan seemed to know exactly what he had asked. "What would have happened if we'd stayed together?"

Lee nodded.

"Yes." Her eyes told him nothing. She turned back to study the painting beside her.

"Come. This way." Giacomo's head appeared out of a stairwell. His hand waved them to follow. "You are missing this most unusual hiding spot."

Meghan's eyes hovered on Lee's face for a long, silent moment. Then, without another word, she turned and followed Giacomo up the stairwell.

"Me, too," Lee whispered at her retreating back.

Lee couldn't quell his guilty feeling about Merry. He took the easy way out. During the afternoon break, he found an Internet store not far from their mansion.

Hi Merry.

It's good to see everyone again. They've all gotten old (as if I haven't).

Have there been any more issues with Max's Spanish teacher?

I'm thinking of planning another trip to Florence to check into the potential for a visiting professorship at the University. I know I haven't mentioned this to you before, but I corresponded by e-mail with the University Department Chair before this visit. If nothing else, a little time here would do wonders for my Italian language skills.

His fingers pounded against the keyboard with his lies.

Maybe I should extend my visit now to see if I could work out details in person.

Lee

Lee realized after he clicked on "Send" that he hadn't told his wife he loved her. And he knew that would be the first thing that Merry noticed.

Lee left the Internet café and headed back to the palazzo. Everywhere Lee looked, people touched each other—mother and daughter, teenaged girls with arms linked, senior citizens, horny twenty-year-olds and their sex interest for the night. When had he last touched Merry?

That night, Lee tossed and turned on the too-hard mattress. His butt found the crevice where the two single beds had been pushed together. He couldn't stop thinking about the potential of living here, in Florence, for a year. A sabbatical.

He knew that Max wouldn't care if the family moved to Italy, as long as he could play soccer here, too. Anne, his daughter, wouldn't want to leave high school, so that might be a problem. And Merry? She had her thriving private practice. In fact, she had canceled her discreet ads in the theater programs because her patient load kept her as busy as she liked. Now, new patients, if she took them on at all, came solely from referral. Could Lee move here without his family?

The excited sensation he had felt standing in the studio this morning kept returning to him. He imagined himself in such a studio, his hands creating new work, starting with a blank slate, rather than treating patients with deformities, or those that had been mangled and damaged.

A soft knock startled him. Early morning light lit the room.

Lee padded to the door in his boxer shorts and T-shirt—Max had teased him out of pajamas.

"May I come in?" Meghan stood in the hallway, her thin frame wrapped in the complimentary white bathrobe, the width way too generous for her build. She looked like a young girl, dressed in her mother's robe.

Lee stepped back, opening the door wider.

Seeing her here, in his room, made all the years fall away. Suddenly, he was young again. Lee cupped her cheeks with his palms and brushed his lips against hers. He felt her quivering response. He made himself pull his head back, away from those tender lips.

Meghan's face relaxed into a comfortable smile. "That was very nice, but not why I came."

Lee gulped air. Shit.

The fingertips of her left hand came up to silence his words. "I wanted to talk to you. Alone."

It took Lee an agonizing ten seconds to recover his composure. "Of course."

Meghan grabbed his hand and led him to the bed. She perched on the edge, took in an audible fortifying breath, and motioned for him to sit next to her. "You asked me yesterday if I ever wondered what would have happened if we hadn't broken up. I did. I obsessed about it for a while. After a few years, I met someone, and we got engaged." She frowned. "That was a huge mistake." She looked at her lap, and then into Lee's eyes. "He cheated on me. Made a fool out of me."

He told her the truth. "What a jerk. He was the fool."

"Are you happy in your marriage?"

The question took him by surprise. Was she still attracted to him? What about Giacomo? His breaths quickened and his groin perked with interest.

She drew a big breath. "I'm sorry. That's not my business. But I've been afraid, you see, to love anyone. Rune told me he and Karen had hooked up that summer we were here. I always thought she and Ed had the perfect marriage, and before that, the ideal relationship. Now I wonder if it's possible to be committed to only one person. That's why I wondered about you and your wife."

Oh. He went limp. Meghan was falling in love with Giacomo and wanted his advice on relationships. What could he tell her about his marriage? He chose his words carefully. "I do believe it's possible to commit to only one person and be happy with them, when it's the right person."

"You didn't answer my question."

"No. I didn't."

Meghan gazed into his eyes. She squeezed his hand. "If that means what I suspect, then I'm sorry."

Lee didn't speak.

Her eyes cast down, and then they lifted and locked onto his. "Rune was blunt with me. He implied that I'm afraid to live. Do you think I act that way?"

He didn't answer.

Meghan nodded. She stood and moved to the door, then turned to face him. Her hand trembled. She reached over and dead-bolted the door.

The click of the lock sent a shiver racing down Lee's back.

"I'll be honest with you," she said. "I'm very attracted to Giacomo. But I can't explore that yet because I've never forgotten you."

Without a word or a moment of hesitation, he moved to join her. This time, her lips reached up to his. He was young again.

When their lips parted, Lee tilted his head back, and his eyes lingered over her face, her eyes, her lips. Kissing her made him lose all sense of time and place. Damn it. Now that he had stopped, even for a moment, his mind started buzzing. He felt like he was being ripped in two. As much as he wanted her, he knew he had to stop. "Meghan—"

"Shh." Meghan's fingers silenced his lips.

Lee clasped Meghan's hand and lowered it. "I want you." He trembled. "I do." His hand caressed her cheek. He forced himself to say the next words. "My wife and I have grown apart, but," he drew in a deep breath, "I made a commitment to her. I can't be with you the way I want. Not yet."

"I know. That makes me love you even more." Her smile verified her words. She reached up and stroked his cheek. "You'll always be more than merely my first lover. Kissing you is … lovely."

Her words were sweet, but Lee's heart plummeted. Meghan didn't say she'd wait for him to untangle his marriage. She didn't say she wanted him, too.

"Come." She grabbed one of his hands and pulled him toward the bed. "Let's talk." And they did. They confided in each other and shared their fears and dreams—one dear friend to another.

They heard footsteps in the hallway.

Meghan stood up. She leaned over Lee and brushed her lips against his cheek. "Thank you."

Lee marveled at her natural beauty and the glow that kissed her cheeks. "Meg." Lee surprised himself. The nickname he had first used during their night of lovemaking all those years ago seemed so natural to him now. "Rune was wrong. You're not afraid of living."

Meghan smiled. "I've earned the right to really live and to do as I damn well please, and that's exactly what I'm going to do."

"If it works out with Giacomo, you may end up staying in Italy."

She beamed. "Even better."

"Who knows," he said, "after I figure things out with my wife, I may be here, too."

She opened the door to leave but stopped halfway through the threshold. "Good morning." Meghan's confident voice was directed to someone in the hallway.

Lee heard a muffled female voice in reply. A few more words were exchanged between the two women. Meghan didn't move from the door. He heard footsteps retreating down the hall.

Meghan twisted to glance back at Lee. "Bella," she said. She grinned. "I'll bet she thinks we had wild sex all night, and I'm not going to tell her otherwise."

43

After seeing Meghan in Lee's room, Bella wandered through the palazzo. She heard the sound of a child's laughter and went to find the source.

Giacomo stood in the front driveway beside a young boy who looked like he was five or six years old. The Italian boy was playing catch with a baseball—with Phillip! Bella stood in the palazzo's entry and watched.

The boy's throws alternated between being way short of Phillip and off to his side. Phillip jogged to wherever the ball landed and made a grand show of picking it up and fumbling it in the air, crazily flipping it hand to hand, sometimes even dropping it, before gently tossing it back to the boy. Phillip kept up a constant conversation with the boy *in flawless Italian*.

She studied Phillip's face. His relaxed happiness, as he played with the child, was the real deal.

The boy threw another ball that fell halfway between Phillip and himself. Phillip again jogged to the ball, picked it up and pretended to fumble it. He laughed at himself and in Italian declared that the ball must be covered in olive oil, as it was so slippery. He walked to the boy and made a show of placing the ball directly into the child's hands. Phillip gestured back to the spot where he had been standing and instructed Giacomo to take his place.

Phillip demonstrated the proper throwing technique by pantomiming a throw himself. Then, he crouched behind the boy, whispered in his ear and moved the boy's throwing arm once, twice, three times to let the boy feel the proper form. Phillip stepped back, clapped his hands and encouraged the boy to throw to Giacomo. The instruction helped. The ball reached Giacomo, only slightly off to one side.

Phillip alternated between teaching the child and catching the ball. The thing that surprised Bella the most was the joy on Phillip's face as he laughed, joked, and feigned ineptitude.

A sedan drove up and a man and a woman got out of the car. The boy rushed to them and gave each a double kiss. Giacomo greeted the couple in the same manner. Phillip walked over and hugged both the woman and the man. All of them stood and chatted a few minutes. The woman gestured at the ball, and the boy ran to pick it up. Phillip again hugged the couple, and then the boy. He walked toward the palazzo.

Bella stood her ground.

"Good morning," Phillip said when he saw her. "Have you been here long?"

"Long enough to see the results of your throwing lessons to the boy. Who is he?"

"Great kid. He's Giacomo's nephew. He watched television while we were at dinner and then slept on the sofa in Giacomo's room last night. I guess his parents had a wedding to attend."

"Your Italian is beautiful. You never said you had learned the language."

His eyes fastened onto hers. "I couldn't let go of Italy and my memories of our time here together."

Right, she thought. Maybe you couldn't let go of the memories, but you were sure quick to dump me.

"Bella," he said, "I've been anxious to get you–"

"*Buon giorno*," Giacomo said as he entered the palazzo. "*Grazie*, my friend," he said, clapping Phillip on the back, "for playing catch with my nephew. He could not stop laughing and talking about how you could not catch and how much fun he had."

"I'm the one who had the fun," Phillip said.

Giacomo glanced at Bella, and then back at Phillip. "I'm sorry to interrupt, but I've played too long, I'm afraid. Now we must go to the courtyard, as our group will leave from there for today's tour in a few minutes."

Phillip looked at Bella. "Can we talk later today? It sounds like there's no time now, and besides, I probably should change." He gestured to his dusty blue jeans.

She nodded.

He turned toward the stairwell to the upper floors.

"Phillip," Bella said. The thought that had kept recurring to her the night before—the incongruity of his nature—begged to be spoken.

He turned to look at her, with a smile on his face.

"Your offer to help Rune last night was very generous. It was kind of you."

"I meant it. I'm happy to help him any way I can. It's only money." With that, Phillip turned and ran up the stairs.

His sincerity nearly knocked Bella off her feet.

When Bella reached the courtyard, she found Meghan, Lee and Giacomo sitting together. Now this was confusing. Which one was Meghan with?

"Good morning, Bella." Lee touched his lips with his napkin. He smiled at Meghan and patted one of her hands with his.

Meghan winked at Lee.

Lee met Bella's eyes. His shining face had dropped years of age since the day before.

Meghan's face bore a quiet confidence. She lifted her chin. "Lee and I are very good friends." Her face dared Bella to ask more.

Giacomo raised Meghan's hand to his lips and kissed it, before returning it to the table. "And I am your 'very good friend,' too, am I not?"

Meghan giggled. "Most definitely." The look she gave Giacomo said volumes.

"Oh." Bella flushed scarlet.

Meghan met Bella's eyes with a steady face and a soft smile. "Lee and I had a lot to catch up on, just us two. It seems we may both have Italy in our future." Her hand reached out, not for Lee, but Giacomo. She stroked the Italian's strong forearm.

Confusing, Bella thought. One thing was certain, though. All three looked happy.

"I may come back to Italy over Thanksgiving to investigate housing arrangements," Lee said. "I'd like to take a sabbatical."

"You'd move your family here?" Bella said.

"That I'll have to work out with them. Life's a compromise, Bella. It's not black and white. I learn that every day in my practice. I love my wife, but that love has changed over the years, and our futures may take different directions. I'm going to sort that out with her when I go home."

Bella repeated Lee's words in her mind. Life is not black and white.

Stillman walked into the courtyard. "Today," he said, rubbing his hands together, "we road trip. We're heading south, to visit a lovely little village, Radda-in-Chianti."

The sound of heavy, rapid footsteps caught their attention. They pivoted to see Hope stomping into the courtyard. Her breath came in gulps and pants. Her eyes flamed with anger.

"Charlie," Hope said, "that no-good, abusive, jerk husband of mine, dumped all my clothes out in the street yesterday. My next-door neighbor texted me a picture of it. Oh, and he closed all of our bank and credit card accounts, too. Asshole."

Phillip entered the courtyard and stood so close to Bella that she could smell his woodsy aftershave. "I'll cover you, Hope." He pulled out his wallet and extended a wad of euros to her.

Stillman moved in front of Hope. "I've got it." His wallet was out and he pressed an equally large bundle of bills into Hope's hand.

A wave of déjà vu swept over Bella. The competition between Stillman and Phillip had revived.

"Thank you." Hope first kissed Stillman's cheek, and then Phillip's, after accepting his money, too. She looked at them each in turn. "You, all of you, give me strength … and kindness … and friendship."

Tears trickled out of Hope's eyes. "I was an idiot. The thing that haunts me is that my daughter, Erica, saw me take it from Charlie—the words and the punches. She watched for years. I pray to God she doesn't believe that's normal. Have dinner on the table whenever he gets home, don't ask too many questions, and stifle your cries when his words or his fists wound you." She pressed a hand to her lips to suppress a sob. "That's what I taught my daughter."

Hope looked at Stillman. "That's why I finally left him. Because of Erica, and because I had a plane ticket to Italy." She clenched her teeth. "I'm never going back to him. Never."

"We're all here for you, Hope." Phillip's calm words broke the tension. "Now and back in the States, too."

Bella knew two things.

Hearing Hope's story, it was ridiculous to feel sorry for herself. Life without a man was a hell of a lot better than life with someone like Charlie.

Second, Bella knew she had to confront Phillip. Today. Her self-respect demanded that she do it, and she owed it to David. She didn't want to admit it, but seeing Phillip play with the boy, and his being so quick to offer aid to

Rune and Hope, had presented a conflicting picture of the man she had hated for thirty years. And she couldn't allow anything to stop her from facing him.

44

They traveled to Radda-in-Chianti by van, with the group collectively putting together a game plan for Hope. Once there, Hope declared that she had her marching orders and that the discussion about "asshole Charlie" was finished for the day.

A line of Vespas, courtesy of Stillman, waited for them for a ride in the country before their lunch and the drive back to the palazzo. Meghan was the only one who wanted to practice in a parking lot before their ride. Soon, they wound single file out of Radda.

Before they reached the open countryside, they passed a line of ten bicyclists. Their red and yellow jerseys emblazoned with the circular Chianti Classico logo brought hoots of admiration from Phillip and Rune.

I should be enjoying this ride more than I am, Bella thought. The cloudless blue sky, rolling hills that wound through woods, and charming pockets of homes and structures built at the road's edge couldn't lift her anxiety.

She welcomed, and dreaded, her conversation with Phillip. When would it happen? Before or after lunch? Or would it be tonight?

Then she saw the sign. Castellina-in-Chianti. The hilltop town where Phillip stole her virginity and her heart. Thank God, Stillman led them away from that infamous village. Bella tightened her grip on the handles of the Vespa. Her stomach churned.

She thought about David but couldn't stay focused on the good he was doing in Africa. No. Her mind kept replaying how she had almost lost David because of her determination to mold him into a different man from his father. Different from Phillip.

The Vespas slowed behind a tractor, small by U.S. standards. Bella, driving second behind Stillman, could see a line of oncoming traffic approaching. She knew Stillman wouldn't go around the tractor because there wasn't time for the entire group to pass it safely. At that moment, she spotted the sign that pointed toward Radda-in-Chianti five kilometers ahead.

Bella floored her Vespa, passed Stillman and the tractor, and left the others behind. Driving recklessly, Bella barely slowed her Vespa around the turns and kept it full throttle on the straight stretches of road.

When Bella returned to their starting point for the ride, she was shaking. She parked her Vespa, put her helmet and the Vespa key in the unlocked compartment underneath the seat, and scribbled a note. Explaining that she wasn't hungry and had gone to explore the town, Bella suggested that they eat without her. It was true. The thought of food now repelled her.

As much as she wanted to have it out with Phillip, she could do the math. First lunch, then a communal stroll through Radda, and then it would be time to return to the palazzo. No time alone with him now. She'd confront him tonight.

Bella struck off from the parking lot along the busy two-lane road that skirted the edge of the main business section of town. Giacomo had boasted on the drive that tourists from both Europe and the United States used Radda as a base for winery visiting and bicycling the Tuscan hills.

In minutes, Bella reached narrow pedestrian streets crisscrossed with shops. She passed an enoteca, a sundries shop, a kitchen gadget store, and a clothing store. Another time, she would have found them charming, but they held no interest for her today.

Thunder rumbled in the distance. She strolled through one street and then another. Bella reached the end of the stores and kept walking. The street curved downhill, away from where she had started.

Oak and cypress trees lined the edge of a cemetery ahead. Bella picked up her pace. At first, the thought of walking through a cemetery repulsed her. But the charm of Radda's cemetery lured her in. Someone took great care in maintaining the neat, manicured appearance of the centuries-old cemetery. Here, she could say a prayer for her mother.

Bella moved closer. She looked up and down the rows packed with monuments. Many headstones bore pictures of the deceased. The pictures moved her. She reached out to touch the smooth oval picture of an elderly woman buried next to a somber-looking husband. The marker held their names and dates of death, and an etched cross. Bella's fingers traced the indentation of the cross.

Something rustling behind Bella startled her. She glanced over her shoulder.

An old woman in a long black dress and kerchief knelt beside a grave. Her head was lowered, her hands stretched before her on the ground, plucking weeds that had sprouted between the flowers in front of the headstone.

Bella heard the woman's breaking voice sing a melody. Then the elderly woman moved to another stone; again, she weeded around the red gardenias. This time, the woman didn't sing. When she finished weeding, she kissed the top of the stone marker.

After the woman had shuffled off, Bella moved to the freshly weeded plots. The first grave held a child. The picture showed a young boy, not more than three. Next to it, the man on the tombstone had to be her husband. Was the woman alone now?

Bella's eyes blurred. It had been more than two years since she last saw David. Oh, how she missed him. In a breaking whisper, she sang David's song, the bedtime song from when he was a toddler. Her hands covered her face. She felt her tears against her hands. Bella stood in silence and tried to remember David's smell. The leaves of the trees rustled.

Someone's hand touched the back of her shoulder. Bella sucked in her breath and spun around. "Sorry," Phillip said. "I've been walking all over town looking for you."

She wiped her palms over her wet cheeks and steadied her voice. He must wonder why she was crying, she thought. Bella looked down at the grave marker beside her, and then back at Phillip. "I saw an elderly woman weeding here. She planted flowers."

Phillip cleared his throat. "I wondered if you'd even speak to me this week. You're the reason I came, you know."

Bella waited.

"I owe you an explanation. Thirty years too late, but you deserve it, nonetheless."

"And if I don't care to hear it?"

"Bella."

She looked into his eyes. She couldn't read them.

"I got engaged the Christmas before our summer in Italy. Her father promised me a fast track to an executive position in the family business. Then I met you."

"You never told me—told anyone—you were engaged."

"I loved you." His face seemed to sag under the burden of his confession.

Bella couldn't speak. What could she say?

"I meant what I said to you when we left. Nothing could stop me from transferring out East to be near you."

"Liar." Bella's nostrils flared. "Nothing could stop you? Some hired flunky met me at the airport. Not you. No." She shook her head. "You weren't there. You stood me up."

Phillip reached for her hand.

Bella pulled out of his grasp. She looked down; she focused on the red, lacy geraniums and fought the tears.

"Please. Try to listen."

Bella didn't move.

"I told Angel about you the day she picked me up from the airport. I broke my engagement with her." His words came out in a strained tone. "It was a full-court press— Angel, her father, my parents. I know it's no excuse."

That's it? Bella's stomach churned.

"Italy seemed so far away. They claimed you were merely part of the charm of my summer abroad."

She glared at him. "You couldn't call me? Give me a chance?"

He moistened his lips. His eyes cast away. "I wanted to. Oh, God, I needed you."

"Why don't you tell it like it is? Or don't you have the balls to admit you sold out your happiness for money?"

He looked at her with pain searing his eyes. "Angel pulled the trump card. She was pregnant."

"Pregnant?"

"Yes."

Bile crept up Bella's throat.

"I would have left Angel, my parents, my college, the job. Everything. I would have left it all for you." His hands, palms up, begged her to understand. "But I couldn't ... couldn't leave my child."

Bella choked on the tears that stung her eyes and clogged her breath. She turned away from him. She moved to the tombstone of the little boy. She knelt before it and rested her head against the cool stone. She heard Phillip move to stand beside her.

"That was the biggest mistake of my life. I started regretting it on my honeymoon." His words rose in volume and flew out of his mouth as if they'd been under pressure. "My wife detests me, and she takes great pride in showing it. My daughter, Jewel, has learned her mother's lessons well. Too damn well. They keep me around because it's convenient, and because I've made them a fortune through the company."

Bella was paralyzed. She wondered if he'd leave if she didn't speak. Leave her here, in the peaceful quiet of the dead.

"I often thought about leaving. Divorcing Angel and quitting the company."

She had to know. She rose to her feet. Facing him, she forced her voice out in an even tone. "Why didn't you?"

"Work. Stupid reason, isn't it? I've spent my life expanding the company, building something tangible, something to be proud of. My work is all I have."

"What about your child?"

"Hah." The sound came out in a choking burst of air. "Jewel only calls me if she wants something." He clenched his teeth and glanced away. His chest rose and fell with deep breaths.

He looked at Bella and spat out his words. "The breaking news is that, more than ever before, my work is all I have. When Angel found out that this trip was to Italy, for a reunion of *that* summer, she gave me a present. It seems my dear fiancée had burned it at both ends. She shared her love around. There was me, the guy her dad wanted to nurture in the business, and Ian, the punk, part-time rocker and full-time asshole she had met on one of her shopping excursions to San Francisco."

Phillip snorted. "Guess she spent most of that summer shacked up with him, until he found a new girl to screw. Problem was, by then she was pregnant."

Bella stared at him.

"Angel told me the morning I left for Florence. My bon voyage present. She never knew if Ian or I had fathered Jewel, and at this point, I don't care. Jewel is my daughter, and I failed her. I have to live with that every day. She's spoiled, self-centered, and expects someone else to take care of her in grand fashion. Jewel has made it painfully obvious that her only use for me is to pay her bills."

Bella looked at the tombstone, and her fingers rubbed the oval picture of the Italian boy long gone but still loved. Her mouth moved, but no sound came out.

Forgive me, David. I should have fought for Phillip when I had the chance. Either fought for him, or called to tell him to go to hell. I should have done something. Anything. If I had called, I would have told him I was pregnant with you. Phillip would have chosen me because it was *me* he loved. You would have had a father. Forgive me.

45

Bella ignored Phillip, and he walked away. What could she say? It was too late for them. Their mistakes had reaped irreversible consequences.

When Bella no longer could tolerate the accusations of the little boy on the cemetery headstone—that she had robbed her own son of a father—she prayed.

It was part conversation and part confession, to God, her mother, and David. Admitting, out loud, that she had been the culprit, that by inaction she had directed her own fate, was as if she had shoved open a window that dust had turned opaque with time. And what better place to allow the light in than here, in Radda-in-Chianti, less than ten miles from where she and Phillip had fallen in love?

The whine of a Vespa approaching the cemetery brought her prayer to a close. Stillman parked his black scooter on the road and walked to where she stood. "Hey, beautiful," he said. "I heard you were hanging out here."

"I'm not very good company now, I'm afraid."

Standing in front of her, he wiped her cheeks with his thumbs. "Why the tears?"

Bella glanced at the boy's headstone beside her, and then back at Stillman. What she told him was true, but not the reason for her tears. "I miss David. It's been more than two years since I've seen him." She pressed her lips together and shook her head.

"Why so long?"

"David's a physician, in Africa, building a clinic down there. He refuses to leave until it's staffed and running. Every time I tried to go visit, or fly him home, something always came up for him, or for me."

Stillman brushed her hair away from her face. "It must be very difficult for you to be so far away from him."

When it had been Bella's turn to reveal her personal history to the others, she told them that she had never married. Bella let them assume that meant she had no family. Before anyone could pose a question, she had changed the focus of the conversation and had asked Meghan to share some of Karen's story. Only Stillman, because of their love affair, knew that she had a son. "I feel guilty for letting it be so long."

Stillman kissed her forehead. "I don't want you to be sad this week. If you'd like to talk about David, I'd love to hear about him, and his work. Unfortunately, Giacomo's got us on a schedule. It's time to head to the palazzo now. After we're back and have had a chance to freshen up, let's have a glass of wine together before dinner. Just the two of us. I haven't had nearly enough time alone with you. We could visit then, about anything you'd like. How about it?"

"I'd like that."

"Think you can hold onto me if we ride double back to where everyone's waiting?" His eyes twinkled at her.

Maybe there is hope for the two of us, she thought. If she wanted Stillman back, she knew she'd have to work for it. Bella smiled. "You can hang onto me," she said with a wink. "I'll drive."

"I called it first." He chuckled and draped an arm over her shoulders. "Let's go, pretty lady."

As they approached the parking lot where they had started their morning Vespa ride, Bella saw the group standing near the van. Giacomo stood by the driver's door. It was apparent that she had kept them all waiting. Phillip paced off to one side, studying his smartphone. He looked up and stared at Bella.

Stillman stopped their Vespa before they reached the parking lot. She dismounted, and Stillman drove off to park the scooter farther down the street, where the other Vespas were lined up. Phillip walked to intercept Bella.

"Are you OK?" His face bore a look of concern. "I shouldn't have left you at the cemetery, but you acted like you wanted to be alone."

"You're right. You shouldn't have left me." At the cemetery or thirty years ago, she thought. "Guess you have a habit of that."

"Damn it, Bella." He grabbed her hand. "I wish I could change everything that happened after we left Italy, but I can't." He glanced sideways. Stillman was fast approaching them. "Please. I hate myself for what I did to you. Can you ever forgive me?"

"This looks like a serious discussion," Stillman said. He stood next to Bella. "I'm sorry to interrupt, but we have to get going. We've kept everyone waiting long enough."

Bella pulled her hand out of Phillip's. *Forgive you? I can't even forgive myself.*

46

On the drive back to the palazzo, Giacomo, Meghan, and Lee visited among themselves, and everyone else silently looked out the windows of the van. Sitting closest to the three of them, Bella could hear the conversation.

She was surprised, and impressed, to learn that the sabbatical Lee had mentioned earlier was to study sculpture in Florence. Giacomo relayed inquiries he had made about an opportunity with a famous sculptor. Unfortunately, Giacomo reported, the maestro only taught one class each year, and this year's class was already full.

Bella had an idea. She asked a few questions of Giacomo about the maestro and the university offering his class. A spark of excitement lit her, but she kept the reason to herself. She now had a mission beyond her own needs, and it energized her.

When they got back to the palazzo, Bella rushed off to her room and started making telephone calls. In the process of researching one of her novels a few years before, she had cultivated a relationship with a University of Florence administrator.

Once she reached her contact, she reminded him of how she had aided his niece in securing a New York internship. Bella pleaded Lee's case, offering his medical expertise as a University guest lecturer in exchange for being added to the roster of the maestro's class. Bella cajoled the man, refused to let him say no, and finally got the answer she wanted. She called Lee's room, but he didn't answer. All the better. Bella could deliver the good news in person.

Intervening on Lee's behalf had been the wake-up call she needed. Empowered by her success, she took it as a sign. No more letting outside forces determine her fate.

Bella washed her face, put on fresh makeup, combed her hair, and donned the new black low-cut dress she had bought before the trip. It made her feel confident and sexy. Exactly what she needed tonight. She rushed down to the first-floor garden.

The courtyard was vacant. A butterfly flitted low over one of the bistro tables and then moved on. The orange of its gossamer wings matched the Tuscan sunset in the valley below. Somewhere in the trees, a bird sang. Bella closed her eyes. The bird sang with gusto and pleasure, chorus after chorus, not afraid of being heard.

At that moment, Lee and Phillip came into view from around the back of the palazzo. Deep in conversation, they faced the horizon, and she knew they hadn't seen her. The two men ambled away from her, along the garden's far perimeter path. The sound of their voices drifted in and out, but she couldn't distinguish the words. When the path circled back toward the buildings, they would see her, but she refused to wait. Bella rushed to meet them.

It was obvious when they saw her. From the look on Phillip's face and Lee's wolf whistle, she knew her dress was a hit.

She smiled and lifted her chin with confidence but didn't slow her pace. She was too excited. When Bella reached the two men, she hugged Lee. "I have great news for you. You're in the sculpting class with the maestro." She relayed her phone campaign, complete with her volunteering him to be a guest lecturer at the University, and pressed a paper into his hand with all the details.

Lee's arms crushed her in a hug. When he released her, he leaped into the air and yelled with delight.

Phillip punched the sky in celebration, cheered, and congratulated them both.

Lee couldn't wait to share the good news with Meghan and Giacomo and rushed off to find them.

Bella watched Lee leave. She took a deep breath, gave herself a quick pep talk, and turned toward Phillip. Her solemn expression wiped the smile from his face. Before she could allow doubt to creep in, she spoke. "I forgive you."

Relief at accomplishing the first of her admissions made her next words tumble out. "I owe you an apology, too. I hated you for dumping me so callously. But I was wrong." And a damn fool, she thought.

Finish what you have to say, she told herself. "I was wrong not to call you. Not to confront you." She blinked. This was it. Say it. "Not to fight for you." She gulped in air. "I'm sorry, Phillip. I hope, when you know what I was going through, that you can forgive me, too."

Phillip's jaw dropped. He clutched her hands and squeezed them. "You don't owe me an apology. And of course I forgive you. But you didn't do anything wrong." Again, he squeezed her hands. "No. It's all my fault." Pulling her hands, he drew her closer to him. Phillip folded her into his arms and rested his head against hers.

It was a kind, gentle, soothing type of hug. But her body didn't react that way. Not at all. Bella's heart pounded and a shiver of electricity raced through her. Damn it. Did he really have this effect on her? Could his mere touch detonate her body, making her want him after all these years? She needed to know. And there was one sure way to find out, but she'd never have that chance. No. Bad marriage or not, Phillip was married.

Phillip released her and stepped away. "Hoping you'd forgive me, if you even came to the reunion, is why I'm here. Breaking up with you, and using a stranger to deliver the message, has haunted me. I loved you too much to do it in person, so I took the coward's approach. I guess you and I had something in common all these years; we both hated me. Thank you for your forgiveness. That's the kindest thing anyone's ever done for me."

He looked anxious, and Bella wondered why. It was apparent he had more to say, so she didn't speak.

"It doesn't matter as far as we're concerned," Phillip said, his face bearing an earnest look, "but I need to share something. Remember I told you about how Angel goaded me with her infidelity before I left for the airport?"

"Yes."

"I took action at LAX. Before I knew if you'd be here, or if you'd even speak to me. I did it for myself. You were not a factor." His eyes peered into hers with intensity. "Understand?"

What the heck was he rambling about? I'm not a factor. Got it. She nodded.

"I called my attorney and instructed him to file divorce papers for me. Start the paperwork and the clock."

She blinked and kept her mouth shut.

"You were not a factor in my decision."

"You made that point very clear. But is that what you want? To divorce your wife after all these years? Aren't you president of her father's company?"

"Hell yes, I want to divorce her. Should have done it years ago." He shrugged. "As far as being president goes, I had my attorney tender my resignation, as well. I have to believe that there's a company or two that would want to hire me, given my track record. That doesn't worry me at all."

"Why didn't you say something earlier? You told us all you were married, with one daughter. Nothing more. Why?"

He clasped one of her hands. "I didn't want my divorce to affect, one way or another, your willingness to forgive me."

Bella replayed those words in her head. However she rearranged them, his message seemed clear. He wanted her forgiveness but didn't want her. She pulled her hand from his and backed away. How could he send her on such wide swings of emotion? She thought of how his touch had ignited her. At this point, she was more than ready to flush out the truth.

At fifty, Bella didn't need to ask permission. She stepped closer toward Phillip. She leaned in and kissed him. Her lips parted and the tips of their tongues met. Fire raced through her body and she couldn't breathe. Bella pulled away from the kiss. Her breasts, her body, everything, prickled with desire.

"I never saw that coming." Phillip smiled. "Hate is a kissing cousin to love, you know."

"I had to find out," she said, "now that we've forgiven each other, how I feel about you."

"What did you decide?"

"There you are, Phillip," Rune's voice boomed out from behind Bella, "mind if I interrupt?" His voice was jovial, but wrinkles creased his forehead.

Of course I mind, she thought. Her last admission would be the toughest. She would bare all. Tell Phillip he had a son, a son named David. Now that would to have to wait.

"No problem," Phillip said. "What's up, Rune?"

"I hate to bother you, but you, ah, volunteered to help me with the cost of my surgery. It's OK if you change your mind—it's a boatload of dough."

"Of course I'll help. What do you need?" Phillip asked.

"I called to get on the schedule for surgery, since they're booked out at least three weeks. But as I don't have insurance, they won't do anything until I make arrangements for payment."

"I'll come with you now." Phillip rested one hand on Bella's shoulder. "Let's finish this after I'm done helping Rune." He stroked her cheek. "For the record, I'm a huge fan of your testing method. I'll come find you, OK?"

Bella nodded.

Phillip followed Rune into the palazzo.

Bella gazed at the sunset. The oranges had given way to a deep red, with the dark evening sky imposing on the last of the color. With a whirlwind of conflicting thoughts, Bella turned and walked toward the mansion. It was time to meet Stillman for that glass of wine and conversation.

47

Bella saw Meghan and Giacomo sitting at a table by the espresso machine. They waved her over to join them. Lee had found them and had shared with them how she had accomplished the impossible—securing his coveted spot in the maestro's class. They both congratulated Bella on her success.

Meghan patted Giacomo's arm. "After we got back from Radda," Meghan said to Bella, "Giacomo took me to meet his family. He has the cutest nephew."

"If he's the one I saw earlier today," Bella said, "he is a cutie."

Giacomo beamed. "He is like my own son. It was no surprise," he said, gesturing to Meghan, "that he fell in love with this beautiful woman. He is very much like me in that way." Giacomo leaned toward Meghan and kissed her cheek.

Meghan's face flushed pink. She stood up and looked at Bella. "Please excuse us. It's not time for dinner yet. I'm going upstairs to my room." She held out a trembling hand to Giacomo. "Would you like to join me?"

Without a word, Giacomo stood and took Meghan's hand. They walked, side by side, to the stairway that led to the guest rooms.

I guess that answers the question, Bella thought, of whom Meghan had chosen. She walked to the entry where she was to meet Stillman but he wasn't there. Bella saw a folded paper on the center table with her name on it. Stillman had written the note, saying he'd be waiting for her in the library.

Approaching the second-floor library, Bella heard laughter, from Stillman and a woman. Entering the high-ceiling room, she found Hope standing near Stillman. Hope had one hand on her stomach and was wiping tears from her eyes with the other.

"It's obvious I missed some fun," Bella said.

"Hope was sharing some of the crazy antics of her daughter," Stillman said. "Hilarious stories. And we started with such a serious subject, too. How did that happen?"

Hope gestured for Bella to come closer. "I pitched the movie man here on coming to Colorado. Boulder's a breeding ground for documentary films, and I think a documentary on abuse in marriage is overdue. Somehow we veered off the subject, and next thing I knew, I was explaining exactly how Erica and her friends cheated in the Frozen Dead Guy races in Nederland." She gave Bella a meaningful look. "You don't really want to know how they did it. It's nearly as disgusting as what they did in the outhouse races in another mountain town."

Bella laughed. "No, I don't think I want to know." She thought of Hope's clothing in a heap on the street. "On that other subject, where will you stay when you go home?"

"I'll stay with my neighbor, the one who rescued my clothes. She's a feisty widow with a spare bedroom and attitude enough for both of us. That way I can keep an eye on my house and make sure the asshole doesn't burn it down or something. By the way, Bella," she grinned, "you look fabulous. And with that dress on, it's obvious I'm the third wheel. So I'm outta here. I'll see you both later at dinner."

Stillman gave Hope a hug and said, "Let's talk more about your documentary idea this week. I've never spent much time in Colorado."

After Hope left, Stillman offered Bella a glass of Vernaccia di San Gimignano. Toasting her glass with his, he said, "To new beginnings." He took a swallow of the wine and then placed his glass on a nearby table. He made a show of checking her out, including having her turn in a circle so he could have a view of the back of her dress.

"Spectacular," he said. "You are absolutely breathtaking. Come, join me on the sofa." He retrieved his wineglass and motioned to the sofa in front of the lit fireplace.

Bella sat beside him and took a sip of wine.

"Earlier today, you were sad about not seeing David," he said. "I have a solution. When the reunion is over, instead of you returning to New York and me to Prague, let's go to Africa together. I'll arrange everything. We can see David.

Maybe even take in a safari." He gave her a meaningful nod. "It's time for you to finally introduce me to your son."

It was as if a knobby-fingered gargoyle had clutched her throat and squeezed. She bit her bottom lip. "I don't know if it'd be right. Maybe not yet. You and I haven't been together for years. It'd be confusing. Complicated."

"Shh." Stillman's fingertips silenced her lips. "That part about you and I not being together, well, I'd certainly love to remedy that." He leaned forward and brushed his lips over hers. "That was objection one, the 'confusing' argument. And as for 'complicated,' it isn't complicated at all. Coincidentally, Phillip isn't the only one involved in charity work. I'm on the board of a foundation—which means I'm one of their major donors—and we actually fund some projects in Africa."

Stillman's voice was calm and even. "Here." He found a picture on his smartphone and held it out for her to look at. "Take a look at one of the projects we fund." The picture showed the early stages of construction of some kind of building.

Bella's throat was dry. "I don't know if I can get away."

"If you don't have time for the safari this trip, we can limit our trip to seeing David."

"He's always so busy, telling me it's not a good time to visit. I'd have to e-mail him first."

"I've already done that."

Bella stared at him in shock.

"With the Internet, it's not hard to research people. I know a great deal about David. His clinic's coming along nicely. See?" Stillman flipped through more pictures on his phone. When he found the one he was looking for, he held it for her to see.

It was a photograph of Stillman with his arm over David's shoulders, standing in front of the African clinic. The background of this picture was identical to the one he had shown her of his foundation's project. "We're friends, you see, David and I."

Questions pummeled her brain, but she couldn't speak.

"It started as business, when our foundation donated the money for the clinic. After a few trips to inspect the progress, we became friends."

"You were the anonymous donor?"

Stillman nodded, with a pleased expression on his face. "It was easy to locate him. The challenging part was waiting for a plausible reason to go visit."

This was surreal. She blinked and looked again at the picture on Stillman's phone. Handsome David—a younger version of Phillip—standing next to Stillman.

"I have to admit, his looks nearly cost him the donation, but I got over it."

Bella choked.

Stillman patted her back. "Are you all right?"

Her mind reeled. "Why? Why did you do this?"

Stillman cleared his throat. His words were slow and precise. "After you turned down my proposal, I was angry and hurt. I left the States and immersed myself in work. Eventually, I wondered if you had turned me down because of David, that for some reason you were afraid to let the two of us meet. So I searched him out and then waited for an opportunity to fly to Africa and meet him."

"Does David know our history?"

"No. I wanted him to know me without the burden of our collective past."

Two conflicting emotions swirled inside Bella. Relief that she didn't have to keep David hidden from Stillman any longer and fury that he had gone behind her back and basically bribed her son into liking him. Mostly, though, it was fury. "Our collective past? Quaint expression, but one that certainly doesn't do justice to the truth. How dare you bribe my son?"

"You're upset for only one reason. I went off on my own and made friends with your son. Phillip's son. By the way, my dear, it's obvious that Phillip's still hot for you. Have you told him that you have a child and that he's the daddy?"

A noise behind them made Bella and Stillman turn toward the doorway. Phillip stood there, ashen-faced, with a bottle of Prosecco and two glasses in his hands. Without a word, he turned and stomped down the hall.

48

Bella raced after Phillip. She caught up with him in the garden. He had abandoned the glasses and wine nearby on the ground. Phillip faced the twinkling lights of Florence and didn't acknowledge her when she ran up beside him. She placed her palm on his back. He stepped away from her touch.

"I'm sorry," she said. "I should have told you. But I was devastated when you dumped me. And so very angry. I didn't want you to be with me merely because I was pregnant. I was too damn proud for that." Tears tumbled out of her eyes. "I hated you for abandoning me, for abandoning us."

Phillip didn't move and didn't speak.

"What you did to me pales in comparison, though, to my sins. I kept your son from you and wronged both of you in the process. It's inexcusable, but please don't take it out on David. He is your son, and although it should have happened years ago, he deserves to know his father."

Still facing the horizon, Phillip asked, "What's he like?"

"Handsome. Intelligent. Motivated. Athletic, generous, caring, and quick-witted. He's like his father. Like you."

"If I hadn't been there to eavesdrop, would you have told me?"

Bella moved to stand between Phillip and the retaining wall he faced, blocking his view of Florence. "Yes. I came to Italy to tell you about him, about everything."

He gazed into her eyes, but she couldn't read them.

"Why did you kiss me?" Phillip asked.

"Because, damn you, every touch and every look from you took me back to that weekend in Castellina, and I wanted to love you all over again. I had to find out, by kissing you, if it was real or my imagination."

"And?"

Bella nestled his face in her hands and kissed him like it was their last night together, which, for all she knew, it was. Never again would she be too proud to fight for someone she loved. Her pride thirty years ago had cost them all too dearly. She pulled away first.

"I love you," she said. "I never stopped loving you, even when I hated you more than anyone on Earth, I still loved you."

"What about Stillman?"

She looked him squarely in the eye. Bella was done with lying. "Do you remember when the two of you asked me to choose between you?"

He nodded.

"I couldn't, because I was attracted to you both. Well, the truth is, I know now that I love you both."

His eyes lowered.

With one hand under his chin, she lifted his face and made him look at her. "I love you both, but in different ways. I knew that thirty years ago, and it's still true. It's you that I want to be with, and spend my life with. Only you. That's why I kissed you. I needed to know if that was still true, and it is."

Phillip's lips slowly broke into a smile. Then he wrapped his arms around her and there, under a sky filled with stars and the lights of Florence on the horizon, he kissed her, and thirty years of time and mistakes fell away.

49

Bella dreaded facing Stillman, but that dread, like so much of her past, was wasted energy. Stillman knew that she had left him to run after Phillip. He also knew that Bella and Phillip had both missed dinner.

She left Phillip in her room and went to find Stillman by herself. He was at a bistro table in the outdoor breakfast area, smoking a cigar. Funny, she never knew that he smoked cigars. He looked up when she approached the table.

"I guess Phillip won," he said. His expression was calm and noncommittal.

"Was it always a contest for you?"

"Bella, my love," he exaggerated his Southern drawl, "I always loved you, but I have to admit, winning your love would have been that much sweeter because it would have meant I won."

She gestured to the cigar. "How about you put that out and we walk the path around the garden?"

"Hmm. Never knew you were a bossy gal."

Bella laughed. "What happened to the sophisticated Manhattan attorney I know? He kept only a trace of his accent."

Stillman tapped out the cigar and stood up. He tucked her arm into his and said in his normal voice, "He's here, too. Didn't you ever hear that expression about not being able to take the country out of the boy?"

Bella wanted to flush out all of her thoughts, issues, and concerns; it was her new style of dealing with matters. "In chronological order, I resent you going behind my back to meet David. And using your foundation's grant money to basically bribe your way into his good graces? Despicable. Admittedly, his clinic will help thousands of people from the surrounding villages. Because of that, I'm thrilled that he received the grant. I thank you for your generosity."

She stopped walking and faced him. "Deceiving me, and pretending you hadn't met David. Pretending that you didn't know Phillip was his father. These deceptions are inexcusable, if you truly loved me and wanted me as your wife."

"You weren't honest with me about David."

"Yes. I'm sorry about that. I was afraid you'd leave me if you knew the truth."

"So little faith in me."

"That's not true," Bella said. "The truth is that I was a coward. David was my little secret, and I was afraid to face the consequences of disclosing who fathered him. I was afraid to face the fallout, not only with respect to you, but also to David and to Phillip."

She grabbed both of his hands in hers. "I love both you and Phillip, but in different ways. I told him the same thing. He's the one I want to have as my life partner, but you've been my friend for a very long time, and I don't want to lose you." She leaned in and feathered a kiss on his cheek. "Is that possible for you? To be my dear friend, and Phillip's friend, too?" She squeezed his hands and searched his face with her eyes.

"Only if you, and not Phillip, still decides who you hug."

Bella laughed and gave her friend an enormous hug. "Thank you."

Stillman hugged her back and then stepped away. "You know, I'm truly impressed by your son. You should be very proud of him. He's responsible for showing me how gratifying it is to help someone less fortunate. It's about time I embraced philanthropy, because without family," he chuckled, "what am I going to do with it? Bury it with me?" He steered them back toward the courtyard.

Hope, Lee and Rune walked out of the palazzo and waited for Stillman and Bella to reach them. Rune had brought two bottles of Prosecco, and Hope had a tray of champagne glasses.

"We need to celebrate," Hope said, placing the tray on a table. "We have to toast Lee, on taking the leap and following his passion for sculpture."

Rune popped a cork off one bottle and let it soar out it into the garden. He filled Stillman in about how Bella had orchestrated Lee's admission to the University.

"I hate to be the practical one here, Lee," Stillman said, "but if you return in a couple of months for this class, what happens to your wife? Will she leave her work and tag along?"

"Truthfully, I don't know," Lee said. "But Merry and I will talk and then decide if we're staying together, or if it's time to separate. Either way, I'm coming back to study sculpture. If I don't do it now, when will I?"

Meghan bounced into the courtyard holding Giacomo's hand. The Italian had that telltale look and swagger of a well-satiated man.

Rune saluted Giacomo with the open bottle. "Looks like you two have some celebrating to do, as well."

Meghan giggled. "Absolutely we do! I'm staying here in Italy with Giacomo."

The Italian beamed and threw his arms around Meghan.

Rune filled the flutes with sparkling wine and passed out the glasses. They raised their glasses in a toast and took a celebratory swallow of Prosecco.

Phillip entered the courtyard and smiled when he saw the festive crowd. "What are we celebrating?"

"You," Rune said, "for bailing me out. Bad news is that then all of you," he added, pointing to the others with his glass, "will be stuck with me for a while, because, with your help, Phillip, I'm going to beat this cancer."

"You sure as hell will," Hope said. "Besides, I need you to help me talk Stillman into producing a documentary in Colorado. He'll probably need a director, you know."

Stillman laughed. "I probably will."

"I'll drink to that." Rune downed his glass of Prosecco. He set it on a table. "Don't worry," he said, patting the glass, "I'll be back."

Everyone laughed.

Rune moved to Hope and put his hands on her shoulders. "What about you? How are you going to be, returning to asshole-land?"

Hope nodded. "I'll be fine. No, scratch that. I'll be damn fine, because I'll be divorcing the asshole. And if he gives me any trouble, I've got a bunch of successful, kick-ass friends," she grinned, "who I'm counting on to come to my aid."

Everyone cheered and seconded her remark. Rune opened the second bottle of wine and refilled his glass.

"I have a toast," Bella said, handing Phillip a glass of bubbly. She raised hers to the sky. "I'd like to toast a remarkable man, the one of us who had the courage, and the money, to bring us all here for this reunion. To you, Stillman." She smiled at Stillman and then at Phillip.

"Thank you," Stillman said.

Bella took a sip of her Prosecco. "Not to be presumptuous, but do you imagine there might be another reunion?"

"Why?" Stillman asked, smiling.

Bella wrapped one arm around Phillip. "Well, because I haven't told everyone about my son, David, yet. And that can't happen until Phillip gets to meet him, since he's David's father."

All of their eyes were on her now.

She clinked her glass against Phillip's. "Phillip and I are just beginning our lives together." She smiled and sipped her wine. "I love being a rule-breaker. And what did the invitation say, Stillman? 'No spouses, children, or friends allowed.' That rule is begging to be broken."

THE END

ACKNOWLEDGMENTS

My special thanks to my editor, Patti Thorn, whose knowledge and kind but firm wisdom allowed my characters to follow their true paths. My sincere gratitude to Nick Zelinger, who created the beautiful cover and interior that transports us to Tuscany. Thank you, copy editor Michael Rudeen, for keeping me honest and grammatical. Judith Briles, you guided the process with expertise and clarity, and for this I am truly grateful.

I would like to express my deep gratitude to dear friends Susie, Greg, and all of our Vespa group, and you know why. I sincerely thank the charming and hospitable people of Tuscany for their warmth and kindness.

My writing life wouldn't be possible without the love and support of my friends and family. Making time to write with four remarkable sons, Brandon, Justin, Nathan, and Damian, and their loved ones was a challenge, but they were always there for me, with encouragement and understanding. I offer all of my friends and family, as well as those who watch and applaud from the next life, my immense gratitude for their love and constant support.

Most of all, I offer my profound thanks to my dear husband, Ray, best friend and soul mate, inexhaustible reader and unwavering cheerleader. You are my world.

Last, but certainly not least, my heartfelt thanks go to you, my readers, who make this possible.

Gail Mencini is the award-winning author of the debut novel *To Tuscany with Love*. A frequent visitor to Tuscany and a homegrown gourmet cook, she has toured Italy by car, train, bus, Vespa, and foot. She lives in Colorado with her family and dogs, where she cooks up dazzling dishes and spectacular stories. Look for the *To Tuscany with Love* companion recipes—*Bella's Tastes from Tuscany*—on her website. You can find reader discussion questions and book club enhancement ideas on her website, as well as contact information to request your own book club chat with Gail.

Watch for the second novel in Gail's *Tuscany* series, which returns to Italy with a new cast of characters and more hill towns to discover. Updates on the release date will be posted on her website.

To learn more about Gail or schedule a book club chat, visit *www.GailMencini.com.*

Bella's Tastes
from Tuscany

During our college semester in Tuscany, I fell in love with the landscape, the people, the history, the food, and the wine. *And if you've read about our summer in Tuscany, you know how I felt about my classmates.* Returning to New York after that semester abroad, I wanted my kitchen to resonate with the smells and tastes of the food that I loved in Italy.

Bella's Tastes from Tuscany is a collection of recipes I created through the years that capture some of the foods, tastes, and memories from that remarkable summer. They feature American—rather than Italian—ingredients and, by necessity in the early years, were easy on my restricted budget.

You can find more of my recipes by visiting *www.GailMencini.com.*

Salute!

Bella

Roasted Tomato Crostini
16 Crostini

This is an alternative to tomato bruschetta for those days when you don't have time to dice tomatoes. I use a French baguette because it is the perfect size for the tomato crostini, plus it reminds me of that wild, steamy trip we all took to Paris.

8 Roma tomatoes
5 tablespoons olive oil, divided
1/2 teaspoon kosher salt
8 to 10 fresh basil leaves
French baguette
Parchment paper (optional)

Preheat the oven to 275° F. Line a baking sheet with the parchment, if using. (It will ease your cleanup.) Cut the tomatoes in half lengthwise. With a spoon, remove the seeds and core (not the flesh). Arrange the tomatoes on the baking sheet in a single layer, cut side up. Pierce the tomatoes a few times with a fork. Drizzle 1 1/2 tablespoons of olive oil over the tomatoes, and then sprinkle them with the salt. Roast in the preheated oven for 2 hours. Remove the tomatoes from the oven, spill out any juice that has collected in them, and then return them to the oven for another 30 minutes.

Make ahead: The tomatoes can be roasted 2 days ahead and stored in an airtight container in the refrigerator once they are cool. Bring to room temperature before assembling.

Continued on next page.

For the crostini toasts, cut the French baguette into 1/4 -inch slices. Brush both sides of the slices with the remaining olive oil. Arrange them on a baking sheet in a single layer. Bake at 350º F for 7 to 8 minutes, until the edges begin to turn golden brown and the center is a little firm.

Make ahead: The crostini toasts can be stored in an airtight container for up to 2 days after they have fully cooled. A full-size baguette will make extra crostini toasts that you can use for another appetizer.

Assemble the crostini close to the time when you serve them, as cut basil will darken. Place one tomato, cut side up, onto each crostini.

Chiffonade the basil: Stack half the basil leaves into a neat pile. Roll the leaves lengthwise into a tight cigar shape. Using a sharp knife cut the leaves crosswise into very thin strips. Repeat with the remaining basil leaves.

Fluff the strips with your fingers to separate. Add the basil fluff on top of the tomatoes. The cook deserves to sample one crostini before they all disappear!

Tuna and Bean Salad
Serves 4 as a side dish or 6 as a tapas

During our summer in Italy, dining alfresco at a trattoria was always a fun, leisurely event, with much laughter and teasing. Sharing these meals paved the way for our friendship, and we often somehow endeared ourselves to the owners. At one of our favorite spots when Pino—the owner—saw us, he immediately brought out bottles of Chianti and bowls of this dish.

1-14 oz. can of cannellini beans
1/3 cup extra-virgin olive oil
Zest and juice of 1 lemon,
   (about 3 tablespoons of juice)
2 – 5 oz. cans of tuna in olive oil (you can use
   more or less tuna depending on the size of your cans),
   drained and flaked
1/2 of a small red onion, or more to taste
Salt and pepper to taste

Drain and rinse the beans. Quickly heat the beans on the stove or in the microwave until warm. Whisk together the olive oil and lemon juice, season with salt and pepper to taste (you may not need any unless you are using no-salt-added beans). Pour the lemon juice-olive oil mixture over the warm beans and stir to coat the beans. Fold in the tuna and lemon zest. Slice the onion into thin circles and then cut the rings into semi-circle halves. Stir the red onion into the bean mixture and taste for seasoning. Add more salt, pepper, or onion if desired.

Continued on next page.

Chill in the refrigerator until serving. (I always serve myself a tiny portion before I tuck it away to chill—I consider it quality control!)

When ready to use, stir the bean salad to mix in any dressing at the bottom of the bowl. The bean and tuna salad can be served cold, at room temperature, or slightly warmed in the microwave.

Make ahead: The salad can be made 1 day in advance.

"Buon appetito!"
Remember, you can find more of my recipes by visiting
www.GailMencini.com.